THE TRUTH ABOUT LOVE

THE TRUTH ABOUT LOVE

TIA McCOLLORS

MOODY PUBLISHERS
CHICAGO

© 2008 by
TIA MCCOLLORS

All Scripture quotations are taken from the *New King James Version*. Copyright © 1982 by Thomas Nelson, Inc. Used by permission. All rights reserved.

Cover Design: TS Design Studio
Interior Design: Ragont Design
Editor: Suzette Dinwiddie

Library of Congress Cataloging-in-Publication Data

McCollors, Tia.
    The truth about love / Tia McCollors.
        p. cm.
    Sequel to: Zora's cry
    ISBN-13: 978-0-8024-9862-5
    ISBN-10: 0-8024-9862-0
    1. African American women—Fiction. 2. Female friendship—Fiction.
I. Title.

PS3613.C365T78 2008
813'.6—dc22

                                                                    2007047182

1 3 5 7 9 10 8 6 4 2

Printed in the United States of America

To Jayce

That you may always do what the Lord requires of you . . .
to do justly, love mercy, and walk humbly with your God.

Dear Reader

God coexists as a Trinity (Father, Son, and Holy Spirit). God is one in essence, but with three distinct and separate functions. The Holy Spirit is the third "person" of the Trinity (1 John 5:7–8).

When a person accepts the Lord Jesus Christ as Savior, he or she is born again by the Holy Spirit. The Holy Spirit dwells within, convicts people of sin, instructs, and empowers (John 14:17, 26; Romans 8:9; 1 Corinthians 12:13). In *The Truth about Love*, the italicized bold print is used to indicate the internal prompting of the Holy Spirit.

Acknowledgments

I THANK GOD for giving me the gift of writing, and even more so for trusting me to use the gift as a tool and ministry to draw others closer to Him. Oftentimes, Christian fiction authors receive criticism for their works because, as one passer-by told me at a book signing, "How can it be both Christian and fiction? Christians shouldn't lie and make things up." My answer to him and others who question our works is that Jesus Himself taught in parables. That's another reason I'm grateful that I'm able to put pen to paper and craft stories with the ability to transform lives.

MY FAMILY has been indescribable in their support of me. They've probably done more work than the most successful publicists, but the best thing about that is that they do it all for free! I pray my efforts to help blaze literary trails, build a legacy, walk in destiny, and obey God's voice will help pay the price for the sacrifices they've made. I'm blessed that my husband, Wayne, believes in me and wholeheartedly supports the vision of our family. He encouraged me to leave the corporate world so I could pursue my writing career, as well as stay at home to raise our energetic, funny, and amazing son. As I continue on this journey, I hide the words he once told me in my heart. "Believe in the ridiculous. Believe in the incredible, omnipotent, awesome, indescribable God."

The Truth about Love is my third book, and **THE MOODY PUBLISHERS FAMILY** continues to be as supportive and excited about this book as they were about *A Heart of Devotion* and *Zora's Cry*. With each release we all expect and anticipate more, and God continues to deliver. My editor, Cynthia Ballenger, and every person in every department have been critical to the production of my books and the building of my career. As I always say . . . thank you for believing in me. The best is yet to come.

In 2006 I embarked on a journey with a group of six other powerful women in "gospel literature": **THE ANOINTED AUTHORS ON TOUR** (Vivi Monroe Congress, Norma Jarrett, Vanessa Miller, Kendra Norman-Bellamy, Shewanda Riley, and Michelle Stimpson, and myself, of course). We've learned a lot —maybe a little too much—about one another during our treks up and down the East Coast, but more than anything else, it's refreshing and encouraging to be among a sisterhood of writers, comedians, and visionaries. We've been able to find our own "places" in the group, and our personalities fit together like the perfect seven-piece jigsaw puzzle. I'm honored to be with the AAOT, and we encourage visitors to our Web site at www.anointedauthorsontour.com.

Great things are always birthed out of the **FAITH COMMUNITY**, and I thank the churches, ministry groups, gospel artists, and other soldiers of the faith who support me. There's nothing like "your own" having your back—and your front. Thank you for doing your part in the body of Christ, and allowing me to do mine.

It's a joy to be able to say that there are so many **AUTHORS** that I admire that I wouldn't dare try to mention them all here. The list of Christian authors, especially, seems to grow by leaps and bounds as so many scribes take the front line. For those I know personally and commune with from time to time, I appreciate your words of encouragement, your professional insight, and the conversations we have that make me laugh until I cry. And to the aspiring authors, keep pen to paper and fingers to keyboard. Write like someone else's life depends on it—because it does.

Where would an author be without the **LITERARY INDUSTRY**? I extend my appreciation to the libraries, book stores, book clubs, and literary organizations that make sure that my books not only make it *on* the shelves, but make it *off* the shelves!

Last, but definitely not least, I owe a tremendous amount of gratitude to the **READERS** who continue to support me. Your e-mails of support and encouragement always land in my e-mail box when I need them. God operates in perfect timing, and oftentimes He uses you to give me the extra push I need or to assure me that I'm pressing in the right direction. Please continue to keep in touch with me through the guestbook via my Web site, or by dropping me a line to Tia@TiaMcCollors. com.

Now turn the page to find out the truth about love . . .

paula manns

I still can't believe he insisted on taking a paternity test.

Paula Manns shut out the absurd thought. Darryl would come to his senses as soon as he heard his daughter's first cry. None of Paula's tears had worked with him. She'd cried out many nights—not just to Darryl, but to God too. It seemed as if both had turned a deaf ear to her.

"Push, Paula. Just one more push and you can see your baby girl," Dr. Seagroves coaxed from behind the hospital sheet. She patted the side of Paula's thigh. "Relax your legs."

Paula dug her nails into her husband's hand and gripped the bed rail with her right. Darryl winced in pain. *Good.* It paled in comparison to the writhing contractions she'd been enduring over the past four hours, not to mention the heavy burden from carrying their crumbling marriage on her shoulders over the last year and a half. At the point when she'd seen the light at the end of the tunnel, it was snuffed out by his attitude. She'd only held on this long because of the promises she'd made to

God. To fight. To honor the vows she'd made before Him.

The anger Paula used to harbor toward Darryl had dissipated, but it had left the residue of hurt on her soul.

Another contraction pierced Paula's lower back. She didn't know how much more she could endure. She'd determined to have a natural birth experience this time. The side effects from the epidural from her son's delivery left her with back pain for nearly two months afterwards. Micah was five now, and she still remembered the agony, although the obstetrician said her epidural wasn't the culprit. Whatever. Paula planned to endure the labor without any help from drugs, but when she changed her mind and requested the epidural an hour ago, the resident looked at her apologetically and said, "Eight centimeters. You're too far along."

Too far, Paula thought. Too far is telling a committed wife that he's going to take a paternity test when he's the one stepping out in the middle of the night. Paula's legs begin to quiver, keeping pace with her trembling bottom lip.

Everything. Everything was too much. Tears spilled from her eyes.

"It's okay," Dr. Seagroves said, not realizing Paula wept about more than the contractions. "Push and hold it for ten," Dr. Seagroves nearly whispered. "She's almost here."

Paula grunted while the nurse helped push her knee to her chest. "You've been saying that for the last thirty-three minutes," she said through clenched teeth. She looked at the large, round, white-faced clock on the wall. The red second hand lapped past the six again. Paula tucked her chin into her chest and bore down.

The nurse counted. "One, two . . . four . . . nine, ten."

"I can't do it anymore," Paula said, falling back against the back of the raised hospital bed. She pushed back the sweaty bangs from her forehead and used the oversized sleeve of her hospital gown to wipe her face. Exhaustion had stolen her strength and reason. "Do what you can without me."

The moment the comment left her lips, Paula realized how ludicrous it must've sounded. Even though Dr. Seagroves'

14

mouth was hidden by a surgical mask, the obstetrician's smile surfaced through the twinkle in her hazel eyes.

"Come on, honey," Darryl said, leaning in close to her ear. "You've gotten this far. You can do it." He looked around at the labor and delivery team in the room. Their eyes were all focused on the event happening under the green sheet below Paula's waist. "Besides, you can't walk around with a half-delivered baby," he said with a half chuckle.

She couldn't believe he was amused at a time like this. Paula cut her eyes at Darryl and decided not to slash him with words. Besides, another contraction paralyzed her thoughts before she could think of what to say. A groan like a wounded bear rose from Paula's belly, and she pushed with the last ounce of strength left in her fatigued body, delivering her daughter into the world.

"Five-oh-three p.m.," one of the nurses said.

Through her blurred, teary eyes, Paula watched Dr. Seagroves suction fluid from the baby's mouth and nose. After her daughter's first cry screeched from her tiny lungs, Dr. Seagroves wiped a jelly-like substance from the baby's face and body, then lay her on Paula's chest.

"Does this cutie-pie have a name yet?" the doctor asked.

"Gabrielle Elise Manns," Paula said.

Looking at Gabrielle, she knew the name was perfect. What made it even more precious was that Gabrielle's initials announced what a priceless jewel she was to the world—GEM. Neither her emerald and diamond pendant nor any of the expensive stones she'd racked up in her jewelry armoire over the years compared to the experience and joy of giving birth to another child. Memory of the labor pains vanished. The only thing she felt was love.

Darryl bent over and kissed Paula's forehead; his lips lingered —soft and tender. She couldn't believe it. She guessed the moment had gotten to him too. Paula couldn't remember the last time she'd felt such a genuine touch from him. At times like this she saw the hope for their marriage's restoration. This could be the moment things changed. The fruit of her prayers was within fingertips' reach. She wanted to reach out and grab it before . . .

Darryl's cell phone rang, and the vision dissipated. He unclipped it from his waist just as he accepted the sterile scissors from Dr. Seagroves to cut the umbilical cord. The lifeline between Paula and her daughter dangled between two metal clamps waiting for Darryl to disconnect it.

I don't believe this. He better not answer that phone.

Paula glared at him, her facial expression speaking the words that her mouth didn't. A musical tone played, signifying that he'd powered his cell phone off. Her silent threat had worked.

After Darryl cut through the rubbery cord, a nurse scooped Gabrielle from Paula's chest. The labor and delivery team worked methodically in the corner of the room to check the baby's vitals and administer a series of tests to measure her responsiveness. Paula had read enough in her baby magazines to know what all of the poking and prodding on her newborn was all about.

"Seven pounds, nine ounces," the nurse announced. She lifted Gabrielle from the scale, the baby's head now donned with a pink and blue striped knit cap pulled down to her eyebrows.

"I'll get your mother," Darryl said, his voice flat with little enthusiasm. He pecked Paula on the forehead, but this time the kiss was dry and rehearsed. More for show than anything else.

The drop of hope that Paula had now fizzled away.

Darryl zipped the jacket of his fleece pullover up to his neck, then tightened the drawstring to the matching black fleece pants. He had his cell phone powered back on and up to his ear before the delivery room door closed behind him. The chill that emanated through Paula's body wasn't from the thirty-eight-degree February weather.

Paula's mother, Rosanna Gilmer, had been camped out in the waiting room with Paula's five-year-old son, Micah. He was overly anxious to see his baby sister and had been asking about her every day and checking the calendar Paula had tacked on the refrigerator. Micah kept a countdown of the number of days until the date Paula had marked with a smiley face. Gabrielle came eight days early.

The nurse brought Gabrielle back to Paula. The infant was wrapped tight as a burrito, swaddled up to her chin in a white receiving blanket. Paula lifted the child to her face and kissed Gabrielle's perfect pink lips. Only minutes before she'd been detached physically from Paula's body, but from the moment Paula found out she was pregnant, Gabrielle had been attached forever to her mother's heart.

"What number is this for you?" the nurse asked in a Jamaican accent. She rolled away a silver tray of sterile tools.

"Gabrielle makes two," Paula said. "And probably the last."

"You're a young lady," the nurse said, flicking her hand in the air. "If you can do two, you can do three. No problem. I've got six. All of them two years apart. Four boys, two girls."

I haven't even gotten stitched up yet and this woman is talking to me about having another baby.

The hospital door pushed open, and Micah bounded inside. Darryl grabbed his arm before his eager son could make a beeline for the bed.

"Hold up a minute, son," Darryl said. "Let the doctor finish with Mommy, and you can see your little sister."

Micah stood on his tiptoes, craned his neck, and tried to wrestle his arm out of Darryl's grip. There were days it seemed he grew taller from the time she dropped him off and picked him up from kindergarten.

"Hi, sweetie," Paula said. She blew a kiss to her son, who returned one of his own. "Remember how important it is for you to be a big boy now?"

Micah jutted out the strong and angular chin that he'd inherited from his father. He nodded his head and pulled at the bottom of his blue T-shirt. "That's why I get to wear this," he said, standing proudly with his shoulders back and chest out.

"That's right," Paula said.

While shopping at one of her favorite online children's boutiques, she'd found him a shirt that said, *I'm the big brother.*

She'd even bought Gabrielle a newborn pink onesie that said, *I'm the little sister.*

Paula outlined the shape of Gabrielle's eyebrows with her index finger. It seemed like just yesterday that she'd held Micah the same way. Loving him unconditionally. The way she thought Darryl would always love her. She looked over at Darryl, who was busy texting messages from his cell phone.

Life was different when Micah had come along. Darryl had hovered over his first son as if his life depended on the baby's breath. Instead of his cell phone, he'd had a camera strapped to one hand and a video camera in the other. Somewhere along the way the frame to their picture-perfect life had shattered, and Paula was still trying to salvage the pieces and put them back together again. She'd made a promise to God that she'd do whatever it took. That was before she knew how much it would take.

My strength is made perfect in weakness.

"Okay. That'll do it," Dr. Seagroves said. She pulled the mask off her mouth and slid back on the rolling stool. "Congratulations. You can go ahead and nurse her if you'd like. They'll come from the nursery to get her shortly."

Micah ran to the bed as soon as Darryl let go of his arm. After three minutes of examining his sister's face and asking a barrage of questions, Micah stretched out on the pull-out couch and forgot about everything except his new handheld video game and the iPod his father had surprised him with.

"Come on, Grandma," he said with his feet propped up on the arm of the couch. "You want to try and play again?"

"I can't half see that thing, Micah," Rosanna said.

"Okay," he said, content to play by himself. He stuffed the buds of his headset into his ears.

Rosanna crept to the hospital bed once the staff cleared the room. The recent flare-up of her arthritis had temporarily stolen her quick steps, brought on, she said, by the rainy weather.

"Grandbaby number four," Rosanna said, her chest puffed out just as much as Micah's had been. "You don't know how blessed you are, little muffin." She tapped the tip of Gabrielle's

18

nose. "Now if you can only get your daddy to act right," she whispered. Rosanna grunted and crossed her arms. The slits of her eyes were sharp enough to cut Darryl straight down the middle of his personal-trainer-toned body.

"Don't do it, Ma," Paula said. "Now's not the time."

Rosanna hoisted her fake leather purse farther up on her shoulder. She'd directed her comments toward Darryl even though she didn't so much as cock her neck to look in his direction. "And I wish you would try to pull that mess about she's not your baby," she mumbled, looking over to make sure Micah didn't hear her. "I'll lose what Christianity I have left."

"Seems like if you can lose your Christianity that easy, you never had it in the first place," Darryl said to his mother-in-law, not once looking up from his electronic gadgets.

Paula hoped her mother would call a truce.

She did.

Rosanna looked at Darryl. He looked smug that he'd delivered the final blow. He rocked back on his heels and leaned against the eggshell-white wall. From the look of the smudges around him, other fathers had taken residence at the same post.

Paula pursed her lips and blew out a stream of air. She didn't realize she'd been holding her breath.

"My baby, Gabrielle," Paula cooed, soothing the newborn and the storm around her.

Darryl finally walked over to hold his daughter. Paula lifted Gabrielle up to him. She had the same thick eyebrows as her father. He touched his forehead to hers. He seemed to be breathing in her innocence. If only he was as guiltless as he looked, Paula thought.

belinda stokes

Belinda Stokes jolted forward in her bed. She thought she heard someone call her name. Her heart raced. Even with her eyes wide open, she couldn't escape the eerie darkness. Something wasn't right. She threw the duvet off her legs and nudged Thomas on his back. Her husband didn't budge, and Belinda's touch didn't disturb the steady rhythm reverberating from the back of his throat. She shook his arm. It's a miracle he didn't wake himself, because he was close to disturbing one of the quietest neighborhoods in Danville, Virginia.

Pray.

Belinda shook Thomas's shoulder until he roused with a heavy snort.

"What is it, baby?" he asked. He turned over and wrapped his arms around her waist. He tried to bury his head in the small of her back. "You better be waking me up for something good," he said, his voice groggy with sleep.

Belinda peeled off Thomas's grip. "Stop it. I'm serious." Her eyes had adjusted enough just to see the pewter cross that lay on top of their cherrywood dresser.

Thomas heaved his tired body up against the headboard and clicked on the bedside lamp. "What is it?" He ran his hand across the stubble of his unshaven cheek.

The light hadn't changed a thing. Belinda still felt as if her heart were trying to pound its way out of her chest cavity. "Where's T.J.?"

Thomas squinted at the digital clock on the nightstand. "I guess he's still out with Donovan. It's only eleven thirty. I told him he had until one o'clock."

"Something's not right," Belinda said, shoving two pillows behind her back.

"Something like what?"

"I don't know. I've got a feeling." Belinda tossed one of the pillows to the foot of her bed.

"He'll be here. Maybe a little late, but he'll be here."

Her husband's words did nothing to assure her.

Thomas turned off the light and disappeared under the crumple of sheets. "Call him on his cell phone if you feel that serious about it," he said, then clicked off the light. His covered mass was snoring in less than a minute.

Belinda's nervousness for her stepson was temporarily replaced by annoyance because of Thomas's nonchalance. She sat in the dark again, surrounded by her roaming thoughts. The shadows taunted her. There was an anxiety she couldn't explain.

Pray.

True enough, T.J. was eighteen—and about to graduate from high school this year—but he was still living under their roof. She and Thomas often had a war of wills and words about the best way to raise T.J. At eighteen, Belinda thought, he should show more responsibility. But then again, a child couldn't emulate what he'd never been taught.

Belinda knew some of Thomas's leniency was attributed to the way T.J. was dumped on their front steps by his mother, Juanita. Unfortunately, *dumped* was the operative word. Five months earlier, T.J. was unexpectedly added as a member of their household. Consistent misbehavior had pushed his mother to drag him from his life in Pittsburgh. While in Baltimore dealing with her mother's blood clot scare following a mastectomy, Belinda received the news. It had been a long night that ended with her family being expanded in a way she'd never imagined.

"Thomas Jr. is here," he said.

"Thomas Jr. is where?" Belinda's grip on the phone loosened, and she had to steady it with two hands. "What do you mean?"

"He's here. At our house. Dropped off on the doorstep."

"The doorstep?" That was a fate reserved for orphaned puppies and abandoned postal packages, not for a teenage son who hadn't seen his father in ten years. "Make sense of this," she begged.

"I wish I could. His mother drove him from Pittsburgh and left him. Remember the boxes of clothes we thought were for the clothing drive? They're his."

Not only did a box of clothes come before him, but T.J. brought the drama with him. Ten years had passed since both Belinda and Thomas had laid eyes on the boy. Some days Belinda's heart melted for the seven-year-old boy she'd fallen in love with. The way he called her Ma 'Linda and begged her to walk him to the playground still held a place in her heart. He'd always run ahead of her, chasing a runaway ball until she scolded him for getting too far ahead.

Those were the small acts of disobedience.

Then there were days like last week when she could begin to see how Juanita's frustration had led her to leave her only child.

"It's a family feud of testosterone and estrogen in here," she'd told Paula one day. "I pray Micah doesn't go through the same phase." That's why Belinda prayed so fervently that Darryl would pull together whatever issue—or person—was keeping him from his marriage, especially now with two children.

One morning during her devotion time, Belinda realized that

she'd been praying more for her friends and the couples she counseled than she had for her own household. That had changed, but God knew she wanted quicker results.

The red digital numbers on the alarm clock teased her. Only fifteen minutes had passed.

Should I call? He probably won't answer.

Pray.

Even though T.J. fought tooth and nail about his curfew, he was on time for the most part. No matter how sleepy he was on Sunday mornings as a result of his Saturday night escapades, T.J. was required to go to church. On that, Thomas didn't budge.

Belinda hadn't given up on her prayers for T.J.'s salvation. He slumped on the back pew with boredom sketched across his face from the time he walked into the church doors until the benediction. At least he'd stopped falling asleep.

Belinda swung her feet over the edge of the bed. Her toes sank into the plush carpet as she moved her feet around in search of her bedroom slippers. She shuffled to the bedroom next to theirs where her seventeen-month-old daughter, Hannah, slept.

The ladybug night-light in the corner of the room shed just enough light for Belinda to see Hannah's face. Ever since she'd gotten a doll dressed like an angel for her first birthday, Hannah wanted to drag it wherever she went, including to bed. It was the cutest thing, but had faded from being washed in the weekly laundry loads.

Belinda gently rubbed her finger on Hannah's chubby cheek. It seemed Hannah's hair was growing faster than her body, and before going to bed, Belinda had brushed it into a frizzy mound on top of her head.

Hannah stirred slightly, hugging her doll into her chest. More than her doll, she loved T.J. Despite what T.J. did, Hannah was infatuated with her older brother. She followed behind him around the house until he grew tired of entertaining her. She'd even had her share of tantrums when he cut their playtime short to go hang with his boys.

Boys like Donovan Ramsey. The thumping bass from his

Chevrolet Impala always announced his arrival in the Stokeses' driveway. Instead of blowing the horn once like a respectable human being, he laid on it until T.J. appeared.

Belinda could see through Donovan's innocent facade. There was something about the constant smirk on his face and the deception lurking in his eyes.

This evening he'd come inside, but only because Thomas wouldn't let T.J. leave until he finished cleaning the kitchen. Donovan had slumped inside holding up one side of his baggy jeans. He watched while T.J. rinsed the dishes and loaded the dishwasher, slipping in a smart comment or two when he thought Belinda was out of hearing range.

The gum Donovan had been smacking did nothing to camouflage the smoke reeking from his breath. His dark lips told that he was a regular partaker of tobacco products, and God only knew what else.

There were plenty of things that God only knew, and God was who Belinda was relying on to protect her stepson in the midst of his negative peer influences. She and Thomas encouraged T.J. to befriend a couple of trustworthy teens at the church, but T.J. seemed to live to do the opposite of what they wanted.

Belinda sat down in the glider rocker in the corner of Hannah's room. She'd bought the chair the week after she adopted Hannah to help soothe the baby's nighttime colicky episodes, but it usually worked better to calm Belinda's nerves.

Pray.

Belinda heard the voice as clear as the one that had awakened her, but this one calmed her.

"God," she whispered. "I know I've got some growing to do in the parenting department, but I care about T.J.'s well-being. That's one of the reasons why I ride him so hard. Don't let him hate me. Let him see I act overprotective at times because I love him. And when I can't keep an eye on him, watch over my son."

She sat. And waited. And prayed some more.

Belinda was drowsy, but her spirit wouldn't let her sleep. At least she felt a sense of peace now, much of it because of the

Scripture she'd been meditating on from Psalm 91.

"He who dwells in the shelter of the Most High shall abide under the shadow of the Almighty. I will say of the Lord, He is my refuge and my fortress; my God, in Him I will trust."

The ringing phone pierced the silence.

Something happened. Belinda rushed back to her room and to Thomas's side of the bed. She could see the shadow of his hand groping for the phone.

"I'm not hearing any excuses about why he's going to be late." Thomas's irritation about the probable excuse surfaced on the voice from the first word when he answered the phone. "No excuse tonight, T.J.," he said with a grunt.

Evidently the response wasn't what Thomas expected. He shot forward.

"Yes." Thomas threw off the down comforter he'd been bundled in all night. "Yes."

"Who is it? What is it?" At first Belinda's voice quivered as the words fell from her lips, but the peace she'd experienced after her prayer swept over her again. She slid closer to her husband, touching his arm as if she could lend him her strength. She could hear a male voice, but couldn't discern whether it was T.J.'s or not.

"Which hospital?" All signs of sleep had left Thomas's voice and actions. He jumped from the bed and headed toward their walk-in closet, the phone lodged between his chin and shoulder.

Belinda was two steps behind him. She instinctively shed her nightgown and changed her clothes in sync with Thomas. The calm demeanor that usually held his wits together seemed to fall off with each piece of clothing. He yanked a turtleneck sweater and pair of jeans from their hangers, while Belinda pulled on a grey jogging suit.

The seconds felt like minutes before Belinda finally got an answer to her question.

He clicked off the phone and dropped it on the closet floor.

"T.J.'s been shot."

belinda

Shot?" Belinda's hands trembled. "What did they say, Thomas?"

Thomas shoved his feet into his boots and pushed past Belinda, his untied shoelaces flapping at his feet. "They didn't tell me all the details," he said. He reached back into the closet and snatched his overcoat off a hanger. The hanger fell to the floor.

"All I know is that they're taking him into emergency surgery."

Belinda unknotted the satin scarf wrapped around her natural twists. Thomas was on his way downstairs before she had the chance to put on her shoes. By the time she'd dressed Hannah, Thomas was waiting in their Jeep. The garage door was already up when she jumped into the backseat of the Cherokee. Belinda buckled Hannah into her car seat, all the while praying.

Thomas threw the car into reverse and backed out into their

cul-de-sac. The single light they'd left on in their bedroom was one of the few signs of life on the quiet street. The neighborhood slept while their family had been awakened to a tragedy.

Hannah's head swayed back and forth in the car seat as the Jeep hugged the curb.

"Honey," Belinda said, adjusting her seat belt. "We don't need two accidents tonight."

"Not now, Belinda," Thomas said. His words seemed to accelerate their speed by another ten miles per hour. He turned on the hazard lights and screeched onto the highway.

Belinda bowed out. Now was not the time to bark back. She closed her eyes and added their safety to the prayers she was whispering for T.J. God's peace kept her until they stood at the nurses' triage desk in the emergency room.

"Thomas Stokes Jr.," Thomas said. He didn't seem to know what to do with his hands. He stuffed them in his coat pockets for a few seconds, ran them across the waves of his hair another, then drummed his fingers on the nurses' station desk.

Belinda hoisted her sleeping daughter higher on her hip, then wrapped one of her hands around her husband's forearm. He looked prepared to bypass the logistics and bolt behind the door designated *Hospital Staff Only*.

After a few taps on the keyboard and directions through the maze of corridors, they were sitting in the surgery waiting room. Belinda found temporary reprieve from the weight of her daughter bearing down on her tired arms. She sank into a small chair covered with mauve fabric and sitting on wooden legs. Thomas paced back and forth between the room and the sterile white hallway, looking up with anticipation every time a staff member walked by.

Hospital waiting rooms were all too common for Belinda. She'd spent most of the previous summer in the hospital with her mother. A miracle, prayers, and God's grace had pulled her mother, Bernice, through her mastectomy and the complications with blood clots that followed. Belinda expected nothing less with T.J.

It was thirty minutes before a doctor arrived to give them

an update on T.J.'s condition. Dr. Patel's scrubs hugged his protruding belly, and his eyes bulged out just as far.

Dr. Patel rushed through his synopsis of T.J.'s status, and Belinda noticed the blank stare on Thomas's face.

Belinda disregarded Dr. Patel's medical jargon and asked, "Which means what?" The jargon and his thick accent made it difficult for her to comprehend his words.

"The bullet went into his side and is lodged in a muscle near the rib cage," Dr. Patel said, poking his stubby fingers into his side.

"Did anyone else come in with him?" Belinda asked. "He was with a friend. A boy named Donovan Ramsey."

The doctor took off his surgical cap to reveal a partially bald head. "As far as I know there's no one else that came in injured with him. The nurse did tell me that a boy came running inside yelling for help to get his friend out of the car."

Dr. Patel stopped to hear the announcement sounding over the intercom, then proceeded. "But after the nurses got your son out of the car and into a wheelchair, the boy sped off. I believe it was a young man around the same age as Thomas Jr., so maybe that was his friend."

Hmph. Belinda shook her head and let Thomas take over the questioning. She sat down at the end of a small couch where she'd laid Hannah. Belinda wanted to stretch out beside her. This was unbelievable. Hopefully when T.J. pulled out of this, he would finally realize that God had spared his life and that bad company wasn't worth cutting his life short.

"Someone will come to get you when your son comes out of recovery," Dr. Patel said. He nodded toward Thomas and Belinda before leaving the room and being summoned by a resident studying a white board attached to a nearby wall.

"I can't believe this is happening," Thomas said, finally taking off his coat. He slouched into the rigid waiting room chair. With his broad frame, there was no chance for comfort for him, but he slid down until his head rested on Belinda's shoulder.

She patted the side of his greying temple. He'd probably added a few worry strands since they received the call from the hospital.

"I should've listened to you," Thomas said. "You knew something was wrong. I'm his father. Why didn't I know?"

"God knew, sweetheart. I'm beating myself up saying that I should've called him. Maybe it would've kept him out of the way of danger some way. I don't know." Belinda shook her head. "But I prayed for God's hedge of protection around him. He's wounded, but he's alive."

"You're right, baby. God's going to bring us through this. He's never failed us." Thomas lifted his head and circled his arms around his wife.

"And He never will," Belinda added.

Hannah stirred awake for the first time, stretching out in her yellow pajama-clad body until she was stiff as a board. She squinted from the glare of the white fluorescent lights and looked around, aware for the first time that she'd been moved from her cozy crib. Her face scrunched into a grimace.

"Hand me her sippy cup, Thomas," Belinda said, aware of the signal that a piercing wail was about to disturb the hospital waiting room's stillness. Belinda had the cup to Hannah's lips before she cut into the silence of the third floor.

Belinda swayed side to side, soothing Hannah back to sleep in the curves of her bosom. And to think, Belinda had been rejoicing earlier that day with Paula about the birth of her daughter, and her son had barely escaped death. She couldn't think about what *could have* happened.

A television bolted to the corner wall ran prerecorded health segments. The Stokes family sat in silence until a nurse in blue scrubs stepped in the doorway.

"The Stokes family?" Her tiny voice fit her even tinier frame.

Thomas stood.

"Your son is in recovery," she said. "You can come see him now, but you should know that the police are waiting to talk to him as well." Her statement almost sounded like a question, but Belinda had a question of her own.

What in the world had T.J. gotten himself into?

✢   ✢   ✢

30

Belinda and Hannah sat in the cold corner of the hospital room until the two police officers finished questioning T.J. There was still no sign of Donovan, who evidently had escaped major injury, if any. Bullets weren't the only thing Donovan had dodged. It seemed now he was also dodging the law. Belinda prayed, it was only a case of being in the wrong place at the wrong time.

More fear than pain bathed T.J.'s countenance after the police left and he was alone with his parents. He barely spoke, and when he did, they were one- and two-word responses to his father's probing questions.

"He's a very lucky man," Dr. Patel was saying when he returned to give Thomas and Belinda an update. He flipped a switch and slid T.J.'s X-rays on top of a light box. He pointed to the black film with a small stylus held between his small sausage-shaped fingers. "One inch to the right and the bullet would have pierced his liver."

"Luck didn't prevent that," Thomas said, his eyes focused on the white blur that was the bullet. "That was God." Worry lines framed the corners of Thomas's eyes. He swayed like a pendulum while the Dr. Patel explained T.J.'s prognosis again.

"So he's going to have this bullet lodged near his rib cage for the rest of his life?" Thomas asked.

"That seems like the case," Dr. Patel said. "Moving it would do more harm than good, and believe it or not, it's stuck in a safe place." Dr. Patel stuck the stylus in the pocket of his white coat. "He'll always remember what he's been through, even if he can't physically see it."

Like the thorn in Paul's flesh, Belinda's thought.

Medical jargon ran out of the doctor's lips again, but this time he was talking to a staff associate at his side. His tone and movements were so methodical. Belinda sensed that he could emotionally disconnect from the people and treat them only as cases.

Belinda looked up at her son. T.J. moaned and pulled the white bedsheet up to his neck.

Thomas rolled the IV pole out of his way so that he could

sit in the chair beside T.J.'s bed. He didn't say much, and T.J. seemed stuck between emotions. Too scared to comment and too tough to cry.

zora fields

Zora Fields kicked off the comforter when the alarm clock blared for the third time. She stood up and adjusted her faded black sweatpants that had worked themselves until they'd twisted snug around her midthighs. She slapped off the shrill of the blaring alarm, wishing she'd set it to awaken her with music from the gospel station, instead of the abrupt beeping. Cool air rushed across her body. Three snoozes were the limit if both she and Preston planned to make it to work on time.

Zora slid back in bed and wiggled her arm under her husband's side so she could wrap him into a bear hug. They always started the night close enough for her to feel his breath on her neck, but by morning they were stretched out on opposite sides of the king-sized bed.

"It can't be time to get up," Preston said, pulling Zora's arms tighter around him.

"Oh, it's time."

Preston reached down and pulled the comforter back up over his legs. "You've got to stop keeping me up late."

"Spare me. You can barely keep your eyes open past ten o'clock." Zora stretched out her arms and legs as if she were making snow angels in Baltimore's first six-inch snowfall.

Last week's blizzard had caught the city by surprise, but Zora was more than thankful for the three days school had been cancelled. Preston was off of work for two of the days, and they'd had a great time doing what newlyweds do.

Preston lifted Zora's arm off his face, then propped himself up on his elbow. "Baby, can I tell you something without you getting offended?" He slid his arm through a rip in the side of her T-shirt, rubbing her side and lower back like an expert masseur.

"I see you're trying to soften me up first," she purred. Zora kissed his shoulder. "I think we should start the morning a little different."

She sat up and threw one of her legs over Preston, straddling him as he lay on his back. As she rubbed Preston's chest, she could tell he'd tossed his conversation to the side. Only God could create such a beautiful and intimate love like this between a husband and wife, Zora thought.

But a few minutes after the loving was over, the conversation was back.

"I'm not sure I want to hear what you have to say, but go ahead," Zora said. She crossed her arms and leaned on the edge of the dresser.

Preston finally got out of bed. He pulled a navy tie off of his rack and tossed it on the bed. "Why do you have to look so defensive? You've got a brother scared to say anything."

"Man up," Zora said, picking up his tie and wrapping it around her hand with a tight grip. "But remember, anything can be used as a weapon."

"I'll take my chances if it means I get to see some sexy lingerie again."

"You mean something from my bridal trousseau?" Zora

asked, rolling the word off of her tongue with a French accent.

"Whatever you call it," he said. "Just put one on. Tonight." He picked off a lint ball from the faded imprint across her chest. It used to read *Baltimore Ravens*.

Zora knew she was a pitiful sight. It was only four months into their marriage and she'd slipped into a rut that she'd promised herself she'd never do—not this early anyway. The dreaded raggedy sleepwear. Her tattered sweatpants from high school had replaced the silk camisole teddies. A safety pin took over the duties of the stretched elastic.

"Tonight," she promised. "The honeymoon attire is back."

Preston pumped his fist in the air. "Let the church say amen."

"Speaking of church," Zora said. "Your dad called after you fell asleep."

Preston walked into the bathroom and turned on the shower. It seemed as if his mind had moved on to another subject. "Do you have plans for later on this evening?"

Zora opened her bureau to find a pair of black trouser socks. She held up two and realized she'd mismatched them after doing the laundry. "I was thinking about going to see Paula and the baby at the hospital, but I wasn't sure if I should wait until they get home and settled a little bit."

"Can you go see the baby later?" Preston yelled over the running water. "I wanted us to have a nice dinner tonight. I'll cook for you."

You're cooking? Now this was something Zora couldn't pass up. While they were engaged, Preston suggested they alternate cooking dinner so they could save money to pay for the wedding. But since jumping the broom, he'd fallen into the routine of letting Zora handle their evening meals. She didn't mind, seeing that she was usually home before five and he rarely pulled into the driveway before seven o'clock.

"How romantic, baby. I'll come home then and see Paula later whenever Monét can go with me." Steam covered the shower door, but Zora could see the silhouette of her husband.

35

He was brushing his teeth in the shower. She hated that. Now he was rubbing the soap under his armpit without using a washcloth. She hated that too.

Even being a newlywed for barely four months, she'd already learned that the small things weren't worth pitching a fuss over. Preston didn't see the big deal about his nasty habits.

"Speaking of dinner," she added. "We're supposed to go out with Monét and Jeremiah later this week."

"Can you add that to my phone and set the alarm for a reminder?" he asked. "I'll forget by tomorrow."

Wife and official secretary, Zora thought, picking up Preston's phone. Her best friend, Monét, was the expert of all these high-tech gadgets, like cell phones that could basically perform everything that a computer could.

Zora made up the bed, then tossed on the embroidered pillows that gave it the extra flair she loved. Preston thought it was overkill, but that was coming from a man who'd only had one flat pillow and the same overwashed sets of bed linens for at least five years. Zora picked up the ringing phone and lay out her slacks and blouse she'd ironed last night.

Whenever the phone rang early in the morning it was usually one of Preston's parents. This morning was no different.

"Good morning, Baby Z," William Fields said. "How are you doing this blessed morning?"

"I'm fine, Pop," Zora said, smiling at the way her father-in-law always talked like he was addressing his congregation. "How are you doing?"

"Couldn't be better, couldn't be better," he said. "Mama is over here with my honey-do list taped to bathroom mirror, so I've got a long day ahead of me." He chuckled. "But I can't complain. She's been a good wife to me for forty years."

"Well, I hope I can keep Preston loving me that long," Zora said.

"Forty years and longer," he said. "Keep God first and you'll be able to endure any storm."

Zora heard the shower turn off. If Pop got started, he'd be preaching for the next twenty minutes, and she needed to get ready for work. "Preston just got out of the shower. Hold on for a minute and I'll put him on the phone."

Preston walked out of the bathroom with a towel wrapped around his waist. She knew she'd hurried off the phone so she could get ready for work, but seeing her husband with water running down his chest changed things. It wouldn't hurt to be a few minutes late.

Zora walked behind Preston, wrapping her arms around him from behind. She kissed his back. "Your father is holding you up from getting another dose of morning ministry," she whispered.

"Yes, sir," Preston said, pushing Zora's hands away as she ran them down his chest and under his arms. "Okay, I can do it." He tried to smother a laugh and covered up the phone's receiver. "You're wrong, baby," he said.

Zora snatched the towel from his waist. "And you're right. All right," she said, falling backward on the bed. She had been able to give Preston the most precious gift of her virginity on their wedding night. Zora beckoned him with her pointer finger, then slipped her entire body under the covers. Her husband ended his call in less than a minute.

✢ ✢ ✢

That evening when Preston arrived home, Zora was ready for him again, dressed in one of his favorite lingerie sets.

Preston dropped his briefcase and keys at the door. "How do you expect me to get any cooking done with you greeting me looking like that?" He picked her up and spun her around. Preston put her down, then loosened his necktie on the way to the bedroom.

"I've got to get started on dinner now," he said, "and I'll get started on you later."

Zora unhooked her robe from the back of the bathroom door and retreated to check her e-mails in the office until Preston called her out to eat. Much to her surprise, he'd moved the coffee table and laid out a fleece blanket in the middle of the floor.

"I don't think there's a comfortable way to eat salmon while sitting on the floor, but I wanted to do something different."

"Aren't you sweet," she said, sitting down Indian style while he served her. Along with the meal of salmon, yellow rice, and green beans, Preston doled out questions about how Zora felt about his family's ministry. Too many.

"Why are you asking me all of these questions?"

"Because I want to know how you really feel. It's not easy being part of the first family. Probably more drama than you expected," Preston said.

"Tell me about it." Zora rolled her eyes. "Oh, sorry, baby." But he was telling the truth. She felt as if she was on trial whenever she missed a service or somebody's committee meeting. Sacrifice went to another level being a Fields woman. She never had this kind of drama as a Bridgeforth.

Preston moved their empty plates so he could slide closer to her. "Baby, I need you to be in prayer with me about being called to the ministry."

What? Zora nearly swallowed the garlic bread she was chewing.

"I know it's a lot to handle all of a sudden—and something you didn't expect."

"You just don't wake up one morning and decide you want to be a minister," Zora said.

She knew that, and Preston knew that. Zora was so stunned at his announcement that she said the first thing that came to mind.

"Trust me, it didn't happen like that. Come on, Zora. You know your husband."

They had been sitting shoulder to shoulder before, holding hands. Zora turned her body so she could face him. "People said that you don't really know a person truly until you marry them. I just can't believe you never mentioned this before."

Zora couldn't wrap her mind around the idea. Or maybe it was that she didn't want to accept it.

"If you're going to be a minister, then I'm going to be a minister's wife," she said, shaking her head. "That role doesn't fit me."

Another thought hit her. Pop wouldn't lead the church forever, and she was sure one of his sons would step up as pastor. "I'm not interested in being anybody's first lady," she said. "Nobody but yours."

"Zora, you're getting panicky, and nothing has happened yet," Preston said. "I haven't said anything about being the pastor. Calm your nerves."

Now he was making her mad. "Don't say that. You know how I hate it when you say that. My nerves are calm. I'm just expressing my thoughts. When did that become a crime? It's called communication."

Preston pushed himself off the floor and sat on the couch. "Okay, this conversation wasn't meant to be an argument. Just like I'm tired of these internal arguments with God. He's got me, Zora, and He's not letting me go until I answer."

"What can I say when you put it like that?"

"Say you're by my side," he said.

Zora joined him on the couch. She cupped his chin in her hands. "I'm by your side," she whispered, studying his face. He was sporting a new look—a tapered beard that gave his face more maturity. He held a striking resemblance to his father.

Zora climbed into Preston's lap and let him hold her like a baby. The shock was wearing off, but the nervousness of being lifted to another level of accountability hadn't. "Why didn't you tell me earlier?"

"Baby, you were dealing with your parents' deaths and then finding out you were adopted," he explained. "We had the wedding on top of that, and I couldn't add that kind of weight to what you were already carrying."

As always, Preston had her best interest in mind. "Thank you. I appreciate you." They weren't just words. She really meant it.

"And if it's God's will that I pastor the church one day, you're more than equipped to handle it."

"God's going to have to help me with that one."

"And He will," Preston assured her.

Zora closed her eyes. She could hear her mother now. "*This is an honor, Zora. God knows what He's doing in your life. You've got to trust Him.*"

Zora wished she could sit on her mother's bed while they ate the chocolate-covered raisins they loved so much. After a day of bargain shopping at neighborhood yard sales and antique stores, her mother would assure her that she was capable of being a minister's wife, and possibly one day, a first lady. But that would never happen. Her days with her parents were stolen last year at the hands of a drunk driver on New Year's Eve night.

"Are you crying?" Preston lifted her head.

Zora let the tears run freely. It was how she handled the remembrance of their deaths, and the memories. "I'm fine," she said. "I'll be fine."

monét
sullivan

Monét Sullivan pulled on her leather gloves as she waited in the atrium of the cultural arts center for Jeremiah Hartgrove. He'd insisted on chauffeuring her to and from work today, saying that she didn't need to be alone with her thoughts on the last day of a job she loved. But her thoughts had been on God's plan for her life. She'd been hit with the reality this morning while enjoying a cup of Earl Grey tea during her morning devotion time. With her regular paychecks coming to an end and few leads for a new position in event planning, her faith was being catapulted to another level. God spoke to her through today's meditation Scripture in Jeremiah 29:11: "*For I know the thoughts that I think toward you, says the Lord, thoughts of peace and not of evil, to give you a future and a hope.*"

"Let me take you out to dinner to celebrate your new freedom and venture into entrepreneurship," Jeremiah had suggested this morning when he'd dropped her off.

"We're going out with Zora and Preston in a couple of days," she said. "I can wait until then."

Monét's best friend was always making sure her first matchmaking success was progressing. Monét's relationship with Jeremiah was built on a strong friendship. Zora kept saying that marriage would be the next step, but it was Monét's fear of the long-term commitment that had their relationship at a crawl. Jeremiah had learned to pace himself with her. Still, Monét's heart was moving faster than she wanted it to. Her heart had run ahead of her mind before, and it had only led to heartache.

Jeremiah interrupted her thoughts. "Tonight is just for us."

"Fine. Let's go for Thai," she said.

He didn't object, even though he was a meat-and-potatoes man. He'd always compromise on the small things, especially if he knew it would make her happy. It was one of the small things that made him more attractive to Monét, almost as equally as the way his deep-set eyes drew her into his world.

"A woman who knows what she wants too. You'll be in some magazine's feature about great women in business in no time. Or maybe we'll be on a cover featuring married couples with innovative business minds."

"Great women in business," she repeated. "I can see that." Monét ignored his other comment, knowing that if she gave him an inch to run with, he'd take a mile.

Jeremiah let her out of the car that morning with a kiss that lifted her spirits and her body temperature. She was going to have to put the brakes on those kisses. They were way too tempting. And to think, she had regular access to those lips since they now lived with his muscular physique just two floors above her. It was a good and bad thing. She loved the fact that she and Jeremiah could spend time together at a moment's notice, but they'd had to take the Scripture "flee fornication" literally a few times.

Monét wrapped her scarf around her neck until the fabric gathered under her nose, then went to sit on a nearby bench. She'd walked through the current exhibits during lunch and reminisced about the challenges of pulling off extravagant events on a shoestring budget. She had watched the financial situation of the cultural arts center where she'd worked for the last four years head downhill. The director tried to salvage her job, but the executive board was set on axing any position they didn't deem necessary. Her job as events coordinator was one of the first on the chopping block.

Monét's savvy business instinct kicked in, and she'd used the last thirty days since her separation notice to gather reference letters from artists who had displayed their works at the center. She had worked hard to build her Rolodex of some of the city's most affluent artists, foundations, and business owners, and had taken the stuffed card file home last night along with two cardboard boxes of office decorations and desk accessories. Today she only wanted to walk out with memories.

Jeremiah honked the horn twice to get Monét's attention. She scuttled outside against the push of the brisk February wind to the passenger door that Jeremiah held open. With his help, she climbed up into the warm cab of his black double-cab truck that she often called "The Monster," because of the oversized tires he'd bought to replace the manufacturer's standard ones. Growing up in Texas gave him a cowboy's heart that hadn't been changed since his move to Maryland from Houston two months ago. Jeremiah was quick to remind her that "they do things big in Texas."

"Ready for the next level?" Jeremiah asked as he adjusted the heat up another notch.

"Always," Monét said, looking back one last time as they pulled away from the curb. Her prayer over the last few months had been for God to expand her career opportunities. He'd done it, just not in the way she expected. The same thing happened when Monét sought God for direction concerning her relationship with Jeremiah. At the time, she was against trying to maintain a long-distance relationship. She'd tried and failed at it before. Her college boyfriend, Terrance, upped and moved to California to pursue his dream of being a movie producer, and what had lasted for two years when they were in the same city was snuffed out in less than a few months when their commitment was tested across the miles. Monét hadn't been able to see herself trying to build a relationship with Jeremiah with an entire coastline between them. Then God intervened. A merger and job transfer later, Jeremiah was living in the same condo building. Monét could only attribute that to divine intervention. God always had a way of showing her that He was in control of her life. *If only I can let Him take the wheel of our relationship.*

Monét glanced over at Jeremiah, who was focused on merging over into the highway's car pool lane.

"Why are you looking at me?" he asked, without turning to her. A Honda Civic with its share of dings and scrapes slowed down so that Jeremiah's monstrous vehicle could get over.

"No reason," Monét said, unwrapping her scarf. "Just thinking."

"About me, I hope."

Monét adjusted the air vent on her side so that the heat blew toward the roof of the car. "It's getting hot in here," she said and unbuttoned her coat.

Jeremiah looked at her as if she were the woman he wanted to spend the rest of his life with. "I guess you were thinking about me."

✦   ✦   ✦

Monét sat down on her shag rug with a coaster and a ceramic mug filled to the rim with hot cocoa. She'd pulled back the sheer panels that ran across the wall-length patio door in her living room, hoping that the winter sun would give her an extra boost of energy. During the first week of unemployment, she stayed up late into the night, often falling asleep on the couch while flipping through redundant infomercials or sitcom classics that she used to watch as a child. Jeremiah's standard eleven o'clock telephone call had been her alarm clock for the day. But this week, she decided to shift into another mode and prepare herself like a woman on a mission. She felt as if something was about to jump off. And she was right.

Savon Perry was well known in the Baltimore city area and was becoming more prominent as he traveled around the United

States, performing as the spoken word voice of The Four Winds, a four-man group of musical artists. She'd contracted him several times as the entertainment for events at the center, and he'd graciously reduced his fee so she could stay within her budget. Like she'd done with all her business associates, she'd sent Savon an e-mail with her contact information in case he or anyone else needed her event coordination services.

It didn't take him long to take her up on the offer.

Savon had left a message earlier that morning, but Monét was determined not to switch into business mode when she first cracked open her eyes. She took time meditating on her daily devotion, read her Bible, and cooked herself a hearty break-fast of oatmeal, egg whites, wheat toast, and turkey bacon. It was a nice change from juggling a protein bar and cup of or-ange juice on the way out the door.

When both her stomach and her spirit were fed, she called Savon.

For the first thirty minutes, he rambled about the fundrais-ing event he wanted to host for his nonprofit, The Savon Perry Foundation, founded to establish and support self-esteem-building programs for inner-city youth. Monét typed furiously on her laptop, trying to capture his ideas and vision so that she could revisit it later.

It was a combination fashion show and art auction and would require her incessant attention to pull off the event in the four-month time frame he suggested.

I wouldn't have to worry about what to do in my spare time, she thought. The logistics of the event would be overwhelming, but Monét thrived on details.

"I've never done an event like this, but I'm up for the chal-lenge," Monét said, when Savon finally stopped to breathe.

"I called you because I believe in you. Trust me," Savon said. "You'll love doing your own thing. Getting kicked off the job won't be so bad."

"Do you have to make it sound like they were happy to get rid of me?"

"Say what you want. As long as you're free to work with me, that's all I care about."

Monét muted the volume on the television and flipped through the channels. "Of course you realize this is a non-binding verbal agreement until you agree to my proposal and consultant fees."

Savon dropped his baritone voice another octave. "Let's rewind what I said earlier, Monét."

Here we go, Monét thought. Savon could use his voice like an instrument, reciting verses of memorized poetry and dropping words on stage that sent his female audiences into a girly fit. But she wasn't one of his groupies pining for attention. This was business.

"Your ideas and your fees won't be a problem," Savon said. "You have my word on it. Words pay my bills, so I don't have any to waste."

"I'll e-mail everything over by Friday, then give you a follow-up call," Monét said. She saved her open document. After a little research on similar events, she could draft a proposal fitting his needs and financially appropriate for the amount of work she'd have to put in.

"How about we meet for lunch on Saturday and I'll pay you the retainer fee?" Savon said. "We can get this ball rolling next week. Do you like Japanese?"

"One of my favorites."

"Let's make plans to meet on Saturday. I'll call you back and let you know where."

"Saturday it is."

Monét disconnected his call but held the phone, trying to think of who else she was supposed to call. *That's right. Belinda.*

Zora had taken on the role as liaison for their group of girlfriends so Belinda wouldn't be flooded with phone calls checking on T.J.'s progress. From Zora's last update, the doctors planned to release T.J. to go home this weekend if his parents promised to limit his activity.

Monét knew the doctors had nothing to worry about. With the law laid down at the Stokes household, she doubted T.J.

would be able to leave the house until he was thirty, especially if Belinda had anything to do with it.

There was no answer at the Stokeses' house or on Belinda's cell phone.

"Hi, Belinda, it's Monét. Hope all is well," she said, leaving a message on the voice mail. "Just wanted you to know I'm thinking about and praying for you all. Call me when you get a chance."

Monét prayed Belinda was holding it together. Even before T.J.'s accident, Belinda had missed their last few prayer circle phone calls because of the demands on her at home. The transition of having a strong-willed teenager in the house had already been a roller-coaster ride of emotions for Belinda. She'd been used to a toddler who wasn't old enough or crazy enough to challenge her parents' authority.

Even though Monét had known Belinda for less than a year, her relationship with her—as well as Paula—was knitted tighter than some of the close friends she'd had since college. God had brought them into one another's lives for a reason—Monét, Belinda, Paula, and Zora.

Zora had been Monét's childhood friend since they were three, but all of the four women's hearts were connected when they participated in a multichurch women's discipleship group —Purposed Ordained Women Equipped and Righteous. When they were assigned to the same prayer group, the covers were eventually thrown off the issues they'd attempted to hide from one another. After nine months, the discipleship group ended, but their friendships didn't. When busy schedules didn't collide, Monét, Zora, and Paula got together for those much-needed girls nights out, but it always felt like there was a missing link with Belinda living in Virginia.

They needed to get together and pour their hearts out to one another. Soon.

belinda

I miss you guys so much," Belinda said, surprised that her eyes were beginning to water. At times like this, it was a comfort to hear the voices of all her friends and prayer partners at one time. As soon as things settled down a bit, she was hopping on the highway to go and visit them and her new goddaughter, Gabrielle.

"Give the baby kisses from her Auntie Belinda," she told Paula. "I'll be up there as soon as I can steal away for a weekend. I need it," she said. "Really need it. Love you all."

"We love you," they chimed back.

"Kiss Hannah for all of us," Paula said. "And pass a little to the men in your life."

"Hannah I can do." Belinda lowered her voice. "Those other two I'll have to think about. Talk to you guys soon."

Belinda went to the kitchen and heaped enough lasagna on a plate for two people. T.J. may have been shot, but there was nothing wrong with his stomach. It actually seemed like he'd been eating more since he returned from the hospital. He'd probably realized the value in having a home-cooked meal. Belinda doubted he'd be begging for a combo meal from a fast-food restaurant anytime soon.

With food in hand, Belinda went upstairs and stopped outside of T.J.'s bedroom door. She'd quickly learned that carpet and socks worked wonders for snooping parents.

"Nah, man. I'm straight," T.J. was saying. "Wasn't nothing but a little battle wound." He went on bragging. "Couldn't take me down though—know what I'm saying?"

Belinda knew what T.J. was saying, all right. That he'd lost his mind. He saw the scar from his operation as more of a mark of honor than a reality check. She could tell by the way he was mumbling his words together that he was talking to one of his running buddies.

"Donovan, man. Stop tripping."

Donovan! Oh no, he wasn't talking to that . . .

"You gotta do what you gotta do. I would've done the same thing."

What? Be a coward and run away? First of all, you know better than that, even if you don't act like it. Belinda took a five-second break to calm her rambling thoughts. This boy was making her talk to herself. *God, give me strength,* Belinda thought, peeking through the crack of the door.

T.J. had his bare feet propped up on the bed's headboard. He'd stacked three pillows under his head, and for the first time Belinda noticed he was in desperate need of a haircut.

"Yeah, man, the police were asking me all these questions," T.J. said. "I didn't know nothing, and that's what I told 'em too. It's like they were trying to trip me up to see if I was lying. You know how they are. Always trying to take somebody down."

Belinda turned around and crept back down the stairs and into the kitchen. She didn't want to hear any more of T.J.'s conversation. She put the plate of lasagna in the microwave and covered it with a napkin. If T.J. got hungry, he could drag himself downstairs or wait until Thomas got home from his meeting at church. They'd agreed not to leave T.J. at home so soon because of his physical state. Now, Belinda thought, it would be a matter of trust.

While Hannah busied herself throwing wooden blocks in a plastic bucket, Belinda folded the baskets of washed laundry by the couch. She finished the towels before working on the heaps of Hannah's clothes. Pretty soon they'd be boxed up with the others she'd outgrown and mailed to Paula for Gabrielle. Not that she needed them. Gabrielle's closet was probably overstuffed with designer boutique wear with prices outside the reasonable budget of a magazine editor and electrician like she and Thomas.

When Thomas arrived home, Belinda was just finishing folding his undershirts. She swore those things mated and had children overnight.

"One of these days I'm going to have a maid," she said, giving him a welcome-home kiss before he headed for the kitchen. The bottles on the inside of the refrigerator door clanked against each other as he swung the door open.

"You sure are, baby," Thomas yelled back. "It's going to happen the same day you agree to let me buy a motorcycle."

"On second thought, folding laundry isn't really that bad," Belinda said, getting up to answer the doorbell. The impatient visitor rang it twice before she had a chance to finish her sentence. "You expecting somebody?"

"Probably one of the neighbors," Thomas muffled through a mouthful of food. "They were collecting dues for the homeowner's association earlier this week, but they caught me when I was on the way out the door. I told them to come back."

Belinda peeked out of the peephole. *Juanita?* She immediately recognized the face of T.J.'s mother and opened the door. Juanita's hair was shorter, and she'd gained about twenty pounds, but there was no mistaking the scowl that framed her face. Belinda had seen it plenty of times when she and Thomas were dating. Over the last ten years, it hadn't changed.

Belinda unlocked the storm door, and Juanita swung it open so fast and hard that Belinda thought she heard the metal spring pop. She staggered to regain her balance when Juanita pushed past her.

51

"T.J.?" Juanita yelled at the top of her lungs as soon as she barged into the house. Seeing no sight of her son, she screamed in the direction of the steps, making the hairs stand up on the back of Belinda's neck. "T.J., are you up there?"

She's still crazy, Belinda thought. She was so stunned that it took her a minute to respond.

"Now wait just a minute. I know you're worried about your son, but you need to calm down. There's no need to disrespect my home."

Juanita jerked her neck back like she was offended. "This is between me and my son's father," she said. She pointed a red acrylic fingernail at Thomas who'd appeared from around the corner. Astonishment wasn't even fitting to describe the look on his face. He scooped up Hannah, who was crying louder than Juanita's tirade.

"Which means it's between all of us, because there's no separation here," Belinda said. She stepped close enough to Juanita for their toes to touch. "So you have a decision to make," Belinda said. She was keeping her cool as best as she could. "You can act like you've got some sense and have a cordial visit, or you can reverse your behind out of my front door."

Okay, God. Maybe that wasn't the best way to say it.

Belinda's heart raced. It had been a long time since the former Belinda, who used to have all the bark with no bite, had surfaced. In her midtwenties she'd sent that bad attitude packing and hadn't seen it since. She thought it was gone for good, but then again, she'd never been challenged in her own house by her husband's ex-girlfriend.

Belinda's heart settled to its normal pace when she saw Juanita cower, especially when she realized Thomas—even in his silence—was in agreement. Hannah clung to Thomas. Her dried tears had left white streaks down her cocoa brown face.

"Please let me see my son," Juanita said, massaging her temples. They were the first words she'd spoken in a normal speaking volume.

"Sure," Belinda said. *That's what I thought.*

Juanita moved toward the staircase, assuming— Belinda

thought—that she had free rein to the house. Belinda held out an arm to block her. A minute before that same arm would've easily trapped that woman in a headlock. *Okay, God. I'm sorry.*

"Thomas will get him for you. Have a seat over there."

Juanita rounded the corner of the end table and plopped down on the brown leather recliner. Belinda started to protest. Of all the places to sit, why did she have to park herself in Thomas's favorite chair? The imprint from his backside was practically etched in it.

"Can I get you something to drink?" Belinda offered. She was trying—really trying—to be cordial.

"I'm fine," Juanita said. She crossed her arms and her legs, subconsciously shutting Belinda out.

Great, Belinda. Tell the woman off, then offer her something to drink. Not likely she'll be sipping from any cup I give her.

"How are you doing, Juanita?" Thomas asked. Hannah wiggled out of his arms and ran to the toy box in the corner of the room.

"All right." She didn't look at Thomas. Instead, she seemed to be taking in the setting around her.

The candles lit on the fireplace mantle made it smell like there was a fresh apple pie baking in the oven. Family pictures in silver frames, the most recent taken at Christmas, were arranged on the end table beside Juanita.

For a brief moment, Belinda felt compassion for Juanita. Did she feel that the Stokeses had given T.J. a secure family environment that she couldn't? There was more drama behind the smiles of those photos than Belinda had ever expected. Despite what she saw, Juanita must've known too. She'd been a single mother trying to raise a son whose testosterone levels often got him into more trouble than the both of them could handle.

Belinda tried to conjure up some small talk, but fortunately the struggle didn't last long. She heard the labored thud of T.J. coming downstairs.

"Ma?" He sounded like he couldn't believe it.

"T.J." Juanita stood but didn't move past her self-imposed boundaries. "Look at you. I can't believe you look so much like a man." Tears streamed down her cheeks. "Don't scare me like this anymore, boy." She finally ran over and kissed him on the face. T.J. had to lean down so she could wrap her arms around his neck. Her affection didn't last long. Juanita punched him in the arm.

"I didn't bring you down here to mess around and get yourself shot. I almost killed myself trying to get here."

In such a rush that it took you six days, Belinda wanted to say.

T.J. rubbed his bicep. "What took you so long, Ma? I've been trying to call you."

"I was on a cruise with Larry. My first cruise ever in life," she boasted, then seemed to realize her timing was wrong for bragging. "I didn't know until I got back on land and checked my messages."

Larry's name brought a grimace on T.J.'s face that matched his mother's earlier expression. "You still foolin' with that busta, Ma?" he asked, shaking his head.

Juanita smacked her lips. "Keep your mouth off of Larry. He's never done nothing to you besides make you try to do right."

"Whatever," T.J said. "So what's with you out in the middle of the ocean? You can't even swim."

"Boy, what's that got to do with anything?"

"What if the ship would've sunk?"

"Well, it didn't, so don't even talk about it," Juanita said. "Larry asked me to go, so I said yes. I'm the parent; you're the child. I don't have to answer to you."

Belinda could tell that Juanita wasn't interested in putting her business out on the table.

"I came down here for you," Juanita said, redirecting the conversation. "Nothing else matters."

Juanita hugged T.J. around his waist in an awkward sort of way. They sat down together on the couch. T.J. slumped so low that he was practically on the floor, while Juanita sat up like there was a steel rod in her back.

Belinda tugged at Thomas's shirttail and motioned for him to follow her to the kitchen table. Even with the television on, they'd still be within earshot of their conversation. T.J. wasn't the only one she didn't trust.

T.J. caught Juanita up with what had been happening since the last time they saw each other around Thanksgiving. They'd spent time together that weekend since she claimed she'd have to work overtime through the Christmas holidays. His Christmas gift from her arrived in the form of a card more fitting for an eleven-year-old—covered with green and red glitter and candy canes.

"Are you taking me back with you?" T.J. finally asked.

"Not right now, T.J. You need to be here with your dad."

Belinda opened the back door and walked out on the deck with Thomas. He'd put on Hannah's coat and taken her outside to play with her ball. "She just wants him here so she can run the streets without feeling guilty, Thomas," Belinda said, watching Hannah stumble over her own feet while she chased the ball in the backyard. "She's gotten a taste of freedom, and it's too sweet for her to turn it down."

"If that's the reason, so be it," Thomas said. "It's better than him being with her and having no supervision."

"He has supervision here, and he still managed to get shot up. The evidence is still stuck in his side, remember?"

"What do you want me to do? Make her take him home anyway?"

Belinda looked past Hannah and out into the bare tree branches. What kind of wife and mother would she be if she answered, *Yes*?

paula

Paula didn't want to put a damper on Monét and Zora's visit, but she felt like she was going to explode from the pent-up emotions. She was relieved for the moments when their fits of laughter brought tears to their eyes. At least then Paula was able to let the tears fall.

Crushed ice from the automatic dispenser clinked into the gold-stemmed flutes. Paula poured green tea over the cold chips until the liquid danced close to the brim. After adding warm spinach dip into the center of a sourdough bread bowl, she served her girlfriends refreshments and a confession.

"Darryl insists on a paternity test. I've been telling him no, but he won't let the issue rest. I might just agree to it to shut him up."

"Paula, are you serious?" Zora asked, her mouth hanging open. She set her drink on the end table without taking a sip.

Paula had never seen a time when her spinach dip specialty sat on the coffee table without being touched, but evidently both of her friends were too stunned to dig into the appetizer they always raved about.

Paula didn't have an appetite, but she made herself eat. It wasn't wise for her to go without food and sleep. With a one-week-old, the lack of sleep was out of her hands, but a few bites of spinach dip would hold her over until she could throw together something for dinner.

Paula lifted her feet up onto the chaise. "Do you think I would make that up? You know my story. I'm not playing."

Zora and Monét were two of a handful of people to whom Paula had poured her heart out to about her dissolving marriage. Before then she'd had an image to uphold, but facades can't last forever.

She remembered the day hers shattered.

The P.O.W.E.R. discipleship group had met at her house that afternoon. With all the preparations for their visit, Paula had failed to study the lesson about marriage that they would be discussing. As one woman—Yolanda—shared her testimony, Paula's emotions erupted.

Paula couldn't stop the tears. She felt the wail rise through the soles of her feet until it nearly choked in throat. Her body slumped over and slid itself onto the floor. She no longer had control.

Someone had knelt beside her, covering her shivering body with her arms. She felt another set of hands on her head and then the voices of women around her. They prayed fervently, sharing her tears and petitions until a peace like Paula had never experienced enveloped her. After a few minutes, she was able to push herself up to an upright position. All of the women were on the floor crouched or sitting around her.

"I must look a mess," she said, running an already soaked tissue across her eyes. It was streaked with black mascara and brown eye shadow.

"Who cares what you look like?" Belinda was sitting closest to her. "You just got a breakthrough."

Paula needed another one cleansing like that one.

Monét bent down to the Moses basket where Gabrielle lay and tucked the bottom edge of the pink fleece blanket swaddling the infant. Gabrielle's eyes peeked open, then drooped closed again. "This face should be proof enough," Monét said. "She looks just like her daddy."

"Tell me about it," Paula said. "He knows it too. He's just doing it to upset me."

"And is it working?" Zora asked.

"Of course, but I'm trying not to act like it is," Paula said.

"Are you going to put the baby through the test? I mean, really."

Paula tore off a piece of bread and put it on her saucer. "Remember that time he ran into me at the coffee shop with that guy Victor from college? I see the man one time in thirteen years, and all of sudden he's my secret lover, if you let Darryl tell it."

"And your baby's daddy. Don't forget that nonsense," Monét added. "Dr. Manns should know better than that."

Zora wore a contemplative look. "One of the things that really stood out to me during my wedding ceremony was when Papa Fields was talking about people staying out of the business of other people's households. So I'm not going to say you should or shouldn't do the paternity test. You need to do what works best for your marriage."

Paula wanted to erupt. "What would work best for my marriage is for Darryl to stop acting like a—"

"You said you were going to fight. Remember that? The last time you hit rock bottom you said you were going to fight until God restored your marriage."

"And I did. And I have been. Over and over again," she said, pounding a fist into one of her palms.

"And it got better."

"For a while. Then it got worse." Paula threw her hands up in surrender. It was an outward sign to Zora and Monét that she'd done all she could do, and an inward cry to God for help. The thought of leaving had been crossing her mind for months, but it wasn't an option for her to waddle out of the house while pregnant, with a son, and ultimately with no plan. Now she was staying for the children.

"Can you hold on to the hope of what it used to be?" Zora's voice was soft like she was dealing with one of her students having trouble with his grades.

"I don't know for how long." Paula cried. It felt good to do it among friends instead of having to do it alone. They didn't interrupt her weeping. When she finished, she wiped her eyes and stared at them.

Paula sniffed. "You look like you want to say something, Monét."

Monét shook her head. "Marriage has me stressed out, and I don't even have a husband."

The hum of the garage door lifting ended their conversation. It was Darryl. Paula reached for another tissue on the end table and patted her face. "Good time for a switch in topics."

Monét shuffled through a set of magazines, looking relieved for the opportunity to change the mood. As a single woman, Paula noticed that she seemed disinterested in marital strife. She couldn't blame her. This was the side of marriage no one had ever talked to Paula about before the words "I do."

"We need to have a ladies' weekend sometime soon," Monét said. "That is, if we can get you married women out of the house."

Paula asked, "So Jeremiah doesn't have the privilege of putting you on lockdown every now and then?" She remembered the blurry dating line that divided the committed weekends with your significant other and weekend romps with your girlfriends.

Monét put her feet up on the chocolate leather ottoman in front of the matching love seat. "Negative. I enjoy my freedom."

"Whatever. She's trying to play that role, Paula," Zora said, finally enjoying the spinach dip.

"I know. I haven't been around as long as you have, but I've just about got your girl figured out."

Monét brushed them off. "The only role I'm trying to play right now is entrepreneur. Your priorities change when you don't have a guaranteed check deposited into your bank account every two weeks." She added, "And you don't have a husband to take up the slack."

"If I had to choose between the two right now I'd take the bank account," Paula said. "That's how a sister is feeling today. Check back with me tomorrow."

Darryl walked in like he not only owned the house, but the entire world. His ego took up all of the empty space in the palatial living room. Paula wondered if anyone else could feel it. His keys clanked and slid across the countertop when he dropped them down along with a handful of mail.

From the outside, Darryl was the epitome of every woman's dream. He was physically fit, easy on the eyes, and his stock tripled because he was a successful cardiac surgeon with influence in the community. Paula fell in love with the package.

Darryl strutted over, intruding into Paula's personal time with her friends. She wasn't sure if he'd noticed the evidence of her tears. He did. She didn't have to look in a mirror to know her eyes were puffy around the corners.

"You ladies having a crying session in here? Whatever she said, I didn't do it," Darryl joked. He was the only one who laughed. He walked over and leaned down to hug both Zora and Monét, passing by Paula.

"Somebody from the association should be contacting you about another fund-raiser this year," he told Monét.

"Oh, I'm not at the center anymore," Monét said. "One month they decide to do structural changes and the next month my job is cut."

"That's a decision they'll regret," Darryl said. "Don't worry—they'll call back for you before you know it."

Monét crossed her legs and her arms. "They never should've let me get a taste of being an entrepreneur. Unless God tells me different, I'm done with the corporate world."

Darryl chuckled. He twisted the signet ring on his left pinkie. The ring finger beside it was still bare. Some days Paula wanted to take off her wedding ring just to spite him. He probably wouldn't even notice.

"I guess God forgot to warn you that they were slicing your job," Darryl said. "He should let people know about things like that."

That was so like him, Paula thought. The chameleon had shown his true colors. Now they'd see what she'd had to live with.

Darryl turned his attention to his daughter. "Is she not the most beautiful baby on the face of the earth?" He scooped up Gabrielle and cuddled her close to his chest. Those deep brown eyes used to look at her in the same loving way, Paula thought. *Would they ever again?*

Patience.

Patience? Sometimes Paula wondered if she heard God's voice correctly. This was one of those times. Her relationship with Him wasn't as close as she wanted it to be, but in the past year, she'd made bigger strides than she had over the six years that she'd lived halfheartedly. If there was one thing she knew for sure, the difficulties in her marriage had driven her closer to the feet of God than she'd ever been.

Zora

Antoinette "Toni" Burkes stomped into Zora's corner office in the guidance counselors' suite. She dropped her flimsy backpack by the door before she slumped into the chair across from Zora's desk. The back of the chair hit the wall, causing a framed certificate above her head to rattle.

Zora acknowledged her presence with a nod, then went back to thumbing through Toni's growing discipline file. The eleventh grader had been in her office three times in the last two weeks. Her grades had dropped from superior to below average, and the principal kept sending the seventeen-year-old to Zora, knowing that Toni's behavior was out of character.

Toni had first been assigned to Zora as a ninth grader who was more interested in socializing than academics. At that time, Toni had never considered college as part of her future, mainly because of finances. Zora, however, saw that Toni held promise and convinced her to consider applying to a community or junior college. When Zora showed interest and concern for Toni, her grades and attitude improved.

Now this.

Toni smacked her lips, then crossed and uncrossed her legs. Zora ignored her. Even when Toni huffed and mumbled under her breath, Zora didn't budge. She wanted to make it clear that Toni was in her territory, and disrespectful attitudes wouldn't be tolerated. Not today. And especially not when she was disrupting Zora's day with nonsense.

After five minutes, Zora held her hand out across her desk. Toni dug into the back pocket of her hip-hugging jeans and retrieved two crumpled pieces of paper. One was a hall pass, the other a note from Toni's history teacher, Mr. Calhoun.

"What is it this time?" Zora asked, before reading the paper.

Toni didn't answer.

"Not today, Miss Burkes. We both have other things we could be doing, and I'm not in the mood." They were close enough that Zora didn't have to beat around the bush.

Zora's strict tone must've worked. When it came to her students, Zora was more patient than the other guidance counselors. She often took the time to talk to the students about their personal lives so she could get to the root of any academic problems. The last thing she wanted to do was add another weight to the emotional baggage they were already dragging.

"Mr. Calhoun doesn't like me. He blames me for everything."

Zora flattened the note out on her desk. "So failing two quizzes in the past two weeks is his fault too, I suppose." It took her a minute to decipher the history teacher's chicken scratch. "It says here you were disrupting the class by arguing with Rashad."

"Rashad started it," Toni blurted out. "He gets on my nerves. I wasn't even talking to him, and he walks up and tries to start some mess. That's why his butt got sent to the principal's office."

"Well, if you had to choose between the principal's office and my office, then it seems like you got the good end of the deal."

"I guess so." Toni leaned over on the chair's wooden armrest and propped her chin up with her palm.

Zora clicked the tip of her ballpoint pen repeatedly with her thumb. "So Rashad is the reason your grades are slipping in your other classes too?"

"No, ma'am."

Zora's tactics eased at the sound of the student's respect. The old Toni wasn't lost after all. "What is it then?"

"I've got a lot on my mind. More than you would understand, Miss Bridgeforth. I mean—Mrs. Fields. Sorry about that. I keep forgetting you got married."

"That's okay. I'm still getting used to it myself," Zora said, leaning back on the headrest of her leather desk chair. "Why don't you try to tell me what's on your mind? I might understand more than you think."

Toni averted her glance to the floor. A single tear fell down the side of her face, but she quickly brushed it away. Zora didn't want to swoop in like a protective mother eagle too soon. Toni guarded her emotions and wasn't quick to share anything that didn't relate to school, even after three years of knowing Zora.

The clock ticked. It was the only sound in the room until Toni answered.

"It's my mama," Toni finally said. "She's pregnant again."

Zora was at a loss for words. *"My mama is getting on my nerves. My mama is always fussing at me."* Any one of those statements she'd been prepared for. There was nothing unusual about a pregnant woman. But Zora knew that Toni's mother was single, and Toni already played surrogate mother to her three younger siblings—a set of eight-year-old twin brothers and a three-year-old sister.

"What gets me is that she's always warning me about being fast and not to get caught up with those 'good-for-nothing' boys. They only want to get next to you, Toni.'" Toni mocked her mother. "All that and she's the one that goes and gets pregnant. Again. The twins are the only ones with the same daddy."

"So much for college, huh?" Toni asked, defeat in her voice.

She picked up her backpack. "Can I have a pass back to class, Mrs. Fields?"

"You can stay and talk if you'd like."

"No. I'm okay."

Zora scribbled a pass for Toni. She'd give her a few days to deal with this news in her own way. She knew Toni would be back to dump a little more of the burden off of her chest. In the meantime, she'd add Toni to her prayer list.

Do it now.

"Promise me you'll come back if you need to talk," Zora said, ignoring her inner conviction to pray for the student now. After all, there were rules about praying in school.

Do it now.

Toni managed a smile, then slipped her arms through the handles of her backpack. "I promise."

Zora knew it was God's voice speaking in her, urging her to step outside of her comfort zone. She stood up before Toni could open the door and disappear down an empty hall carrying the same worries she'd come in with.

"Would you like to pray with me? I think it'll make both of us feel better today."

Toni's eyebrows rose in two perfect arches. "I don't know too much about praying except for when I pray over my food."

"I'll pray. You can just listen."

"Cool." Toni closed her eyes and clasped her hands under her chin.

It wasn't how she prayed, but Zora did the same anyway.

"Dear heavenly Father, first we want to thank You for this day, because it's the day that You have made. And since You made it, You know what would be happening in our lives today and how we would feel. You know everything about Toni, God, and I'm asking You to strengthen her during a time when she feels hurt and confused. . . ." Zora prayed until she felt the burden that was in the room lifted.

Toni pulled out a tissue from the box Zora offered her. "I've never cried over a prayer before. But it was a good cry," she hurried to say. "Thank you, Mrs. Fields. That really did make me feel better."

"Me too." Zora put an arm around Toni and walked her to the office suite door. The school bell rang, signaling the end of second period. Students spilled out into the halls, maneuvering past each other like bumper-to-bumper morning traffic on I-695.

"I should send Rashad in here so you can pray for him," Toni said. "Maybe then he won't act like such an idiot."

"Some things you don't need to say," Zora chastised. "Stay out of Rashad's path and you'll be all right."

Toni blew out a heavy sigh. "Not likely to happen. His dad is the baby's daddy." She rolled her eyes, then disappeared into the ocean of rowdy students.

monét

Echelon Noir was packed to the brim on a Thursday night. If it wasn't for Savon's connections, Monét probably would've had to squeeze onto a bar stool between dawdlers and the women nursing a drink until they were asked to dance. One look around the place and Monét could tell that this wasn't a club for the college students. It was where the mature professionals gathered after taking care of business all week. The saxophonist whined away the stacked in-boxes. The musician tickled the keyboard that massaged away the complaints about supervisors. Tonight was all about jazz.

Monét followed Savon to a back corner booth reserved by a small placard and two chocolate mousse desserts.

"I didn't know your boyfriend would be joining us," Savon said. He waited for Monét to sit down, then slid in beside her. "I'll have them bring out another one."

"Don't worry about it. We can share one," Monét said, rotating the edge of the white porcelain plate. The chocolate fluffy dome was trickled down the sides with hot fudge and dusted on top with white powdered sugar. "I've gained ten pounds just looking at this."

"And it's all landed in the right places," Savon said, eating her with his eyes.

Monét rerouted the direction of his eyes and the conversation. "Speaking of places. This is nice."

"I told you. Now you can see why I want to throw the event here." Savon pulled off his black leather jacket and helped Monét out of her coat.

A couple at the next table clinked wine glasses, then kissed each other with too much passion for public display. Some things don't change, Monét thought. A club was a club no matter what day of the week and who was there. She didn't miss the lame pickup lines, exaggerated resumes, and people pretending to be people they weren't. Business suits could only camouflage so much.

Monét looked toward the door for a sign of Jeremiah. He'd dropped her off at the front door and gone to park her car. As soon as she'd disappeared behind the tinted entryway of Echelon Noir, Savon swept her into the dimly lit room.

"There's a stage behind those curtains," Savon said. "They open them up for special events or when they have a larger band."

Monét pulled a notepad from her red leather bag so she could sketch the club's layout.

Savon leaned in until their shoulders touched. Monét inched over and kept to task. Savon must've gotten the hint. He retreated back onto the booth seat.

"So would your boyfriend mind if we shared a dance? Let me spin you around on the dance floor a couple of times." He touched the middle of her back. "Show you I can do more than recite poetry."

Monét moved his hand. "I pass, whether he would or wouldn't mind. We're in a business meeting."

"All work and no play?"

"For tonight, anyway."

"I can respect that." Savon picked up a spoon and dug it into the dessert in front of Monét.

"What are you doing?"

"You said we'd share," he said, licking the tip of the prongs.

"I meant me and Jeremiah," she said, switching their plates.

"My bad."

Was it worth the money? Savon had never tried to make any advances toward her before when she'd used him at events for the center. Maybe it was the atmosphere of the club that had him a little more relaxed. Too relaxed.

Jeremiah's presence shifted Savon's flirtatious behavior.

"Celebrating the event already, I see," Jeremiah said.

Monét slid their untouched dessert toward him. "Have at it," she said. "Just save me two bites."

Monét sat sandwiched between two men she personally crowned as the best-looking males in the place. Three women at the table across from them must've agreed. Their glances darted to the table—one too many times at Jeremiah.

It had been some time since her jealousy meter had registered in the green zone. Who could blame the women for the extra fluttering of their fake lashes? She slid closer to Jeremiah. She was admittedly cautious about long-term commitments, but she wasn't going to leave the door open for someone else to walk in. She marked her territory in her own subliminal way, unlike the woman walking toward her who looked like she didn't plan on letting her man out of her grip.

Bryce Coleman swaggered like he was the trophy to be paraded.

Bryce!

Monét knew the woman's face too, even though tonight her scowl was masqueraded with heavy makeup. I don't believe this, Monét thought.

Before Jeremiah, there was Bryce, Monét's on-again, off-again, part-time romance. He'd tried to convince her that his desire to have a relationship with God was a personal one and not an act to earn him extra points with her. Bryce's charisma dimmed her vision until God opened her eyes to the pit she was being lured closer to. Jeremiah's persistence and God's grace kept her from falling in.

The woman on his arm was undoubtedly the same one who'd confronted Monét one night after leaving Bryce's apartment. She was more polished and poised tonight, but Monét knew the truth behind the black body-hugging sweater dress.

A mile down the road, Monét pulled into a gas station and the car followed. She pulled up to the gas pump and the car crept by. A girl with tousled hair pulled in a ponytail on top of her head peered into the car. Monét watched the car circle around the gas station, then leave in the direction they'd just come. Evidently a case of mistaken identity, Monét thought. A woman scorned on the hunt for her man. Well, he wasn't in her car.

The gas station was in a well-lit and fairly busy area, so Monét decided to fill her tank. She'd noticed on the way to Bryce's that it was creeping down to just above a quarter of a tank. Her dad wouldn't be pleased. He didn't believe in letting a gas tank drop to under half-full.

She slid her debit card into the automated machine and unhooked the gas pump handle.

Before she knew what was happening, a car screeched to a halt in front of hers. Within seconds, the deranged-looking woman who'd left the scene earlier was in her face, spitting out a string of curse words.

"I don't know who you think you are, trying to sneak around with somebody's man, but don't try to play me."

"I think you've got the wrong woman." Monét shoved the handle into her tank and tried to stay calm. "I don't know anything about your man."

"Oh, so now I'm stupid," the girl yelled. Her eyes nearly bugged from her head.

Monét saw a woman peek her head from around a gas tank from two stations over. The patrons going in and out of the store didn't seem to be paying them much attention.

"*I just saw you hugged up with Bryce outside of his apartment. I just told you, don't try to play me.*"

Monét's defensive instincts kicked in, and she raised her voice to match her attacker's volume. "It seems to me you should be taking this up with Bryce, not me. Trust me, I'm not so desperate that I need to be with somebody else's man."

Calm down.

Monét had to stop herself from going off, and erred on the side of caution. She didn't know what this chick was capable of. Her heart pounded in her chest.

"Is everything all right out there?" A voice from an overhead speaker disrupted their altercation. "I'll call the police."

"Please do," Monét said. She glared at the girl but remained calm.

"Watch yourself," the girl said. She went back to her car and disappeared as fast as she'd come.

For days after that her home and work voice mails were clogged with hang-ups and dial tones. It didn't take long after that for Monét to disconnect the relationship.

Bryce finally noticed Monét and flashed his politician's smile as he passed. "Long time no see, Monét." He paused as if he wanted to show her what she was missing.

Monét made sure there was no spark in her eyes, and was relieved that there was none in her heart either. When they'd dated, Bryce had always been able to make her rethink her decision whenever she tried to walk away from him. But tonight she felt absolutely nothing.

When Bryce realized he couldn't pull conversation from anyone at the table, he retreated. "Take care of yourself," he said.

Please, Monét thought. "You too."

Savon waited until Bryce and the stalker had passed. He leaned in and said, "His woman is a little touched, if you ask me. Man, that chick is bona fide crazy."

"For real?" Jeremiah asked.

"Man. Beautiful as she is, she can act ugly as a grizzly bear.

I've seen her turn it out in the parking lot." Savon shook his head in disgust. "Oh, man. She's brutal."

Out of sight under the table, Monét gripped Jeremiah's knee in warning. Jeremiah didn't need to dig for information. He was well aware of the drama attached to Bryce.

"Let's get back to business, gentlemen," Monét said. "We don't want this to be a gossip queen session."

"Bruh, she went there," Savon said. "You've gotta keep your woman in check."

Monét rolled her eyes. She'd like to see the day any man dared to do that. She flipped to a blank page in her pad. "So did you get the contact information of the other artists that you want to use?"

"Got them right here," Savon said, pulling a yellow sticky pad out of his sports coat pocket.

Men. Monét pulled off the top sheet and stuck it on her page. "I've already started contacting some of the local boutiques, and they're jumping at the chance to have their clothes modeled. For a small donation, of course, that will go directly to your foundation."

"It's basically cheap publicity. They'd be crazy not to."

"I think it would be a good idea to use some of the people who frequent here. Who else better than the regulars to spread the word like wildfire? They'll tell their friends, and the place will be packed."

"Long as their friends have money. It won't do any good to have broke people at a fund-raising event," Savon said.

Monét didn't think it would be a problem to get the people here to put their hands in their pockets and purses for a good cause. If they didn't have money to spare, they sure didn't act like it. Designer handbags and clothes looked to be the norm. The women probably had standing weekly hair appointments, and the men didn't spare a dime to look groomed either.

Monét added, "Well, I've contacted the stations to try to get some local TV and radio personalities involved. Maybe the city's politicians will help us out too."

Jeremiah dropped in his two cents. "If you really want to

74

get in the ladies' purses, get some male athletes in here."

"You got that right," Monét said, a little too enthusiastically. She winked at Jeremiah and patted the side of his face. "You've got 'em all beat," she whispered.

Savon sat forward and dug a spoon into his dessert. "And the men will empty their wallets if you can find some women who look half as good as you, Monét."

"I know what you mean," Jeremiah said. "You rarely find this much beauty and intelligence in one package."

He was doing it to her again. Looking at her in that way. Jeremiah almost seemed too good to be true. But like Zora had told her recently, women needed to expect and accept the honorable men in their lives, instead of looking and waiting for them to mess up.

Jeremiah put an arm around her to pull her closer so he could kiss her cheek.

"Take all of that back to the house," Savon said, gawking at the women across from them that had caught his attention. "I see a little business I need to tend to soon, so we need to keep it moving."

Monét reviewed the items on her task list with Savon until the lights grew too dim for her to read by the single candle flickering on the table. A few couples had taken their groping to the dance floor in front of the live band. Its members, all dressed in black, were illuminated by the blue recessed lights surrounding the stage.

Jeremiah seemed to have grown bored with hearing the event logistics and was fiddling with his BlackBerry. Monét knew he was either texting Preston or checking sports scores.

"I'm gonna order some food to go before we get out of here. Do you want something?" Jeremiah asked.

"Chicken tenders will work for me," she told Jeremiah before he went to place their orders at the bar.

Savon slid closer to her. "So you see the vision?"

"I've got you," Monét said, sliding an arm into her all-weather coat.

Savon helped her. "I don't blame Jeremiah for keeping a short leash on you."

"A leash?" Monét whipped her head around. "Don't talk about me like I'm a pet."

"Hold on, queen."

Jeremiah calls me that.

"You're far from being or looking like a pet. I sincerely apologize. Don't walk out on me now."

"I'm not dropping your project." Monét spooned the last lonely bite of chocolate mousse into her mouth. "Besides, I need the money. And you pay good. Real good."

"That's not the only thing I can do that's real good."

Monét ignored him. If Jeremiah knew about Savon's advances, he'd be against them working together even though Jeremiah had nothing to worry about. Half an hour earlier, Savon had been gawking at the group of women seated near them, and he didn't hide his thoughts about any of the others that caught his insatiable eye. That wasn't the kind of man she wanted. The kind of man she wanted was seated at the bar, ordering her food, and wouldn't be lured away for the sake of temporary gratification.

Monét had what many women prayed for—a good man.

belinda

Belinda opened the front door. It was a scene she hadn't expected to see, and one that she would never see again in her house. Never. She nudged the door closed with her foot, still balancing a sleeping Hannah on one arm and four plastic bags of groceries swinging on the other.

"Let me get those for you, honey," Thomas offered, taking the bags and heading for the kitchen. He was busted and was already scrambling to make good for the mistake he was sure to be hounded about later.

"And I didn't even get an invitation to this little party going on in here," Belinda said. Hannah awakened, and Belinda stood her on the floor. Hannah went directly to T.J., pulling at his jean leg for him to pick her up.

"I'm sorry," Juanita said. "We were just talking about old times and T.J. when he was a baby. He was always into something, I tell you," she said, shaking her head at the thought.

Things haven't changed, Belinda thought.

Juanita scooted forward to the edge of the recliner. She was in Thomas's favorite chair again, and evidently he hadn't found the nerve to evict her like he usually did everyone else.

She cleaned up the glasses and open bag of pretzels on the coffee table. Her V-neck sweater was cut so low that Belinda couldn't believe her twins hadn't already popped out to welcome her home. And although Juanita's skirt was long enough to sweep the floor, it didn't leave much fabric for her legs to move.

Thomas was guilted into silence. He went about unpacking the groceries, then pulled out the electric wok to prepare the Asian stir-fry dish they were having for dinner.

God, I hope You don't want me to entertain her for dinner tonight. Please, Lord, don't make this a test. I'll fail.

"Don't worry about those," Belinda said when Juanita turned on the kitchen sink faucet to rinse the glasses. "We'll wash them with the dinner dishes."

"Are you sure?"

"Positive. Go spend some time with T.J. I know you need to leave early in the morning to go back to Pittsburgh."

Juanita had been in town for a week, dropping by for at least two hours each day to spend some time with her son. As far as Belinda was concerned, she'd worn out her welcome.

"That's a good idea." Juanita turned off the water, then dried her hands on a paper towel. She propped her elbows on the grey granite countertop.

"You always were a gourmet chef," Juanita said, as she watched Thomas tap a few drips of olive oil into the center of the red electric wok.

The oil bounced and sizzled across the deep pan. It was the only response to Juanita's comment, but it wasn't the only thing growing hotter. Belinda's temper was rising.

God, give me strength. I'm trying to represent You, but this woman is testing me.

Belinda balled up the plastic grocery bags and pushed them into one of their recycling bins.

Juanita fiddled with the clasp of her necklace and rotated it to the back of her neck. "Let me get in here with T.J. for a while. Looks like you'll be eating dinner soon, and I don't want to interrupt your family time."

"Okay. Tell T.J. he can put Hannah in her playpen with some of her books," Belinda said without looking at her. "She'll be fine for a few minutes until I come and get her."

Juanita lingered for a moment.

Belinda looked up. *Don't try to invite yourself to dinner,* her face said. Her stoic expression didn't leave room for friendly chitchat. She had the feeling enough of that had happened while she was lugging clothes to the dry cleaners and keeping a busy child calm so she could buy enough groceries for dinner.

Juanita retreated, but Belinda didn't when it came to addressing Thomas later that evening.

+ + +

Thomas lounged across the couch, comfortable in a white T-shirt and his blue and white striped pajama bottoms.

Belinda joined him, stretching out on the opposite end of the couch so that she could prop her feet on his chest. He kneaded the balls of her feet with his knuckles.

He can't massage his way out of this one.

"So how long was Juanita here before I got home?"

"About an hour, I think." He took a deep breath, causing his muscles to flex when he filled his chest cavity with air.

"Well, an hour or whatever. Anytime was too long without me here."

"The woman just showed up. What was I supposed to do? Have her sit outside on the porch?"

Yes. Belinda sat up and swung her feet on the floor. "You could've told her to come back later when I got home," she suggested.

Thomas shook his head in disbelief.

God, is that not a reasonable request?

Thomas turned his attention to the local news anchor who was reporting on yet another act of violence.

"A Pittsylvania County police officer is recovering this hour after a very close call. A bulletproof vest saved the life of thirty-eight-year-old Harold Kellam. He is at home resting tonight,

79

but the alleged shooter is behind bars for attempted murder."

"So you're going to ignore me?" Belinda asked.

"I didn't think it was a big deal." He flipped the channel.

"That's the point. You didn't think." She crossed her arms and cut her eyes at Thomas, knowing that she was acting childish. Belinda didn't remember a time she'd been this disappointed in her husband.

Thomas flipped the channel again.

"And stop changing the stupid channels." She wiped her brow. "Please."

Thomas turned off the television. The cushion shifted as he sat up and scooted so close to Belinda that their love handles kissed.

"Come on, sweetheart." He put an arm around her and whispered in her ear. "Don't be like that. I'm sorry."

His beard scratched her cheek. Thomas was doing it to her. As much as she tried to maintain her front, her marriage counselor role took over. She could hear what she'd say to another pouting wife. *"I know you may not have agreed with what he did, but is it big enough to cause strife in your marriage? There are bigger things in life to use your energy on."*

Belinda jabbed her elbow into Thomas's side, attempting to shove him over. He wouldn't budge. Instead, he wrapped his other arm around her.

"But did you have to kick back with her and reminisce?" Belinda asked. The scene she'd come home to flashed in her mind again.

"It wasn't that serious." Thomas always thought Belinda was overreacting.

"Not to *you*."

Thomas held her so tightly that her side hurt. The feelings she fought constantly to suppress surfaced.

"She's the mother of your biological son. She gave you a child—something I was never able to do."

"I'll say it every day until I die if I have to. In my eyes Hannah and T.J. are no different. It doesn't matter that Hannah was adopted. They're my children and both blessings from God.

A heritage we've been trusted to raise and protect."

Thomas stood up and pulled Belinda to a stand. "The love and honor you give me is something Juanita never did and never will do."

Thomas led her over to his brown leather recliner. She sat down, then surrendered her stubbornness and let him lift her feet onto the ottoman in front of her.

"I'm sorry for bringing up this nonsense to you," she said, slumping forward so Thomas could position a pillow behind her back.

Just the right spot. Belinda arched her back to stretch out her sore muscles. Who needed a membership at a gym with a busy toddler? Muscles she didn't know she had got a daily workout. *I could use a back rub.*

"I trust you more than that," Belinda continued. "I really do."

Thomas kneaded the muscles in her back. "I know my wife. I can discern your thoughts even if you don't say them." He rubbed out a knot in the top of her shoulders. "And you can sit in my chair anytime you want."

Belinda smiled. It was her sanctuary now. She wanted to drift off into an undisturbed sleep, but her peace was interrupted by the rumble of an engine and bass music that made her front windows rattle. It could only be one person pulling up to her house with that much commotion.

"That better not be who I think it is," she said.

Thomas pulled back the corner of the sheer window panels and peeked out the front window. "It is," he announced. "And he comes bearing a gift. The boy has got a fruit basket."

Thomas was clearly amused. Belinda wasn't.

"Donovan's the basket case if he thinks some apples and bananas are going to get him inside this house," she said.

"First you want to leave Juanita outside, and now you want to keep Donovan locked out." He laughed. "I'm gonna have to take you to the altar on Sunday."

We all need to go to the altar, Belinda thought. Just once this week, she wished she'd have a normal day, but it seemed like normal didn't live at their house anymore. *Maybe things will get better next week. Might as well get all of the drama out of the way.*

"On second thought," Belinda decided, "let him in."

paula

W hat are you crying about now?" Darryl was irritated, and his attitude wasn't helping Paula to calm Gabrielle.

The baby's pitchy screams elevated whenever Paula tried to lay her down, so she bounced, sang, and patted her daughter's back, hoping to console whatever was wrong.

"Everything is not about you, Darryl," Paula said, wiping her tears. She was too drained to raise her voice above a whisper. Gabrielle was up every two to three hours for a feeding. Paula knew it was imperative for Darryl to sleep so he could function the next morning, but it still annoyed her that he rarely cracked an eyelid open during Gabrielle's nighttime ritual. He usually had surgery cases booked on Wednesday mornings. She couldn't blame him for disappearing into one of the guest rooms shortly before two o'clock in the morning.

Paula hated the cold feeling of the hardwood kitchen floors on her bare feet, but she couldn't find her bedroom slippers. The chipped polish on her toenails made her long for a bubbling spa pedicure and manicure. Feet like these should never see the light of the day in the summertime, she thought. Thank God it was the end of February.

Gabrielle whined. Paula swayed. She wanted to unwind in the shower with the massage showerhead set on high and water beating over her tense muscles. What she wouldn't give for a chin-high soak in her Jacuzzi tub. Lavender bath salts softening her skin. A loofa brush to reach the itch in the middle of her back. It wasn't happening anytime soon. Over the past week, Paula counted it as a reward to shower before seven o'-clock in the evening.

Paula hummed a melody in Gabrielle's ear. *This little light of mine, I'm gonna let it shine.*

"I don't remember your hormones being out of whack like this after you had Micah," Darryl said, pouring a glass of orange juice.

"I haven't slept in two weeks, so I think I'm entitled to a tear or two. You have no idea what it's like to carry and give birth to a child."

"Thank God for that."

"If you want to thank God for something, thank Him that I haven't gone crazy and left you here with these children." It was an empty threat. She'd never leave her children.

"Whatever, Paula."

Paula paced back and forth in front of the grandfather clock until Gabrielle's crying subsided. She watched Darryl as he flipped through the morning newspaper. Something looked different about him. He was dressed in his blue scrubs instead of his signature starched slacks and white button-down shirt. That wasn't it. His haircut had the same flawless taper. Then she realized. He'd shaved off all of his facial hair. She'd only known him to do that one other time since they'd been married.

"Problem?" Darryl asked, looking up from the business section.

He'd caught her staring. It wasn't like she didn't have the right to look at her husband as much and as long as she wanted to. "Excuse me?"

"Why are you staring at me like that?"

"I'm not even looking at you. I'm just looking in your direction," Paula lied. "Thinking."

"Well, while you're thinking, come up with something for dinner tonight. I'm having a few of my associates over for an investor meeting."

Not that again. During the winter months it seemed like he'd laid aside his dreams of revitalizing dilapidated homes and flipping them for pocketfuls of cash. She tried to understand his rationale, but it wasn't like they needed the money. From the sounds of things, the sleeping giant was about to awaken. His first attempts took more money out of their pockets than they put in. Hidden damages and shady contractors were the causes of most of the drama at first. Then a tenant locator service found them two sets of sorry tenants who didn't know what it was to pay rent on time.

"I can hardly manage to get a shower during the day. How do you expect me to cook dinner?"

"Just get it done, Paula. We could've met somewhere else, but I was trying to stay around here so you wouldn't have to be here by yourself with the baby and Micah tonight." Darryl folded his newspaper and pushed his chair away from the table. "You're always complaining about what I don't do, and when I offer to help, you still act crazy."

"Let me rewind that conversation," Paula said, circling a finger in the air. "I don't recall you saying anything about helping. You only barked out a dinner request, and that doesn't require any help on your end. And yes, you may be home tonight, but what good is that if you're in a meeting? How is that help?"

"I help you every time my check is deposited and you don't have to worry about going to work." Darryl sneered. "That's my help." He tightened the string on the pants of his scrubs. "I never thought you'd be the kind of woman who'd be so ungrateful."

"So *I'm* the ungrateful one?" Paula said. She wasn't going to get worked up any more than she already was. Gabrielle had finally quieted down, and it was the opportunity she needed to steal away with God and her thoughts. More so with God. Her thoughts would've made her go slap Darryl in the face.

✝   ✝   ✝

Paula tossed a pair of khaki pants on the bed. A few minutes later it was topped by a pair of black trousers. Three pair of jeans that usually fit like gloves were heaped on the mound too.

After failing to wiggle the sixth pair of pants past her post-pregnancy waistline and meaty thighs, she grudgingly pulled on a pair of adjustable maternity pants that she'd worn during her first trimester. Too bad Donna Karan didn't specialize in maternity wear. *This has to go. Soon.*

Paula tightened the waist string, then patted down the small pouch in the crotch area. The weight had practically melted off after having Micah. *Of course, I was five years younger,* she reasoned to herself. *It's only been three weeks since I brought a living being into the world.* She pinched the baby roll across her abdomen and the stretch marks she'd acquired for the first time. *I'll consider these medals of honor.*

Paula sighed. *They're rolls of fat. Where's the honor in that?*

Gabrielle napped soundly in the pink bassinet beside the bed. Paula hovered over the basket until she was sure she'd seen the rise and fall of her baby's chest. It was the nervous habit—she thought—of all mothers to constantly check their newborn to see if the baby was breathing.

Even though Micah was five, she found herself peeking in on him during the night if nature called her to the restroom.

Gabrielle whined in her sleep, then stretched her pudgy arms above her head before tucking them under her chin.

A life with no worries. Paula turned on the baby lamb mobile suspended over the bassinet and the comforting lullaby of "Twinkle, Twinkle, Little Star" began to play. Paula balled up on the bed to rest and, like she'd done most of the morning, she cried. The hormonal letdown was more than her emotions could carry. Fear, anger, regret, and sadness knotted themselves between her muscles and in her psyche.

She prayed that her daughter would never have to experience

86

the deep hurt of a heart left scarred by a man. She'd teach Gabrielle not to put her self-worth and total confidence in a man, but to know the woman she was designed by God to be before she dedicated herself to someone. And as for Micah, he would know how to treat a woman.

Paula dried her eyes when she heard Darryl making his way upstairs. She pretended to be asleep until he left for work. It had to be God that caused Gabrielle to sleep for almost two hours so Paula could rest uninterrupted. When they both awakened refreshed, Paula arranged for Micah to go home from school with his best friend, Timothy, until later in the evening. She ordered assorted appetizers, quiches, and cheese trays from the local deli, and stuffed chicken with vegetable sides from the soul food restaurant in the same plaza. Knowing that Darryl would be in surgery most of the morning, she left a message with his secretary, Maxine, for him to pick everything up on the way home from work. She assumed all was well until he walked into the home at six thirty that evening empty-handed.

"Where's the food?" she asked.

Paula took the extra effort to set dinnerware across the bar. Homemade lemonade was being chilled in the freezer. She'd regained her composure after a little rest and her devotion time. God had led her to a scripture in Colossians 3:23: *And whatever you do, do it heartily, as to the Lord and not to men . . .*

God had a way of slapping her hand in private. That was the only reason why the spread looked like it did.

"I should be asking *you* about the food." Darryl had changed out of his scrubs and was wearing a long-sleeved crewneck shirt and corduroy pants. He pulled off a leather trench coat and hung it in the hall closet.

"I left a message with Maxine for you to pick up the food on the way home."

"She didn't give me the message."

"Maxine? I don't believe you," Paula said, reaching for a set of glasses out of the cupboard. She lined them up across the bar. "She's always on top of things. She doesn't forget to give messages. The trays were supposed to be picked up from the deli we always use, and I put in an order for some other platters from that little soul food restaurant."

Darryl opened the door leading to the garage and pushed the button to cause the door to lift. It rose with barely a whine.

"I'll go back out and get it," he said a little too hastily. Paula knew guilt had rushed him out of the door. He hadn't been this agreeable in months.

"Where have you been today, Darryl?" Paula followed him to the door. He smelled slightly like perfume, and it wasn't hers. The only thing she'd been scented with lately was baby lotion, powder, and spit-up.

Darryl ignored her. He opened the door to his black Jaguar, slid in, and cranked it up all in one harried motion.

Paula slammed her hand on the hood of the car. Her actions shook him. They stared at each other through the windshield. This time she was the raging bull.

"Where have you been? You didn't go to work, did you? You never change out of your scrubs on surgery day," she screamed, landing another rage-induced fist on the hood.

She was so angry that she didn't care that two women walking their dogs had paused at the end of her driveway. When they saw they'd caught her attention, they quickened their steps faster than their pint-sized pooches could keep up with.

Darryl let down the window as he backed out of the three-car garage. "Stop it, Paula. You're making a fool of yourself."

"No. You stop," she shouted. "Whatever you're doing. Stop it. Or you will regret it." Her hands shook. "You will, Darryl." Paula whirled around and picked up the closest thing within reach. She slung a plastic bucket. It hit the front bumper and rolled to the bottom of the driveway. "You will."

monét

The Sunday morning rain had taunted Monét. The rhythmic pitter-patter had a voice—begging her to pull the sheets over her head. It was the perfect day to sleep in. But Monét hadn't. The alto section of her choir was already sparse and most of the time uncommitted, especially during the winter months.

Monét sat down on the front pew and unzipped her choir robe. She wished she'd driven her own car instead of riding with Jeremiah, but what woman wouldn't want to be chauffeured on a day when everything in passing looked waterlogged.

Her legs itched through her hosiery. Even though Jeremiah had dropped her off close to the front doors before the service, she'd still managed to step into a puddle at the curbside, splashing water up her ankles and lower calves. She wanted to go home.

Jeremiah's unexpected meeting had delayed Monét's plans to watch and doze her way through flashback theatre movie marathons. Jeremiah was in a circle around the keyboard with other members of the praise band. It hadn't taken much time for him to decide to join Monét's church, and even less time for him to finish the mandatory classes for new members. He'd signed up to serve in the worship and arts ministry the following Sunday after completing his classes.

Minister Odom, one of the seasoned leaders of the church, led his mother to the front pew beside Monét. Sister Maybelle steadied her cane, then slowly bent her feeble knees so she could ease down onto the pew. She laid her cane and white crochet purse on her lap, clutching them as if she were in a dark alley instead of at the church she'd been a member of for almost sixty years.

"Don't get into any trouble, Mama. I'll be back in a few minutes," Minister Odom said.

Sister Maybelle chuckled. So did Monét. If she did manage to get into any trouble, there'd be no way of escape. Monét could take ten steps for every two of Sister Maybelle's.

"It sure is a beautiful day," Sister Maybelle said, tapping her foot.

"I could do without the rain," Monét said.

"Any day that God gives me is beautiful. I'm eighty-six, working on eighty-seven next month."

"That's a blessing," Monét said, feeling guilty that she'd spent most of the morning complaining. Her saggy hosiery twisted at her ankles. As she bent down to fix them, she noticed that they looked like Sister Maybelle's hosiery. The only difference was that Monét's were in a pair of black pumps and the elderly woman's feet were shoved into a pair of black orthopedic shoes.

"Yes, the Lord has truly kept me. I've seen a lot and been through a lot, and God has never left me. I've never seen the righteous forsaken." Sister Maybelle shook her head. "People complain too much these days, but I remember a time when . . ."

Sister Maybelle's trip back in history began with her childhood growing up in rural South Carolina.

Monét concentrated on Sister Maybelle's deep-set eyes. The elderly woman was known to have a slip of her dentures, but it had been at least ten minutes and they seemed to be gripped solid. But her eyes told stories her lips couldn't. Almost nine decades of wisdom rested in the soft bags beneath them.

By the time Jeremiah finished with his meeting, Sister Maybelle had walked Monét through the Jim Crow era, the Civil Rights Movement, and every world-changing event after that. Monét had forgotten a lot she'd learned in her history books, but life and experience had the events sealed in Sister Maybelle's mind.

Monét could see the excitement bursting from Jeremiah's face. She dared not douse his flames with any appearance of impatience. Besides, she'd been both entertained and taught by Sister Maybelle.

"I'll get the car and bring it up front," he said.

"That's okay," Monét said, getting up. "I can use any exercise I can get."

"That's right," Sister Maybelle added. "Use your legs while they're good and strong." She patted the knees hidden under her flowered ankle-length skirt. "Before they can forecast the weather like mine."

Jeremiah helped Monét into her raincoat. "If we can look and move half as good as you do now when we're half your age, we'll be doing all right."

Sister Maybelle smiled wide enough to cause that fateful slip of her dentures. She used her thumb to shift her top plate, but Jeremiah seemed to think she was choking instead of experiencing a dental malfunction.

"Are you okay?" Jeremiah reached over and patted her back.

Goodness, gracious. The lady isn't choking; she's trying to keep her teeth in her mouth.

"I'm all right, baby. It's these old teeth. I'd rather not wear the things at all."

Jeremiah and Monét bid adieu to Sister Maybelle, then headed for the front door of the church. Besides the people who had to stay for the meeting, everyone else had made a run for their cars instead of lingering around like they usually did.

"Jeremiah."

Monét and Jeremiah turned at the sound of his name coming out of Charise Alston's mouth. She sashayed toward them in three-inch-heel leather boots, but it didn't make her five-foot-two frame look any taller than it was.

"I forgot to give you my number." Charise tore off the corner of a Sunday bulletin and wrote her name and number across it with a red pen. "Call me if you're coming over."

"Will do." Jeremiah slid the paper into his pocket without looking at it or Monét.

Hmmm. Caught in the act. And just when I was making myself believe that he wasn't too good to be true.

"How are you, Monét?" Charise chirped. She'd never been that enthusiastic when speaking to Monét.

"Great, thanks," Monét said. "Have a good one," she said, walking toward the door.

Jeremiah opened the door for her. "Stay dry out there, Charise."

Even though Monét had been a choir member for years, she'd never personally connected with Charise. Everything about her was petite and cute. Her short pixie cut framed a round face that housed perfect teeth, the kind tamed by high-school braces. Monét could probably fit Charise's doll-sized pants on one arm.

"Picking up chicks at church?" Monét asked once they were in the car. "And in front of your woman, nonetheless. You're bold."

"The praise band is having a get-together at Charise's house on Friday night." He revved the engine slightly. "And you're more than welcome to come with me. You didn't even give me time to ask you."

Monét looked out the window. The defroster was inching away the fog off the glass. *This isn't going to be good.* "This Friday?"

"Yeah. You and Zora have something planned?"

"Not exactly. I've got a business meeting."

"Seeing Savon again, huh?"

The drizzle outside suddenly picked up to a downpour. Monét was spending more time with Savon, but absolutely nothing was going on besides business. She needed the money, and currently Savon was her only client. She could overlook his occasional advances if it meant her not having to enter the job market right now.

"We're *meeting*," Monét stressed. "He's my client."

"On a Friday night?"

"It's the only time he has available, and we've got some things to take care of."

"The only thing he's concerned about is taking care of you. I watched him. I know his game."

"Even if he wanted more—which he doesn't—there's no chance." Lying on the church grounds couldn't be good, Monét thought. But it was only a half-lie. There wasn't a chance. "Savon's not my type."

"That's the only reason? Dagger to the heart." Jeremiah grabbed his chest and let his head fall against the headrest, then sat up with a serious look on his face. "And what if he was your type?"

"All of that came out wrong."

"Make it up to me."

"How?"

"Say yes."

"Yes to what?" Monét asked. She could barely see out of the window anymore. The rain pelted down on them in horizontal sheets. "I'm not saying yes until I know what it is."

"Okay," Jeremiah said, putting the car in reverse and backing out of the parking space. For ten minutes, Jeremiah purposefully rode in silence. He usually had the radio or one of his jazz CDs playing, but the silence only made Monét wonder more. Jeremiah was a man of surprises, and it was nothing for him to have a date planned that she couldn't have arranged on her best romantic day.

"Yes," Monét finally said after they'd been caught at nearly every red light there was on the street. She'd let Jeremiah win this one. "Are you happy? Now what do I have to do?"

"Come with me to Houston."

"Are you serious?" *There was no way she was going.*

"The last weekend in May. My godparents are throwing my parents a party for their thirty-fifth wedding anniversary."

Monét bit her lip. "I don't know. I'm not ready for the whole meet-the-parents ordeal."

"You met them at Zora and Preston's wedding already."

"No. I spoke to them at the wedding. We had a brief conversation, and that was it. Going with you to Houston is different. Besides, that's the weekend before the fund-raiser and I'm sure I'll have plenty to do."

"Interesting. Savon is the excuse for the second time today."

"It's my job."

"You're your own boss. Give yourself the time off. You act like I asked you to go next week. The party is three months from now," Jeremiah said, slowing down at the yellow traffic light.

Monét knew he was looking over at her, but she didn't look back. Her experiences with the parents of her boyfriends had never been anything to write home about.

"I'll think about it."

"You'll think about it? Is it the money? I wouldn't ask you if I didn't plan on taking care of everything."

"In the past—"

"The past is the past. We need to think about our future."

Our future?

They were the last words in Monét's mind before she heard tires screeching. The impact jarred her, throwing her against the door. It was so sudden that she didn't have time to react. Jeremiah's truck was rammed into the intersection. She felt it spinning, and she gripped the dashboard until the truck came to a sudden stop in the middle of the intersection. Monét's heart felt like it was beating in her throat. They were facing oncoming traffic.

"Thank You, God," she managed to say. She looked at Jeremiah. His hands were still clenching the steering wheel.

"Jeremiah?"

"I didn't really think people's lives flashed before their eyes." He rubbed his forearm. "You all right?"

"Yes." She unbuckled her seat belt. It burned across her neck. Looking in the visor mirror, she saw a small area where the skin had been rubbed raw by the friction of the seat belt locking her against the seat.

"Don't get out." Jeremiah reached behind his seat for an umbrella, opened the door, then stepped out into the pelting rain.

Monét could barely see past the heavy rain cascading down the car windows. Someone with a red umbrella stood at the back of Jeremiah's truck, probably inspecting damage to the two vehicles.

Unlike Jeremiah, her life hadn't flashed before her eyes during the seconds they'd hydroplaned across the two lanes of traffic. But now she was in the car alone, mulling over her last thoughts before the accident. *Our future?* Cars crept past the accident. The police came. And the only thing she could think was, *Was the future of their relationship an accident waiting to happen?*

Zora

It had been raining for three days straight, causing a constant gloom to hover over the city. Unfortunately, it had felt the same way in Zora's house. Tonight was going to be another lonely one. She'd have to eat dinner with the company of the television and the casts of the prime-time dramas for the rest of the week. Church responsibilities had tied up Preston's calendar. Again. This time, his father had appointed him to spearhead a project to revitalize a community recreation center. A month had passed since he began his minister's training, and already Zora was tired of her time with her husband being usurped.

"I suppose next week you'll be sent on a mission trip to Africa," she'd complained on Sunday evening. She'd already begun to feel the sacrifices required of a minister's family, especially one next in line to inherit a church's legacy.

"God's work doesn't have operating hours, Zora. I'm asking you to understand."

"I've been understanding," she said. "But I'm asking you not to forget your responsibilities to your family. God's calling you to that role too, even if it's just me. I make your family. You're supposed to leave your parents and cleave to me," she said.

"Now you want to go all biblical to prove your point."

"That was a good one, wasn't it?" Zora laughed, but she still meant what she said.

Preston suffered through the romantic movie she'd chosen without complaint. She'd felt better.

Until now.

Zora looked at the clock on her office wall. The bell for last period would ring in eight minutes. There weren't any scheduled after-school meetings for her to attend, so as soon as she finished her duty to monitor the buses outside, Zora would be on her way home.

Maybe Monét could use some company, Zora thought. She was probably still shaken up after her and Jeremiah's accident. It had taken her most of that Sunday night to convince Monét that the accident was in no way a sign of the future of her relationship with Jeremiah. God operated through sovereignty, not superstitious acts.

"You up for company?" Zora asked when Monét answered the phone.

"I've got a meeting tonight with Savon," Monét said. "He's the guy I'm planning the event for. We were supposed to meet Friday, but I asked him if we could move it to today instead."

"Savon? That sounds like the name of a romantic pursuer on a soap opera."

"Don't say that in front of Jeremiah. He's already convinced the man has ulterior motives."

"Does he?"

"Probably, but I ignore him. I'm all business."

"Make sure you keep it that way. I'm trying to keep my figure for your and Jeremiah's wedding."

"Marriage is the last thing on my mind right now. There seems to be more drama in the married life than in the single life.

Look at what you're having to deal with."

"Well, it's definitely work. But then again, anything that's worth having is."

Zora made a mental note not to share so much of her marital woes with Monét. It was hard not to divulge all of her business with her best friend. It's what they'd always done—the secret crushes in third grade, the diaries they used to hide in an empty macaroni and cheese box in the back of the closet.

"Speaking of work," Monét said, "I've got tons to do. I'll give you a call later so we can catch up."

Zora could picture Monét sitting behind the desk in her room with lists of action items tacked to the clipboard in front of her. As long as she had a stack of her favorite CDs within arm's reach, her friend could get so pulled into her work that she wouldn't notice the small desktop clock ticking time well into the early morning. Her career had always been a top priority in her life. It was an outlet to escape issues and people she didn't want to deal with. Her relationship with Jeremiah didn't need to be one of those things.

"Definitely," Zora finally said. "It's time for us to have one of our sessions."

"I'm not even going to ask."

"Good, because I don't have time to talk now either. The bell is about to ring. Bye," she said, and hung up the phone.

Since Zora's parents' death last year, she'd needed Monét's advice and shoulder to lean on even more. Even though they were only a year apart in age, Monét could comfort Zora with the motherly advice she needed and at the same time give her the brutal truth like a true girlfriend should.

Recently Zora had shared her anxieties about Preston's call to the ministry and her frustration with him spending more time away from home in the evenings. She wished she would've kept it to herself. Monét didn't need another reason to bury in the back of her mind and bring up later. It was about that time for her and Monét to have a heart-to-heart conversation so her friend wouldn't end up driving away the best man she'd ever had.

A knock on Zora's office door was followed by Toni peeping her head inside.

"Come in, Toni."

Zora studied her student. One day she'd explain to Toni why wearing skin-tight pants every day wasn't the best option for a woman's sanitary health or the way to attract a respectable young man.

"I haven't seen you in a while." Zora crossed her arms. "I take it you've kept away from Rashad."

Toni clapped her hands and did one of those dances Zora had seen while flipping through music videos. Zora couldn't see how anybody could coordinate their body arms and legs to do two totally different things without popping their limbs out of the socket. Looking at Toni dance, life in her thirties seemed light-years away from that of teenagers.

Toni finished her dance and flopped into the chair across from Zora's desk with a grin that spread the width of her face.

"Staying away from Rashad was easy to do. He got suspended last week for fighting," she said with a satisfied look on her face. "And he hasn't been hanging out at my apartment complex either."

"What about your schoolwork?" Zora asked.

Toni unzipped her backpack and took out two pieces of paper. One was a B quiz from history and the other an A grade for an English book report on Richard Wright's *Native Son*.

"That's the Antoinette Burkes that I know. Glad to see she's back."

Toni blushed. Her braids swung in front of her face as she bent over to slide her work into her backpack. "It was that prayer you said for me, Mrs. Fields. I know it was."

Zora was glad she'd followed God's voice.

Toni beamed. "I've been praying every day since then. In my own way, you know."

"There's no other way. It's about a personal relationship," Zora said. "For years I went to church because my parents made me, but the day came when I had the desire to have a relationship with God for myself."

The bell rang signaling school's dismissal. Zora picked up her raincoat and umbrella.

"I know you've got to get on post and watch those knucklehead kids get on the bus," Toni said. "I just wanted you to know that I believe everything is going to work out for my family. It'll be hard, but we'll survive."

"You'll do more than survive." Zora took a slip of paper from her memo cube and jotted down Romans 8:28. "Look this Scripture up when you get home."

Zora opened her office door, as did the other two counselors. Mrs. Ledbetter, the head counselor in the department, took off her purple-framed eyeglasses. They dangled on a silver chain around the collar of a lavender turtleneck sweater. The color of the woman's wardrobe was never a mystery. She wore a shade of purple every day, and no one—even when running into her during summer vacation—had ever seen her wearing anything else.

Mrs. Ledbetter examined Toni from head to toe. Zora was sure the same concern about Toni's pants was running through her fellow associate's mind, along with some other critical observations.

"Miss Burkes, you must want to be a guidance counselor. I've seen you in here quite a bit lately," Mrs. Ledbetter said. She slid her tinted glasses back on her nose and peered over them.

Toni propped her hand on her hip. "Today it was for good news."

Mrs. Ledbetter looked content with Toni's answer. "Keep it up, Miss Burkes. I'm expecting great things out of you. Your brothers and sister are looking up to you too."

"Yes, ma'am. I'm not going to let you or them down." She turned to Zora. "You either, Mrs. Fields. If you hadn't prayed for me I wouldn't have made it through that day. That prayer helped me get my mind focused." Toni lifted her braids out of her coat collar. "I better go. I've got rehearsal for the chorus concert. If you're late, Mrs. Thornton makes you sing the *Star Spangled Banner* standing on one foot. Ain't that crazy?"

"What about your brothers and sister?" Zora yelled after her.

"My neighbor, Ms. Ella, is going to watch them until I get home. I told her I'd wash and roll her hair if she helped me out one day a week."

Toni headed down one wing of the school's hallways, and Zora followed behind the students filing outside toward the buses and student pickup area.

Zora stood under her umbrella even though the rain had dwindled to a mist. If she didn't, her hair would be a nest of frizzy curls before she went back inside. Although she had the evening to herself, she preferred not to spend it trying to tame her wild hairdo back into shape.

A row of buses sat against the curbs waiting for the students to board. Hundreds of students milled on the sidewalk engaging in their usual horseplay. When a large group of students ran in the direction of the back student parking lot, Zora knew a fight had broken out. She followed them, being careful not to get trampled in the middle of the herd. Several teachers were already there looking for the source of the melee.

"Gun!"

zora

The warning came from the middle of the crowd and rippled through the student mass. "Gun!" The shouts came from everywhere now. Students and teachers scattered.

Zora dropped to the ground behind a white car. The loose gravel scraped her knees through her slacks as water from a nearby puddle seeped into her shoes.

Zora heard tires spinning and rocks being thrown as a car peeled out of the student lot. She crawled to the rear bumper in time to see a four-door black sedan with tinted windows heading east. She pulled herself up by the car's door handle and brushed the dirt off her knees. Zora corralled the remaining students back to the front of the school and onto the buses. The students talked over each other, recounting the story as they'd seen it. There were as many versions as there were people. Even when the police arrived, they couldn't find a consistent testimony among the students who'd been kept behind.

"Mrs. Fields! Mrs. Fields!"

Zora was finally headed home when Toni called her from the end of the west wing corridor. Her voice was unusually loud as it reverberated through the empty hallway.

"Were you outside when the shooting went down?" Toni patted herself on the chest, seemingly to calm herself down.

Zora was amazed at how the grapevine of gossip had escalated the incident into a shooting. "Yes, I was outside, but there weren't any gunshots."

Toni noticed the soiled bottom half of Zora's pants. "You were ducking from *something*."

Zora's kneecaps still stung even though she'd treated her scrapes with antibiotic ointment and covered them with bandages from the school's first aid kit. "Everybody was screaming there was a gun," she said to Toni. "What else what I was supposed to do?"

"I wouldn't think you'd care about getting shot and dying."

"What? Why in the world would you think that?"

"'Cause you would go to heaven anyway, right? You pray and go to church and all that," Toni surmised.

"Yes. But that doesn't mean I'm ready to go *now*. Just like God has plans for your life, He has plans for mine too."

Toni attempted to shove her hands in her back pockets. She shook her head like a concerned citizen. "You need to do some extra praying tonight for our school. You know whoever it was is gonna come back again. People are crazy these days. They'll shoot you in front of your own mama. I've seen it happen."

Zora scrounged for keys in her purse. Her feet felt slimier with every step. "I'll definitely do that," she said, wiggling her toes around. "Do you need a ride home?"

"No." Toni walked with her guidance counselor to the front door. "My friend is coming to pick me up."

"Who?"

"Nobody you know. He doesn't go to this school. The boys here are too immature," she said as she smeared a thick coat of lip gloss across her full lips. "For a woman like me, anyway." She smiled, exposing a small chip on her bottom tooth.

"A woman?" That was another thing she'd have to address with Toni, Zora thought. There was a distinct difference between a woman and a lady. Toni's body was definitely more mature than Zora's had been at that same age. Zora didn't have curves like that until she was in her midtwenties. But curves didn't make you a woman or a lady.

They walked past the principal's office, past the cafeteria, and toward the exit.

"So who is this supposedly mature boy?"

Toni stopped before pushing against the metal handle of the double doors. She waved toward someone parked in a rusty heap sitting on rims that probably cost more than his entire car. "His name is Cedric. And he's a senior," she emphasized.

"Oh, he's definitely a man, then." Zora's expression must have relayed a message to Toni.

"Don't worry, Mrs. Fields. I've got three menaces at home that I have to watch and a pregnant mama. I'm not trying to have no babies. I know how hard it is. I live it every day. I'm not going to have sex until I know it's *true* love." Toni threw up a wave as she bounded out the door and into Cedric's jalopy.

Love? A seventeen-year-old mind couldn't perceive true love, and certainly shouldn't be considering sex. Not only was she due for a heart-to-heart with Monét, but it looked like she was going to have one with Toni too.

✢　　✢　　✢

Zora tuned in to her favorite gospel station on the drive home.

"You're listening to Melissa Flint on the station that makes you get your praise on all day long," the radio personality sang. "Before I put on the latest and greatest gospel hits, I'm asking all of the listeners to send up a special prayer for Baltimore City High School. Thank God there were no reports of an actual shooting at an incident there today, but a concerned parent called in and asked for the city to keep students everywhere in prayer. You know how we do it, Baltimore. Let's bombard the air waves with prayer. Honk if you know God is a protector."

Zora pressed her horn down until the commuter in front of her threw his hands up in frustration.

belinda

I'm praying things will be calmed down around here so I can come up to Baltimore for a few days," Belinda told her mother, Bernice. "Remember the P.O.W.E.R. ministry I took part in last year? The women's discipleship where I met the other ladies? They're having a sort of reunion."

"Are you bringing Hannah with you?"

"Don't worry." Belinda rinsed the remains of peas and squash off the dinner plates. "My shadow is never far behind me."

"Where is she? Usually by now she'd be begging for a cup of milk or something."

"I peeled her off of my leg long enough for Dionne to take her up the street to the playground."

"Dionne seems to help a lot," Bernice said.

"She's a godsend. I couldn't have asked for a sweeter girl, and Hannah loves her."

Dionne wasn't only an ideal sitter because she conveniently

lived two streets over from the Stokeses, but Belinda had watched Dionne grow up in front of her eyes. Dionne had first won Belinda's heart as a ten-year-old in the elementary Sunday school class at church. But as good as Dionne was with Hannah, Belinda wished her mother was closer so that she could not only spend more time with Hannah but be close for when Belinda needed a shoulder to cry on.

Belinda flipped the latch on the dishwasher door, and the spray of the water pattered against the dishes. "I'd probably ask Dionne to help more if T.J. wouldn't lurk out of his lion's den whenever she's here."

"You make it sound like the boy is stalking the child," Bernice said.

"He is. He acts like he's going to pounce on the innocent girl. I don't want him tainting her while he walks around trying to pretend like he's a thug. Good girls seem to get caught up with bad boys, and she needs to see he's not the same boy she used to play with at church."

Over the phone, Belinda heard a hum and then the crunching of what sounded like ice. She knew her mother was blending some kind of iced protein concoction. Since undergoing surgery and treatment for breast cancer, Bernice had transformed to a walking cookbook of organic recipes.

"I'm not exactly an expert on raising teenage boys," Belinda said. She opened her laptop bag that was on the kitchen table. "I didn't have those preteen transition years to practice."

"I'm not sure it would've helped even if you had. It sure didn't help me with your brother. Sometimes even children who were taught better will test their limits, although I must say that none of you ever went out and got yourself shot."

"So what am I supposed to do?"

"Stay on your knees," Bernice said after a loud slurp. "Stay on your knees."

✢   ✢   ✢

T.J. sauntered downstairs with his backpack hooked over one shoulder. The stench of his cologne and aftershave was thick enough to slice. With a butcher knife. Belinda resisted the urge to cover her nose as T.J. pulled back one of the kitchen chairs across from her.

She looked at him over the screen of her laptop but didn't say anything. Belinda went back to work sending out a mass e-mail to her freelance writers asking for queries and articles for the upcoming summer issue of *A Healthier You Magazine*.

Under her editorial leadership, the health publication was growing in circulation and popularity in the Northeast region. With her mind locked in work mode, she wasn't up to being disturbed. She pushed her reading glasses up on her nose.

T.J. was either too naive or too focused on his mission to take the hint. Belinda guessed it was the latter.

"Ma 'Linda," he finally said, sounding tired of being ignored.

"Uh-huh?" Belinda's eyes didn't leave her keyboard. Her fingers ticked across the keyboard, and T.J.'s fingers drummed the table.

"Ma 'Linda," he huffed.

She answered him after she clicked the Send button. "Yes, T.J.?"

"Can I borrow the car?"

"No." Belinda tapped her index finger on her wireless mouse. She scanned through her in-box to make sure she hadn't missed anything important.

T.J. turned his cap backwards. "You didn't even ask me why I needed it."

"It doesn't matter. The answer is still no."

"I need to catch up on my school work. I'm having trouble with calculus since I missed so many days, and I was going over to Tasha's for help."

"Tasha?"

Belinda thought it was more likely he had biology in mind for the purpose of his visit. *This boy thinks I was born last night.*

Belinda stood up. She'd been rude to him for no reason. He probably did need help. The school in Danville had been more academically challenging than the one he came from in Pittsburgh, and T.J. had struggled from the beginning of his senior year to keep up. "I'll take you," she offered.

T.J. didn't object immediately, but Belinda knew he would shortly. He was trying to come up with a viable excuse.

"I was going to save you a trip since you're trying to get some work done," T.J. said.

There it was. Belinda closed her laptop cover. "It's no problem. I could use a break," she said, stretching. To be the editor of a health magazine and only forty-one years old, she was always discovering tightness in the most peculiar places. She needed to practice more of what she preached.

"Forget it." T.J. pushed away from the table. The chair legs screeched across the kitchen hardwood floors. "I can't do nothing around this place. I might as well be in jail!" he yelled.

T.J.'s rages were getting out of hand.

"At the rate you were going you were well on your way to jail. And you're wrong. You *can* do something around here. You can act like you've got some sense."

With Belinda standing and T.J. sitting, she towered over him. He refused to let Belinda have the edge. He jumped up with such force that the kitchen chair flew backwards. The force left a small hole in the wall behind it. It seemed T.J.'s street instinct had prevailed over his good sense.

"You can go to . . ."

No you don't. Belinda grabbed T.J.'s shirt around the collar and shoved her fist under his chin. Her aggressiveness surprised them both. "One thing you won't do is disrespect me," she said, her voice low yet filled with authority.

Belinda's face grew warm and tears of anger stung the corners of her eyes. They stared at each other, wondering who would make the next move.

Belinda heard her mother's voice. "*Stay on your knees.*"

It had to be God that had Thomas arrive when he did. He walked through the kitchen door from the garage entrance, obviously stunned at the scene before him. Belinda wished Dionne and Hannah hadn't been behind him too.

Hannah ran to Belinda. "Mama," she squealed, clapping her hands. Her toothy smile brought the tenderness back to Belinda's heart. She loosened her grip of T.J.'s shirt and picked up Hannah. Hannah was the only one who wasn't stunned speechless. T.J. smoothed the neckline of his shirt.

"T.J. and I were reviewing a lesson on what it means to be respectful," Belinda said. She swung Hannah around to her hip, then picked up the overturned chair.

"Dionne, can you come over tomorrow after school? I need you for a couple of hours so I can run a few errands."

"I can be here around three thirty." Dionne spoke so low it was almost a whisper. She looked timid, like she didn't want to be the next person to ruffle Belinda's feathers.

"That'll be fine," Belinda said, walking Dionne to the front door and away from the scene of the drama. "I'm sorry you had to see that." She patted her back and let Hannah lean over to kiss Dionne on the cheek. "We'll see you tomorrow."

When Belinda closed the door she heard Thomas direct T.J. to come into the living room.

"Yes, sir," he muttered to his father's commands.

Belinda hoped T.J. got a good look of the outside and everything else around him. Besides going to school, she figured he wouldn't see much else besides the inside of his room for the next week.

After Thomas finished hurling around T.J.'s list of punishments, both of them retreated upstairs. Slammed doors followed behind the eldest and his son. Belinda sat in Hannah's room and let the toddler dump all the belongings from her toy box on the floor. She shrieked in delight in the middle of them and insisted that Belinda play with every toy she brought her.

"You play, Mama," she said, handing Belinda a pink plate and a fake plastic scrambled egg. Hannah sat beside her and banged a wooden spoon around in a bowl.

Belinda sat Indian style and pretended to eat. The P.O.W.E.R. reunion couldn't come fast enough. Sometimes all a woman needed was a few days away from her regular responsibilities. Her mother and Aunt Wanda would gladly babysit Hannah for the weekend so she could relax and reconnect with her girlfriends. Baltimore was only three hours away, but it seemed so far from the women she'd grown to love as sisters.

paula

One hour, huh? Paula stared at the crystal chandelier suspended over the foyer. She turned it on along with every other light downstairs. The house was lit up like the biggest social event of the year was jumping off inside, but it was only her and the two children there. As usual.

As immaculate and expensive as the décor was, everything that night seemed to have lost its shine. The new photograph of the children that she'd set on the mantle was the only thing that made her smile.

When Darryl had finally arrived, he walked through the house, switching off lights.

"What's done in the dark will always be brought to the light," she said when he finally walked into the enclosed sitting area off the kitchen. Her temper rose from zero to boiling in three seconds.

"Who is she?" Paula screamed. The words burned her throat, but not as much as they burned her heart. She wasn't supposed to be at this place in life. "Who is she that she can take you away from your wife and children?"

"I'm right here."

"Your body, yes. But where's your heart?" Paula pounded her hand on her chest. "Your heart, Darryl." She circled around him. "You know the sad thing? The sad thing is that you're W-E-A-K." She sneered. She'd never heard herself sound like this. She guessed this was the fury of a woman scorned.

Act like a virtuous woman, not a scorned one. A gentle and quiet spirit is what I desire.

Paula ignored the voice trying to calm her. Being the quiet and composed wife hadn't gotten her anywhere.

"It takes a strong man to nurture and satisfy one woman," she continued. Paula stopped in front of him. "And if you really loved her, you wouldn't be here at all. You would call it quits with me and move on. But no, Darryl. You're not man enough to leave."

"What does that say about you?" Darryl asked.

Paula knew she should walk away, try to keep peace in the house, and let God handle it. *Maybe another day.*

"Oh, it's the money, isn't it? You're afraid I'm going to take you to the bank. Well, you're right." In truth, Paula couldn't care less about the money. What she really wanted —joy—was priceless.

Paula followed Darryl upstairs to their bedroom.

"You know what? I have tried. God knows I've tried." She willed the tears back. She wasn't going to give him the pleasure of seeing her cry.

"Tried what?" Darryl slid his perfectly creased slacks onto a hanger and hung it on the rack designated for all of his brown pants.

Everything in his life had to be perfect, Paula thought. *Except for his marriage.*

Paula turned off the light in the walk-in closet, leaving him in the dark. "Tried to keep this marriage together while you treat me like a stray dog from the street."

Hmph.

I know he didn't just grunt at me. "If you're going to say something, say it. I'm tired of this."

Darryl walked out of the closet, wearing only a white V-neck T-shirt and pair of boxers. "Well, leave, Paula. Nobody is making you stay. Even God gives you free will." He disappeared into the bathroom, and Paula heard the buzz of his electric razor.

"You're right," Paula whispered. "He does."

✠   ✠   ✠

Darryl didn't think she'd do it. She knew he didn't. But he didn't try to stop her. Paula wasn't sure herself until she left the entrance of her subdivision and pulled out on the main road. She didn't even look out of the rearview mirror. It was her way of saying good-bye to the past. She wouldn't return to the house as the same woman, if she returned at all.

You'll return.

God, if that's You speaking to me, You're really going to have to work a miracle. I just can't believe this is the life You have for me and my children.

In retrospect, Paula could've waited until morning instead of dragging her children out into the chilly March night in their footed pajamas. But Darryl's cold heart had chilled her more than any dip in temperature. Interstate 695 was spotted with cars zooming past her. She looked at her odometer and saw that the digital numbers ticked between fifty and fifty-five miles per hour. She was barely going the speed limit.

Paula clicked on her Bluetooth earpiece. "Call Monét," she demanded the voice-activated system.

"Hello."

Paula didn't sense a hint of tiredness in Monét's voice even though it was well after midnight.

"Are you busy? It's Paula."

"Not with anything I can't take a break from. What's going on?"

Paula sensed the worry in her friend's voice. "I left Darryl." She said it. She'd done it.

"Left him where? Where are you?"

"Left him, as in walked out on him. Walked out on my marriage."

Silence.

"Are you sure about this?" Monét finally said.

"No. I'm not sure about anything." Paula sighed. *Maybe I should go back. No.* "I had to leave tonight. I couldn't wait until morning, or—" She didn't know.

"Or what?" Monét asked.

Paula thought for a moment. "Or I would've lost my courage," she said. One tear started a waterfall that streamed down her face.

"Maybe you just need a night to sort things out."

"No, Monét. This isn't something that can be solved in a night." Paula wept. "Nights are when I've had to lie alone in my bed and cry. Nights are when I've prayed and nothing changed."

Paula wiped her eyes and runny nose with the back of her coat sleeve. The blur of the road from her tears was worsened by the light misty rain that had begun to fall. She was sick of the rain. She was sick of this life.

"I'm sorry," Monét said. "What can I do?"

"I just needed to talk to somebody." Paula glanced over her shoulder. Her children slept soundly while she wrestled with a decision that could change the way they would be raised. She'd grown up in a single-parent household. She knew how tough things could get. What did she have to fall back on other than Darryl's bank accounts?

Before Paula was a stay-at-home mother, she was a stay-at-home wife. Her career life as a single was unstable as she floated between unfulfilling jobs in search of the one thing that made her want to get up early and stay up late. Four years of study for a degree in business administration and she'd still had no idea.

When she'd become Mrs. Paula Manns, she thought she'd found the job to fill the void. She could handle being a doctor's wife and living lavishly. It was a temporary fix.

"Paula? Hello? Where are you? What's wrong?" Monét

116

sounded panicky. Paula realized she'd zoned out of the conversation.

"I'm here. Sorry."

"Do you need a place to stay? You and the kids are more than welcome to—" Monét stopped midsentence. It seemed she didn't want to ask the question, so Paula answered the obvious.

"Yes, they're with me. We're fine. I'm on my way to my mom's house." She was surprised to hear herself say it. Even more so to know that she was doing it. Even with their distant relationship, it seemed natural to seek solace there.

"I'll call you in the morning," Paula told Monét.

"Promise?"

"Promise."

"Okay. I'll be praying for you."

"Thank you." Paula pulled off her earpiece and tossed it in her purse. Darryl was too stubborn to call so soon. He'd hold off at least until the morning. He knew Paula wouldn't go anywhere where the children wouldn't be safe.

The rubber wiper blades squeaked across the drying windshield until Paula pulled into her mother's driveway. She turned them off. It was too quiet. Even the rain had stopped.

Paula knew better than to bang on her mother's door at 12:30 at night. She'd been warned numerous times about the gun tucked in the back of the overstuffed bedroom closet. By the time Rosanna could dig past the row of outdated dresses from the seventies, any would-be robber would've taken off with every valuable possession in the house. Not that there were that many to choose from.

Paula decided to call her.

"Ma, it's me. I'm outside."

"What? Paula?" Rosanna mumbled. She cleared her throat and asked, "What are you talking about?"

"Come open the door, please."

Click.

The porch light turned on a few moments later, immediately inviting an unsynchronized dance of bugs around it. Rosanna's hippy silhouette took up most of the doorframe.

117

"I can't believe this is my life," Paula said, pushing the automatic door locks. She opened the back door and unhooked Gabrielle's car seat from its base and took her inside before steering Micah inside on wobbly, sleep-weakened legs. Rosanna undressed the children out of their coats while Paula rolled in three Louis Vuitton suitcases.

The screen door creaked closed behind her, then whined when she tugged it until it lined up flush with the frame.

"Don't tell me Darryl put you out," Rosanna said, shaking the screen door to make sure it was secure. "Looks like you plan to stay for a while."

"I left." Paula couldn't bring herself to make eye contact with her mother. "I just threw some stuff in here for me and the kids."

"*You* left?" Rosanna turned on the dim yellow light in the hallway. The bulb barely diffused enough light to matter, even though the light cover was missing. Paula remembered when she'd broken it. She'd hurled a majorette baton at her sister, Kandi, after she caught her reading her diary. The light fixture and a scar on Kandi's left shoulder still carried the battle wound.

"If you want to end a marriage, put the man out. Don't you leave." Rosanna shuffled down the hallway, her wide hips rocking side to side like an ancient pendulum. "And then you're out in this weather with your children. Gabrielle is not even two months old, for heaven's sake."

I should've gone to Monét's.

Paula followed her mother into the small bedroom that she used to share with Kandi. Her master bathroom at home was four times the square footage than the cramped space. Rosanna's efforts to transform the bedroom into a family room had stalled before completion. One side of the room was a dingy pale pink and the other a soft beige color. Two trophies from Paula's high school dance squad were perched on top of a wooden entertainment system that the self-proclaimed handyman of the family, Uncle Lonnie, had built.

"Tomorrow you need to *blah, blah, blah.*" Paula tuned out

118

most of her mother's ranting. Only the sound of Paula's cell phone ringing shut Rosanna's mouth—for about two seconds.

"Hmph. I know that's not Darryl calling. I wouldn't answer the phone. I bet he let you walk out and didn't try to stop you, didn't he?"

Paula clicked the talk button without looking at the phone. She had to hear what Darryl had to say.

"Yes?"

"I'm just making sure you're okay," Monét said. Her voice sounded flustered. "I didn't want to wait until morning. Did you get to your mom's?"

"Yes. We're fine. Thanks for calling, Monét."

"Good. I'll talk to you later. Love you."

"Love you too."

Rosanna peered over at Paula's phone. "Monét? What's a Monét? That's not some man you're seeing, is it? Is that why you left Darryl? Men don't change; they just come in different wrappings."

"Monét is a friend of mine. A female friend."

"And you told her your personal business like that? I've never known you to have any close female friends since that one roommate, Jeanette, in college." Rosanna paused as if the thought of Paula having friends had stumped her.

"Things change, Mother."

"Can't argue with that," Rosanna said, setting her crossed arms where the fullness of her now saggy breasts used to be. "And don't call me Mother. Call me Mama, like you always did. No sense in trying to walk around trying to act so uppity and everything."

Paula turned up the volume on her cell phone, then put it on the dresser, covering the small heart Kandi had etched into the wood. The initials KP were surrounded by a heart. Kevin Paschal was one of her sister's high school flames. He'd lasted about three months, like the rest of them. The only one with a long-standing record was her children's father, Ronald, better known on the streets as Big Ro. He only made appearances when a job loss sent him down on his luck. Paula's niece and

119

nephew, Yvette and Javon, deserved better than an invisible father. So did Micah and Gabrielle.

"So," Rosanna was saying. "What are you going to do now?"

zora

Zora unbuckled her seat belt and waited for Preston to come around and open the car door. "I still don't see why your mother won't drive on the highway. What does she do if she has to go somewhere that's not on this side of town?"

"She waits for Pop to get home," Preston answered, like it made perfectly good sense for a woman to steer clear of every street more than five miles away from her own house.

Zora shook her head. When her mother was alive, she would hit the road in a hot second to go around the corner, or a cross country road trip with Monét's mother, Josephine—who also happened to be her best friend. Zora and Monét had grown up to be just as close as their mothers had been.

"And what if there's an emergency?" she asked. "She won't be able to wait for somebody then."

Preston held the door open for her while she put her shoes back on. Zora could tell Preston was tired of her complaining. She'd whined about the standardized exit exams the students were preparing to take in May. She wasn't satisfied with the greasy Chinese food buffet Preston wanted to eat for dinner. And the last thing she wanted to do was drive out to her in-laws'. They'd made this trip at Mother Diane's persistent request. Her excitement was too high to wait until Sunday to bring the gift she'd bought for Zora to church.

"You're going to love it. I can't wait to see your face," she'd said.

The doorway seemed to shrink when William "Pop" Fields stood in it. He dwarfed most things with his monstrous size.

"Hey there, Baby Z," he bellowed. As always, his arms swallowed Zora like a cub caught in a papa bear's clutch. He smelled like fresh mountain-scented soap and musk oil. "Mama kept looking out for you all. She was acting like Jesus was coming back or something."

Pop finally let her go and went straight to his son. They slapped hands so hard that Zora could feel the sting in her palms.

"Mama's in the kitchen putting up leftovers from dinner. Did you eat yet?"

Unfortunately, Zora wanted to say. Her stomach turned at the thought of the fried egg rolls and what was supposed to be chicken floating in sweet and sour sauce.

"I've always got an inch of space left for Ma's cooking." Preston slid his coat off and tossed it across the back of the love seat in the den.

It was unfair. Preston could devour twice his weight, and muscle seemed to take over his body instead of fat. It wasn't uncommon to find him straddled over his weight bench before his morning shower, or catching a pickup game of basketball with Jeremiah at the gym. His gym visits, however, had waned recently since church business took precedence.

"Son, I think we can get the interest rate we need on the loan we need to rehab that building we were looking at," Pop said. They'd barely had time to get in the door, and Pop was at it.

I'm not going to spend all night over here, Zora thought.

Mother Diane shoved the last of the plastic containers onto

the bottom shelf of the refrigerator and wiped her hands on a dish towel. "Come with me, Zora. Let's leave the men in the kitchen for a change," she said and headed for the steps.

Diane Fields was never found in raggedy loungewear like the pants and T-shirts Preston had convinced Zora to trash. Her hair was impeccably styled, and she donned a full regalia of gold bangles on her wrist, a cross necklace, and a tiny pair of hoop earrings on a daily basis. Even her house shoes had faux fur and a tiny heel. No wonder Preston wanted Zora to step it up a notch—he'd grown up with his mother walking around like she was in a beauty pageant.

Zora didn't dare try to pull her hand from Mother Diane's grip on their way upstairs and past the groups of family photos lined down the hallway. She'd only been in her in-laws' room once before, when Mother Diane had taken her upstairs to pray for her after her parents were killed.

When Zora walked into the room, she immediately saw the two huge boxes on the four-poster bed. The top mattress was as high as Zora's waist and tall enough that Mother Diane needed a step stool on her side of the bed.

One of the boxes was round with a rope carry handle. *Is that a hatbox? I hope that's not a hatbox.*

"This is an early Easter gift," Mother Diane said, sliding the first box toward Zora. "Honey, talk about stylish. It's from my favorite boutique."

Zora hoped her smile looked genuine as she lifted the box top. Her shock was delayed by a bed of white tissue paper, but under it was a suit in the true fashion of Mother Diane. It was the color of a ripe Georgia peach. The top was adorned with a row of bejeweled buttons, and the long asymmetrical skirt was ruffled around the hem.

"And to top it off," Mother Diane said, opening the hatbox herself.

She can't be serious, Zora thought. "Mother Diane, you shouldn't have." *Really shouldn't have.* Zora couldn't force a smile.

Mother Diane put the hat on Zora's head, then swung her

around so she could see herself in the full-length mirror in the corner of the bedroom.

"This will add a little color to your wardrobe. And it looks so good with your complexion. Much better than those drab beige suits you like to wear."

I like my suits. And they're not drab; they're classic.

"Well, what do you think?"

You don't really want to know. "It's different from my usual taste. I definitely don't have anything like it."

"I knew you'd like it."

I didn't say that.

"With Preston being called to the ministry at church, more eyes will be on you than ever before."

That was the problem. Zora wasn't interested in living up to anyone's expectations but God's. She felt caught in the middle of Preston's family and church tradition.

"Why don't you try the dress on?" Mother Diane suggested, rubbing her hand across the sparkling buttons.

"I'd rather wait." Zora rubbed her stomach. "I'm feeling a little bloated. We had Chinese for dinner."

Mother Diane scrunched her nose. "That stuff doesn't sit well with me either."

Kind of like this outfit, Zora wanted to say. She put the hat back on the bed of tissue paper, and they each carried one of the boxes downstairs to the kitchen. All of a sudden Zora didn't feel too well.

Zora leaned over the kitchen island while Preston sat at the kitchen table with his father. Pop had a row of papers lined in front of Preston, who looked like he was trying his best to stay awake. He'd been crunching numbers all day doing his job as an accountant at one of the city's tops firms, then had to be his father's consultant on business matters tonight.

Mother Diane rummaged through one of the kitchen drawers. "You don't look too well, Zora. Maybe you should go lie down on the couch in the living room."

Preston jumped at the chance to leave. "We were only coming for a minute anyway. We better get home if my baby's not feeling well."

Zora beat Preston to the car.

✦   ✦   ✦

"Junk, phone bill, mortgage, junk." Preston dropped the mail on the bar as he sorted through it. "Bank statement." He paused and held one of the envelopes to Zora. "Department of Human Resources."

Zora looked at it but didn't take it.

"Want me to open it?" Preston asked.

Last year a letter had changed Zora's life. Could it be an answer to the question she'd been carrying for over a year? She remembered the day. It was the second time that year that her life had been hit with a life-changing blow. First, her parents were killed. Then when she went to start cleaning out their belongings at their house in search for insurance papers, she'd found it . . .

Zora flipped past the folders tabbed for the household utility bills and car insurance. She came across an unmarked manila folder and pulled out the single sheet of paper inside. Zora panicked as she read the words that followed. She was sure that her eyes had deceived her. She read the paragraph again. And again. And again. She could feel the blood rush to her face and the aching like bile in her stomach already beginning to swirl. Her fingers gripped the letter, and for a moment she considered ripping it to shreds along with any evidence of the secret it held. Tears rolled down her cheek and salted her lips. How could she be adopted?

Zora found herself too shaken to stand and, with trembling hands, finally managed to call her fiancé, Preston Fields. She could barely understand her own words through her sobs.

It couldn't be true.

Every imaginable emotion fought to push itself to the surface. She succumbed to her agony and balled herself into a fetal position on the plush tan carpet of her parents' bedroom floor. She didn't move until she heard Preston ringing the doorbell and banging on the front door. She opened the door, handed him the letter, then slipped into the arms of the only truth she'd known.

Those same arms held Zora now as she stared at the white envelope. A mediator had been assigned to her case and was supposed to contact her if he was able to find any leads to her biological parents. So far, there had been nothing.

"You open it," Zora decided. Her hands trembled as Preston's finger slid across the envelope flap. This letter could very well change her life.

belinda

T.J. was supposed to be earning their trust.

Then where is he? Belinda thought to herself. She couldn't for the life of her understand why Thomas had let T.J. go off this morning with Donovan. When it came to his trust account, he had a negative balance. The peace offering fruit basket and apology attempt hadn't changed anything for her.

Even though Donovan and T.J.'s names were cleared of any connection with the random shooting at the teenage club they'd been in the night T.J. was shot, Belinda still felt Donovan was bad news. Thomas was more open to giving second chances, but Belinda didn't believe in that when the first affected her family.

The volunteers from Agape Love Christian Church milled around the Love In Action Community Center. The building, attached to the sanctuary by a glass-enclosed atrium, was the location for the church's monthly community outreach. The men's ministry had been assigned the project for March, and Thomas was one of the lead volunteers. He'd rushed from the house at seven o'clock that morning and waited until then to inform Belinda about his decision to let T.J. go with Donovan to an intramural basketball game at their high school. She was too tired to object, but she'd had most of the morning to think about it, even when she tried not to.

Thomas walked over to where Belinda was stuffing toothpaste, deodorant, and other personal care items into plastic sandwich bags. He lifted his baseball cap and wiped his sweaty forehead with the back of his arm. "Have you seen T.J. yet?"

"No," she muttered under her breath. "Surely you're not surprised."

"I hope you plan on having a better attitude by the end of the day, Belinda. You're letting too many things rule your emotions instead of trusting God."

Belinda dropped a finished toiletry bag into a box. "What I've been doing is trusting that you'll come to your senses."

"What's that supposed to mean?"

"It means you walk around letting T.J. play his trump card. When T.J. first came to us you were the hand of discipline in the house, and now you've slacked up. The boy acted like he was going to jump up in my face. You grounded him for two weeks, and then it's back to business as usual."

"There's a science to discipline. The more I say don't do something, the more T.J. does it. Sometimes you have to let hard heads suffer for their mistakes. It's the only way they'll learn."

"He doesn't need any kind of science or reverse psychology. He needs God. And he needs his father to try a little tough love. When he's under our roof he shouldn't have choices. Wrong choices almost got him killed."

Belinda noticed Thomas's jaw tighten. "This is not the place for you to preach to me about what kind of father you think I am or wish I'd be," he said.

Belinda fixed a toiletry bag of women's items, then dropped it in the box marked *WOMEN*, clenching her comment between closed lips.

A soft answer turns away wrath.

"You're right." She didn't look up from her work station.

"Thomas and Belinda!"

The couple turned toward the sound of their names, at the same time turning off their sour expressions and turning on inviting grins.

Jackson and Catrese Welch held hands so tightly they looked fused together. Their cheek-wide smiles were the only similarities between the husband and wife. According to Jackson's story, it was his bald head and butterscotch complexion that had captivated Catrese the first time their paths crossed six years ago. To hear Catrese tell it, it was her almond-shaped eyes and West Indian heritage that had him on one knee eleven months after they met.

Just eight months earlier, they'd sat on opposite ends of the couch in the church's counseling office while Thomas and Belinda walked them through their first session at marriage restoration. As the counseling sessions progressed, the physical and emotional distance between Jackson and Catrese closed.

Belinda's shoulders were tense, but Catrese's warm embrace seemed to lift her load. There was something nurturing about her that Belinda had never felt before.

"We've got good news." Catrese patted her midsection. "We're expecting. I'm twelve weeks."

Thomas slapped Jackson on the back. "Man, congratulations. This is going to be one of the biggest blessings in your life."

"Twice as much." Jackson squeezed his wife closer.

"We're having twins," Catrese said.

Belinda was elated. During one of the roughest periods in their life, God already had a blessing in store for them on the other side of the storm.

"Are you kidding me?" Belinda asked. "Twins?"

"That's the same thing I asked the doctor when she told me." Catrese laughed. Her happiness was contagious. "I'm already twice as tired and twice as hungry."

"You're pregnant. You're entitled to whatever you want," Belinda said.

At twelve weeks, Catrese had no noticeable weight gain.

By the end of nine months, Belinda couldn't see how her petite frame was going to handle being the home for a set of twins.

"We know it was God who sent you into our lives. Even before we came to marriage counseling, I watched you from afar," Catrese said. "You have the marriage and family I've always wanted for myself. I just hope we can be half as good parents as you've been."

Catrese was tearing up. "Sorry," she said. "I think my hormones are kicking in already."

"Don't do that," Belinda said. "You'll make me start too."

Before the couple was pulled away to assist with wrapping another tray of turkey sandwiches, Jackson and Catrese promised to come to the Stokeses' house for dinner. Belinda used to regularly invite couples over for dinner when she and Thomas first married. It was one of the ways they were first drawn to join the church's marriage counseling ministry.

Belinda stood beside Thomas as they watched the couple float back to their station and continue stuffing bag lunches.

"I don't want to fight like this. Not at church, not at home, not anywhere," Thomas said. "In eleven years our marriage has never been like this, and I don't want to start now."

Belinda nodded. "We'll get through it. Together. All of us."

Thomas kissed her forehead.

"There's part of our family now," Belinda said.

T.J.'s baseball cap was pulled so low that it masked his eyes and the bridge of his nose. He was growing his usual low-cut tapered style into a mini Afro. Belinda preferred a clean cut look, something like Dionne's brother, Stephen, would wear—starched khakis and a nice polo shirt. That, of course, was coming from a forty-one-year-old mother whose daily attire rarely ventured past jeans and a solid T-shirt.

The cuff of Donovan's jeans dragged on the floor. They were starched stiff enough that they could've stood up on their own.

"Hey, Dad. Hey, Ma 'Linda."

"Hello, T.J.," Belinda said. "Glad you could make it to help us, Donovan. There's plenty of things left for you guys to do."

"But first come with me, gentlemen," Thomas said, taking

Belinda's hand. "We've got something to take care of first."

T.J. and Donovan walked behind as Thomas led them through the connecting pathway from the community center into the church. The sanctuary was dark except for the small lights by the altar and an illuminated cross suspended over the pulpit.

In such a reverent, peaceful place, Belinda knew the boys wouldn't dare object when Thomas knelt down and looked at them to follow. T.J. had removed his hat once he entered the sanctuary, but Donovan's was still perched on his head.

T.J. hit the bib of his friend's baseball cap. "Take your hat off, man. Don't you know nothing?"

Belinda heard Donovan whisper, "I ain't never done this before. Is the preacher coming out here?" He sounded frightened.

"Just get down on your knees, man." T.J. knelt beside his father.

Although Thomas led the prayer, Belinda still prayed silently on her own. It was a prayer she'd said many times before.

Father, give me the wisdom to handle the children You have given to us. Help me handle my emotions so I won't be sucked into the trick the Enemy has to take my mind off of my focus to raise a godly seed for You. Strengthen my faith, hope, and marriage during this time. Everything, and I mean everything, is in Your hands.

Zora

Zora couldn't get out of that place fast enough. As soon as the last bus left its trail of black exhaust fumes and puffed down the road, she went back to her office to gather her belongings.

This morning had been their first faculty meeting since their new principal started last week. Since it was so close to the end of the year, Zora didn't understand why they hadn't appointed an acting principal from one of the administrators already on staff.

Stewart Gaines had a different modus operandi than their former principal. He had no intention of making friends with the teachers or students. He didn't talk; he grunted. He didn't walk; he stomped the halls.

And today, Mr. Gaines had succeeded in souring everyone's day.

Zora turned on the car radio. "Sex and singleness," the radio personality whispered into the radio microphone. "Don't act like it's not happening."

Zora wheeled her car through the student parking lot. *Is that Toni?* She drove up to the school's entrance to see if the burgundy braids and black quilted jacket belonged to her beloved student. It did.

How Toni scaled the high brick wall to sit on the entryway sign was beyond Zora. Her legs swung over the edge, blocking one of the Os of the word SCHOOL. A textbook was opened across Toni's lap.

"Antoinette Burkes," Zora said, putting down her car window. "What are you doing up there?"

Toni clutched her book to her chest and jumped to the ground. "Doing my homework," she said.

"Okay. And why not do it on the ground?"

Toni shrugged. "Change of scenery, I guess." She bent down beside Zora's car and shoved the ragged biology book into her bag. "My stupid locker gets jammed all the time and won't even open. I put all my books in here so I won't get written up for not bringing my books to class."

Toni slid her arms through the backpack straps. It bulged from her frame like a camel's hump. It was a miracle she didn't tip over, Zora thought.

She didn't want to, but Zora turned down the radio so she could hear better. Today's hot drive-time topic was going to bring in some interesting comments from listeners.

"So what are you still doing here?" Zora asked Toni.

"I thought I had chorus practice, but it was cancelled." Toni unhooked her cell phone from the clip on her belt. "I've been trying to call Cedric to see if he can pick me up, but he's not answering."

Zora moved her attaché to the backseat. "Get in. I'll take you home."

Toni put a hand on her hip and cocked her head. "Are you sure, Mrs. Fields? Don't you need to get home to your husband and cook dinner or something?"

"Get in the car, girl. I'm going with one of my girlfriends to dinner tonight."

"Only because you insist." Toni walked around to the

passenger's side. Heaving the backpack off her shoulders, she dumped it in the backseat, then buckled herself up in the front. "Nice leather," she said.

Zora propped her arm on the middle armrest and watched in amusement as Toni pushed nearly every button and gadget to adjust her seat. "I'm ready now," she said, slapping her thighs.

Zora reached above her and slid back the sunroof. "Sure?"

"Yes." Toni reclined her seat a bit. "Please drive slow. I'm loving this."

Zora couldn't believe the comments of some of the callers to the Melissa Flint Show. These people were bold to mix their personal opinion and their stretched interpretation of the Bible. Toni was amused for other reasons.

"And this lady actually thinks that people can hold off having sex until they're married?" Toni was sucking greedily on a watermelon lollipop. The sweet smell took Zora back to middle school and when Monét's mother made her older sister, Victoria, walk them to the convenience store. When Toni offered her a sour apple lollipop, Zora ripped the paper off.

"Waiting to have sex until you're married is not just this woman's opinion. It's in the Bible," Zora explained.

"It is?"

"Yes."

"I wouldn't know anyway. I've never had a Bible. We don't even go to church."

Zora remembered the day she'd given Toni a Scripture to look up. She'd probably been too embarrassed to mention that she didn't have a Bible.

"You've never been to church?" Zora asked. She'd been to church enough for two people. Her family rarely missed church, and her parents kept her involved in the youth ministries until she became old enough to choose extracurricular activities at high school that they would approve of.

Toni nibbled the tiny remains of candy off the white stick. "Mama sent me a couple of times with Ms. Ella when it was Easter. We were in that place all day. I thought I was gonna starve."

Zora laughed. "You'll have to go to church with me one Sunday. And you won't be there long enough to starve, trust me. My father-in-law is the pastor."

"So you *really* gotta be at church every Sunday," Toni said. She shook her head like she was apologetic, then went back to listening to the radio personality's and listeners' comments.

Now's the perfect time for that talk.

Zora felt God's urging. She knew the topic and her driving Toni home weren't coincidental. There were already too many messages being pushed into Toni's head about sex—and most of them were wrong. Toni needed to know she deserved more respect than the way women were being portrayed in the media and in the streets.

"I was a virgin until I got married," Zora said. She could see Toni's stunned expression from the corner of her eyes. It seemed she'd leaned forward so she could get a clear look at Zora's face.

"Seriously?"

"Very."

"How old are you, Mrs. Fields?" Toni held up her hand. "Oh, wait, I'm sorry. That's rude to ask a woman."

"It's okay," Zora said. She counted every year a blessing and had never hesitated in telling her age. "Thirty-one."

Now Toni was chomping on a piece of bubble gum. She's a walking candy store, Zora mused.

"That's a long time not to have done 'the do,'" Toni said, blowing a bubble.

"'The do'? That's what it's called now?"

"I thought that's what people your age called it." Toni snickered.

"Do you want to get put out on the side of the street?" Zora joked. She slowed down.

"Stop playing, Mrs. Fields." Toni pointed at a street sign. "Turn right here."

Even though the sun brightened the blue cloudless sky, the earth's colors seemed to fade to grey when Zora turned in to Toni's apartment complex. Street lights and faded fire hydrants

136

were more numerous than oak and maple trees. Scanty patches of dry, brown grass jutted up between the sidewalk cracks. Four girls jumping rope beside a fire hydrant didn't seem to be aware of two men chugging back beverages from a brown paper bag.

An elderly woman sat in a rusted metal chair on her stoop, watching it all.

"Pull down by the woman wearing that red scarf. That's Ms. Ella. My brothers and sister are at her house."

"Is that them?" Zora pointed to a group of children at the corner.

"No. They're probably inside doing homework or watching some kind of educational cartoon. Ms. Ella won't let them come outside until I get here. She said she can't be running after children with her bad knees and arthritis."

Zora was relieved that Toni and her siblings received some sort of supervision. People didn't always abide by the adage that it took a whole village to raise a child, but one concerned person could influence a child more than a group of disinterested ones. Ms. Ella seemed to be the overseer of the neighborhood children.

Toni moaned. "Great," she said, smacking her lips. She had one leg out of the car door and was about to step out. "This is not what I wanted to come home to."

Rashad Tatum was an object of infatuation at the high school. His attractiveness and bad-boy image attracted most of the girls—freshmen, seniors, and everyone in between. Except for Toni. She couldn't stand him.

"I wish my mama wasn't having a baby by his dumb daddy. They're two sorry men, and I've seen enough of that in my life. My daddy included."

Whoa. Zora had never heard Toni mention her father. She was sure years of hurt were pent up behind that comment.

"Talking about them isn't the best way to handle it. Keep praying for them and be cordial. You prayed about Rashad last time, and didn't you feel much better?"

"Yes." She smiled at the memory. "And God got him suspended."

"I don't think it was God that got him suspended," Zora said. "That was a consequence of Rashad's own actions."

When Rashad got close enough to realize it was Toni getting out of the car, a smirk spread across his face. "Your mama actually let you come out of the house looking like that? That's like secondhand smoke. Bad for the health of everyone around you."

"Get a life, Rashad," Toni snapped.

"Mr. Tatum. That's not the way to treat a lady."

Rashad shielded his eyes and ducked his head low enough to see inside the car. "Oh. Hey, Mrs. Fields. I didn't know that was you. You might have to get your car sprayed down after letting Toni ride with you." He clapped his hands, then patted his own back. He was clearly amused at his mission to work Toni's nerves.

He wasn't going to let up on Toni, even in Zora's presence.

Toni got back in the car and slammed the door, closing out Rashad's pestering. "See what I mean?"

Zora reached over and picked up her hand, resting it together with hers on the middle armrest. "He'll keep trying to annoy you as long as he gets a reaction. Ignore him and he'll be like a barking dog. He'll go away."

"Okay, Mrs. Fields." She flipped down the sun visor so she could see the mirror. Zora didn't know how Toni saw herself, but Zora saw a kitten who masqueraded as a tiger for survival in her tough world.

"I better go," Toni said. "I've got tons of homework, and I still gotta fix something for dinner."

Speaking of dinner, Zora needed to hurry to Monét's place. She wasn't the kind of woman to keep waiting when she was hungry.

monét

It's heartbreaking," Monét said to Zora. She clicked off the television and put the remote on the stack of fund-raiser solicitation letters she'd prepared for mailing. "We take it for granted that everybody grows up the way we did."

"Not the case," Zora said. "It's another world they're growing up in now. They deal with stuff as teens that I wasn't even thinking about until I was in my twenties."

"The sad thing is that I don't know if it's getting any better. Daytime TV needs to be R-rated. Now that I'm home during the day I see all the junk the networks call quality programming." Monét got her jean jacket out of the hall closet and picked up her purse. "Are you ready to go?" She put an extra whine in her voice on purpose.

"Why do you have to sound like that?"

"Because I don't see why we have to go all the way out to the Harbor to eat. I'm in pout mode," she said, poking out her bottom lip.

"It's not going to do any good, so get over it," Zora said. "We haven't been since last summer, and I like the restaurants down there."

"Remember when we first saw Paula last summer at the Harbor? We never knew we'd cross one another's paths again. God is so strategic, isn't He?"

"Yes," Zora said. "And speaking of meeting Paula last year, did you get that letter about the P.O.W.E.R. reunion?"

"Yes, and I wouldn't miss it for the world. I can't wait to see everybody again."

"Me too," Zora said.

Monét locked the door behind them and stuck a red envelope in the door crease.

"What's that?" Zora asked.

"A card for Jeremiah. He usually stops by on his way upstairs when he gets home from work. I'm leaving a little something for him."

"So sweet," Zora gushed.

Monét pushed Zora toward the elevator. Her friend could be a hopeless romantic at times, especially when it came to her. Zora was the kind who would give twelve creative gifts to represent the twelve days of Christmas. For Monét, that was equivalent to giving a card that had taken her thirty minutes to analyze in the store to make sure it said the right thing, the right way. It had taken her forever to find the perfect one for Jeremiah. She needed it to relay to him how much she cared for him, yet tell him to be patient with her.

Monét realized one thing. She wasn't used to Jeremiah's kind of love.

"I hope you realize what a good man you have in Jeremiah," Zora said, as if she'd read Monét's mind. "Don't try to sabotage this relationship by comparing him to the men you've dealt with in the past. He's not Bryce, and he's not Terrance. Don't forget that."

"Even if I did, I'm sure you'd remind me," Monét said. She clicked the keyless entry for her car. "Jeremiah is so serious."

"What you really mean is that Jeremiah is too mature to

play those games you're used to. So tell me the real deal. What's your problem?" Zora asked. "Everyone around you has successful relationships—your mother, your sister. Me. It's not like you don't know it's possible to be happy and in a relationship at the same time."

"You're right, but it's all been at the expense of the woman losing herself," Monét said.

"What? That's not true."

"Victoria used to be a successful businesswoman, and she gave it all up to stay at home with her children." Monét snapped her seat belt. "What about the dreams women have for their lives?"

Zora looked at Monét like she had two heads.

"I can't believe you said that. Victoria is a stay-at-home mother by choice, and I can assure you that she still has dreams. Sometimes our dreams aren't God's dreams, and later on we realize what's more important in our lives. That doesn't mean you've lost yourself. Sometimes it really means you've found your true self."

Monét waited to back out of her parking space until her neighbor had unloaded her children and groceries out of the car. "So your true self is being a minister's wife and possibly a first lady?"

"It's being a committed and supportive wife to my husband and the calling God has placed on his life. Sometimes that entails things you don't expect, but that's life," Zora said, turning on the radio.

"Oh yeah," Zora added. "I want to stop by the bookstore and find Toni some kind of teen devotional. One more book can't hurt in that overstuffed backpack of hers."

Monét waited in the car while Zora went into one of the community's popular Christian bookstores. She ended up texting Zora on her cell phone with a warning that she'd leave her at the store if she didn't hurry up. Monét had only eaten grapes and cheese most of the day because she'd been too lazy to go to the grocery store.

"Let's eat and get out of here," Monét said when they finally arrived at the Harbor.

"We won't be here long. You're not exactly good company tonight."

"I've got a lot of work to do. I want Savon's event to be a success. He can open a lot of doors for me in Baltimore's echelon, so to speak."

"If anybody can plan a stellar event, it's you. There's nothing to worry about, and you know it. I, on the other hand, have got the in-law blues." Zora held her hand in the air. "Let me preface this by saying I am not losing myself over all of this."

"Point taken. Now what did they do? You and Preston haven't been married long enough for you to be at odds with the outlaws."

"To start things off, Mother Diane is trying to whip me into shape with a new wardrobe. She bought me a suit."

"That's nice," Monét said, picking up her pace against the March wind. What's wrong with that?"

"I'll tell you what's wrong with it," Zora said, giving Monét a detailed rundown of the suit in question.

"That's scary," said Monét. Inside she was cracking up, but Zora looked like she was truly devastated. Regardless, Zora's wardrobe could stand a little sprucing up. Her best friend's style was bland, or as Zora liked to say, "classic."

Tonight she was wearing a pair of black trousers with dress socks and black loafers. Under her pea coat, she wore a button down blue shirt with no element of style whatsoever. All she needed was a red scarf tied around her neck and she could double as a flight attendant.

"Well . . ." Monét pushed against another brisk wind that seemed to swoop down from nowhere.

"Well what?"

"Mother Diane went a little overboard, but she had good intentions."

"So what are you trying to say?"

"A little pizzazz here and there could do you some good."

She pinched two fingers together. "Just a little bit. Don't act like I haven't told you before."

"What is this? Some kind of 'Makeover Zora' mission?"

Monét rolled her eyes. "Stop being so sensitive. You're too fashionably safe, and you know it. You never want to step outside of your comfort zone or safe shoes." Monét looked down at Zora's loafers.

"I'm not a stiletto kind of girl. So sue me."

"I give up. But I don't think loafers are going to look good with that peach suit."

Their shoes clicked across the bricks on the walkway as they made their way to their favorite eatery. There was little activity down at the Harbor tonight, and they only passed one person on their short trek to the restaurant.

"I'm having a déjà vu moment," Zora said. "Don't we know that guy?"

Monét looked back. The admirer had turned around. "I don't think so," she said, and realized he was moving to catch up with them. *Then again, he does look familiar,* Monét thought. *Chocolate complexion. Deep eyes. Alluring smile.*

"I hope you didn't forget our promise," he said as he walked up to Monét. He sounded sure that he hadn't forgotten her face or their conversation.

"Would you like to introduce yourself before you approach me with pickup lines?'

"Solomon." He held out a hand.

Monét shook it, and before she knew it he'd lifted her hand to his lips. His lips were wet. Too wet.

Monét yanked her hand from his and wiped it on the leg of her jeans. When she finally looked straight into his eyes, she remembered him from their last trip to the Harbor. She'd sideswiped his knees with an oversized shopping bag.

"No problem. You can just make it up to me." His smile invited her into his world.

"I'm sorry, but I've got to go," Monét said. She turned to walk away, but he reached out and tapped her arm.

"We can't even talk for one minute?" He held up an index finger in front of his lips. They seemed to move in slow motion. *"Just one."* He stepped in front of her to help clear a path through the crowd.

Monét didn't accept the invitation, though it would have been easy with a smile like his. It was alluring, even with the barely noticeable knick on his front tooth. She was sure he'd flashed it on a number of women through the evening. His cell phone was probably full of new numbers.

"If it's meant for us to talk, our paths will cross again—" Monét paused when she realized she didn't know his name.

"Solomon," he said. *"But they call me Solo. And you promise you'll give me a minute?"*

"Monét," she introduced herself, *"and I'll give you ten minutes."* She smoothed back one side of her hair. *"If you don't mind me asking, why do they call you Solo?"*

"Because I live in this world alone until I'm blessed with a beautiful woman like you."

Here come the pickup lines, Monét thought. *"Well, nice to meet you, Solo."*

He held out his palms, and Monét placed a hand between them. *"Nice to meet you too, Monét. And I'm holding you to that ten minutes."*

"You said that if it's meant for us to talk, out paths—"

"I remember what I said," Monét said. "But that was before I had a man."

"Lucky man," Solomon said.

Zora butted in. "Blessed man."

Solomon zipped up his jacket and lifted the collar. "I guess I was a day late and a dollar short," he said. He walked away, but not before blowing Monét a kiss.

"Mr. Solomon's ego was deflated." Monét laughed. "I guess he'll be living solo for a little longer, or whatever he says of himself."

Zora stopped in her tracks.

"What's that look for?" Her friend was clearly puzzled.

Zora turned and watched Solomon walk away. He did seem to have an effect on people, but this effect on Zora was unusual. The only man who ever left her speechless was Preston.

"Living solo?" Zora's eyes flashed to Monét, then back to Solomon's disappearing figure. "Does he call himself Solo?"

"I don't recall him saying that. I just remember him saying something about solo 'cause he was in this world alone."

"That's him," Zora said. "I know it. I've got that funny feeling in my stomach." She yanked Monét's arm. "Let's go."

Monét dug one of her heels into the cobblestone pavement. "What? I'm not going anywhere until you tell me something."

"Solo. The guy." She pointed but couldn't seem to get her words together.

"What guy?"

"The guy from the adoption chat room that I used to talk to last year when I first started looking for my biological family."

"The one you were supposed to meet that time down here until Preston found out?"

"Yes."

"Are you sure?"

"No, but how many people named Solomon relate themselves to living solo, or whatever?"

Then, as if he'd heard his name, Solomon looked back. When he saw them watching him, he posed as if they were the paparazzi and he was a washed-out celebrity starving for attention.

"He stopped," Zora said.

"I know." Monét hoped it wasn't who Zora thought it was.

"He's coming this way."

"I'm looking at him, Zora."

"What do I do?" Zora answered her own question. "I'm going to talk to him," she said.

Zora left Monét in the middle of the walkway and in the middle of her thoughts. She couldn't let this happen. Preston had forbade Zora to talk to him over the Internet, so she knew he wasn't down for any face-to-face camaraderie. Solomon looked puzzled as to why he was being approached by Zora instead of Monét, but whatever Zora said to him had locked

145

him into a conversation. At first, they shook hands like new business associates, then shared an awkward hug.

Monét was two seconds from prying them apart. Should she stand aside and let them share a private moment?

Zora's search for her biological family had begun last year in the state's adoption records and adoption Web site chat rooms. Masquerading as "Baby Z" from California, Zora regularly visited chat room sites for people who shared her stories and her fluctuating emotions. Her cyberspace connection had been the strongest with Solomon, aka "Solo." That was, until Preston discovered their virtual date and possible plans to meet in person. The plans had been cut then, but it looked now like they were coming full circle.

No, Monét decided. There was no such thing as a private moment between strangers. The only thing they shared was a somewhat similar history. Zora still had her future to be concerned about.

Monét walked over and put an arm around Zora's shoulder. "I'm starving. You ready?"

"Sure." Zora squeezed Solomon's arm. "I can't believe I finally met you. Live and in color."

"You've got a grip on you, Baby Z," he said, rubbing his shoulder. "Now I've got a sore shoulder *and* a growling stomach."

Monét got Solomon's hint, but she wasn't falling for it. There was no way she was going to let him invite himself to dinner.

"You know where you can find me if you ever want to talk," Solomon said to Zora. He reached into his pocket and pulled out a business card, handing it to Zora. "Now you know how to reach me too," he told her.

This time when he walked away, Monét hoped that would be the last time they ever saw each other.

"Don't do it," Monét said, getting inside Zora's head. "My daddy would say, 'Let sleeping dogs lie.'" She looked Zora dead in the eyes. "You don't want to start some kind of emotional attachment to Solomon. Preston didn't like it then, and he definitely won't like it now. You were his girlfriend at the time, but being his wife is another level."

146

"Before we got here we were talking about how God ordered our steps for us to cross paths with Paula."

God, what can I say to that? Drop down some wisdom. And I need it fast.

"Meeting Paula was to open a door," Monét said. "Tonight seeing Solomon was to close one."

"But I haven't been thinking about Solomon, and I haven't been in adoption chat rooms."

"No, you haven't, but you did get that letter from your mediator, and that's enough to show you that God works out things in His way and His time, and it's not the way we think it's going to happen."

paula

Four weeks had passed since Paula had left home, and she still slept and awakened with the question her mother had dropped on her the first night of her arrival.

"What are you going to do now?"

Get through today. That was her daily prayer and Scripture from Matthew 6:34. She'd written it on an index card and taped it up to the dresser mirror.

"Therefore do not worry about tomorrow, for tomorrow will worry about its own things. Sufficient for the day is its own trouble."

Paula wasn't going to worry that Darryl hadn't called and asked them to come home. At least he'd called once a week to talk to Micah and ask about Gabrielle. Evidently he thought it was easier to communicate through Rosanna, even though they'd never gotten along. But Darryl's first call to speak to his children was a disaster and ended in an argument with Paula. She'd thought the time away from him would make him realize what he'd been missing at home. Instead, it seemed to be widening the rift in their marriage.

"When are you going to stop acting like a child, Paula?" he'd asked.

They weren't the words she'd wanted to hear. She wished he'd said, "I'm sorry, baby. These past four weeks have been the worst of my life. I can't live without you. Please come back. Our family is worth fighting for."

Instead, he'd hung up in her face. She called him back repeatedly, but he never answered. She finally decided to stop making a fool of herself and have a little dignity.

Paula usually spent most of the daytime hours tending to Gabrielle. When she wasn't doing that, she was walking on eggshells to make sure she wasn't doing or saying anything to disrupt her mother's daytime television routine. She kept her cell phone clipped to her hip, just in case Darryl called with the words she wanted to hear.

Once or twice Paula thought about going back, but she couldn't bring herself to do it. She knew some women who'd think it was a ridiculous move for her to leave if there was no physical abuse. But they hadn't walked in her shoes, and honestly, at this point Paula didn't care what anyone thought.

Paula closed the door to her old bedroom and went into the kitchen.

"Really, Ma," Paula said, hoisting her second laundry basket of dirty clothes on her hip to carry out to the car. "Nobody goes to the Laundromat anymore."

"Good then. It'll just be nobody and you there, so you'll be finished in no time." Rosanna clicked on the kitchen television with the remote, its batteries secured by a strip of grey electrical tape. She ignored Paula's huffing.

Paula missed her housekeeper, Estelle. She made their clothes smell like a fresh spring breeze rolling over country hills. Housekeepers always knew the deepest secrets of the families they worked for. They could tell what was going on by the slightest change in routine—like the lack of dirty clothes in the washroom, or the fact that none of Micah's toys were strewn around his playroom. What was Estelle thinking now?

Paula covered her undergarments with a towel. She couldn't remember the last time she'd had to wash, much less drag a laundry basket into a sweat-evoking Laundromat. On top of that, Paula's backside ached just thinking about the plastic steel-legged chairs.

"I don't see why you don't go to your own house to wash if you've got to grunt and complain so much," Rosanna said. "You've got a right. Your name is on the title too."

Actually it wasn't. Never had been. Paula's life had mistake written all over it.

Rosanna slapped her hand on the end table. "One dollar higher. You're supposed to bid one dollar higher so you won't go over," she screamed at the floundering game show contestant. "This woman knows nothing about *The Price Is Right.*"

Paula opened the front door. "I'm going straight from the Laundromat to pick up Micah from school. Are you sure you'll be all right with Gabrielle?"

"Two children and grandbaby number four," Rosanna stated matter-of-factly like there wasn't a need for further explanation. "Get some quarters out of that Mason jar on the counter. And while you're out, buy yourself another dose of courage so you can go back to *your* house to wash."

Paula closed the door. Going to do laundry seemed a lot more appealing now.

After thirty-six years, it would seem Paula would be used to her mother's snide remarks. "The world's going to treat you much worse than I ever could," she used to say. In Rosanna's house, you did what you had to do to survive. Tears were for the weak and were meant to be shed behind closed doors.

✣ ✣ ✣

"I'll kill you." The words spat from the mouth of the man blocking Paula's exit. Past his rough, snarling face, he still looked to be in his early twenties. It was evident he'd been dealt or taken life's rough hand.

Paula couldn't believe she was trapped between two rows of industrial washers. Four of them held six dollars' worth of

151

her laundry. The only weapon she had was a can of grape soda that she'd beaten out of the machine when it threatened to steal her sixty-five cents. It wasn't likely she'd escape by spraying a stream of purple soda in their faces.

"You owe me a dollar," said a woman, the other half of the impending brawl. "Give me my money." The hair slicked into a knot at the top of her head was pulled tight enough to slant the corners of her eyes. She followed her demand with a string of insults about the man and his daddy.

"You gave me that dollar," the man hissed. The black head rag tightened around his forehead as the veins on his face pulsed through his skin. "You better back up off me. I'll kill you. I ain't playing."

Paula couldn't believe it. She scolded herself for not having the guts to return to her own house to do laundry. Maybe her mother's cutting remark had been a warning from the Lord. She hadn't heeded it, and now she was praying she wouldn't lose her life over a dollar. Ten dimes. One hundred stupid pennies.

I can't die like this, God, Paula thought. *My children barely have a father; You can't take their mother too. I'll do better. I'll pray and read my Bible every day. I won't miss another church service. In fact, I'll be there as soon as the doors open this Sunday.*

The feuding couple was still blocking Paula's exit. She didn't trust that her post-pregnancy body was as agile as it was eleven months ago. As soon as Paula was able, she was putting in a call to Cordell, her personal trainer. Six weeks with him and she'd be able to skim the washers as easy as the hurdles she'd jumped during her high school track meets.

The words the man and woman hurled between each other grew louder and more vulgar. When they stepped nose to nose to each other, Paula grabbed the opportunity to squeeze past them and make a calculated dash to the door.

Once outside, Paula noticed that she was the only one disturbed by this scene. A short-haired woman added a folded blue washcloth to the other fraying towels in her laundry basket. The same guy who'd had his ear glued to his cell phone for the last twenty minutes hadn't taken his eyes off his growing stack of plaid boxers. Even patrons from the neighboring cleaners and nail shop had their noses pressed against the Laundromat window, going toward the action instead of running away from it.

Paula sat in her Land Rover and watched the rowdy couple take their argument down the street and toward the convenience store. The way people could act over a little money was amazing. She knew from experience that even an abundance of it couldn't guarantee happiness.

When she'd left this kind of drama in her old community, Paula had no intention of returning to it. She also hadn't intended on being a single mother with two kids, but the possibility loomed over her more every day.

At least in her gated community people didn't take their arguments to the street—unless you count her and Darryl's garage scene. She was living proof that money, prestige, and dysfunction could reside behind the same walls.

Paula waited in the car while her clothes finished washing. By the time they'd finished drying, she had just enough patience to dump them in the clothes baskets with a promise to fold them all that night.

She looked at her watch. Before she picked up Micah she had the time for one last errand. She'd stayed reasonably calm in the face of danger about an hour and a half ago. That was courage, she thought. And she had enough of it to go to her house.

Paula used to wonder what would make a person have a conversation out loud with themselves. She was finding out.

"It's your house, Paula," she said to herself.

"But it hasn't felt like home for over a year."

"What about the courage you claimed to have?"

"I have it. If I didn't, I wouldn't be turning down Three Oaks Lane right now."

Paula crept to the end of her cul-de-sac and came to a stop in front of her neighbor's house. She shouldn't have come. If she hadn't, she wouldn't have seen the red BMW parked in her driveway with the license plate that read LADY DI.

153

belinda

Belinda had been counting down the days until the P.O.W.E.R. reunion and was elated to finally spend the weekend with her friends. She, Paula, Monét, and Zora had all bunked in one hotel suite, and before they knew it, seven o'clock in the evening became three o'clock in the morning.

Even though she'd only had five hours of sleep, Belinda felt as refreshed as she did after a restful eight-hour slumber.

"You don't know how much I needed this," Belinda said. The April morning beckoned her out onto the hotel balcony.

"I bet I do," Paula said. "Last night was the first time in about three months that I've slept all the way through the night —what sleep I did get." She squeezed a lemon over her water, then wrapped the juiceless rind in a napkin.

Belinda slid her shades down on her nose and put a bookmark to mark her place in a novel she'd been engulfed in since Friday morning. The joy of reading, she thought. It was amazing how she could escape into the pages of a good book when an incorrigible teenager and demanding toddler didn't soak up her extra time.

"I could stay here—"

"Forever," Paula finished.

"Well, not that long." Belinda laughed. "Three days and I'd start to miss my family too much."

"Four days for me," Paula said. "I guess forever is a bit much."

Belinda tucked her legs in under her ankle-length Bohemian skirt.

"Secret question," she said to Paula. "Just between us old married-with-children women."

"Ask away while I still fit the categories."

"Do you ever wish for the days when you were single?"

"Do I?" Paula took a long drink of water. She rested her head in her hand. "At least once a week. Isn't that terrible?"

Belinda pulled at one of her natural twists. She loved that they'd grown longer. On a whim a few weeks ago, she had added some streaks of color. Now that they were down to her chin, she could pull them back into a hair clip. "Then we're both guilty," Belinda admitted.

"Not you too?"

"Yes, me."

"I thought you counseled married couples at your church."

"What's that got to do with anything? Counselors need counseling," Belinda said. "Twice a month I'm the spiritual advisor to couples trying to keep their families together. And the stitches of mine have started looking mighty raggedy."

"I know what you mean," Paula said.

They sat in contemplative silence.

Paula crossed her legs and wiggled her toes. They had a fresh coat of fire engine red polish and the daisy design that each of the friends had gotten painted on their big toe. Instead of red, Belinda had chosen a soft pink color for her pedicure and manicure. With all of the typing she did working on articles for the magazine and editing other people's work, her nail polish would be chipped off by next week. Belinda held out her hand to admire the manicurist's work.

"You know the crazy thing?" Paula said. She shook crushed ice around in her glass. "When I was single I was praying for a husband and children."

"Honey, I was fasting, praying, laying at the altar, and everything else." Belinda clasped her hands under her chin. "Lord, if You give me children, however You give them to me, I'll train up them to follow You." She chuckled.

"Girl, you are too funny," Paula said.

"Some days I have to laugh to keep from crying. But it's getting better. I only want to send T.J. back to Pittsburgh twice a week instead of every day."

Paula stood up and looked over the balcony railing. Belinda noticed how her midsection barely told of her recent pregnancy, while Belinda's clothes hid a stomach comparable to a woman who was three months pregnant. Her favorite comfort foods had become a mainstay in her pantry and refrigerator. Cinnamon and raisin bread. Salt and vinegar potato chips. And her most delightful, guilty pleasure—strawberry cheesecake ice cream. She bet none of it had ever touched Paula's lips.

"Paula, you look good," Belinda said.

"Are you trying to give me hope that another man will want me someday?"

"I'm serious. You've got a body like one of those women on those Pilates videos."

"Tell that to my old pants that I can't wiggle past my thighs."

"Oh, please. You had a baby three months ago." Belinda pinched her love handles. "I can't attribute this to anything but being greedy. Why do you think I only have a head shot for my editor picture in the magazine? I don't want people to know I'm not practicing what I preach."

Paula put her hands on her hips and twisted around to see her backside. "So it really looks like I'm losing weight? I've been taking Gabrielle on stroller walks in the morning and some evenings."

"Yes. I wouldn't lie to you."

"Good. I need to get back into all those clothes that Darryl's money bought."

They laughed at Paula's comment, but Belinda knew Paula laughed more to keep from crying. Last night they'd kept the conversations light, and the only tears shed were happy ones. No one wanted to kick off the reunion they'd been anticipating by putting all of their drama on the table.

Zora pushed open the glass door that led out to the patio. "What's all the cackling about out here? You must be conspiring to do something."

Monét's voice trailed from somewhere behind her. "Either that or you're talking about somebody."

"Good thing we're having a speaker at the morning session," Zora added. "She might need to review our lessons on taming the tongue."

"Well, listen to First Lady Fields," Belinda said. She waved her hands in the air like there was a chorus of "Amens" and "Hallelujahs" in pews behind her.

"Don't start, Belinda."

"Face it, First Lady. You're in training to take the reins from the front pews of the church." Paula fanned an imaginary over-sized church fan in front of her face.

"I'm ignoring both of you." Zora stepped back inside the hotel room. "We only have fifteen minutes before the session starts, so Monét and I are going downstairs. We'll hold two seats," she said, and she slid the door closed behind her.

"I guess we better get going," Belinda said. She took off her shades and hooked them on the front of her tank top.

Paula sat down in the reclined lounge chair beside Belinda. "Guess so."

Neither woman moved. They looked at each other.

A mischievous smile lined Paula's face. "You better get a move on," she said.

"Yeah. You too," Belindea agreed, reclining her chair back even farther.

A siren whined in the distance. Belinda listened to the hum of passersby in conversation four stories below her. She slowly exhaled, closing her eyes. Even with the city noise, it was the quietest time she'd experienced in months.

"I'm not going to the first session, but don't let that deter you."

"I'm not going either," Paula said. "And you had nothing to do with my decision."

"I need some peace and quiet for a change," she said, just as another siren whined in the distance.

"I might get the quiet, but I'm not sure about the peace."

Belinda slowly straightened her legs as she attempted to sit up. The feeling of prickly pins danced across the bottom of her feet that had fallen asleep. "Still thinking about that car at your house, aren't you?"

Paula stood back up and went back to the balcony rail. There was nothing spectacular to see, but Belinda knew she was looking into her life and not at the silhouette of the city's building landscapes.

Even though Belinda was only five years older than Paula, her friends looked at her as the matriarch of their prayer and friendship circle. They'd connected so deeply last year during the P.O.W.E.R. women's discipleship group, and Belinda often wished she lived closer than the two hundred miles that separated them. Prayer kept them close, but sometimes there was nothing like a sister's hand to hold.

Belinda walked over to Paula. She put an arm around her shoulder. "Let's go to your house. We've prayed it up before; we'll do it again," recalling the time when their entire discipleship group had walked through Paula's house to pray for her marriage.

"I can't. I told you."

"You can, and you will." Belinda grabbed both of Paula's shoulders, shaking them gently. "This is the counselor in me. God has not given you the spirit of fear, but of power, love, and a sound mind. Now don't you believe God?"

"Yes."

"Isn't He always true to His word?"

"Yes."

"Didn't He say that you could have an abundant life?" Belinda spoke to Paula, but she found that her words were strengthening her own spirit.

159

"Yes."

"Are you living an abundant life?"

"No," Paula said.

"So what are you waiting for?"

Belinda wasn't giving up on Paula. She could see both the desire and the apprehension in her eyes. Only God knew what awaited them behind the house's doors, but Belinda couldn't stand to see her friend living like this. Belinda often saw—more times than she wanted—couples who endured a period of separation before God restored their marriage.

Paula turned and picked up her sunglasses from the patio table. "Let's go."

paula

Paula held her breath until she heard the click of the door latch. *Why should a woman feel like an intruder in her own home?* To her relief, Darryl hadn't changed the locks. The brass doorknob felt unusually cold. Or was it her clammy hands?

Paula wiped her palms on the legs of her capris. She swallowed slowly, then exhaled the anxiety smothering her chest. The arched frame of the doorway towered over her by at least four feet. She looked at Belinda, then back at the door that separated her from the truth.

Paula turned the knob.

Sunlight bounced on the spotless marble floor of the foyer when she pushed the door open. The smell of lemon-scented household cleanser overtook her senses.

"I see he's still got the housekeeper coming," she said, filling the tense atmosphere with empty words.

"How much of a mess can a man make by himself?" Belinda asked, closing the door behind her.

Paula walked past the study and into the kitchen. The house was eerily quiet without the sounds of their everyday life. The only thing she heard was the flip-flop of Belinda's sandals in sync with her own steps. Micah's fingerpainted masterpiece of himself playing basketball still clung to the stainless steel refrigerator by two bright magnetic alphabet letters. She soaked in the scene.

An unfinished mug of coffee sat beside the automatic coffeemaker. She was certain the slow and steady drip had started at six thirty this morning for Darryl's groggy descent to the breakfast table. Next, he'd staggered to the end of the driveway for the newspaper so he could lose himself in the business section while he ate a routine breakfast of cream of wheat, two boiled eggs, wheat toast, and orange juice.

Paula dumped the leftover coffee into the sink, which was empty except for two dinner plates and two wine glasses.

Two?

Paula looked at Belinda. She'd noticed it too, but didn't say anything.

"Can you come upstairs with me?" Paula asked.

Belinda nodded.

Paula didn't know if she truly wanted to go, but her feet were already taking her there. She needed to look. She had to see if another woman had entered the sanctity of her bedroom.

They walked upstairs in slow motion. The flight seemed endless even though there were only fourteen steps. She'd counted them hundreds of time with Micah.

Paula could hear Belinda whispering behind her. She was already praying. The only prayer Paula could muster was, "Lord, help me . . ." She repeated it over and over again until she stood in her bedroom doorway.

The bedroom was in disarray, a stark contrast to the neatness of downstairs. It was, however, the only room in the entire four-thousand-square-foot house that Estella never entered. Today, it showed.

The five pillows that were usually propped neatly against the headboard were hunched together in the middle of the king-

162

sized bed. It seemed that the imprint of Darryl's head was impressed upon each one and that he'd been in a tousle with the sheets. Half of the linens were strewn on the floor.

"He can't find peace without his family here," Belinda stated confidently. "He might be stubborn, but he's a miserable man right about now."

Paula stepped over the comforter, then picked up its corner. Belinda lifted the other end, and when she did, a Bible fell from the bunched-up duvet.

"I told you," Belinda said. She picked up the Bible and placed it on the nightstand. "God is working on him."

Paula couldn't remember the last time Darryl had picked up a Bible. It looked like the family Bible they'd received as a wedding gift from one of Darryl's aunts, because Darryl had never owned his own. Until her marriage started to crumble, Paula's own Bible pages had been crisp and clean. Now, the pages were used so much that they seemed to turn themselves, and the highlighter she used sometimes bled onto the other pages.

Paula and Belinda worked together—smoothing the sheets, tucking the corners, straightening the comforter, fluffing the pillows. When they finished, Belinda sat at the foot of the bed and went back into prayer.

Paula surveyed the bathroom, then walked back into her room. Thoughts rushed into her mind. Has another woman been in my bed? Shared the Jacuzzi bathtub that she'd spent at least one day a week in with Darryl during their first years of marriage? Before more questions swept in, the Holy Spirit dropped a Scripture in her mind to crowd out the negative thoughts. "... *whatever things are noble, whatever things are just, whatever things are pure, whatever things are lovely, whatever things are of good report, if there is any virtue and if there is anything praiseworthy—meditate on these things.*"

Paula looked around for something else to fix. With the drapes closed, it was no wonder that the leaves and vines of her ivy plant drooped lazily over the edge of the where it sat. She opened the drapes and sheers, then moved the plant closer to the window after giving it a showering of water from the bathroom sink.

God breathed another Scripture into her. "*I am the vine, you are the branches. He who abides in Me, and I in him, bears much fruit; for without Me you can do nothing. . . . If you abide in Me, and My words abide in you, you will ask what you desire, and it shall be done for you.*"

I want my family back together, Paula prayed silently. Her thoughts were so hypocritical. She wanted their marriage restored, but she couldn't bring herself to come back home. Not yet.

Belinda had stopped praying and sat on the settee by the bed, waiting for Paula's instruction.

"Could you get some more clothes together for the kids?" Paula asked her. "Just a couple of things."

"Sure," Belinda said. She rubbed a silver pendant from her necklace between her fingers. Paula had noticed the habit surfacing whenever Belinda seemed contemplative.

Think, Paula, she told herself.

"The baby's room is the first door to the left down the hall, and Micah's room is the second door," she said, realizing that Belinda didn't know where to go. "There should be a duffle bag in the top of Micah's closet. You can throw their things in that."

"Okay."

Paula clasped her hands together under her chin.

"*What are you going to do now, Paula?*" Her mother's words never seemed to leave her. It was like a call to action, and Paula had yet to step up to the challenge. "I'm going to pray," she said aloud. "And pray some more."

Paula walked into her closet and unhooked a handful of suits and dresses from the top rods. Hopefully in the next few weeks, she'd be able to fit back into them. "I'm going to get myself together and let God handle Darryl in His own way." She neatly zipped them up in a garment bag, then threw a few casual shirts, pants, and shoes in a shoulder tote bag. Paula lifted her bags up onto the bed.

That's when the door chime sounded from downstairs.

A woman's voice echoed from the empty foyer. Paula froze.

No one would've known she was here. They'd driven Belinda's car and parked at the end of the cul-de-sac at Paula's insistence.

Belinda appeared at the doorway with the blue duffle bag draped over her shoulder.

"Who's that?" she whispered.

"I don't know."

Belinda dropped the bag by the door and pointed her fingers to the stairwell. "Don't just stand there. It's your house, your husband, and you don't have the spirit of fear."

Paula whizzed past Belinda so fast that she didn't know whether her friend was behind her or not. She didn't care. She'd been anticipating this confrontation for over a year. She was about to meet the woman that Darryl claimed didn't exist.

She took the stairs by two, maybe three. Everything in front of her was a blur.

"And you're in my house, why?" Paula said, screaming before she rounded the corner to the voice she heard in the living room.

"Mrs. Manns!" The woman's long black braid whipped around as fast as her stout body. "I'm sorry. I didn't know anyone was here. I left my cell phone yesterday, and I need it so my children can call me." Her words were so fast that they tumbled over each other.

"Estella." Paula held her hand up to silence her housekeeper.

"I didn't know where I'd left it, and then I remembered, so I called Dr. Manns and he said it would be all right if . . ."

"Estella!" Paula interrupted loudly, then dropped her tone to calm them both. "I apologize. I promise you it's okay."

"I really need this job, Mrs. Manns."

"Estella, how long have you been working for us?"

"Four years."

"And do you actually think I'd fire you over a small mishap like this?"

"I didn't know what to expect." Estella threw up her hands and paced back and forth in front of the fireplace. Paula had worn the carpet thin along the same path many nights waiting for Darryl to come home.

Estella continued, "Dr. Manns said you had some things going on and needed to go away for a while."

So that was his explanation.

In two quick steps, Estella had her arms around Paula, locking her arms by her side. "I'm so glad you're back. I've been praying every night for you." Estella rocked, swaying Paula's body side to side. "I said, 'God, do a special work in the life of Mrs. Manns.'" She clasped her hands together and said, *"Oro para mi amiga buena. Bendiga, por favor."*

"That's sweet, Estella. A person can never have enough prayer."

Estella finally loosed her grip, but her rambling didn't let up.

"That's the same thing I was telling Mrs. Manns. Well, the other Mrs. Manns, yesterday." She cocked her head to the side. "I see where Dr. Manns gets his good looks and charm from. She's such an elegant woman. She definitely doesn't look like the kind of woman who would stand over a stove."

Estella's mouth ran like water, and this was one leak Paula would let drip.

"When I came yesterday she was busy cooking dinner for Dr. Manns, and it was only eleven o'clock in the morning."

Drip.

"She said she was going to be here until this Sunday."

Drip.

"She talked about a surprise visit she needed to make before she left, but she never said where. I had a time trying to guess, but she wouldn't tell me."

Drip.

Belinda had retreated to the kitchen table. The only time Paula was aware of her presence was when she heard her leafing through the pages of a magazine.

"Forgive me for being so rude." Estella finally spoke to Belinda. "I'm Estella Garcia." She slid the cell phone into the front pocket of the black smock she was wearing. Paula noticed that instead of the flesh-colored hosiery she usually wore, the rising spring temperatures pushed Estella to wear a pair of footies with her customary white tennis shoes.

Estella shuffled to the door like she didn't want to leave any scuff marks on the spotless floor. "Don't worry, Mrs. Manns. I'll lock the door behind me," she said. And she was gone.

"So much for the mystery of the two plates and wine glasses," Paula said, relieved.

Belinda closed the magazine. "God is good. Sometimes He won't give you time to let your imagination run too wild."

"Speaking of imaginations, I wonder what Zora and Monét are thinking."

Belinda looked at the grandiose grandfather clock in the living room. "If we leave now we can make it back in time for lunch and our friends' interrogations."

"Let me grab the bags from upstairs and I'll be ready."

Paula shuffled through the designated junk drawer on the kitchen island. Inside were take-out menus, coupons, grocery list pads, and a few sheets of stationery. Occasionally, she used it to write thank-you notes to Estella, or draw a picture that she'd hide as a lunchtime surprise in Micah's Spiderman lunch box. This time, she used it to write Darryl a note. She went upstairs and tucked it in the Bible he'd been reading.

zora

They definitely played hookey," Zora said. She and Monét had scanned the auditorium until the crowd thinned. Now they stood in the hotel's atrium with no sight of their two friends. Most of the women had scurried in different directions, heading for the closest restaurant to scarf down lunch between sessions.

"I'm close to playing hookey myself," Monét said. "Jeremiah is coming with me to my parents' house tomorrow, and I need to go home and wash my hair."

"Please, Monét. Find another excuse. Your hair is the picture of perfection." Her friend had recently dyed her lush tresses jet black and was flaunting a new look, as she usually did every week. "I like the curly look on you. It looks so healthy and full of body."

An armful of gold bangles clanked when Monét pushed her hair off her forehead and pinned it back with a small clip. "It's been a week. I'm over it." She adjusted the straw bag on her shoulder. "I think I want to get it cut. Try something short and sassy." Monét pointed to a pregnant woman wobbling by sandwiched between two elderly women. "Like that. Maybe a little shorter."

"Does Jeremiah like short hair?"

Monét rolled her eyes. "What does the hair on my head—that *I* have to do every day—have to do with Jeremiah?"

"Men have preferences. That's all I'm saying."

"I do too. And I prefer to be able to change my hairstyle without having to worry about whether Jeremiah's feelings are going to change about me."

"You're taking it too deep, Monét," Zora said. "And Jeremiah is attracted to you as the entire woman that you are—the physical, intellectual, and spiritual sides. He likes the entire package and what comes with it. Just like my package looks good in my clothes, my style."

With Preston's help on how to address the sensitive issue, Zora had convinced Mother Diane that the choice of attire for her daughter-in-law was a bit too flashy for Zora's taste. They'd compromised on another suit that was less flamboyant and dumped the satellite-sized hat altogether. On Easter Sunday, she'd sat on the second row with a suit that was the same color as Mother Diane's, but fortunately far from the same style.

Monét draped a light blue cardigan around her shoulders. "Well, summer is around the corner, and some things—like style—could stand to change with the season. Everybody could stand a little refreshing every now and then."

Just then, Belinda and Paula rounded the corner.

Zora curtsied as the ladies approached them. "Well, look who decided to join us," she said. "The queens have arrived."

"And where have you ladies been?" Monét asked.

Belinda hooked her arm through Paula's. "Didn't I tell you the investigations were going to start as soon as we got here, Paula?"

"Well?"

"We'll talk about it at lunch," Paula said.

"See?" Zora shook her finger at Paula. "You're the one who's always keeping secrets. It's time for another confession session."

Zora waited for the hostess to clean the clutter and crumbs from the restaurant table. She'd purposely chosen the same restaurant and table where they'd bonded almost a year ago after being grouped together as prayer partners. Even the hostess, with her bleach-soaked washrag, couldn't wipe away the memories.

"I feel like I'm coming to a group therapy session," Paula said, taking the first seat.

"Call it what you want. All I know is that when two or three —and we have four—are gathered in His name, God said He'd be in the midst." Belinda melted into the chair beside Paula.

She looked tired. Drained. But not as much as Paula, Zora noticed. On the ride over, Zora had been able to drag out of them that the two had taken a trip to Paula's home. By the time the hostess came to clean their table after lunch, the rest of their stories and struggles would be out on the table again.

The women took their time eating. With all of them ordering deli sandwiches, it was no worry that their food would grow cold. They weren't in a rush to leave. At times, they were comfortable in their own silence. Zora longed for a time when they had nothing but good news and triumphs to share. Life was lived in seasons. The comforting thing about it was that their tribulations were perfecting them. When she thought about the winter season Paula was experiencing in her marriage, Zora's attitude toward being a minister's wife was selfish. Through continuous prayer, she was learning to accept it. This calling was helping her spiritual growth.

Paula sliced a piece of red velvet cake and slid it to the middle of the table. "Did you ever think about leaving Thomas?" she asked Belinda.

"What? No."

"Not even now?"

"Hasn't even crossed my mind. My situation isn't bad enough to make me leave my husband. Nowhere close to it. You can't compare our situations."

Monét probed. "What exactly *is* your situation, Paula? We

know Darryl has a nasty attitude, but unless I'm wrong, you've never been able to prove that he's having an affair."

Paula put down her fork. "When you're married, instinct can be stronger than proof. Of course, it's easier for me to point at Darryl and call out his faults, but I think I'm justified."

Zora agreed about the instinct thing. More like discernment. It was getting to the point where she and Preston could predict each other's actions. She prayed her womanly instinct would never have to be used in a situation like Paula's.

Paula brushed a wisp of hair off of her forehead. "You can't make somebody love you."

"And you can't turn love on and off like a faucet," Zora put in. Even as close as they'd grown, Paula had always veered their conversations away from Darryl over the last three months. Unless she brought it up, Zora didn't touch the subject.

"Did you feel any kind of love from Darryl before you left? Or now?" Monét asked Paula.

"Hardly. He loves something or someone else more."

"Love is a strong word," Belinda said. "He loves you. I know that for sure. But someone may be trying to get a grip on him, and it's clouding his vision. But God is working on him. You saw the Bible with your own eyes."

Paula nodded. "I wouldn't have believed it if I hadn't." She looked at Zora and Monét. "I didn't tell you about the intruder in my house."

Zora held her breath through the entire story. "I didn't know who you were going to say was in your house. Then, the dishes in the sink." She shook her head. That was a real-life soap opera.

"I wonder why your mother-in-law didn't try to contact you," Monét said.

Paula shrugged. "She's like that. She's never liked me, but I didn't care. I wasn't marrying her."

"Wouldn't she want to see her grandchildren?"

"You never know what Darryl told her. As far as she knows, she could think we moved to another planet. The woman believes anything her son tells her no matter how crazy it sounds. He's an only son and a big-time mama's boy."

Umph, Zora huffed. "Tell me when you find some scissors big enough to cut him loose. I'm trying to help Mother Diane snip the strings to her baby boy."

Everyone laughed but Belinda, who wasn't paying attention.

Belinda had been looking thoughtful during most of their time there, Zora noticed. That's what counselors did. Listen. Take it all in. Drop a nugget to make you think.

"Do you ladies want to know the truth?" Belinda finally asked. She took a sip of her coffee that she'd missed enjoying at breakfast.

"Love," Belinda said.

Zora wasn't the only one wearing a question mark on her face.

"These things we're going through. It's all about love." Belinda clasped her hands and placed them over her heart. "Love is patient. Love is kind. It's long suffering. It can heal a marriage, build a marriage, show us we're equipped to handle our calling, and get a knuckleheaded son to act like he's got some sense."

They chuckled softly.

"Seriously, though." Belinda reached for Paula's hand. Paula grabbed Monét's, who covered Zora's hand.

"Love," Belinda continued. "Love bears all things, believes all things, hopes all things, endures all things."

All of the women finished the Scripture in the thirteenth chapter of 1 Corinthians. It had been one of their memory Scriptures during P.O.W.E.R., hidden in their hearts for such a time as this.

"Love never fails."

paula

Paula slid her foot into her pump and buckled the strap around her ankle. She closed the bedroom door and looked into the mirror hooked on the back of it. Her image was slightly crooked because of the crack running down the left side. The two-piece baby blue linen suit fit her with no fabric to spare. Ellen Tracy would be proud of how she was working her design, even though Paula was still a few pounds from her usual size eight.

She hadn't forgotten the promise she'd made to God in the Laundromat, but last Sunday she'd had to miss church because Gabrielle was getting over a cold. Today she'd even planned on going to Sunday school, but Gabrielle had awakened for two feedings during the night and Paula was too pooped to pull herself out of bed to make it to church by nine thirty.

After a final examination, Paula stepped into the hallway, tapped on her mother's door, and eased it open.

"I'm getting ready to go, Ma. You sure you don't want to come?"

Rosanna looked up from her crossword puzzle. "I'm at church right now," she said, nodding her head toward the television. A local preacher on the public television station was walking out an illustration for his congregation. He wiped a white handkerchief across the bridge of his nose, then stuffed it in his suit pocket.

"You're not even paying attention."

"I can do more than one thing at a time," Rosanna said, and tossed the folded newspaper on the lumpy pillow beside her. "Now go. No sense in being late if you're going to go to church at all." Rosanna waved Paula off with a flick of her hand and picked up the remote to turn up the television. The voice of the pastor drowned out Paula's attempt to say anything else to her mother.

Paula lifted Gabrielle out of the playpen she'd bought and managed to squeeze into the living room. In the excitement of her mother's presence, Gabrielle flung her arms around and bonked Paula in the side of the eye with the rattle she was holding. Paula's eye was still watering when she pulled into the parking lot of the church just a few miles away.

It was a parade of families in their Sunday best. Women dressed in suits the color of dyed Easter eggs with matching wide-brimmed hats sauntered inside the church with their suited men and energetic children by their sides.

Paula paused and turned around, holding on to the black iron handrail after hearing someone call her name. His face looked vaguely familiar. Her mind ticked through how she might know him.

"Have I changed that much?" he asked when he caught up with her. He extended a hand to help Paula up the remaining three steps.

Paula accepted his act of chivalry. "Evidently so," she said, shifting Gabrielle from over her shoulder to a cradled position. She straightened out the baby's lavender jumper and lace-collared white undershirt.

"Wayne Edwards," he said, opening the door that led to the church vestibule.

"Not Wayniac Brainiac." She laughed, recalling the well-known rhyme that had followed him through elementary and middle school. The maturity of his running buddies had finally swept the rhyme under the rug when they went to high school. Like most boys, they grew more interested in trying to impress the girls—however futile their efforts.

Wayne's face blushed in amusement and embarrassment. His honey-toned skin was dotted with freckles, and his hair was still as red as the horizon of the setting sun. The braces that used to hide the crooked teeth during high school had transformed into a smile as straight as a white picket fence.

The thirteen years since I've seen him have definitely done him some good, Paula thought.

Then she remembered. Just that quick, her mind took her back. The last time she'd run into an old friend had resulted in a confrontation when Darryl accused her of having an affair. Her instinct had thrown up a red flag that she ignored when Victor suggested they grab a bite at the coffee shop inside the mall. Then out of nowhere . . .

Darryl began again before Victor could speak. "So you must be the father of my wife's baby?"

Paula's heart found its way back from her toes and up into her throat. Her shock matched the look on Victor's face. Her hands trembled.

"Evidently you're mistaken," Victor said, shaking his head and shoving his hand into his pocket. He was calm and unmoved by the confrontation, unlike Paula. "We ran into each other in the parking lot. We went to college together. I'm Vic—"

"Is that the story you two concocted?" Darryl's words were slow and steady, easing out of the subtle smirk on his face. "Really, Paula," he said. "I thought you were more intelligent than that. And to think you said you were going to meet with a women's church group so you could sneak out. Is that what this

group does? Teaches women to cheat on their husbands. Can I get an Amen, Paula?"

It's not what you think.

Darryl hovered over her, waiting for a response. Her body betrayed her. She couldn't get her lips to move or her legs to stand. She almost wished he'd cause a scene. At least then she'd be sure of where his head really was. His impassive reaction was more threatening. He was calm. Too calm.

"Her things will be packed tonight so you can pick her up," Darryl said, landing a heavy-handed slap on Victor's back. "I'll see you then." He walked out and took Paula's courage and ego with him.

Darryl had appeared from thin air that day, and there was no telling if and when it would happen again. The sanctity of the church grounds wouldn't stop him from cutting the fool. Of all days that he'd show up, she wouldn't be surprised if today would be the one. She skimmed the parking lot for signs of her estranged husband. Today might be the day.

Paula and Wayne exchanged a few minutes of small talk before going their separate ways to take their seats when the thump of the drum and voices of the praise team signaled the start of service. Paula had never been a regular attendee of Oak Cliff Church but went enough for them to present her with an engraved Bible and fifty dollars when she graduated from high school. She, a boy named Garrett, and a girl named Danita had to tell the church about their aspirations that Sunday. Paula remembered making something up about becoming a lawyer, then went to the back pew repenting to God for lying in church. She wasn't much of a public speaker, and nervousness had caused her to ramble off the first thing that came to mind. Besides that, saying she wanted to be a lawyer sounded more intellectual than saying she had no idea what career path she'd follow.

If Pastor Earnest Tidwell handed her the microphone now, she'd say she wanted to try something new like be a personal trainer, or start an exercise program for busy mothers to get back in shape after having children.

Pastor Tidwell entered the pulpit and approached the large mahogany podium that dwarfed his small stature even more. The collar of his robe hid his short neck, making his head seem to wobble.

"We're going to begin service a little different today, church. Is that okay?"

"Go 'head, Pastor," rang throughout the congregation in agreement.

"All day yesterday, God kept talking to me about the importance of fathers," he continued. "And I don't think you have to wait until Father's Day to give men a special message about fatherhood—whether they have their own children or not."

"Amen," some answered in unison, the male voices louder than usual.

When it came to fathers, Paula didn't have her biological dad to look at for a frame of reference. She didn't want it to be that way for Micah and Gabrielle, and it made her pray that her children could spend some time with Darryl soon, even if he didn't want to see her.

Then the thoughts came. She wondered if he was somewhere playing daddy to someone else's child—or even worse, his child that she knew nothing about. Paula scolded herself. She'd been watching too many talk shows with her mother.

Paula tried to focus on what Pastor Tidwell was saying, but events kept replaying in her mind.

Last week after school, Micah had jumped into the backseat of the SUV clutching a picture frame constructed with macaroni noodles that had been painted blue.

"It's a gift for Daddy," he'd said, holding it proudly over his head. "Can we take it to him?"

"Not today. We'll do it later, okay?" Paula stalled like she always did.

"I'm ready to go home. I'm tired of spending the night at Grandma's."

Paula went through conversations like that with Micah at least once a week and usually ended up buying him another toy to tide him over. "Soon, sweetheart. We'll go home soon. Mama and Daddy are trying to work some things out."

"Okay." Micah pressed his nose against the back window and stretched open the sides of his mouth with his fingers. A boy standing on the sidewalk did it back to him.

"Micah, don't do that."

"Okay. Can we go get a cheeseburger?" He'd stuck his tongue out at the boy when he thought Paula wasn't paying attention.

And that was the temporary end of his whining.

✦ ✦ ✦

Paula lifted Gabrielle and kissed her nose. She hugged her as much as possible, because before she knew it, Gabrielle would be the hormonal teenage girl who Paula might have to beg to show her some affection. Gabrielle basked in the extra attention, holding on to her mother's cheeks before being distracted by the spectrum of lights illuminating from the stained glass window.

"Everybody always remembers the mamas," Pastor Tidwell was saying. "We go overboard for mamas during the holidays and on special occasions. And what do those football players shout out when they win championships?"

"Hi, Mom!" the congregation answered in sync.

"Ooohhh, but the men," Pastor Tidwell moaned. "On Father's Day we get the recycled ties and the shirts that don't fit over our stomachs, don't we?" Pastor Tidwell winked at the deacons seated on the front row, and they pumped their fists in agreement. "Don't get me wrong. Our mothers deserve everything they get and then some. 'Cause if mama ain't happy, ain't nobody happy."

"You got that right, Pastor," an overly expressive woman shouted from the back, sending another round of chuckles rolling through the sanctuary.

"But seriously," Pastor Tidwell said once the parishioners quieted down. "God has put an extraordinary mandate on the lives of men. Not just fathers, but all men have a responsibility to raise a godly seed, whether they have biological children or not. I want every man to make his way to the altar. Bring the

180

baby boys too. It's never too late to speak God's Word over the lives of our future."

The men spilled out into the aisles and crowded the altar as the women erupted in thunderous applause.

Paula shouldn't have let Micah's temper tantrum sway her decision in letting him stay in bed. He could be manipulative when he wanted to.

A young father, his pudgy son in his arms, squeezed past Paula and into the aisle. Paula had never known her father, and her mother always played clueless about his whereabouts. When Paula had been seven, her mother married a man she knew as Uncle Stan. Three years later he'd been sent packing with a trunk and two suitcases. Paula lost the only semblance of a father that she'd ever known, if you didn't count Uncle Lonnie. By the time Paula's puberty set in, Uncle Stan's involvement in her life had diminished to yearly birthday cards and the occasional Christmas phone call. Then nothing.

Paula wiped the tears rolling down her face. Pastor Tidwell's fervent prayer for the men shook Paula's pain to the surface. When the prayer concluded and she opened her eyes, Gabrielle was staring at her. When she laid her head on her mother's chest, Paula felt the ache leave her heart.

✝   ✝   ✝

Wayne caught up with Paula again after the service and escorted her to the car. He'd always been a gentleman when they were younger, and his ways hadn't changed. Back then, Paula hadn't paid much attention to him. Not only was he an awkward teenager, but he was three years younger than she was. That was against the rules then, and this conversation was against the rules now. She scoped the parking lot again. The possibility of Darryl's presence caused anxiety—almost fear. *A woman shouldn't feel that way about her husband.*

Paula double-stepped it to her car and buckled Gabrielle into her car seat. Gabrielle whined and stretched her body, resisting Paula's attempt to buckle her in.

"That's my cue," Paula told Wayne. "I'd better get out of here before she really turns it out."

181

"It was good talking to you." Wayne tucked his Bible under his arm. "Maybe I'll see you the next time you're in Baltimore."

"Next time? I live here."

"Oh. For some reason I thought you'd moved. I haven't seen you around here in years."

"Playing wife and mother. You know how having your own family can be."

"Not really. But I pray that one day I will," he said, opening her car door. "Take care. Good seeing you. I'm sure baby girl's daddy is waiting for her to get home." He put his forehead to the back window and shielded his eyes so he could see inside to Gabrielle.

Paula waved, then inched her car through the parishioners dawdling in the parking lot. She seemed to be the only person in a rush to leave. And to go where? Home?

Paula thought it would be nice to let Micah take his macaroni frame to Darryl today. When she heard her cell phone ring from the glove compartment, Paula pulled over in one of the parking spaces.

It was Darryl.

monét

James Sullivan treated Jeremiah like he was the second son he never had. The novelty of his first son-in-law had worn off, and Monét's father had turned his attention to inducting the man he saw as the next potential male member of the family.

Monét and her sister, Victoria Watkins, rinsed the dinner dishes, then stacked them in the dishwasher. Cleanup duty was the least they could do since their father had cooked nearly the entire Sunday dinner. He'd refused to give up his chef's hat and let someone else man his grill. Nobody could put down a steak like chef extraordinaire James.

"Daddy's got Jeremiah on lockdown, doesn't he? Same thing he did to Scott," Victoria said, closing the dishwasher door.

"I know. He's already got a hook in him."

Victoria slid the latch, and the whir of the dishwasher began. "You're the one who needs to make sure you've got a hook in him. Don't let him get away."

Monét wiped her hands on a dishcloth, then hung it on the hook on the refrigerator beside a picture of her twin nephews standing on their heads.

"He asked me to go with him to Houston for a party for his parents' thirty-fifth wedding anniversary." Monét sat down at the kitchen table.

"That's nice. When are you leaving?"

"I'm not sure if I'm going yet."

"Why? It's not like you have to ask off of work."

Monét rolled her eyes. "No, but I still have *work* to do." She worked harder as an entrepreneur than she ever had at the cultural center. She had two other projects she was bidding for, in addition to working on Savon's fund-raiser that was just around the corner.

"Go with the man to see his parents. Men don't just take any woman home with them, especially to another state. He's never had a problem coming over here, has he?"

"No. But that's different."

"How?"

There really wasn't a difference, but Monét had to think of something to prove her point to Victoria. It was like she was ten again and Victoria was the thirteen-year-old know-it-all who was trying to be her mama.

Monét's nephew, Aaron, whizzed past the window with his identical brother, Tyler, an arm's length behind him. Their screams were loud enough to hear through the closed windows and over the grumbling of the dishwasher.

"Leave me alone," Aaron screamed.

"Give me the ball. I mean it."

When Tyler finally caught up with Aaron, he grabbed the tail of his shirt, turning them both around in a circle until they eventually hit the ground like a sack of rocks. Punches followed.

"Don't you see your sons out there thrashing each other?" Monét asked Victoria, who didn't seem to be moved that her sons were battering each other.

"They'll be all right. Scott is out there somewhere, probably with his head under Daddy's Corvette. He'll straighten them out."

184

Victoria was right. When Monét's brother-in-law finished his scolding, the two boys wiped the tears, dirt, and grass from their faces, then shook hands.

Monét contorted her arm to try and reach an obnoxious itch in the center of her back. "Children are too stressful for me. I don't have the patience to be a mother."

"Trust me, God will give you everything you need *when* you have your own children," she said, reaching over and scratching Monét's back. She clawed so hard that Monét had to slap her hand away.

"I don't know. I might need to stick to borrowing yours."

"Does Jeremiah want kids?"

Here we go again. "Why does everybody try to measure every decision for my life based on what Jeremiah would want?"

"Because that's life when you marry someone, and you know you love the boy, so stop trying to play so hard. Don't start with this commitment phobia stuff. You're almost thirty-one."

"I do not have a fear of commitment."

"Yes, you do."

"No, I don't." She knew it, but did everybody have to bring it to her attention?

"You don't what?" Josephine Sullivan always walked into the room when conflict was brewing. She looked cute from head to ankles. On her feet was an ugly combination of a pink fuzzy flip-flop. "They let my feet breathe," she claimed. Monét had never seen anything so horrid and had planned to trash them as soon as she could get her hands on them.

"Nothing, Ma." Her mother was the last person Monét wanted in on the conversation. Her mother was as traditional as they came. Despite Monét's many accomplishments, no reward would seem greater to her than for Monét to march down the aisle in a pure white A-line princess gown.

Victoria couldn't let it go. "Monét is denying that she has a fear of commitment."

Monét shook a playful fist at her sister. "Some people just don't grow out of being tattletales."

"Well, you definitely do have a fear of commitment," Josephine said. "A blind man can see that." Josephine lifted the glass cover off of a cake dish. Her signature German chocolate cake made Monét's mouth water, especially after a week of eating only fruit and fresh steamed vegetables.

"You keep it up and the only thing you'll be married to is your career." Victoria had gotten their mother started. "Then you'll be old living with a bunch of cats and no children to visit you on the holidays."

"Probably dogs," Monét said sarcastically. "I don't like cats."

Aaron and Tyler ran in from outside, laughing like they hadn't been in a scuffle just ten minutes earlier.

Josephine warned her grandsons before they could get more than a few steps inside. "Don't run in the house, and leave the football outside."

"Yes, ma'am," they said together. Aaron opened the door and threw the ball outside to the backyard.

"Wash your hands," Josephine said, "so you can have dessert."

Monét found the small paper cake plates that her mother kept in the back of the lower cabinet. She put them on the table with some plastic forks. She didn't plan on washing another round of dishes.

Victoria sliced into the thick layers of the chocolate mound. She lifted two thin slices off the plate for her boys, then cut thicker ones for the adults. "Remember what you said about borrowing your nephews every once in a while?"

Monét ran her finger along the side of her slice, then licked the icing off of her finger. Cucumber slices and tomatoes had never tasted this good. "Now you want to sound sweet because you want something. I know that voice."

"The boys want to stay with their wonderful aunt next weekend."

"So this is the boys' great idea? Somehow I don't believe that."

"Uh-huh. It was." Victoria batted her eyelashes.

"And why would they want to do such a thing?"

"Because they want nothing more than to see their parents have a romantic weekend. Alone."

Monét took one more bite of her cake, then slid it away. The hunk of cake was meant for a man, not a woman who was trying to watch her weight and adopt a healthier lifestyle. "Let Mama watch them."

Josephine wiggled her hips from side to side with her hands up in the air. "I don't think so. Your dad and I are going out to a birthday party."

"Do me a favor and don't do that in public, Ma," Monét said, before turning back to Victoria. "I don't know. What am I supposed to do to keep two eleven-year-olds entertained?"

"They're not three. They can entertain themselves."

"I've seen their idea of entertaining themselves. They'll turn my living room into a wrestling ring."

"My boys have more home training than that. As long as they have enough food and video games for two days, they'll be fine."

Aaron and Tyler hopped out from around the corner, jumping up and down in a synchronized chat. "We're going to Aunt Monét's house." They gave each other a high five, then ran over to wrap their arms around Monét.

"I feel like a piece of turkey meat between two slices of wheat bread."

"Aunt Monét is a turkey," Tyler said, making a gobbling sound. As always, when one twin did something, the other mimicked his brother.

Monét covered their mouths. "Stop gobbling or you're not stepping foot in my house."

Immediate silence.

"Your mother put you up to this, didn't she?"

"No, Auntie," Aaron tried to say with his mouth still covered up. "We love you."

Tyler peeled three of Monét's fingers off his mouth so he could talk. "Yeah. We never get to go to your house. You're always working."

187

"Uh-huh." Josephine joined her family at the table. "Out of the mouths of babes."

James's voice bellowed from the living room. "Mama! Daddy is missing you. Come in here with me for a while."

Josephine stood up as quickly as she'd sat down. "My king is calling. Come on, ladies. You need to get in here with your men." She swatted at her daughters' backsides as they carried slices of cake into the living room. "Especially you, Monét. I need to have a talk with Jeremiah and teach him how to deal with you."

"Ma. Please don't meddle." She said it with seriousness, but respect.

"Calm down. I'm not saying anything to Jeremiah. You need to remember you're almost thirty-one. Open your eyes one day and you'll be forty. The older you get, the faster time flies."

That was a song Monét had heard sung before.

Jeremiah was no stranger to the Sullivan household, and he'd already kicked off his shoes and made himself comfortable. He set his cake aside for later, and Monét found a comfortable spot in the crook of his arm that was stretched out across the back of the couch. There was no sense in suggesting they leave until the last minutes ticked off the clock of the Los Angeles Lakers and Detroit Pistons game. She had nearly nodded off completely when she heard the beginning of an embarrassing conversation.

"Are you going to marry Aunt Monét?" It sounded like Tyler's voice.

"Do you want me to?"

"Yeah. She needs a husband so we can have some cousins and stuff."

"Oh, really?"

"Uh-huh. Plus, I think she looovveeess you," Aaron said. Monét heard kissing noises.

The whole family is in on it, Monét thought. She cracked her eyes enough to see the boys rolling on the floor in laughter. Jeremiah's side trembled as he tried to contain his amusement.

"I'm not asleep, by the way," Monét said.

"No, but you're sleeping on love," Tyler said, and everyone in the room cracked up.

This was going to be a long evening.

paula

Darryl picked up the children at three o'clock that Sunday afternoon. As soon as Paula returned home from church, she had just enough time to feed them, change their clothes, and pack their bags. There were so many things to get ready for a five-year-old boy and a three-month-old newborn who was liable to need any random thing, even for a short stay. Paula wasn't ready for Gabrielle to go off without her. She knew the meaning of her different cries, how she liked to be held when gas rumbled through her stomach versus how she liked to be bounced when she was sleepy.

Darryl didn't know, but she prayed he'd figure it out so her baby wouldn't be miserable. When Darryl arrived, he didn't bother to come into the house. He honked the horn, and Rosanna helped snap the children into their car and booster seats.

Paula had been watching from the closed-in patio. She walked outside before he backed out of the driveway.

"I'm glad they're getting to spend some time with you today."

"Me too." He drummed his fingers on the steering wheel.

Paula stood there, not knowing what else to say. The worst thing was the awkward silence between her and Darryl. The children were their common thread, but now they couldn't even conjure up a conversation about them.

Didn't he wonder who'd come in and made the bed that day when she went to the house with Belinda? Had he read her note? Why didn't his mother call to come see her grandchildren? If she asked any of those questions, an argument was sure to erupt. They could find an argument if she asked, "Is the sky blue?" This Sunday was her children's day, and she didn't want to mess it up.

Darryl released the emergency brake. "We need to go." He adjusted his rearview mirror, and as he looked at his children, his stern expression softened.

"Okay," Paula said. "Bye, Micah. Take care of Gabrielle, okay?"

"Yes, Mommy." Micah grinned, clutching the paper bag he'd decorated that held his macaroni frame. Micah was the one who'd received the true gift today. That was what mattered most.

Darryl shifted the car in reverse. "We'll be back before long."

Paula had watched the car with her family in it disappear around the curve. That "before long" had now been five hours, and she was trying to ward off the thoughts that her children were enjoying a family outing with another woman.

Darryl wouldn't do that. *Would he?* If he actually had the audacity, Micah will divulge all the information she needed to know.

Rosanna didn't bother to knock before she opened the bedroom door. "You plan on staying inside this room all day? Even an ostrich comes up for air every now and then."

Paula twisted the cap back on the top of the ruby red fingernail polish. It was too thick and sticky to go on smooth. Adding a drop of nail polish remover hadn't been the cure to thin out the cheap polish she'd scavenged from the back of the closet in the hall bathroom.

"I'm thinking," Paula said, sliding her body down until her heels reached the foot of the bed.

"About what?"

"Darryl."

"What about him?"

"Why and how we ended up here."

"Because my doors are always open to my children, no matter how crazy their babies' daddies are."

"Not here. Not this house. Here, as in this place in our marriage when I'm wondering if he'll ever love me again."

"He's got some love in him for you somewhere."

"And how would you know that?"

"'Cause you can still go to the bank and get out money. A man who don't love you ain't giving out the dollar bills," Rosanna said, rubbing her fingertips together.

Paula laughed inside. Her mother had been watching too many urban television programs.

"That's because of his children."

"Even with the kids, he'd give you what he wanted you to have. You wouldn't have open access."

Her mother was right. She'd been able to withdraw money at her whim. There was still the same amount being electronically deposited every month in her personal spending account.

"I don't care what happens between me and Darryl," Paula said. "I just want him to have a relationship with his kids. They can't go through what I've been through."

"What do you mean by that?" Rosanna sounded offended.

Paula didn't know why. It's not like her mother didn't experience it firsthand when times got so tight that they had to choose between electricity and groceries until she could make it to payday Friday. Rosanna had refused to apply for help from the government, so they made do.

"Nothing, Ma. Just forget it." Paula wasn't going to try to relive the stories when she knew her mother knew good and well what they'd gone through. It hurt that Rosanna would try to act like it hadn't affected her children.

Paula changed her mind. She was going to say something.

For thirty-six years, she'd had to pretend as if it was okay. "I mean growing up without a father. I don't want my children to go through that like I did."

She didn't want to cry in front of her mother, but the tears she'd tried to hold back betrayed her. Paula pulled her legs up to her chest and wrapped her arms around her knees. "You don't know how I've carried the pain of not knowing who my father is. Fathers are one of the most important people in a girl's life. And a woman's. Pastor Tidwell was talking about that today."

The mood in the room was solemn. Rosanna shuffled back and forth like she was going to walk away and go back to sit on the back porch like she did every Sunday evening. The only company she wanted on Sundays was a jug of red punch and the day's sale papers.

Rosanna walked into the room and looked into Paula's swollen eyes.

"If you want to meet your daddy, I can tell you where he is."

The room was so silent and still that Paula could count the beats of her heart. One thump. Two thumps. How much more could she take?

"What do you mean?" Thump. Her heart pounded twice the speed.

"I mean . . ." Rosanna pulled the belt of her cotton house dress tighter around her midsection. She clutched the collar at her neck as if she was debating about whether to let the words rise from her throat.

"Just what I said, Paula. I know where your daddy is." She walked to the corner window of the room. "I don't know why I just said that," she muttered to herself. Rosanna pounded her hand on the windowsill.

"Since when? Did he come back to find you?" Paula stared at her mother as if she'd never seen her before. She hadn't expected to hear those words. Rosanna's expression didn't change; neither did her voice quiver. Her mother had spoken in the same tone as if she'd said, "We're having meatloaf for dinner."

Rosanna had always held it together. She wasn't one to show emotion and had told her daughters to do the same. Paula always failed at it.

Rosanna spilled the facts with no emotion attached. "I was young and stupid, and Floyd Raymond was a ladies' man. I thought I could change him, which was a lie. You can't change any man. Only God can do that."

Amen to that.

"He told me he loved me and played the part like an Oscar winner until I got pregnant." Rosanna smacked her lips. "Then he didn't want anything to do with me, but he couldn't just go about his business. He wanted to run my name through the streets like I was common with all the men.

"I told him he'd never set eyes on his child if he didn't show me some respect. Do you know what he said?"

It wasn't a question Paula wanted to hear the answer to. After all, this was about her.

"He said he didn't care," Rosanna said, rolling her neck. "And from what I hear, he's got children all up and down the East Coast." The sentimental side of her was gone as quick as it had come.

Paula had smudged the polish from her toenails onto the daffodil yellow comforter. She nervously picked at the mess she'd made around the cuticles of her toenails while her mother looked like she'd regretted her confession.

"He owns the shop up the street. The Oil Pit and Repair Shop. You can go see if he's changed his mind, but if I were you, I'd let sleeping dogs lie. And I do mean dogs."

But Paula couldn't let it go. For the past thirty-six years she'd wondered about him, and he'd worked blocks away from where she'd grown up. In college, she'd had a tire on her old Nissan Sentra patched there once before heading back to school after spring break.

"I can't let it go, Ma," Paula said. "I'm going up there tomorrow."

belinda

Bernice had begged Belinda to stay longer. Her mother's pity party had only earned her one more day, and then Belinda headed back to Danville at six o'clock that Monday evening. She pulled into her driveway shortly after nine o'clock and noticed that the fifteen-year-old Toyota Camry Thomas was repairing wasn't in its usual spot. He's finally taken it to the professionals, instead of tinkering under it himself, Belinda thought. *Good.* She already had an oil leak stain at the top of her driveway.

"Hey, baby." Belinda pressed her lips against Thomas's and lingered there until his kiss made up for the four days she'd been away. "Where did you take the Camry?"

"What do you mean, where did I take it? It's by the side of the house where it always is."

"Unless it magically appeared in the last thirty seconds since I walked in the door, it's gone."

Thomas slapped the magazine closed and tossed it on the glass-top coffee table. It knocked over a half-full bottle of water, sending the water splashing across the magazine and seeping toward the floor. He was outside and standing in the spot where the Camry was usually parked. Thomas picked up the balled-up blue tarp that was jammed behind the garbage can. "That boy has pushed me to the limit."

"You don't actually know if T.J. took the car. You haven't even been upstairs yet."

"Do you think I need to? If you thought it was stolen, you would've called the police yourself by now."

"I thought you'd taken it someplace to get it fixed," she said, kicking a green garden hose closer to the house. "Give the boy the benefit of the doubt."

Thomas headed back inside with Belinda close behind. He threw the tarp in the garage before heading upstairs to T.J.'s room.

The door was locked.

Thomas's heavy-handed fist landed on the door hard enough to crack the wooden frame. Hannah shrieked from her bedroom two doors down. After calming Hannah's nerves, Belinda tucked her back in for a peaceful night's sleep. At least one person in the household needed one.

Downstairs, Thomas sat in the dark with only the light and the low sound of the television.

"You can go ahead to bed. I'm staying here until he comes home."

"How did he get out in the first place? And what makes you think he's coming back through the front door? Evidently he didn't leave that way."

Thomas held up a screwdriver. Belinda assumed he'd jimmied open the door with it. "He slid down from the window with a rope tied to the leg of his bed. Can you believe that? Like some foolishness he's seen on television."

"Inventive." Belinda chuckled.

Even Thomas couldn't contain a quick chortle. The smile fell from his face, and he said, "I untied the rope and dropped it out the window. Trust me. He'll just think it came loose and fell down."

Belinda sat down on the couch and surfed through the television channels. Before she walked in she'd been exhausted from the P.O.W.E.R. weekend and the drive home, but this proved to be more exciting than sleep.

"What?" Belinda answered Thomas's questioning look. "I'm not missing this one. If I fall asleep, wake me up before the action goes down."

"You're so pitiful," he said, taking the remote from her.

"No. Climbing out of the window on a rope is pitiful."

Thomas turned the television to a late-night movie classic. And they waited.

✛　　✛　　✛

"Belinda." Thomas called her name just above a whisper, nudging her out of a light sleep.

"Your son's home." T.J. was always "her son" whenever he was in trouble—which was most of the time.

The porch's motion light cast his lurking shadow onto the front window. The click of the lock was so quiet and slow that it was barely audible.

Belinda held her breath as if she were a nervous teen who'd missed her curfew.

Thomas waited until T.J. closed and locked the door before he said, "I hope it was worth it."

T.J. froze.

With a quick flick of Thomas's finger, the light came on. Before she knew it they were all flooded by the light from the overhead ceiling fan. T.J. reached for the doorknob, as if for a split second he was deciding whether to make a mad dash. Evidently his feet betrayed him. He thought better of it. At a time like this, his father could've taken him down.

T.J.'s countenance turned from one of worry to conceit. "Yeah, it was worth it. Look, I'm a grown man. You run this house like I'm a convict."

"Grown man? Grown men don't have to sneak out the window." Thomas took a step forward.

T.J. matched it with a step backward, not realizing subconsciously that his toughness had been diminished by the action.

Thomas stood wide legged, daring his son to push through the human blockade he'd set with his wide shoulders. "You're acting like a convict. You stole my car."

And our trust, Belinda thought. Again.

"I borrowed it. I brought it back."

"You took it without permission. That's stealing." Thomas took another step forward. "You think you were in a prison before? I've been more than easy on you when you didn't deserve it. You'll see what lockdown really means over the next month. Get upstairs."

T.J.'s sidestep to get past Thomas didn't put him far enough out of his father's reach.

Thomas yanked T.J.'s arm and pulled him to his face.

"Don't think I was born yesterday," Thomas said. "Everything you can think of trying, I've already done, or thought of doing. There's nothing new. Nothing." The cold stare followed—the one that said the last straw had been pulled.

T.J. jerked his arm from Thomas's grip, then bolted upstairs to his bedroom. His door slammed.

Hannah cried.

Thomas flew up the steps.

Belinda went too. *So much for the peace.*

Zora

For over a year, Zora had kept the letter she found revealing her adoption folded into thirds inside her purse. Now there were two letters in the zippered compartment. The other was from the Department of Human Resources, and it held the promise she'd hoped for. The mediator had finally found the contact information to Zora's mother. The only problem was the high probability that her mother had moved and would never receive the letter sent by her mediator, asking her for permission to reveal her identity.

Zora looked up at the sound of sniffing at her office door. Toni stood in the doorway in tears. She didn't wait for her guidance counselor's invitation. She eased the door closed behind her.

Zora left the supervisory position behind her desk to sit beside Toni. She pulled Toni's head to her shoulder and let her cry until her tears ran dry. She pulled two tissues from the box on her desk and put them in Toni's hand.

"I tried, Mrs. Fields. I did. I read the Scriptures you showed me and everything in my new Bible. I even showed them to Cedric. It's all I can think about today, and everybody thinks I'm pregnant or something because I started crying in class."

Toni was blubbering so hard that Zora had to listen closely to make out her words. Toni's eyeliner, which was too thick and dark for her small eyes, was smeared across the tissue, her face, and Zora's sleeve. Zora pulled a few extra tissues again and patted her student's face.

"Now," she said when Toni had gained some of her composure. She smoothed her student's braids back off of her forehead so she could look into her troubled eyes. "What's going on?"

"Cedric is pressuring me to have sex, and I told him no," Toni explained through a stuffy nose.

"That's good. You did the right thing."

"He doesn't think so. He told me last night that if I didn't give it to him, there were plenty of girls who would."

Zora didn't know what to say. Unfortunately, Cedric's threat was probably true. It was easier for teenagers to get sex than it was for the school system to get new textbooks.

"You're more of a woman—no, a lady—for saying no."

Toni sniffed. "I know you mean well, Mrs. Fields, but that doesn't make me feel better. My heart hurts so bad that it's making me feel sick. He's going to dump me."

Zora wanted to say, "Let him go. He's not worth the tears you're crying."

Toni stared at the chipped polish on her nails. She picked away at what was left on her thumb. Zora knew to choose her words carefully. There were few incidents more traumatic than a teenage girl's first heartbreak.

"You and your body are so precious that God wants to protect you from people who don't value it. If you really have it in your heart to save your virginity, then God will help you honor that, even if it means taking people out of your life."

Toni filled up her shredded tissue with one blow of her nose. The look in her eyes said she needed more to be convinced that the celibate life was worth losing her man.

Zora handed her the tissue box. "What class did you leave?"

"Chemistry. We're reviewing for one of the exit exams."

Zora reached for a hall pass. "Maybe you should go back to class and drop by to see me after last period. I'll wait for you."

Toni hesitantly took the pass. "I was going to stay after school for a study group for history, but now I don't know if I can."

Zora rubbed Toni's back. "You'll be all right. It may be hard to focus at first, but once you get started you'll be fine."

"No, that's not the problem. Cedric was supposed to pick me up, but the way he was talking last night he probably won't come. I've texted him three times already today, and he hasn't returned any of them."

Zora needed to finish some work after the faculty meeting. She was sure she'd have to stay at least two hours after school. "I'll be here until five. I can take you home if you want me to."

Toni's nose was still red and swollen. "I'll meet you here," she said with a nasally tone. "Thank you, Mrs. Fields. I can always count on you."

+   +   +

"I need to talk to you for a few minutes, Mrs. Fields," Principal Gaines said. His voice was loud enough to turn the heads of the teachers on the other side of the room even though he was less than five steps from Zora. "I'll be with you shortly."

"Sure, Principal Gaines," Zora said, with a smile on her face, even though she felt irritated inside. She didn't want anyone to think that some kind of reprimand was in order for her. The truth was, she rarely crossed paths with the man. Principal Gaines was too busy terrorizing the teachers instead, making surprise appearances in their classrooms, then suggesting alternate teaching techniques that they should consider implementing in their classes next year. Zora was thankful that her corner office in the guidance counselors' suite didn't get many visits. Out of sight, out of mind.

"What did you do to ruffle his feathers?" One of the teachers, Mrs. Concord, lightly jabbed Zora in the side with her elbow.

203

"That old rooster just has to crow at somebody all the time or his life wouldn't be complete."

Zora just smiled. She wasn't about to be pulled into a gossip session with Mrs. Concord. She was always looking for a complaint partner, and most of the faculty had learned to keep their comments to themselves unless they wanted them to come back up later.

Once most of the faculty thinned out and the remaining department cliques were left whispering about preparing the students for their state-mandated exit exams, Zora followed Principal Gaines to the administrative offices at the front of the school. She could see through the frosted glass window that it was dark inside. Good. She would've avoided going with him inside of his office, anyway. Being an only child—and a female —her father had taught her to be overly cautious.

"Please have a seat," he said to Zora. Principal Gaines sounded too cold and professional, even outside of school hours. Principal Hartman had been nothing like that. After the school's dismissal bell, she'd insisted the faculty call her by her first name, Elaine.

Zora sat down on the hard wooden bench bolted to the wall. During school hours, it was the waiting area for students who'd become too much for their teachers to handle. Principal Gaines would come out of his office and stand over them, much like he was doing to Zora now.

"It's come to my attention that you've been conducting prayer sessions during school hours." His hands were crossed across his broad chest, subconsciously signaling that he'd already shut out anything Zora had to say.

"Prayer sessions?"

"Yes, Mrs. Fields. Praying with students."

Zora's eyebrows lifted. It was amazing how stories seemed to grow when they traveled between mouths. Her question was, Whose mouths had taken her time spent with Toni to the next level?

She stood up to put herself on the same playing field with Principal Gaines.

"Well, I have prayed with one student a few times in my office, but I'm not conducting prayer sessions, as you call it. The student has come to me with some of her problems, and I've been there to help."

"You're supposed to help her with her academic problems, not her personal problems," Principal Gaines said. "There is such a thing as separation of church and state, Mrs. Fields. Trust me, you don't want to mix the two, and honestly I'm not sure what God has to do with children and their school-work."

Zora took a step back from him in case God wanted to strike a bolt of lightning through the school's roof. "In all due respect, Principal Gaines, these children actually have problems that reach outside of their academic lives. Some of them carry more burdens at home than you and I could ever imagine."

Principal Gaines loosened the blue and yellow striped tie around his neck. "If home is where the problems are, then that's where they need to be handled," he said, unbuttoning the top button of his starched white shirt. "It would be in your best interest if you let the parents handle their own children. Maybe someday you'll have your own children to parent if you're looking to run someone's life. Unless of course you've got a hen-pecked husband and you can get all the practice you want." He laughed.

Zora didn't.

"So now that you know where I stand with that, I don't expect to hear anything else about these prayer sessions. Let's make the rest of the little school year we have left pleasant for us all." Principal Gaines patted Zora on the back like she was a rebuked child, then walked away.

Zora stood there for a moment in utter disbelief before going back to her office. Toni was waiting outside of her door.

"Whew," Toni said. "I was hoping you hadn't left me, but I saw your car was still in the parking lot."

"I had to talk to Principal Gaines for a minute," she said, unlocking her office door.

Toni scrunched up her face. "I didn't know that was possible.

I've never heard the man talk. The only thing I ever hear him do is yell at everybody."

Seems like the students notice it too, Zora thought. Zora took her purse out of her desk drawer. After what she'd just experienced, she had some comments of her own, but Toni would never hear them. She'd save those for when Preston got home.

"I wonder if that talk show on that gospel station is going to be playing on the way home," Toni said, swinging her purse against her legs. "I can't wait to see what they're talking about today. I need to hear some more reasons about why I shouldn't have sex before marriage," she confessed. "It's not as easy as it sounds, especially since everybody's doing it."

"Not everybody," Zora said. She put her arm around Toni as they walked outside to the car. "There's one virtuous lady I know who's making the right decision."

Toni wrapped her arm around Zora's waist.

Not praying whenever Toni needed it was not an option, even if she needed it in the middle of a school day. Zora needed prayer herself from the time she opened her eyes in the morning until the time she closed them at night. Prayer had always lifted her during the good times and carried her through the bad.

Zora knew that the steps of a good man—and woman— were ordered by the Lord. She finally felt prepared to walk her path, even if she had to do it in a First Lady's shoes.

zora

On the ride home, Toni was too involved with the flash cards she'd made for her history class to worry about Melissa Flint's topic for the day. Zora turned off the radio so that Toni could concentrate while she read her notes aloud.

Frustrated, Toni slapped her stack of index cards against her bare legs. Her skirt didn't pass the school district's policy that skirts be no more than two inches above the knee when sitting. As long as the students could get away with it, they ignored every rule for the sake of fashion.

"Mrs. Fields, how much of this history stuff do you remember from school?"

Zora didn't answer, and Toni didn't let up.

"I mean, do you really need to know this stuff?" she asked, thumping one of her cards. "Is it important for you to do your job? That's all I wanna know."

This is a setup. I've got to think of a clever way to swing this one. Zora was no history buff herself. In school, she'd always struggled with the dates of most events pre-1900. The historical context and events of the Bible were so hard for her to keep straight that she'd signed up for one of the Bible enrichment classes at the church. Not only did she need it for personal study, but wasn't a minister's wife expected to be more mature in the Word? The title she could handle, but the clothes Mother Diane was still trying to push on her would never happen. Ever.

"You have to know where you've been so you'll know where you're going," Zora said, turning into Toni's apartment complex.

"Nice try," Toni said, smiling at Zora.

Zora winked at her and pulled against the curb, again in front of Ms. Ella who was at her post on the porch. The metal chair she was sitting in last time had been replaced by a wooden chair that looked like it belonged at the kitchen table. The same as last time, the curbside was jumping with activity, but the hot temperatures had driven twice as many children outside to play instead of inside locked in a trance in front of the television.

"I guess this is the end to my study time." Toni put her index cards in her fake designer purse and picked up the handle of her backpack.

"Why?"

"Because my brothers and sister don't get the meaning of quiet. My mama is going to her second job tonight, so I'm going to have to do everything tonight, including getting them in bed—which is about impossible."

Zora looked at her watch. It was five thirty, and Preston said he wouldn't be home until close to seven thirty. She had plenty of time to get home and make dinner. "Do you think Ms. Ella would keep the kids for another thirty minutes?"

"I don't think she'd mind."

Zora tapped her watch. "Time is the only thing you spend that you can't get back. So let's go. I'll help you study."

Toni opened her door. "Just like I don't need to waste time with knuckleheads like Cedric." She slammed the door at the mention of her boyfriend's name.

208

Hopefully his name would be moved to the "ex" category, Zora thought.

"Sorry, Mrs. Fields. I got a little carried away."

"I'll let you pass this time."

Zora's pump heel got lodged in a crack on the sidewalk as she walked to Toni's apartment, causing a small tear in the leather. That's what she got for wearing high heels to work instead of her comfortable loafers. Monét's suggestion to upgrade her work style was going to be hung back on the closet shelf along with Mother Diane's attempts.

"Hi, Ms. Ella," Toni said.

The elderly woman was trying to cool herself with a church fan from the funeral home, but Zora doubted it was helping much. The forecast was predicted to be in the eighties, and it didn't seem like it had cooled off much since this afternoon. When Ms. Ella swatted at a swarming insect, Zora realized the fan had double duties.

"Hey, baby. The children are inside watching a movie." She tapped on the screen door with the wooden handle of the fan. "Your sister's here. Get your stuff together." She looked back at Toni. "You know how long it can take them to get it together when they're wrapped up in the television."

"Actually, Ms. Ella," Toni said. "I was wondering if you could watch them for thirty more minutes so I can study a little longer. Mrs. Fields is going to help me."

Ms. Ella fanned out the bottom of her sundress and stretched out her legs, rubbing the left kneecap. "So you're Mrs. Fields. I'm glad to get to meet you. Toni loves herself some Mrs. Fields."

"I love her too," Zora said. She held out her hand and Ms. Ella grabbed it with a grip of a woman half her age. "Zora. Please call me Zora."

The roadmap of wrinkles on Ms. Ella's hands foretold years of wisdom, but they were some of the plumpest and softest hands Zora had ever felt. She wanted to ask her what her secret was.

Ms. Ella shook her finger at Zora. "Zora. That's like that woman author, isn't it?"

"Yes, ma'am. Zora Neale Hurston. That's who my mother named me after."

"That's nice. I had a sister named Cora. Cora Mae Bennett, but she died a few years back. Who are your people?"

For years she'd announced herself as being in the proud lineage of the Bridgeforths from her father's side, and maternally from the family of the Walters. Zora thought about the letter in her purse and how she was close to finally knowing the truth. Her heart jumped in excitement at the thought of it.

"My maiden name is Bridgeforth, but my husband's family lives in the area."

"Fields?" Ms. Ella seemed to shuffle through the endless memory bank of families that all elderly people seemed to have. Before Zora's grandmother's dementia progressed to Alzheimer's, she could connect two people she'd never met before through six degrees of separation in a matter of minutes.

Ms. Ella finally asked, "Are you related to Pastor William Fields?"

"Yes, ma'am. That's my father-in-law."

"Oh. Well, you're all right with me. I've never been to his church before, but I've heard good things about it over the years. Bad news travels, but good news gets around too." Ms. Ella swatted at a fly that had landed on the edge of the empty plate beside her. "One of these days Pastor Fields might pass the mantle on to your husband to lead the church. That's what pastors do these days while they're still alive and kicking and can choose who'll lead their congregation."

Ms. Ella twisted the rubber band holding her short salt-and-pepper hair into a small knot at the nape of her neck.

"It's a lot better than waiting until you cross the chilly Jordan and watching from heaven while everything you built falls down in shambles." Ms. Ella shook her head in pity at the thought, then her eyes lit up.

"You might end up being a first lady. Wouldn't that be nice?"

"Only God knows," Zora said. "Whatever He says."

Zora glanced at Toni, who she could tell was growing impatient. She was digging her house key out of her purse while she held open the screen door with her shoulder.

"Yes, Lordy," Ms. Ella said. "Living your life like that makes things a whole lot easier. In my years on this earth I've learned that for sure."

Toni had gone inside the apartment, and Zora could hear her reciting the notes from her flash cards. "It was nice meeting you, Ms. Ella. Maybe we'll talk again sometime."

"Come see me anytime you want to, even if Toni is not here." She lowered her voice and covered the corner of her lips with the church fan. "And you keep doing whatcha doing with that girl. I've tried talking to her mama about the Lord too, but she don't wanna hear it. I just do my part by staying here instead of letting my son move me up to Chicago with him. The Lord told me to stay and pray over this neighborhood, and that's what I'm gonna do. So you do what the Lord tells you, no matter what."

"Yes, ma'am."

Zora opened the screen door, and like every screen door she'd ever touched, it creaked. Somebody—the children, she assumed—had decorated the doorframe with glittery star stickers and smiley faces. When Zora walked into apartment B-11, things didn't look like she'd assumed. She'd had a stereotypical assumption that the house would be unkempt and that she'd have to lift her feet every now and then for a crawling visitor.

Zora couldn't have been wronger, and she felt God's conviction for being judgmental. What may have been an outdated or worn sofa and chair covered by tan slipcovers and decorated with two burgundy throw pillows. Two glass end tables with brass legs sat on either side of the sofa. On one was a single candle that had never been lit, and on the other was a picture of a group of children. She recognized one as Toni, although her hair was pulled into one ponytail on the side and she looked about five years younger. Zora had never seen her student without a head full of braids.

"You can have a seat, Mrs. Fields," Toni said. "Let me run

211

to the bathroom, and I'll be right back. I know time is ticking."

"Okay," Zora said, sitting down on the couch. Her rear end nearly sunk down to the floor. She scooted over until she couldn't feel the hardness of a spring, then flipped through one of the *Jet* magazines on the coffee table. She was reading about the latest city government fiasco in Atlanta when Toni returned.

"Okay, I'm ready." Toni handed Zora her set of flash cards, then sat down Indian style near Zora's feet. "Just read the first sentence and I'll give you the year it happened and tell you something else about it."

Zora drilled Toni for twenty-five minutes straight until she'd quizzed her on the entire set of fifty cards. "You'll pass this test with no problem," she said.

"Wish I could remember the math formulas like this."

"You'll do fine," Zora assured her. "Just pray for God to bring everything you've learned all year and what you've been studying into your remembrance. When all else fails, go with your first thought and don't try to second-guess your decisions."

Toni nodded. "That's when you usually mess up. When you start trying to think too hard." She got up from the floor and sat on the couch with Zora. "Can you pray with me now?"

Zora hesitated for a moment. Principal Gaines's words came back to her, but he didn't have any jurisdiction at somebody else's home. "Sure," Zora said.

Even after Zora heard the screen door open a few minutes later, she kept praying. When she didn't hear the patter of feet or anyone speak, she opened her eyes.

"... and God, we thank You that You'll help Toni remember all that she has studied ..."

Toni was the younger spitting image of the woman standing at the door rubbing the underside of her round, protruding belly. She even had the same look on her face now that Toni had whenever Rashad had irritated her.

Zora closed her eyes again. The woman's piercing stare had made her feel uncomfortable, so Zora sped up the prayer so she could hit the door. "... You've given an intelligent mind to a great young lady, and I ask that You bless her and her entire family in a special way. In Jesus' name. Amen."

"Amen." Toni stood up and wiped off the back of her jeans. She didn't realize her mother was standing at the door until her mother said her name.

"Oh, Ma. I thought you had to go to your other job today. What're you doing home?"

"What are *you* doing?" Her mother asked, ignoring her daughter's initial question.

"Mrs. Fields was helping me with my history test." She looked at Zora. "This is my mother, Marjorette Burkes."

"Nice to meet you." Zora stuffed her foot back into her shoe. "These are not shoes you want to wear all day," she said nervously.

Marjorette didn't accept Zora's handshake offer and looked at Zora's hand like it was contaminated. She hooked her silver oversized purse on the back of one of the kitchen chairs and popped a piece of gum around in her mouth. Zora could see where Toni got it from.

"It didn't look like you were studying to me."

"We just finished a few minutes ago."

She walked to where Zora had been sitting and dropped a plastic bag with a pair of shoes inside. "If you spent more time studying, you wouldn't have to do so much praying." Marjorette looked down her nose at Zora. "I doubt all this praying is in the school's curriculum, and I know it ain't goin' a help Toni pass no tests."

"I apologize, Ms. Burkes. I didn't mean any harm," Zora said. "It won't happen again."

Marjorette opened the door for Zora, then slammed it behind her. "Better not," she sneered behind her.

Zora smiled sheepishly at Ms. Ella. "Have a good day."

"Don't stop praying, anyhow," Ms. Ella whispered. "Keep praying and keep loving."

paula

I can't let it go, Ma. I'm going up there tomorrow."

Paula was sure about it when she'd spoken the words, but now she wasn't. Monday came and went. "I'll do it tomorrow," she told herself. And then Tuesday. "I'll do it tomorrow." Finally a week had passed and she still hadn't gone to confront her father.

Paula tiptoed down the hall, led only by the dim streak from the streetlight that seeped through the windows. She popped two aspirin, chased it with a glass of orange juice, and then headed out the door. Her eyes were swollen and her head throbbed from crying all night. Again. Something about night-time forced all of her emotions to the surface. It was the same way when she'd been at home waiting to see if Darryl would come home.

Paula knew God's Word said that weeping would endure for a night, but joy would come in the morning. She was still waiting for her morning.

The infamous screen door that always screeched and announced her arrival when she missed curfew as a teen announced her departure that morning as well.

"I'm going to my father's shop," she'd said after rolling Gabrielle's bassinet into her mother's room.

"You're what? What's wrong with you?" Rosanna had rolled over and propped herself up on one elbow. She clicked on her bedside lamp and squinted at the small crystal clock under it. "It's six o'clock in the morning," she said, rubbing sleep from her eyes.

Paula wouldn't let her mother sway her decision. Rosanna had made a decision for her thirty-six years ago that Paula had to face today. "I'm sure I'll be back before Micah wakes up."

That's when she'd closed the bedroom door and headed for the medicine cabinet.

Last night Paula had managed to write a letter to her father. She flipped the sealed envelope over in her hand and then stuck it above the car visor. If her words were anything like her thoughts, the letter was surely a rambling mess.

Paula backed out onto the dark street and drove toward the Oil Pit and Repair Shop. She pushed the button to turn on the radio, but Micah's CD of Disney songs blared from the speakers. She turned it down. It hadn't seemed that loud last night when they were singing it together on the way home from taking him out for pizza. Paula let the radio tuner scan until it stopped on a station playing morning jazz.

Breathe in. Breathe out. In through the nose. Out through the mouth. She'd been reading recently about how proper breathing could rid the body of toxins, but she wasn't doing that. She was reminding herself to breathe.

The sign of daybreak was just beginning to paint itself across the sky. The only sound of the morning was the scratching of her fingernails across the nylon fabric of her windbreaker pants. Confrontations were never easy, no matter how well planned. That's why Paula decided this morning to leave the letter and let it speak for itself. She wasn't ready to meet him face-to-face.

Paula rounded the bend to her father's repair lot. *My father.* The title seemed inappropriate considering he'd never fathered her. He'd missed teaching her how to ride her bike with the white tassels attached to the handlebars. When she'd crashed into her neighbor's metal mailbox and had to get stitches, he'd missed holding her hand at the hospital. There had been no one there with warnings and clenched fists when her first date picked her up at sixteen, and no one but Uncle Lonnie to help pack her car when she'd left for college.

Paula's car rocked as she bumped across the broken pavement and potholes scattered in the parking lot. Bumper stickers were pasted across a closed steel garage door and a rickety grey sign with red letters reading OIL CHANGES hung above it. She pulled so close to the garage door that her front bumper nearly touched it. Two other doors were stations assigned for BODY REPAIR and TIRES.

There was a rusty metal mailbox on the door. Maybe I should leave the letter there, Paula thought. She breathed in the stench of motor oil and gas as it seeped through her car vents. To escape the odor, Paula decided to back up and squeeze between two rusty cars in obvious need of major repairs.

She second-guessed whether she should even leave the letter. She didn't know why she was still sitting there. Traffic in the community was becoming alive as commuters started their daily trek to work. A few early risers were leaning against the bus stop signs, no doubt hoping that their dusk departure would get them to work on time. Paula hadn't thought about whether anyone would arrive at the shop early, but then she noticed the square lights of an older model car pull into the shop.

Paula's SUV was camouflaged among the line of those in need of repair. She pushed the automatic button to slightly recline the driver's seat. She couldn't see the face of the man that stepped out of the white Cadillac. A navy work shirt hung out on top of his cargo pants of the same color. He barely lifted his feet as he walked, perhaps the sign of wearing heavy steel-toed shoes for most of his working life.

Is that my father?

Paula watched him until he disappeared into the darkness behind the office door. She kept off her headlights until she pulled back onto the main street.

Maybe tomorrow.

+   +   +

Paula propped Gabrielle across her shoulder and patted her back. If she didn't prime at least one good burp from her, Paula's visit would go from a pleasant one with Monét to a crying disaster.

"I can't believe she just out and told you that," Monét said. "She's probably been wanting to tell you about your father for years."

Paula tried laying Gabrielle across her lap, but Gabrielle wasn't happy with that position either. "You don't know my mother," she said. "She can hold a grudge to the grave." Paula stood up to bounce Gabrielle. "I didn't even want to say anything to anybody until I had a chance to process it all. I'm living a life filled with drama right now, in case you haven't noticed."

Monét nodded her head in disbelief. "I've noticed." She pushed back the white sheers that were hanging in front of the wall-length balcony door.

Paula loved the airy feel of Monét's place. Everything was so crisp and white with just the right amount of color. Monét rotated the look of her home accessories with every change in season. Single people can do that, Paula thought. If Monét had children, everything in the room would already be smudged with grimy fingerprints.

Darryl was particular about his house and would rather pay money for an interior designer than to let Paula express herself and make their house a home. At first it was exciting to have a designer in her home, but every now and then she wanted to test her decorating skills.

Of course, she didn't have to worry about that now. Her mother's taste was beyond repair.

Monét bit into a crisp apple. "I wonder why she chose to tell you now."

"Probably pity," Paula said, choosing a deep red apple out of the fruit bowl Monét offered to her. "My mother does have a heart, even if it's cold sometimes."

"You're going through a lot right now, Paula. But God is faithful. You're holding up well, and you're definitely looking good too."

"You know how it is. When you look good on the outside, it makes you feel better on the inside."

Paula had successfully lost another ten pounds over the last three weeks. It was a cinch after she started cooking more of her own meals and not indulging in the junk food and processed meals that her mother kept in the house. It also didn't hurt that she'd been in shape before having the baby, but this time she'd gotten her body back without Cordele's help. She'd even gone out and bought a week's worth of new clothes to celebrate and didn't mind that in another three weeks from now, she probably wouldn't be able to wear them.

"Mmmmm." Paula let the fruit's sweet juice roll around in her mouth. "Now this is a good apple."

"Supposedly organic and pesticide free," Monét said, taking another bite. "I'm not trying to be in your business—well, yes I am—so why don't you want to see your father face-to-face?"

"I'm not ready." Paula reached down in Gabrielle's diaper bag and pulled out the envelope holding the letter she'd written to her father. "I wrote a letter," Paula said, holding the letter up.

"What does it say?"

"I can't remember it all. I wrote it one night when I was having a moment."

Monét laughed. "That could be dangerous."

Paula stuck it back in her bag. "All I remember is that I didn't bash the man. I'm not trying to scare him off before I get the chance to meet him," she said, as Monét's phone rang.

"You should give it to him," Monét said, getting up to reach the cordless phone. "Life is too short," Monét said.

"What's too short is that skirt." Paula knew Monét would smack her lips and ignore her when she asked, "Has Jeremiah seen it?"

"Hello? Yes. We're ready now. Paula needs to pick up Micah by five, so hurry up." Monét opened and closed her hand like a lobster claw to signify that Zora was rambling away. "Okay, bye," she finally said.

Monét put the phone on the table beside her. "That was Zora. She claims she'll be here in the next twenty minutes after she drops Preston's lunch by his job."

"Okay." Gabrielle had finally fallen asleep on Paula's shoulder. "I'm going back tomorrow to take the letter," Paula said.

Monét didn't look convinced. She propped her feet up on a red leather ottoman that doubled as a storage cube.

"I really am." Paula spread out a pink receiving blanket on the couch and laid down Gabrielle. She was changing the subject. She was starting to get another headache.

"So what's going on with you and Jeremiah?"

"Nothing really."

Paula picked up a picture of the couple that was sitting on the end table. Jeremiah and Monét were standing at the gate in front of the White House wearing leather jackets and knit skull caps. If Paula remembered correctly, it was the trip they'd taken to Washington, D.C., shortly after Jeremiah moved to the Baltimore area.

"Are you going to Houston with him or not? If I can meet my father for the first time, you can go with your future husband to meet your in-laws."

"I've met them before."

"But you never know what you're getting into until you go spend some time with them. Trust me, you need to go check them out."

paula

Paula loved shopping with other people more than she liked going alone on clothing excursions. At least then she had honest opinions from friends instead of biased sales associates trying to fatten their purses from commissions. But she had never known anyone who disliked shopping more than Zora.

"It looks too tight," Zora complained, turning around in the three-way mirror.

"No, it's not," Paula said. She'd picked out a turquoise blue jersey knit dress for Zora that fell three inches below the knee. The cap sleeves and scoop neck perfectly accentuated Zora's shapely arms. She'd worked hard to get them fit for her strapless wedding gown, and it still showed. But she knew Zora was more concerned about her hips—which was ridiculous, Paula thought. "It fits you to a tee," she told her friend. "It looks great, and you know I wouldn't lie to you."

Monét nodded her head as if they'd completed a successful

science experiment. "It looks perfect. The First Lady is stepping out of her shell some more."

Paula gave her a high five. "I say we start an image consulting business. We have everything we need to turn a tarnished woman into a polished woman."

"I'll take you up on that," Monét said.

"For one thing, I'm far from tarnished," Zora said, looking in the three-way mirror. "And secondly, before you two start writing a business plan, I need you to get a size ten in this." She held up a sky blue blouse. "I can tell by looking at it that it's not going to fit."

Paula hung the blouse back on the hook in Zora's fitting room. "Hold on to the eight for now. I'll get another one." She pushed Gabrielle's stroller to the front of the women's boutique. There were only two blouses left that were the identical style and color to the one they'd chosen for Zora, and fortunately one of them was a size ten.

Paula threw it over her arm as she spotted a mannequin in the store window wearing another dress that would flatter Zora's figure, but still had the conservative style that her friend liked. The mannequin looked so real that it looked ready to walk off of the display and to the cocktail party that it was dressed for.

That would be perfect, Paula thought, and looked around until she found one on the round garment rack.

Then she saw him.

Darryl.

He preferred to buy his suits at the shop that was located across from the boutique where Paula and her friends had been shopping for the last hour and a half. He was standing on a raised platform while the tailor pinned the hem of his pants. The suit looked custom made, as most of Darryl's suits were. Since scrubs or slacks and a crisp dress shirt were his usual work attire, Paula knew he had to be getting ready for a special event. For the last four years, he'd chaired a regional cardiology foundation and sat on the board of two other civic organizations.

Maybe we can have a cordial conversation today.

Paula hustled to the dressing room, shoved the two items through the drawn curtain, and scooped up Gabrielle.

"I'll be back," she told Zora and Monét. "Watch my stroller."

Paula strode like she did during her evening walks to burn off those extra pounds. She rounded the corner and saw . . .

Her.

She was running a hand along Darryl's shoulder, as if admiring the fit of his suit. Paula watched the woman pick up a tie from the display table beside them and wrap it around Darryl's neck. She moved slowly, tying the knot like it was an act of seduction. This wasn't an employee. She was the woman Paula had wondered about. Now she didn't have to wonder any longer.

Paula was standing in front of them before she had time to think about what to say.

"That's a nice tie," she said. "But frankly I've seen better." She looked at the tie and then at the woman. She glared at her from the tip of her designer sandals up to her flawless hair. "A whole lot better," she said, punctuating each word. She lifted the tie, then let if fall back onto Darryl's chest. "I'm sure you have a tie similar to that in your closet that you haven't worn."

She turned to the woman, who had stepped away from the scene of her crime.

"You see," Paula said, eyeing her, "wives know everything about their husbands. Like Darryl, for instance. Unless it's golf, he gets easily bored with a new recreation. And it's not long before he's dumped his extracurricular activity." She shoved Gabrielle into Darryl's arms. "He always returns to his first love of golf."

Paula paused and let her analogy sink in. "I am golf." She said it slowly so her words would pierce them. Inside, she was as surprised at herself as the woman seemed to be. The "other woman" was fumbling with her purse. Even Darryl had loosened the tie around his neck. A few moments earlier it had been a source of entertainment, but now it was probably choking him.

You don't have to do this. Let Me be in control.

223

Paula knew it was wrong, but it felt good being in control. The salesman and tailor had retreated to their safe posts—one behind the counter and the other behind an opening covered with tan linen curtain panels.

Darryl's voice was so low it was nearly a whisper. "Paula, don't make a scene. You don't know what—"

She didn't want to hear it. "*You're* telling *me* not to make a scene? So you want to have a selective memory today, is that what it is?"

Darryl opened his mouth to say something, but she didn't give him a chance.

"Whatever you do, remember this. And *you* remember this," she said, turning around to the woman. She was gone.

Good. Only God knew what would've transpired if she'd still been there.

"You have a family that you're responsible for—not just to take care of, but to love. Because we love you. I love you. And I'm not giving up."

Paula started crying. She hadn't wanted to, but just like her love for him, she couldn't turn it off. Despite all they were going through, she loved Darryl. God had made them one. Nothing—and no one—was going to change it.

Paula lifted Gabrielle out of her father's arm. Darryl leaned over and kissed Gabrielle on the top of her head before Paula turned to walk away.

She took her time leaving the store. She wanted Darryl to take in what he was missing. She looked back once more, feeling Darryl's eyes watching her.

Paula wiped away the last tear lingering on her cheek. "You *will* love me again."

monét

I am golf'?" Monét didn't believe so much had transpired while she was in the fitting room helping Zora spruce up her wardrobe. "Now, that's one for the books."

"It's the first thing that came to my mind," Paula said, letting Zora and Monét out at the front of Monét's condo building.

Monét turned around when she heard a car horn followed by two voices screaming her name.

"Auntie Monét. We're over here."

Her nephews swung open the backdoors to her sister's Volkswagen Passat station wagon. Monét liked it much better than the family minivan Victoria had been driving for the past six years, even though at the time Victoria claimed the van was state of the art. Monét vowed that she'd never drive a minivan. Ever. There was nothing cute about a miniature-looking bus with bucket seats that could fold down and convert to booster seats.

Monét looked at her watch. Victoria was at least thirty minutes early dropping them off. Sometimes Victoria seemed to forget that, single or not, Monét actually did have a life.

"What are you guys doing here?" She hugged the boys as they ran up. Then Tyler had the ludicrous idea to jump on her back.

Is this what my weekend is going to be like? Me playing the part of a walking jungle gym?

Victoria popped open the trunk and lifted out two rolling suitcases—one red, the other blue. "Come get these bags, boys. Your mother isn't being your personal assistant today. I'm officially off duty," she said, slamming the trunk closed. "And we're here early because we were already on this side of town and I knew you'd be home soon, so we just came and waited."

"And this is only until Saturday, right?" Monét asked, looking at the two overstuffed suitcases sitting on the sidewalk.

"No, Sunday. Don't get amnesia." Victoria lifted the handles of the rolling bags. "Believe it or not, I made them unpack some things. They were overly excited, because you know they *never* get to spend the weekend with their aunt."

"Okay. You can stop singing that song now," Monét said, helping Aaron hoist his bag onto the sidewalk. "Now go help your Aunt Zora real quick," she told her nephews.

Since Monét and Zora were like sisters and spent so much time together, Aaron and Tyler had taken to Zora like they were her biological nephews. They gladly assisted her, because they knew—and Monét knew—that Zora would slip them some money, just because.

It had taken Zora the most time to gather her purchases and put them in her trunk. After it was all said and done, Zora seemed pleased about the items she was adding to her wardrobe. Monét and Paula had added just enough flavor to spice up her style and give Preston a taste of refined woman.

Zora walked over to Victoria and tried to dip her like a salsa dance partner. Zora claimed Victoria as the second sister she'd never had. Like all siblings, they'd had their fair share of fights, but nothing but time and miles ever came between them.

226

Victoria screamed. "Girl, don't mess around and throw my back out. This is the first weekend I've had alone with my husband in a long time, and I need every part to be in top working condition." After Zora helped her to an upright position, Victoria squeezed her.

"So what's been going on? I miss you so much," Victoria said. "You got married and deserted the poor Sullivan family."

"Other than Preston being called to the ministry?"

"Are you serious? Monét didn't tell me."

"It slipped my mind," Monét said. "I was going to let Zora tell you."

"She's too busy being in love to remember anything, anyway," Zora said.

Paula rolled down the passenger side window. "Don't forget this," she said, handing Monét a shopping bag.

Monét had decided that she needed to put her best attitude —and fashion—forward for her trip to Houston. Paula and Zora had ganged up on her during their entire shopping spree. They even had the nerve to call Belinda and put her on intercom from Zora's cell phone. They verbally backed her into a corner until she had to face her commitment issues. Belinda called it "speaking the truth in love," but Monét called it harassment.

Regardless of their friendly beat down, Monét had already decided to go to Houston. Jeremiah sacrificed for their relationship all of the time. It was about time for her to drop her emotional baggage. Or at least try.

At first she thought Jeremiah would tell her it was too late for him to buy a ticket for her, but it hadn't seemed to matter. By the time the girlfriends had returned to Monét's place, he'd chalked up a buddy pass for their flight out next Thursday afternoon.

Paula had taken her to one of her favorite semiformal shops, where she'd found the perfect red dress for the anniversary gala. It had a fifties flair to it with a tight bodice and an A-line cut to the skirt. She already had the perfect pair of open-toe sandals that strapped around her ankle—courtesy of the bridesmaids' attire from her cousin's wedding two years prior. Monét also couldn't resist buying two pairs of lightweight cotton Yoga pants for the round-trip flight. Other than that, she planned to wear sundresses every day. Jeremiah had warned her of the sweltering Houston humidity.

"You're going to be a knockout at the party," Paula said. "If Jeremiah has any cute cousins, bring one of them back for me."

Monét shook her head. "And get me in trouble with God? I don't think so. You know God is putting your marriage back together." Every sign pointed to no, but Monét had to stand with her friend and believe in a miracle. "Since we walk by faith, and not by sight, you don't need to analyze what you saw today."

"You know, I'd already started letting my mind get away from me."

"So now you can stop," Monét said. "Call me—call somebody —if you need to talk. Okay?"

"You know I will," Paula said. "Have a good time with the boys."

Jeremiah pulled up just as Paula and Zora were driving off. It was perfect timing. With the silent auction and fashion show just two weeks away, Monét wanted to make sure she'd tied up all of her loose ends. The boys had already planned some kind of video game competition with Jeremiah that was supposed to last all night. She had no doubt that Aaron and Tyler could stay awake to the wee hours of the morning, but Jeremiah wouldn't last past one o'clock, especially since he'd pulled late hours at the office for most of the week. After ordering them pizza and buffalo wings, Monét would pour her time into one of the most prestigious and extravagant events in her event planning career. By nine o'clock, she'd retreat to her bedroom with one of the novels she'd borrowed from the library. Saturday was going to be a long day.

✦   ✦   ✦

"Guys, don't go so far ahead of us," Monét told her nephews for what seemed like the fiftieth time. They hadn't even gotten to their seats yet and her patience was wearing thin. It was hot. Too hot to sit in the baking sun for five hours and watch the Baltimore Orioles play the Texas Rangers. As far as sports were concerned, Monét's interest didn't go past football, and that wasn't until the Super Bowl.

Jeremiah strolled like he was in heaven. He was happy in any sports arena. He hadn't said anything to the boys until they tried to push past two elderly women.

"Aaron and Tyler."

It was the first time she'd heard Jeremiah raise his voice in irritation at them. It stopped the two boys in their tracks, and they waited until Monét and Jeremiah caught up with them.

"Didn't you hear what your Aunt Monét said?"

"Yes, sir," Tyler started. "But we were trying to see what—"

"There's no excuses. Listen to your aunt, or we're going back home to watch the game on television."

"No," they pleaded.

Aaron pulled on Monét's arm. "Don't take us back to the house. Please. We'll act right."

Monét pulled the brim of Aaron's baseball cap down over his eyes. "Well, you better be obedient. Do you know what *obedient* is?"

"Duh, Aunt Monét," Tyler said. "Of course we do. Do you think we're going to second grade, or something?"

Monét laughed and playfully pinched Tyler on his cheek. "You'll always be Aunt Monét's little boys." She stole a kiss from his cheek, and he wiped if off like her lips were poison.

"Not in public, Aunt Monét. That's embarrassing."

"Whatever," she said.

Jeremiah grabbed Aaron from behind and held down his arms so Monét could kiss him across the forehead and on both of his cheeks.

Tyler heckled him. "Ewww . . . you're going to have spit all over your face. And you can't wipe it off. You're only rubbing it in."

"You want some more too, Tyler?" Monét grabbed for him, but he dodged out of her reach.

"I'll take his," Jeremiah said. "You've been so busy lately I've hardly had time to steal some sugar from you."

"Sugar? You sound like somebody's grandma."

Jeremiah wrapped his fingers through Monét's. "That's what my Grandma GiGi used to say. You'll meet her next week. She's a trip. She's in a senior living community, and she had the nerve to say she *wanted* to go so she could have more freedom."

"Can't wait to meet her," Monét said.

Once the boys were distracted with the happenings going around them at Oriole Park, Monét kissed Jeremiah twice on his cheek. "Two lumps of sugar for your coffee."

"I like my coffee with lots of sugar."

"Don't get carried away. Kissing leads to other things, and you know we're not going down that road."

"I'm a patient man," Jeremiah said, lowering his voice. "As hard as it is, I can wait until God joins me with my wife. But if I keep feeling like I do, you're going to have to move out of the building."

"I was there first. You need to move."

"Maybe I should make you my wife so neither one of us has to move very far."

Wife? Why was her heart racing? "Are you as hot as I am?" Monét asked.

"Now you know how I feel all the time," Jeremiah confessed. "Monét, I know what I want and who I want."

His gaze was seductive. *This heat is going to Jeremiah's head.* Monét tightened the sun visor that matched the Orioles T-shirt Jeremiah had bought her to boost her home team spirit. She'd never been more grateful for one of her nephews to interrupt her conversation.

"Can we get something to eat?" Tyler asked.

"We just ate before we came," Monét said, amazed at how the boys' stomachs seemed to be an endless pit. She thought she'd fed them enough to last them at least until they got home, but the smell of roasted peanuts, buttery popcorn, and cotton candy was hard for anybody to ignore.

A redheaded toddler passed riding on his father's shoulders. The man's grip on the child's knees held him steady for the ride while the boy smashed a pink and blue fluff of cotton candy into his sticky mouth. Monét was trying to keep the boys off sugar while they were under her supervision, but she could tell that was going to be one of their first requests when Jeremiah took them to the concession stand.

"Let's get to our seats first," Jeremiah suggested. "If you can wait until after the first inning, I'll buy you guys whatever you want."

They seemed satisfied with the answer, and when Monét thought about it, she wondered how she was going to survive the game without filling up on processed junk food. Her dress for next week's trip was the perfect fit and would reveal any deviations from her current eating plan.

Jeremiah pointed to a restroom area. "Let me make a pit stop before we go to our seats. You guys need to go?"

"Nope."

"Are you sure?" Monét prodded. "Don't wait until after the game starts and ask to come back out."

Tyler and Aaron looked at her like they did when she was treating them like babies. She wasn't going to push the point. If they had to go later, she'd make Jeremiah take them.

Monét felt her cell phone vibrating through the miniature backpack she was wearing in place of her purse. She dug past the novel she'd brought in case of boredom to see that it was Savon calling her cell. She wasn't surprised. As the days ticked away, so did his patience. He wanted so badly for the Savon Perry Foundation fund-raiser to be a success that he was calling her at least twice a day.

"Don't add any last-minute changes. Things are going to work out fine," Monét said, without saying hello first.

"I'm glad you think so, because our emcee just cancelled."

"Cancelled, why? And why did she call you instead of me?" Monét had just spoken to the city's most popular news anchorwoman last week, and everything seemed to be fine. She'd even decided to showcase three custom outfits from her personal seamstress's collection and would raffle off a prize for a custom-designed man's or woman's suit at her own expense.

"I don't care who she called and why. It just needs to be

fixed. Her father had to have triple bypass surgery, so she's flying out to Indianapolis for at least a week. Evidently her mother just had heart surgery less than two months ago, and she's hardly well enough to take care of anybody but herself."

At least she had a valid excuse, Monét thought. "I'm sorry to hear that. We'll have to have something delivered to her office when she returns," Monét said, while her thoughts began ticking through a replacement she could find at such short notice.

"That's nice," Savon said. "I wouldn't have even thought about anything like that. I need a woman like you for my personal assistant. Why don't you think about that?"

Savon could definitely use somebody to keep him focused once in a while, and Monét knew she could use whatever pay he offered. "Let's take care of one thing at a time," she said.

Aaron and Tyler were entertaining themselves with seeing how hard they could punch each other on the shoulder. *Boys. They find fun in the strangest ways.*

"Oh, and did I tell you that we have to move the fashion show rehearsal from the Tuesday during the week of the event to next Saturday?" Savon asked.

"When did you find that out?"

"Last week."

"And you're just now telling me?"

"I just remembered. The manager at Echelon Noir called me when I was getting ready for two poetry slams. She interrupted my practice. I forgot."

"You better be glad I like you," Monét said, shooing away one of the boys. "Yes," she told Tyler, then went back to her conversation with Savon.

"So I finally got you to confess," Savon said with a seductive laugh in his voice. "What are you doing tonight?"

"Focus, Savon. I'm going to be out of town next Saturday. I need to call the manager and work something out."

"Why would you go out of town the week before the event?"

"I *do* have a personal life, Savon. And as far as I knew, everything was going smoothly."

232

"So I guess you're going to have to pull out that plan B you're always saying everybody should have."

If I had a plan B. "Don't worry about it. It'll get done," Monét said, then hung up. She slipped her cell back in her bag and looked around for the boys. They were nowhere in sight.

Jeremiah walked up beside her. "I'm ready. Where are the boys?"

Monét saw nothing but a sea of orange and black, and no sign of the red shirts the boys were wearing. People hustled in every direction, squeezing through the crowd past her while she stood in the middle of the bustle. She began to panic.

Jeremiah must've sensed her alarm. "Stand right here so you'll be here when they come back. Don't worry about them. They're old enough to find their way back."

Victoria had entrusted her children to her for two days, and less than twenty-four hours later they were missing. The people around her passed in a blur until two identical brown faces approached her.

"Jeremiah isn't back yet?" Tyler asked.

"Man, what's he doing in there? I'm ready to go."

Tyler snickered. "There's only one thing he could be doing if he's gone that long."

Monét found her voice. Her panic was swept away with the Oriole fans filing past her. "He's looking for you. Where have you been?" she fussed. "Don't ever leave again without telling me."

"But we did, Aunt Monét," Aaron said with a confused look on his face. "We asked if we could go look at the people hitting in the batting cage, and you said yes."

Monét remembered them asking her something, but she'd been so caught up in the conversation with Savon that she hadn't paid attention. "I'm sorry," Monét said. "Just stay with me."

She spotted Jeremiah in the crowd and waved him over. *And this man would actually trust me with his children?*

paula

Paula pulled against the curb in front of her mother's house. The driveway wasn't wide enough to fit her SUV along with her mother's Buick Regal and the car she recognized as her aunt and uncle's Cadillac. For as long as she'd remembered, Uncle Lonnie had driven a Cadillac. You couldn't convince him that there was a better car ever made.

Every time Paula replayed the incident at the mall yesterday, her heart beat faster. She couldn't believe she'd finally seen her. She'd seen her face all night in her dreams. Yes, the woman was beautiful, but Paula didn't believe her looks were enough to keep Darryl. In her heart, Paula knew the woman was giving Darryl something beyond the physical. While Paula had questioned and complained about all of Darryl's decisions when he was considering leaving medicine for real estate, she probably gave him support. Even after Paula had tried to be supportive of Darryl's new business ventures, she was too impatient and pessimistic. Now she saw her mistake. She'd put more trust in Darryl as her provider instead of God as The Provider.

Yet and still, she wouldn't forget the look in Darryl's eyes before she walked away. He was coming back to get her. She just didn't know when and what would cause him to change his mind. She needed it to be strictly his decision, and not something she manipulated out of him by threatening to take him to the bank, or by using his children as a pawn.

Yesterday Paula had held up remarkably well. As she drove to pick up Micah, she'd reminded herself of Monét's words: "We walk by faith, and not by sight."

Both Micah and Gabrielle had fallen asleep on the ride home. Micah's face was sun-kissed from spending most of the day outside. The sports camp he was attending was teaching the children the fundamentals of soccer.

"Next week I get to learn about golf," he'd announced earlier, jumping into the car with a pair of shin guards bouncing around his ankles. "I can't wait to tell Daddy. I think we can go play together, and I bet I'd beat him." He held an invisible golf club between his hands. "See, Mommy?" He swung his arms back. "I can probably hit the ball so high into the air that it would knock the sun out of the sky."

"Now, that would be a good swing," Paula had said. She rotated her body in the driver's seat so she could see Micah. She leaned on the middle console and asked, "The last time you went with Daddy, did you go and see anybody? Like maybe one of Daddy's friends that's a lady?"

Micah was using his shin guards as a drum. "No, Mommy."

"Are you sure? You can tell Mommy anything. I won't be mad."

"No, Mommy. You told me to always tell the truth."

"That's right," Paula had said, studying Micah's face. The strong genetic bone structure he'd inherited from his father was growing more prominent as he got older.

Paula had decided not to belabor the point. She didn't want to be one of the mothers who dragged her children into the middle of the parents' mess.

"I love you, Micah."

"I love you too, Mommy," he'd said, using his tongue to wiggle his bottom tooth that was loose enough to twist around.

He'd pulled that same tooth out on the ride home this afternoon, wrapped it in a napkin, and shoved it in his pocket.

Paula got out of the car and opened the passenger door. She shook Micah until he was aroused out of his nap, then steered him to the door with Gabrielle's car seat carrier hooked on one arm. The repetition of lifting Gabrielle and lugging more infant stuff around was starting to put more definition in Paula's arms. She could've socked Ms. Lady one in the face with no problem, she thought, opening the screen door.

Paula.

Okay, Lord. I'm sorry.

Aunt Edna and Uncle Lonnie were sitting around the kitchen table cracking the shells of a pan full of boiled peanuts.

"Hey there, Peanut," Uncle Lonnie said. He'd given her that name as a baby and still called her that to this day. He was the only one who did, and he refused to let go of the nickname, even when Paula announced her adulthood after high school graduation.

"Hi, Uncle Lonnie." She bent down and let him kiss her on the forehead just like he'd always done since she was a child.

Micah balled himself up on the couch, and Paula unlatched the harness straps of Gabrielle's carrier but didn't take her out. She set the carrier down near Uncle Lonnie's size-thirteen foot. His toes seemed to take up half the space of his sandal.

He peered over into the carrier. "I'm gonna leave her alone for now, but I can't wait until this baby wakes up. She needs to get her first good look at her favorite uncle."

Aunt Edna cracked a shell between her open palms. "Let the baby sleep. If she's anything like Micah was, she'll just be taking a bunch of catnaps." Aunt Edna popped open the top of a ginger ale, drinking down the fizz that bubbled out of the top. "When I walked in I thought your mama had opened a nursery in here or something," she said, dusting her hands over a napkin on her lap. "Times sure have changed. We didn't have any of these contraptions when y'all were babies."

Paula had to admit that Gabrielle's swing, bouncer, and

convertible playpen took up most of the empty space in the crowded house. What wasn't covered by Gabrielle's things was littered by Micah's action figures and child-sized sports equipment.

Rosanna walked inside from the back porch. She had a trowel in her hand, so Paula knew she must have been digging around in her array of potted plants outside. Either that or she'd finally planted the hydrangeas she'd bought from the home improvement store last week.

They hadn't talked much since Rosanna told her about her father, unless it was out of necessity. There was an unspoken tension whenever they were in the room together, so Paula tried to avoid conversation as much as possible. Rosanna did too.

Her mother hadn't asked her about her trip to her father's repair shop. She didn't know that Paula had backed out. For all she knew, there had been a blissful reunion of a daughter with her father. It hadn't happened yet, but Monday would be the day. Paula had the rest of today and all day Sunday to work up her nerve.

Aunt Edna was still talking about the simplicity or lack thereof of baby gear during her time. "Who's going to help you pack all this stuff back up today? Or is this stuff just for the children when they come over?"

Paula looked at her mother, who was pulling off her gardening gloves. She caught her mother's eye, and Paula knew that she hadn't told Aunt Edna or Uncle Lonnie that she'd been staying there. That in and of itself was a major feat. There wasn't much that didn't pass through the grapevine of the two sisters' lips.

"I thought it would be nice for us to come and stay with Mama for a while," Paula said. "How often do I get the chance to do that?"

"You're a stay-at-home mother, with a housekeeper, at that. You can find time to do what you want to do."

Uncle Lonnie spoke up for Paula like he always did. "Mind your business, Edna. You don't know what she has to do in a day."

Aunt Edna didn't want to let it go. "That big old house

you got, and you're coming over here? Seems like it would be the other way around. What you need to do is take your mama over to your house and get her from in front of this television all day. I came right inside and turned it off. Sometimes you just need a little bit of peace and quiet in the house."

Like now, Paula thought. She wasn't sure how that would ever be possible with Aunt Edna in the house. She felt sorry for Uncle Lonnie.

"I told you one time," Uncle Lonnie warned. He dropped some peanuts into his mouth. "Paula's a grown woman, and you don't need to meddle in her business. You've got enough troublesof your own."

Aunt Edna didn't respond. She tapped her foot on the linoleum floor, perhaps pounding out a rebuttal that she wished she could say instead.

Paula sat down on the couch and looked at Uncle Lonnie, her eyes saying, "Thanks." Before she knew it, she was awakened by an impatient rapping on the screen door. She looked around the room through squinted eyes. Aunt Edna was nodding at the kitchen table. The sound hadn't moved her in any way. Uncle Lonnie had disappeared with Gabrielle, an empty carrier sitting where they'd been.

Paula's sister, Kandi, pulled on the locked screen door. "Open the door. I've got to use the bathroom." Paula unlocked the screen, and Kandi pushed past her. Her children, Javon and Yvette, rushed in behind her. There went the peace.

When Micah heard his cousins, he was up and out the backdoor behind them by the time Kandi returned from the bathroom.

"I thought you would've gone back to Darryl by now," Kandi said. She was talking loud. Loud enough to wake Aunt Edna and provide her with the information she was probably curious about anyway. "Evidently he hasn't stopped your cash flow. 'Cause I know if it was me, I would make sure my pockets would stay full before I filed for divorce."

"Nobody's filing for divorce," Paula said. There was no need to whisper. Aunt Edna was as awake as a person could be in the middle of the day.

239

"You've been here for three months. You must be doing something."

"I'm being patient while God puts my marriage together."

"I never known God to take this long doing nothing," Kandi said, opening the refrigerator door.

"You know what? You don't have room to say anything, because Roland won't even marry you. He's content with dropping by like the postman and leaving you a baby every now and then."

"I know you're not talking about my kids." The refrigerator door—which was already having trouble staying closed without an extra push with the hip—slammed shut.

"No," Paula said. "I'm not talking about your kids. I'm talking about you."

"Whatever, Paula. You used to walk around on your high horse, and it seems like somebody came and finally knocked you right off. Maybe now you'll finally get some sense knocked into you. Maybe you'll see that a woman like you never was fit for a man like Darryl. Even his mama didn't think so. She didn't even have the decency to come and see you when she was in town. She snuck over here to see Gabrielle and Micah as soon as you left that Friday night to go to your little prayer group reunion. Mama didn't tell you that, did she?"

Every word slapped Paula in the face. It was like an open palm had landed heavily against her cheek, making it burn, but it was really her temperature rising.

Rosanna appeared from nowhere. She'd always done that when they were having arguments growing up. "Don't come in here raising sand in my house. I'm not in the mood for it, and I don't want to hear it," she said, shaking a finger in the air. "Now, I mean that."

Aunt Edna shook her head. "Sisters shouldn't act like that toward one another. You need to apologize."

Kandi walked out of the living room. Paula heard her open up the backdoor and yell for her kids.

"Yvette and Javon. Let's go. Come to the car. I better not have to come back and get you."

Kandi went out the door without a word to anybody.

Micah was the first to come flying through the backdoor. He jumped on Paula's lap, with the hot smell of summer on his skin while his cousins ran out the front door.

"Bye, everybody," Yvette yelled behind her.

Micah hugged Paula's neck. "Mommy, can I go with Javon and Yvette?"

Paula lifted his legs up on the couch so he could sit across her lap. He was getting tall for his age, but his weight had yet to catch up with his height. "Not this time," she said, rocking him side to side like he was a baby. Every now and then, he liked getting the special attention, especially since Gabrielle had stolen most of his lap time.

"Can they stay here with me? I won't have anybody to play with," he whined.

"I'm sure they'll be back in a few days. Mommy needs you here with me today. Maybe we can go to the park."

"I don't wanna go to the dumb park. I wanna go with my daddy," Micah pouted. He crossed his arms and pushed out his bottom lip. "I wanna see my daddy."

Fathers had a unique ability to rescue their children from pain. Micah usually clung to Paula like glue, but there were times when even her sweet talk and warm embraces couldn't take the place of Micah's yearning to be with Darryl.

What excuse would Darryl have if she called and he was with that woman? Paula didn't want to get Micah's hopes up, and she certainly didn't want anybody else playing a makeshift mother to her children.

"Let the boy call his daddy," Rosanna said. "It's still his daddy, no matter what."

paula

It was Monday. Paula had watched Sunday come and go and had still been awake when Monday was ushered in. She remembered the Monday from her first day of high school. It was the first time she'd been able to wear a completely different outfit to school each day for an entire week, because she'd picked up babysitting jobs during the summer for extra money. Micah had been born on a Monday. But this was a different Monday, one she was sure she'd remember years from now—no matter the result.

Paula waited for Micah to jump into the backseat of the car. He'd woken up this morning without whining. She'd only had to call him once. Even Gabrielle must have sensed something. It was the first time she'd slept through the entire night.

Paula had thought about the approach she'd take when she met her father today—in between praying, crying, and praying some more. But it wasn't just about her father. It was also for Darryl. His face came into her mind whenever she closed her eyes. Her feelings for him wouldn't leave her alone. Even when she'd wanted to go to sleep, she couldn't. She'd never had an experience before where she'd prayed all night, and she'd never petitioned God with such intensity. She prayed for Darryl beyond his role as her husband. She prayed from him as one of God's children. Paula had asked God to bring him in right relationship with Him.

She'd earnestly prayed for the scales to fall off Darryl's eyes by whatever means necessary so that he could free himself from the woman's alluring grip. By searching her Bible's concordance, Paula had come across a passage in Proverbs 6 that warned of the perils of an adulteress. She highlighted verses twenty-three through thirty-three in her Bible.

"Reproofs of instruction are the way of life, to keep you from the evil woman, from the flattering tongue of a seductress. Do not lust after her beauty in your heart, nor let her allure you with her eyelids. For by means of a harlot a man is reduced to a crust of bread; and an adulteress will prey upon his precious life. Can a man take fire to his bosom, and his clothes not be burned? Can one walk on hot coals, and his feet not be seared? So is he who goes in to his neighbor's wife; whoever touches her shall not be innocent. . . . Whoever commits adultery with a woman lacks understanding; he who does so destroys his own soul. Wounds and dishonor he will get, and his reproach will not be wiped away."

Paula fought God when she felt Him leading her to pray for the woman. Paula couldn't be sure she was the same "Lady Di" who owned the red BMW that had been parked in front of her house, but it didn't matter. She didn't want to know her name. She preferred to refer to her as "the woman."

Then God led her to another verse in the sixth chapter of Luke that talked about praying for your enemies. Paula read it, closed her Bible, then tried to sleep. She tossed and turned for over two hours. She thought Gabrielle would wake up for her middle-of-the-night feeding, but she didn't. She was sound asleep. Paula wished they could trade places.

She finally prayed for the woman. She knew in a tussle with

God she'd never win. Besides, she'd needed any rest she could get. Just before Paula had drifted off to sleep, she'd heard God speak.

It's time to go home.

Paula pulled up at Micah's camp and veered into an area marked for camper drop-off.

"Mommy, I'm going to learn golf today. Did you remember?"

"Yes, sweetie." How could she forget? Micah had been talking about it all weekend.

Micah pushed the button to unbuckle himself from his booster seat before Paula came to a complete stop.

"Micah, you know better," she scolded. She let down the window and took the sign-in clipboard from the camp counselor.

"How are you doing, Mrs. Manns?"

"I'm fine, Shawn."

"You're definitely that," he said under his breath, but loud enough for Paula to hear. He leaned in on her driver's side window.

Paula knew he could take in every piece of her attire with one glance—the way men do when they're checking out a woman. Even though she was at least fifteen years older than the college student, Paula knew she could turn his head any day on the street.

"You look nice today. I mean, not like you don't look nice every day. You must have something special going on."

"You could say that," Paula said. But that was all he was going to get. Only her close friends and her mother knew she was going to her father's shop. Last night she'd finally admitted to Rosanna that she hadn't had the guts to leave the letter the first time. Paula thought she'd looked relieved. Her countenance changed when she followed with the next blow.

"But I'm going back tomorrow after I drop Micah off," she said last night.

Rosanna wrung the dishcloth out in the sink and draped it over the faucet. "You're grown. Do whatcha wanna do," she'd said. She picked up the washcloth again and started scrubbing the spotless countertop. A few minutes more with that much fervor and she would've rubbed a hole straight through the laminate—much like Shawn was still boring a hole through Paula's clothes with his eyes.

Boys his age had no shame whatsoever, Paula thought. It was definitely a change from the workout pants and T-shirts she usually wore to drop off Micah at camp. Most mornings she headed back out for her daily stroller walk with Gabrielle as soon as she returned to her mother's house.

But this was *that* Monday.

The dashboard clock showed that it was twenty-three minutes past eight o'clock. If Floyd always started his mornings as early as he did the first time she saw him, then he had been at work for almost two hours. What would he say to her? What would he . . .

"Bye, Mommy." Micah waved. His water bottle and thermal lunch tote were hooked on his shoulder. "Can you call Daddy to see when he's bringing his golf clubs to Grandma's house? He said he would."

Shawn patted the top of Micah's head. "A Master's champion in the making."

Paula shifted into drive. "Yes, I'll call your daddy," she said to Micah. "And try not to be so obvious when you're looking at women," she whispered, winking at Shawn as she pulled away.

He winked too, but in a more flirtatious manner.

Lord, I hope that little boy didn't think I was coming on to him.

✝   ✝   ✝

Paula had no doubt that God had piloted her straight to her father's repair shop. She hadn't remembered driving there.

The three metal garage doors that had been closed last time were lifted. At two stations, cars were hoisted above the ground on lifts with workers tinkering under each. The hood of a midnight blue Honda Accord was popped open, covering the faces of two men behind it.

Paula pulled up in front of the office door. Through the light tinted film on the window— some of which had been scraped

246

off at the top—Paula could see that no one was inside. But he was here. She was parked beside the car she'd seen him driving last time. If that was even him.

Paula called Monét from her cell phone. "I'm at my father's shop. Tell me I can do it."

"You can do it. Get out of the car."

Paula pulled down the visor mirror and looked at her face. Even with less than three hours of sleep, she looked amazingly refreshed. God was amazing. She didn't feel tired at all.

"How did you know I was still in the car?"

"I had that feeling. Do I need to call in the troops?" Monét asked.

"Yes. I need all the prayer warriors I can get right now."

"Hold on a minute. And don't you dare put that car in reverse."

"Well, you better hurry up," she said before Monét clicked over to another line.

Paula watched who she suspected was Floyd Raymond walk from the front of a car around to the side. He lay down on a wooden plank with wheels and slid under the car. A knock on the window nearly made her jump out of the window. She put down the window to a man with a greying beard that was just as thick and wiry as the hair on his head. The name Walter was stitched on his faded blue work shirt.

"How can I help you, pretty lady?" he asked. "This ride looks like it's in tip-top shape. Watcha need? Directions or something?"

"I'm actually here to see someone." She held up her cell phone. "But I'm taking care of a phone call first."

"All right, pretty lady. I gotta see who's lucky enough to have you come see them. I need to give that man a pat on the back."

My daddy is the lucky man. But we'll see what he thinks about it since he hadn't so much as seen my face in thirty-six years.

Walter moved a worn toothpick between his teeth with his tongue. He waved his dirty hand and walked away.

"Are you still there?" Monét was back on the line.

"Yes."

"I'm here too," Zora said.

"And me too," Belinda added.

Paula felt strengthened already.

"I'll take us to the throne," Belinda said. "This won't take long. Faith without works is dead. And your next act of faith is getting out of that car and going to meet your earthly father, because your heavenly Father has opened this opportunity to you," Belinda said, before leading them in prayer.

Paula gripped the steering wheel while Belinda prayed. "Thank you, guys. I'll call you later and let you know how it went."

She opened the door before she had time to change her mind. She walked over to the Honda Accord and to the man she'd seen that first early morning. "Floyd Raymond?"

"Yeah, that's me."

Paula extended her hand. It seemed so formal for a daughter and father, but they were strangers. And she was frozen. The words she'd rehearsed on the walk from the car had vanished from her memory.

"I'm Floyd," he said, when she didn't respond the first time. He rubbed his oily hands down the side of his soiled pants. "What can I do for you? Gotcha self some car problems?"

"No, my car is fine." *I'm the one who's a wreck.* Paula swallowed the lump in her throat. "Do you know Rosanna Gilmer?"

Floyd wiped the sweat from his forehead with a red bandana he'd pulled from his back pocket. He leaned against the car.

He's stalling. He knows something is up.

"Rosanna Gilmer?"

Paula had the feeling the sweat running down his nose wasn't a result of the heat. Sweat began to trickle down her back too.

"I remember somebody by that name," he said. "Why? What happened to her?" He wore suspicion on his face.

"Nothing happened to her," she rushed to say. "She's my mother."

Floyd stared at her blankly.

"I'm Paula Gilmer Manns."

He fidgeted with his belt buckle.

He knows.

"This is awkward," Paula said, wringing her hands. "Very awkward, I know."

Floyd took his hands out of his pockets and crossed his arms across his stomach. "What's that got to do with me?" He began coughing like he'd inhaled too much exhaust fumes in his day.

"I'm your daughter," Paula blurted when he caught his breath. It didn't feel like she thought it would. There was no sense of relief. She felt like she'd opened a door to more pain.

Floyd wiped his forehead again with the dingy red bandana. He furrowed one of his brows; the other stood at attention.

Funny. She could do the same thing.

"And what makes you think that?" Floyd asked.

"My mother told me."

"And that's supposed to make it the truth?"

Paula had never considered that it could be a lie. Her mother may lie about other things, like telling the telephone company that the check was in the mail. But this? Never. "Yes," she said to Floyd. "She wouldn't lie about this."

"After thirty-six years you expect me to believe some random woman that shows up at my shop and tells me she's my daughter?"

Paula paused. She wanted him to realize what he'd just said. She'd never told him how old she was. He'd counted the years, probably thought about her with each passing one, wondering how she looked.

"So you've wondered about me? I've wondered about you too. I know we can't start over from the beginning, but we can—"

His silence turned to rambling.

"I don't know what you're talking about. The only thing I'm wondering is why you chose me to be your daddy. Can't you look around here and see I ain't got money?"

"But Mama told me—"

Floyd shook the sweaty bandana in her direction. "You need to go back and straighten things out with your mama," he growled. He exhaled, and his expression softened. "I'm not your daddy."

He turned away.

Paula followed him. She wouldn't let him walk away. He'd already done that to her mother. "I didn't choose you to be my father. God did. For whatever reason."

Sometime during their conversation, Walter had walked up. He picked up two tools and hung them on his belt loops.

"Put it up on the rack, Walter," Floyd said, kicking the front tire on the passenger's side of the car.

And that was it. The Monday morning she'd always remember as the first time she met her father.

Paula's chest heaved from anger at his denial, and from hurt because of his rejection. She pushed around the loose gravel under her feet; it seemed to mix with fragments of her shattered heart.

She hurried to her car, getting in and slamming the door.

"God, why me?" Paula asked. "The two men who should be the most important to me are rejecting me." She put her car in reverse, hoping that the car behind her would get the hint. When she looked over the seat behind her, Paula realized the vehicle blocking her exit was empty.

She held down the horn, but the driver of the car didn't appear.

Paula pulled down the sun visor, and the letter she'd written to Floyd dropped in her lap.

Leave the letter.

Floyd had already made his thoughts clear. Paula couldn't stand to think that she'd poured her heart out on pages that may be crumpled and thrown in the trash if she gave the letter to him.

Leave the letter.

Paula felt the unction. She heard His voice speaking quietly to her spirit. Maybe Floyd was in shock. Who was Paula to think she could show up unannounced and introduce herself to a man who hadn't heard anything about his daughter for over three decades?

She hesitated, then opened her car door. She'd leave the letter on his office desk, giving him the choice and the time to make the right decision.

A bell clanked against the wooden door when Paula opened it.

"Oh, excuse me," Paula said to a woman bent over a red and white cooler.

The woman pulled out several sandwiches in plastic wrap and set them on the desk on top of a wobbly stack of clipboards. Condensation from six bottles of water dripped onto a stack of yellow invoices.

"I've never seen a group of men who could eat so much." The woman huffed. "They always want a midmorning snack, and my breakfast hasn't even digested yet." Her slender face was nearly hidden among the oversized flowery shirt she was wearing. "Now," she said, closing the cooler lid. "My husband is outside in the garage. He can help you with your car. Go out there and ask for Floyd."

"Actually, I've already talked to him." She handed the woman the letter. "You can give this to him."

"I sure will."

Paula opened the door. "Oh," she said, turning back. "Is this your car? It's blocking me in."

"I'm right behind you," the woman said. She slid Paula's letter in her purse. "I'll make sure Floyd gets this personally," she said. "If I leave this check on the desk it'll get lost forever."

Check? Paula didn't tell her any different. Let her believe what she wanted. Before it was all over, his wife would know the truth too.

✢ ✢ ✢

Paula noticed the missed call indicator on her cell phone. She'd missed three calls: Monét, Belinda, and Zora, no doubt. She pushed the button to scroll through the phone's missed call log. All three were from Darryl's office.

Paula called in without checking her messages.

"Hi, Maxine. I think Dr. Manns has been trying to get in touch with me. Is he in?"

"Mrs. Manns?" Maxine's voice quivered. "I was trying to get in touch with you. Are you in town? Please come to the hospital right now. Dr. Manns was in a terrible accident last night. I didn't know until I got in this morning. The hospital has been trying to reach you all night and morning at home, but they said they couldn't get an answer. Is there any way you can catch a flight back home?"

All of Maxine's words were running together, tumbling over each other in nervousness.

That was why her prayers for him last night had been so fervent, Paula thought.

"I'll be there in thirty minutes," Paula said, flooring the gas pedal to run through a yellow light.

paula

The machines beeped. Nurses crept in on their padded clogs. Some spoke. Others acknowledged Paula with a sympathetic nod and let the door float closed behind them.

Darryl groaned in his restless sleep. He was being pumped with meds to abate the pains from his cracked ribs, broken left arm, and bruised hip bones. The black eyes and slight burns on his face were a result of the deployed side and front air bags of his Jaguar.

Paula was standing at the head of the hospital bed when his eyes flickered open. She softly rubbed her fingers along his hairline, following down the side of his tapered beard.

"I'm here, Darryl," she said, meaning much more than her physical presence. Their wedding covenant wasn't broken because their marriage was temporarily broken. What God had joined together, no man would put asunder. She'd said, "*In sickness and health.*" She'd said, "*For better or for worse.*"

"Hey," he managed to say.

"Relax. Don't try to move right now, okay?" she said when Darryl tried to sit up. Paula put a gentle hand on his shoulder. It was rock-hard. It had been a while since she'd touched his body, and it was unfortunate that it had taken this accident for him not to coil away from her touch. She wanted to crawl in the bed beside him. Hold him. Have him hold her.

It looked painful for Darryl to nod his head. He settled back into the pillow and closed his eyes again. The blue and black bruising under his eyes looked like half moons. There was a small laceration diagonally across his neck that the doctor attributed to the seat belt.

There was a soft knock on the door. Dr. Goldstein came inside, followed by an intern who looked too young to treat anything except her ailing baby dolls. He had been the first person to give her an assessment of Darryl's injuries when she'd first arrived an hour and a half ago.

"He'll still be in and out for a while longer," Dr. Goldstein said. "Can I get you anything? Maybe a cup of coffee?"

Paula shook her head. "I'm fine, but thank you for the offer." She held up the purse-sized Bible she'd brought out of her car. "This is all I need to sustain me right now."

"Buzz the nurse if you need anyone to get something for you. Dr. Manns is part of our family, and you are too."

"Thank you so much," Paula said.

When Dr. Goldstein and his walking shadow left the room, Paula felt a tickle on the side of her hip. She'd set her cell phone to the vibration mode from the time she walked into the hospital's double automatic doors.

It was Darryl's mother calling for the fourth time since Paula had called her. As any mother would, Delores was panicky and was waiting at the O'Hare International Airport to hop on the first available flight from Chicago.

"Hello?"

"How's my son? Please tell him I'm on the way. He's got to hold on until I get there. Jesus, help me," Delores cried.

"Delores." Paula waited until sobs subsided. "Darryl isn't going to die. He's hurt pretty bad, but he's going to be okay."

It was just like her mother-in-law to exaggerate a situation, although this reaction was certainly justified.

"Are you sure they checked out everything? We don't need to skimp on anything. Darryl deserves top-notch care, and I plan to see that he gets it."

And what am I doing? Trying to patch him up with a second hand first aid kit?

"You know Darryl works at the most reputable hospital in the city, and he's receiving the best care they have to offer," Paula said. "Even in his condition now, he'd call them to the carpet if he thought they weren't doing their jobs."

Paula heard the muffled voice in the background through the phone.

"I think they're calling my name," Delores said. "I'll call you back." She hung up the phone.

"Paula?" Darryl cleared his throat and tried to speak louder. "Paula?"

Paula left where she was standing in the room's corner near the window and bent down close to Darryl's lips.

"Was that my mama?"

"Yes. She'll be here as soon as she can."

"Where are the kids?"

"Gabrielle is at Mama's, and Micah is still at camp. I didn't want to go and get him. He doesn't need to be here right now. I'm having Monét pick him up and bring him this evening."

"Okay."

"Do you need anything?"

Darryl shook his head. He used the free arm that wasn't attached to an IV to pull the single hospital sheet up to his neck.

"Do you need a blanket?"

"No." Darryl looked at Paula, then looked away quickly. "When I was asleep . . . I thought I heard you reading the Bible."

"I was," Paula said.

"Can you read some more?" He closed his eyes.

Paula pulled a chair closer to the bed. A burgundy ribbon marked the last page she'd been reading from. The Psalms were becoming one of Paula's favorite books. Over the last few weeks she'd realized that many of the songs that moved her during praise and worship at church were based on the Scriptures.

Darryl's chest rose and fell in a slow, steady rhythm. Paula knew she'd grown in her faith. Less than two years ago she would've crumbled from Maxine's first call. Honestly, she would've done the same at the beginning of last year. But she felt like she was tapping into her spiritual reserve tank for times like these.

Paula ran her fingers under the words as she read from the fourth chapter of Psalms.

"Hear me when I call, O God of my righteousness! You have relieved me in my distress; have mercy on me, and hear my prayer. . . . The Lord will hear when I call to Him. Be angry, and do not sin. Mediate within your heart on your bed, and be still. . . ."

And she read.

Paula read until the lines of words blurred together. She couldn't have been asleep very long when she heard the creak of the door opening. Paula opened her eyes in time enough to see her. The woman.

Then her face was gone. Maybe she thought she'd make a safe exit. Maybe the woman thought Paula wouldn't accost her with Darryl in the shape that he was in, when they were in the hospital.

The woman was wrong.

Paula set her Bible on the chair and went out the door as quickly and quietly as possible.

It was like a movie. The woman was pushing the elevator button and nervously looked over her shoulder, when their eyes met. Paula had been so zeroed in on the woman's face that she didn't immediately notice that the woman was wearing nursing scrubs. And a wedding ring.

"Does your husband know that you're having an affair, or am I the only one seeing his family torn apart?" Paula glanced at the woman's name badge. Diane McClean. Lady Di.

Diane looked around the shuffling nurses' station, as if she could send out a secret honing signal for one of her colleagues to rescue her. She tucked her badge lanyard down the front of her shirt.

"Listen, *Diane*," Paula said, letting her know that her name wasn't a secret. "Let that be the last time you lay eyes on Darryl or ever try to make any kind of contact with him. You've done enough to *try* to destroy my family. But you won't win. Remember that."

"I'm sorry, Miss." Diane pushed the elevator button again. "I'm not sure what you're talking about."

"Oh, you don't know?" Paula asked, intentionally raising her voice. She didn't look behind her to see the reaction of the staff behind them, but she could imagine someone gawking in their direction. There was always someone who was the department busybody. Word about any sign of drama between the women would spread before Diane could get on the elevator.

The elevator doors opened. Diane rushed on, and Paula went in behind her. Diane pushed the button for the lobby level three times. Before the elevator doors could close, a hairy arm shot through the crack between the doors.

"Going down?" the man asked. He whistled and rocked back and forth on his heels.

Something is going down all right, Paula wanted to say.

"I've got to go out and soak up a little sun," he said to no one in particular. "It's cold enough to freeze an Eskimo in this place."

The man looked at Diane. "What floor do you work on?" Paula could tell she didn't want to answer.

"Who, me?" she stammered, looking up at the lighted numbers counting down from the fifth floor.

"Yes, you," the man said.

Both his shameless gawking and Paula's breathing down her neck were probably about to make Diane faint.

"Second," she finally said, looking down at her watch.

"Oh, you're wearing a wedding ring. No need for me to visit that floor," the man said, stepping out into the hospital lobby as the elevator doors opened.

Diane walked off with Paula on her heels. They passed through the lobby and out the exit doors.

"I'll follow you to your car, Lady Di," Paula said. "The red BMW. Don't make me do it."

Diane stopped.

"I'm sorry," were the first words the woman spoke.

What? Paula didn't expect an apology. She wanted the woman to give her a reason to land a punch. Just one.

"I needed him," she said. "But we didn't sleep together. I didn't cross that line."

"You actually expect me to believe that." Paula felt insulted. It made her even madder.

"I'm married."

"And guess what? So is my husband," Paula said sarcastically. "But neither of those facts has seemed to matter to you. Or to Darryl," she added. Paula wasn't ignorant. She knew it was just as much his fault.

"My husband is in Iraq. It's been hard for me not having him there."

"I hope you don't expect any sympathy from me," Paula said, rolling her neck with each word. "You took my husband away. He might as well have been in Iraq, but I was the one fighting the war."

"I just needed him," Diane said again.

Did this woman know how she sounded? "You needed him?" Paula tried to think of a way to tell her off without using the curse words that were in her mind. If she ever needed a Scripture to raise in her spirit, it was now.

Paula was audibly panting. "And you think I don't?" she asked, flailing her hand in the air. "You think his five-year-old son and his three-month-old daughter don't need him?"

"I never intended for it to be like this. I was never trying to—"

"Trying to what? Tear a family apart?"

"You don't know the whole story."

"I don't need to. What I know is enough. And I'll tell you how this story ends. You won't so much as stick your head through that door again or try to contact Darryl in any way, or I'll have you arrested."

Paula didn't know if she actually could, but it sounded good.

Guilt seemed to have Diane paralyzed. She couldn't say a word. Her white tennis shoes were stuck to the sidewalk. Instead of her chestnut hair waving loosely at her shoulders like the first time Paula had seen her, it was pulled into a low ponytail at the nape of her neck. She hardly wore any makeup, only a light bronze sheen of lip gloss.

"Today marks the end of your little clandestine romance," Paula continued. "For whatever reason, God used an accident to bring Darryl back into my arms." Paula grabbed Diane's arms before she could realize her actions. "And he will never be in yours again. Never."

Diane jerked her arm out of Paula's grasp. They glared at each other. Paula thought she saw more fear than anything in Diane's eyes. The woman turned and ran, bouncing like a pinball between the parked cars in the parking lot.

That's when the tears began to fall. Paula hadn't even cried when she first saw Darryl lying in that hospital bed. She'd been holding herself together all of this time, but this confrontation had taken its best stab at her spirit.

"God," she cried. "God." All she could do was call His name. She didn't care about the passersby staring at her. One woman looked like she wanted to stop and comfort her, but the man with her ushered her forward, probably thinking that Paula was mourning over the death or illness of a relative.

Paula ignored the car horn when she heard it the first time. The second time she looked up to see Monét swinging into a no-parking zone. Monét jumped out of the car, then opened the back passenger's door for Micah.

Micah jumped out, running to Paula's side. He wrapped his arms around Paula's waist and buried his head into his mother's side, saying, "Please don't cry, Mommy," his voice cracking.

She looked down into his wide eyes, then knelt down beside him.

"God will make it better, Mommy," he said. He squeezed her neck as hard as his five-year-old arms would allow.

Paula felt a hand on her back. Knowing it was Monét comforting and praying, she held on to Micah. She held on to God's promise to her about her marriage. She held on to Him.

ZORA

Two people had been on Zora's mind all night—Paula and Toni. She didn't want to overcrowd Dr. Manns's hospital room, so Zora stayed home while Monét dropped off Micah at the hospital. She did, however, call Rosanna to see if there was anything she could do to help her with Gabrielle. She declined, but wrote down Zora's cell phone number in case she wanted to take her up on the offer later.

Zora's heart ached with all that Paula was going through—her marriage troubles and now Darryl's accident. Praying for Paula had taken Zora's mind off of her own worries. She couldn't even complain about the fact that her mediator from the state hadn't heard back from her biological family.

When she, Paula, Monét, and Belinda had hooked up via phone last night, Paula had only briefly mentioned the visit to her father's shop. Paula had gone in with no expectations, she'd said. That way it wouldn't hurt as much if he rejected her. At least that's what she thought. It did hurt. The only reason Paula hadn't taken the time to acknowledge the pain was because she had to exert her energies elsewhere—specifically, to Darryl. And from what Zora could tell from what Paula told her, Maxine was going to be a handful.

When Zora wasn't thinking and praying for Paula, it was for Toni.

According to the attendance reports, Toni had been absent from school for the past two days. This wasn't the week for her to play hookey. Although she hadn't had exams in physical education and home economics yesterday, today's fifth and sixth period exams would have meant testing for Toni in history and chemistry.

When Zora tried to call Toni at home, the phone was disconnected. After last Friday's confrontation with Toni's mother, Zora wanted Toni to know she had no ill feelings.

Zora's best judgment told her that an unexpected visit to try to find Toni would cause more problems than she already had by being in Marjorette's home. Zora would have to wait until Toni returned. She prayed it would be tomorrow.

Zora looked up when someone tapped on her open door. If she had one prayer now, it would be that Principal Gaines's visit was as short as possible. He walked in and closed the door. He stood, like he always did. Zora knew it was his way to intimidate.

"Please have a seat," she offered.

He hesitated—not wanting to give up the power—but he did anyway.

"I received a call from Antoinette Burkes's mother this afternoon."

Zora exhaled. Finally she'd know what was going on. "Where's Toni? I've been so worried about her."

"It seems maybe you care a little too much about her," Principal Gaines said, unbuttoning his suit jacket. "And her mother isn't happy about it."

Here we go. "Would you care to elaborate?"

Principal Gaines was nearly sitting on the edge of his seat. Zora knew he'd do more than elaborate. He'd arrived to give a warning.

"Let me put it like this, Mrs. Fields. You don't have the right to go and pray in anyone's home without their permission." He propped his left leg over his right knee. "Just like you can't do it here," he said, punctuating each word with a tap on the side of his shoe.

Zora sat back in her chair. "Toni needed a ride home, so it was my pleasure to drop her off. It wasn't my intention to pray when I went over there, but I do what the Lord tells me to do," she heard herself say. She wasn't one to usually put her religion on the table, but the words flowed out, and she didn't try to muzzle them.

Principal Gaines laughed in a cynical sort of way. It was more of a snort. "I suggest you limit your conversations with God to home and church."

It was like he couldn't take sitting down for long. He stood up and opened a file folder, laying it in front of Zora.

"This is an acknowledgment letter that you need to sign." He took a silver Montblanc pen from his suit jacket pocket and put it on her desk.

Zora took her time reading the disciplinary letter. This wasn't something to be skimmed over. The letter mentioned their past conversation following the faculty meeting and outlined the discussion he'd had with Toni's mother.

Except for the conversation she hadn't heard between Principal Gaines and Marjorette, the contents of the letter were accurate, so there was no reason for her not to sign it. It was the first of its kind that would be added to her file, and she knew it would be lonely tucked among the other glowing yearly reviews.

Zora signed the paper and closed the folder.

"Like I said before," Principal Gaines said, picking up the pen and the folder, "just because it's the end of the year doesn't give you license to do what you want to do."

The phone couldn't have rung at a more appropriate time.

"Thank you, Principal Gaines." She tried to dismiss him as kindly as she could without pushing him out the door and slamming it behind him. She wasn't going to give him what

263

she knew he wanted—a reaction. "Have a good day."

Zora picked up the receiver, and Principal Gaines let himself out.

"Zora Fields, how may I help you?"

"Do you really want me to answer that question?" Flirtation was in Preston's voice. He had been more affectionate since Zora had let her lingerie reemerge, and was pleasingly impressed with the additions to her wardrobe.

Preston had even given her a romantic card with quite a bit of cash tucked inside. He liked what he'd been seeing—especially her nighttime attire—and he wanted to see more of it. More and more he was the first in bed—and sleep was the last thing on his mind.

"Don't start, baby. You know I'm at work." The student assistant walked by, and Zora motioned for her to close the door. "I just had an interesting visit."

"Really?" Preston sounded excited. "From who?"

"Principal Gaines."

"Oh. What did he have to say?"

Zora hadn't painted the best picture of her supervisor. She'd honestly tried to find something about Principal Gaines to like, but since fashionable suits didn't count toward character, she always came up empty.

"He came to tell me that the mother of one of my students called to complain about me praying with her daughter. You remember Toni? The one that I always talk about?"

"Yeah, I remember her. Well, you *have* been praying with her."

"Yes. But I know God was telling me to do it. She was always going through something and would always come to me for help."

"If you know you heard from God, don't worry about it."

"But I have a letter of reprimand in my file."

There was a short silence. Zora knew he was shifting from being her husband to her spiritual counselor. "God sacrificed His only Son. When you consider the cost He's paid, a letter in your file isn't a big deal."

"You're exactly right. It's nothing but a letter."

"And you might not do it out loud with everyone, but nobody —not even the principal—can stop you from praying. You've prayed for those students, your school, and the entire school system more than anybody I know. Don't let one incident and one parent stop that."

Zora opened her center drawer and pulled out a stapler. "I know. But things like this make me want to apply to work at one of the private Christian schools instead of in the public school system. I want to be free."

"You're where you're supposed to be, right?" Preston paused when Zora didn't say anything.

It's something Zora knew without a shadow of a doubt. Before she'd accepted the position, she'd prayed for God to order her footsteps.

"Right?" Preston pressed her.

"Yes."

"There's no reason to talk that nonsense that you want to leave the school. They need you, and they need your prayers more than anything. One day they'll see that."

zora

It's not your fault," Zora said, embracing Toni. Zora was happy to see Toni back at school, but sorry to hear about the circumstances that had kept her out of school for two days and brought her back on the last day before summer break. Fortunately, Toni's teachers had arranged for her to take make-up exams later in the week.

"I kept wishing Mama wasn't pregnant and God would let the baby die. If I hadn't said anything, she wouldn't have lost the baby. I didn't know prayer had that much power."

Toni was right; prayer was powerful. But how could Zora help Toni see that what happened was a sovereign act of God, and not a result of a selfish wish?

"I ain't never seen my mama this sad before," Toni said. Her eyes were swollen from so much crying that they nearly looked closed. She wiped her nose again and stuffed the dirty tissue in the pocket of her jean shorts.

"Your mother will make it through this, and you will too.

It may not seem like it right now, but each day it will get a little better."

"It's been three days since it happened, and I don't feel better at all. Every day I wake up, I feel worse. Please pray for me, Mrs. Fields."

"I will, Toni. I was praying for you when I didn't even know what was going on."

Toni had closed her eyes and had her hands clasped under her chin. She wanted Zora to pray now.

Mrs. Ledbetter walked past Zora's open office door, pausing for a moment when she saw Toni in her prayer position. She moved a few steps away, hovering near the copier machine. Zora listened. There was no hum from the machine making copies. She knew the sound well because the outdated equipment made a painful whine whenever it was duplicating.

"Do you need help, Mrs. Ledbetter?" Zora called out.

"Oh, no." She peeked her head in Zora's office. Her hair was pushed off of her face with a purple headband. Purple hoop earrings dangled from her ears. They shook as her head shook.

She held up a piece of paper. "Just making some copies."

"Okay," Zora said.

Mrs. Ledbetter scooted past the door.

Zora got up and pushed the door together, but didn't close it all the way. She sat down beside Toni and rested her clasped hands on her lap. She thought of the best way to say it. She couldn't say, "I'd already gotten reprimanded once by Principal Gaines for praying with you during school hours; then your mother had the nerve to call him and made the situation worse." Now that Zora knew Marjorette had probably called the school out of heartache and backlash from her loss, she didn't feel irritated at Toni's mother like she had before.

"School policy prohibits me from praying during school hours with students," Zora explained.

Toni looked puzzled. "We've always prayed during school hours."

"And I broke the rules. It was something I shouldn't have

done. So whenever you realize you're wrong about something, you make it right."

Toni was visibly disappointed. Her shoulders slumped, and her eyes became teary again.

"That doesn't mean I can't pray for you at all," Zora rushed in to say. "Just not here. And nobody can stop you from praying yourself."

"It's not the same. God knows you personally."

"He knows you, too," Zora reassured her. "And He knew you'd be going through this situation."

Toni wiped her eyes with the back of her hand. "If He knew I'd be hurting so bad, why did He let it happen?"

Zora shook her head. It was a question she couldn't answer. She knew God was sovereign, but how she could relay that to Toni in a relatable way?

"I asked God the same thing when my parents were killed."

"You're so strong, Mrs. Fields. I forgot your parents had died. I never saw you walking around crying or anything."

"Oh, I cried, and screamed, and was mad at God. All at the same time," Zora said. "I've only made it through with God's strength, but I still have my moments. And you know what I do? I look at the people that God left behind who love me."

Neither Zora nor Toni expected to see Rashad walk into the office. Without knocking, he walked in and stood beside Zora's desk. He fumbled with the memo cube on the corner of her desk. Toni turned away from him and stared out of the blinds.

"Excuse me, Mrs. Fields. I was looking for Toni. Her girl, Amber, told me she was probably in here."

Toni stood up and stomped to the window. "Don't come in here startin' no mess, Rashad. I got enough on my mind as it is, and the last thing I need is for you to be up in my face." Her sorrowful eyes were now raging in anger.

Any other time, Rashad would've bitten back at her with a harmful and ruthless comment, but Zora could tell that he'd come to her office with peaceful intentions. He sat down in the chair that Toni had abandoned. He even took off his baseball hat and hung it on the edge of his knee.

"Look, Toni. I know you don't like me. It's not like you're one of my favorite people either, but we need to talk."

Zora got up to close her office door, then pulled her desk chair back for Rashad to sit instead. She knew asking Toni to sit in the chair beside Rashad was a bit much. Anytime they were that close in each other's personal space, there was always an argument.

Rashad sat down in the seat and looked at Toni, but Toni studied her nails, never looking up at Rashad the entire time he talked.

"I wanted you to know that I'm sorry about what happened to the baby too. I was mad at my pops for getting your mom pregnant, but what was done was done, so I let it go. I was actually looking forward to having a little brother."

It was a boy? Toni had never mentioned that to Zora.

Rashad pounded a fist into an open palm, although not in an angry way. He rubbed his knuckles. "You know . . . maybe I could've done for him what my pops never did for me. Man, who knows how long my dad was going to stay around to be in the baby's life? He's hardly in mine. But I'd already made up in my mind that he'd always have his big brother around."

Now Zora was the one with tears welling in her eyes. She prayed that Toni would at least be open to Rashad's apology. She could tell it was sincere and that it had taken him more guts to show his feelings than it had ever taken to rough up anybody in a hallway fight.

Toni crossed her arms over her chest. "Just tell me why," she demanded. The fight was still in her voice. Rashad's plea had yet to soften Toni's resolve. "Why do you always have to mess with me? This has been going on for three years, and you can't seem to get enough."

Rashad set his hat backwards on his head. "Man, I mess with everybody. I don't give anybody slack. That's Rashad. That's how I roll," he said, sitting forward like he'd made a grand announcement. "Plus," he added, "I know you can take it. You not gonna go home and be crying and stuff."

"You don't know what people do behind closed doors," she

told him. "You remember that the next time you wanna hash somebody," she said, rolling her neck.

"I'll think about it," Rashad said. "Look. I'm sorry. You ain't gotta like me, but at least forgive me."

"And I'll think about forgiving you." Toni paused for a moment. "No. I *do* forgive you." She looked at Zora and smiled. "I read in my devotional last week about forgiveness."

Zora beamed. The seeds she'd planted were bearing fruit. Despite the hardships that always seemed to rise in her student's life, she knew God's intentions for Toni would prevail.

Zora clapped her hands. "It took all year, but we've finally got a peace offering. Now, that's a good way to start the summer break," she said, opening the door.

Zora was the first to hear the popping. "I knew somebody would give us some excitement today. I wonder who's popping firecrackers?" She moved toward the window.

"I don't think those are firecrackers," Rashad said. His eyes were the size of saucers. "Somebody's shootin'."

Zora

Zora heard the frantic screams of the students who'd congregated outside for lunch.

"Gunshots?"

Three more pops confirmed Zora's biggest fear.

Zora crouched down by the window and motioned for Toni and Rashad to do the same. Fear stole her voice as she peeked through one slat of the blinds. The students scrambled across the side of the building, scattering themselves behind trees and between cars in the student parking lot.

Then Zora saw him. A masked gunman heading toward the front of the school.

God help me.

Her protective instincts kicked in, and Zora ran to close the door to the guidance counselor suite. "There's a man with a gun outside," she said to everyone. "Lock yourself in your offices. Now!" she screamed. Doors slammed. Locks turned. Zora closed her door and turned the dead bolt with a loud thud.

Her mind clicked through the emergency drills. Inclement weather. Fire. Nothing for a crisis of this nature.

Toni cried, "What are we going to do? I can't die like this!"

"Nobody is going to die," Zora said. "Just stay down and be quiet." She peeked out the window again and saw at least two students who hadn't escaped the apparent rain of bullets. They weren't moving. She'd just said no one would die. Zora prayed she hadn't lied.

"Man, this is crazy." Rashad unclipped his cell phone from his waist. "I'm calling my mama."

911. Why hadn't it hit her earlier to call? "Keep your voice low," Zora said, picking up her phone. She didn't want Rashad to do anything but lie low, but now wasn't the time to deny him a call to his mother. The emergency dispatcher answered on the second ring.

"We have an emergency situation at Baltimore City High School. Someone is outside shooting." Zora looked at the students' panicked faces and tried to keep herself calm. She felt a quiver rise on the inside, and it came up to her voice. "And it's possible they may be headed inside of the school. If they aren't in here already."

"The police are already on their way, ma'am. We do have reports that the gunmen are in the building."

There's more than one?

"Where are you, ma'am?" the dispatcher asked.

"Locked in a guidance counselor suite. We're on the west wing of the school."

"Stay there and don't move until the police come in for you."

Zora watched the terror on Toni's and Rashad's faces grow as a loud pop was heard inside. It was followed by three more. Toni was cowered in the corner, her backpack hugged against her chest as if it were a life-support system. Rashad had leaned against the grey steel file cabinet. His voice was barely audible, but Zora still heard the screams of a female voice coming through the other end of his cell.

"Ma'am. Did you hear me?" The dispatcher's voice was

so calm. Zora knew they weren't supposed to be shaken by emergency responses, and this woman was doing an excellent job at it.

"Yes. I'm here. Certainly. We'll stay put."

By the time Zora hung up her office phone, Rashad was handing over his cell phone. His mother was hysterical. It wasn't helping Zora keep a hold of her sanity.

"Please take care of my baby. I can't lose another son," she pleaded. "I'll be there in thirty minutes." She hung up.

She'll be out there among a slew of other parents, Zora imagined. Zora had always thought cell phones and all those communication gadgets were a nuisance in the classroom, but under this circumstance, she hoped the students were calling and texting everyone they knew.

"Turn off the light," Zora mouthed to Toni. She didn't want any signs of activity to show through the frosted glass window of her door.

Toni didn't budge from her crouched position, so Rashad crawled to the door, flipped the switch, then squeezed himself into a small space beside Toni. When she bit her bottom lip, appearing to hold in the scream that showed in her eyes, Rashad awkwardly patted her knee.

Sirens.

Zora looked out the window again. A line of police cars was barreling into the parking lot. The officers jumped out of the squad cars—some corralling the students who were outside into a holding area away from the building and near a grove of oak trees. A black-uniformed defense line armed with guns circled the school.

The two bodies Zora had seen earlier outside on the grass were being whisked away to the ambulance on stretchers.

"The police are here," Zora told Rashad and Toni. "We'll be out of here in no time."

This isn't real. This can't be happening to me. I'm a new wife. I—Preston!

Zora crawled to her desk and pulled her phone to the floor.

"There's nothing you can do now but pray," Zora told her

husband once she'd given him the update. "Pray until we're out of here safely."

Prayer wasn't enough for him. Zora knew her husband would be joining Rashad's mother and the rest of the frantic parents and loved ones. From what Zora could see when she peeked out of the window again, no one who wasn't already on the premises would get very far. Orange barricades and yellow police tape set up at the school's entrance would impede their progress.

Zora looked at the wall clock. Ten minutes had passed. She looked at the students. At her hands. They were shaking.

"You don't have to put up a front for us, Mrs. Fields," Toni said. "It's okay to be scared."

"You're right."

"So are you? Scared, I mean."

"Yes. But we're going to get out of here unharmed."

Zora wondered what was happening in the hallways. The cafeteria? The locker room? Classrooms? She hadn't heard a gunshot in some time. Zora's imagination kicked into high gear. Perhaps the gunmen were holding students in one of the classrooms hostage. The horrors of the national media coverage of past shootings at high schools and colleges began to flood her head.

The Holy Spirit battled it by bringing Psalm 91 to her remembrance.

"He who dwells in the secret place of the Most High shall abide under the shadow of the Almighty. I will say of the Lord, 'He is my refuge and my fortress; my God, in Him I will trust.' Surely He shall deliver you from the snare of the fowler and from the perilous pestilence. He shall cover you with His feathers, and under His wings you shall take refuge. . . ."

"We need to pray, Mrs. Fields," Toni said. "Bump school policy. We need God's help, because I'm telling you right now, you can't depend on the police."

Zora crawled down on the floor beside the students. She put an arm around each of them. They crouched so that their heads touched in the middle.

And Zora prayed.

belinda

The entire Stokes household was awake even though it was six o'clock in the morning. Belinda wished Hannah would've at least slept until she'd awakened her at seven o'clock like she planned, but once she'd heard everyone else traipsing around in the kitchen, Hannah called for her daddy at the top of her lungs.

Their overnight bags were stationed by the door. Belinda had placed them there last night after asking Thomas if the family could go to Maryland to support Paula and Zora. Not only did she want to stand by her friends, but T.J. needed to see how needless acts of violence affected his peers. Reality had a way of causing teenagers to change in a way that a parent's scolding couldn't.

"Are we going straight to the school or to Zora's house first?" Thomas asked.

"To the school. Zora doesn't know we're coming." Belinda dropped two pieces of wheat bread into the toaster. "I'll see her when we get to the school. I printed out directions from the Internet last night."

Hannah squealed with impatience when T.J. didn't scoop her cream of wheat into her mouth quickly enough.

"Hold your horses, little woman. I'm not an expert at this stuff," T.J. said. Most of Hannah's breakfast had dropped on the front of her pajamas and on the tray of the high chair instead of making it into her mouth.

"And you don't need to be an expert at it anytime soon," Thomas said.

Thomas was the only one already dressed, being used to waking up at the crack of dawn for work. You could've knocked Belinda over with a pinkie when she walked downstairs this morning and saw him wearing jean shorts with a Miami Heat basketball jersey.

"Reclaiming your youth?" she'd asked him, pouring them both a cup of strong, black coffee.

"I want to connect with the youth. I can't approach them and have them looking at me like I'm an old man."

"Be you. You'll be fine, and the Lord can use you like He always does."

Thomas tapped a drop of cream into his mug. "I'm still keeping on this jersey. T.J.'s gonna have to give this to me."

"That'll be the day. You know how that boy is about his clothes."

Two weeks ago, T.J. would've staged a protest at the suggestion that he wake up before noon. His behavior had drastically improved, but Thomas and Belinda were still trying to rid him of his slothful attitude about life. The principal at his school had made it possible for T.J. to be able to walk across the stage during graduation, but it turned out that he needed to finish three credit hours during the next school year so he could officially earn his diploma.

Thomas had stopped giving him an allowance, unless it was for necessities. Sooner or later he'd realize that getting a job was the only way he'd be able to buy the childhood luxuries he wanted, like a pair of shoes to match every outfit.

"Ma 'Linda, can you finish feeding Hannah so I can go get dressed?"

"No," Thomas interjected. "She told you that was your responsibility this morning, so you need to follow through. And you can wash your sister's face and put her clothes on when you finish."

Hannah stuck her hand in the bowl, then slung her breakfast in her hair.

"Aww, man. Look at this junk." He wiped off the side of her head. "This is a conspiracy to make my job harder."

Thomas's eyes lit in amusement. "Wait until you're out in the real world, son. This ain't nothing."

With frustration, T.J. survived his morning feeding Hannah, and his ride in the backseat with her to Baltimore, but the look on his face when he had to stand amidst the mourning students spoke volumes. He sat on the curb with the backpack Belinda had asked him to watch.

Belinda tied the strings to Hannah's sun hat under her chin. She forced the small wheels of the umbrella stroller over the grass, looking for Zora.

"I don't think she's here yet," she told Thomas.

"But every television station in the city is." Thomas blew a stream of air. "I hope they don't forget. After all the news stories are told, I hope these kids realize that nobody knows when it's their time to go."

"If nobody else gets it, I know one person who does."

T.J. was flipping through a Bible. Belinda had stuck it in the front pocket of Hannah's pink and purple backpack in case she needed her sword at a time like this. He ran his finger along the page as if looking for a particular verse. Evidently he found it. He pulled the Bible close to his face, no doubt to read the small print. Belinda couldn't make any of the words out herself without her reading glasses.

Belinda let him stay to himself until her motherly conduct couldn't keep her away. She handed Hannah to Thomas. "I'm going to go sit with T.J. for a while. Am I overstepping boundaries?"

Thomas looked over at his son. "If you feel led to, go ahead."

279

"I do." Belinda walked off to the son God had sent her. He hadn't come into her life when or how she expected, but nevertheless, he was there. Belinda hadn't prayed, cried, and gone through changes in her marriage for nothing.

"What are you reading?" Belinda asked T.J., squatting on the curb beside him.

"Umm . . . Psalm 91. Umm . . . It's taped on the wall in my closet."

"It is?" Belinda had never seen it, but then again, there wasn't much she could ever find inside T.J.'s closet.

"I put it in there after I got shot. I memorized the first two verses, but that's all." He closed his eyes. "'He who dwells in the secret place of the Most High shall abide under the shadow of the Almighty. I will say of the Lord, He is my refuge and fortress; my God, in Him I will trust.'"

Belinda was amazed. The son she'd only heard rap around the house was reciting Scripture. One of the most moving experiences in life was to see the fruit of your prayers manifest. Knowing how hard she'd prayed for her children, Belinda knew the best was yet to come.

A cameraman walked by with his equipment hoisted on his shoulder. Two steps behind him, a field reporter flipped through a steno notepad before stopping to look around.

She slung her glossy brunette mane over her shoulder as she called to her colleague. "Roy." The woman pointed toward a cluster of people holding hands. They wore identical blue T-shirts with a boy's face and the words *Forever in Our Hearts* screenprinted across the front. Their bodies slumped in despair the closer they walked toward the vigil site.

"I think that's the boy's family," the reporter said.

The woman approached cautiously at first, then more aggressively when she noticed the other reporters from competing stations turning in their direction.

"Man, that could've happened to me," T.J. said.

It was hard to think about, but it was true. Belinda wrapped her arm around him. "But it wasn't. God gave you a second chance. A lot of people don't get that."

One of the women in a victim's family fell to her knees, screaming in agony. Even when the others tried to help her up, she was too stricken with grief to stand. "Why my baby?" she screamed, tears watering the ground below her. "Tell me why."

"I don't want to mess up any more of my chances, Ma 'Linda," T.J. said, leaning his head on Belinda's shoulder.

It had taken a year, but Belinda knew her family was finally having a breakthrough.

zora

Zora turned to another television station, but couldn't escape the news story. It was all she could do to keep down three sips of apple juice and a few spoonfuls of bland oatmeal. Her stomach churned. But nothing hurt as much as her heart. Stephen Motts, a student she hadn't known personally but had seen in the halls, was the only fatality from yesterday's shooting. The two bodies she'd seen whisked to the ambulance had suffered injuries, but none of them were life threatening. They'd both told reporters that they'd played dead in case the gunman was watching them.

It had been more than an hour before the two teenage gunmen, dressed in black with the bottom halves of their faces covered with orange bandanas, attempted to escape out of the school's back hallway exit. The teacher and students in Stephen's English class were forced to stay in the room with their classmate's dead body.

"You could tell they were terrified," the teacher said,

speaking of the gunmen. "After they shot Stephen they didn't know what to do. They were in shock, so they started yelling for us to get on the floor in the back of the room and put our head between our knees."

"What were the other students doing?" the reporter asked.

"They did what they were told. We were all crying. Praying. That's all we could do. We didn't want anybody else to be killed."

The camera shot jumped from the English teacher's tear-streaked face to a B-roll of police herding students and teachers out of the building once the two gunmen had been apprehended. Zora saw herself, holding the front door open as students passed through. Toni had refused to let go of her hand the entire time.

Yesterday had been such a traumatic experience that she'd come home and gone straight to bed. It was three o'clock in the morning before she was actually able to fall asleep, and even then it was a restless slumber. Preston called in for a day off even though she'd tried to convince him that she would be fine. He didn't listen. Zora was glad he didn't.

Zora flipped the station to another network. She hadn't known that Principal Gaines had been interviewed until she saw this morning's broadcast.

"A prayer vigil is being held today following the Thursday afternoon shooting at Baltimore City High School," the reporter was saying. "One student was fatally shot, and two others were injured. They are recovering at Union Memorial Hospital from their physical wounds, while the other students are recovering emotionally. It is thought the gunmen are the same suspects involved in an incident at the same school earlier this year."

Principal Gaines stood under the flagpole near the circular driveway in front of the school. The cameraman focused on the flapping American flag before panning down to his face. Instead of his usual overly starched look, the principal was dressed in a polo shirt bearing the school's blue and gold colors with the mascot—a panther—stitched on the chest.

"We didn't want one day to pass by without showing the students, their parents, and the community how much we're concerned about what has happened. Although the school year has come to a close, our guidance counselors will be here over the next week to help grieving students. We'd like to ask that everyone pray that God be with us during this time."

Zora almost choked on the oatmeal she was forcing down. "What? So now he wants to know God. I can't believe that man," she said, dumping the rest of the oatmeal down the garbage disposal. She rinsed out the bowl, then put it in the dishwasher with the rest of the dishes that had been piling up all week.

"What are you talking about in here?" Preston walked in carrying his tennis shoes. He dropped them on the floor at the foot of the chaise longue that he refused to let Zora donate to the local charity.

He walked over to Zora and hugged her, holding her as tightly as he'd done last night. When the police officers had finally released the students and teachers from the school yesterday and pulled down the barricades, Zora noticed Preston dashing from the streets where hundreds of cars were lined.

Zora had fallen apart before he was in arm's reach. Her body shuddered against his as she wept.

"You don't know how grateful I am to God for protecting you," Preston had said. "It was terrible not being able to get to you. I never want to experience that again."

Preston stopped to look at the newscast. "You feeling all right this morning?"

"Principal Gaines is making himself look like a saint instead of the prayer police that he really is." Zora was on the edge of being livid.

Preston opened the refrigerator and pulled out a carton of eggs. "Baby, tragedy will drive anybody to their knees. You never know. He might have meant that sincerely after all that's happened."

"If you think so," Zora said, wishing she had the stomach to handle one of Preston's omelets. There had never been a time when she turned one down. But today, even the look of him

285

whisking the whites around in a bowl made her queasy. When he dropped the eggs in the frying pan with his diced peppers and mushrooms, the smell overtook Zora's nose.

"I'm going to the bedroom to lie down," she said, hanging her purse on the umbrella stand near the door. "Call me when you're ready to go."

"Are you okay?" Preston asked, using a spatula to flip over his eggs.

"I'm fine. My nerves are really shaken up. I'm going to read my Bible."

Zora felt better after getting away from the kitchen cuisine aromas and taking in the Word instead. Following ten minutes of rest and twenty minutes of travel time, she was pulling into the school parking lot. She was met at her car with a group of students, led by Toni.

"Mrs. Fields, we've been waiting for you," Toni said.

Toni's entourage stood behind her with sullen eyes. Most of the teenage girls at the high school usually overdid it with make-up. But today their faces were bare and told the stories of the children they really were. It was as if the tears of the students had formed a grey mist that hovered in the air.

Zora stuffed her purse under the front seat and closed the door. She hugged Toni first, and the other students—most of whom she knew by face, but not by name—huddled in around them. When they loosened their embrace, they began wiping the tears from one another's eyes.

Toni took the hand of one of the girls. "This is Amber," Toni said. "My best friend and Stephen's girlfriend."

It only took one tear from Amber to cause the floodgates of her friends to open again.

"I told Amber you're the person to come to for prayer," Toni said. "I know we can pray for ourselves," she put in, "but there's something about your presence that's so calming."

Preston had already excused himself away from their group, and Zora saw him congregating near a group of boys. Zora knew Preston was waiting for an open door to go and minister to them. Their eyes were rimmed in red, but they appeared now to be holding their emotions inside. It was a rare instance to see a group of young men in complete silence.

Sometimes that's what was needed to hear God speak. His voice would come through Preston. When her husband sat down on the grass amidst the group, Zora led the girls to a quiet shaded area. The instrumental version of hymns played through the school's intercom system.

She talked and prayed with the girls until Principal Gaines walked over to them.

"Can I speak to you for a moment, Mrs. Fields?"

Zora stood, wiped off the back of her jeans, and joined Principal Gaines a few footsteps away.

"We're going to reflect with a moment of silence, but would you mind leading us in a word of prayer afterwards?" It looked like it was hurting Principal Gaines to ask her.

He looked away as he said it, fumbling in his back pocket.

"Of course I will," she said.

Relief washed over his face when Zora agreed without bringing up any of their earlier confrontations. He pulled out a scrap piece of paper, and Zora watched him scribble her name beside the word *PRAYER*. Principal Gaines shoved the paper back in his pocket.

"Thank you. We'll go ahead and get started now."

He walked away.

Principal Gaines's voice sounded over the intercom, asking all of the supporters to gather in the circular grassy area with the flagpole staked in the middle. Although the music volume was lowered, Zora could still hear the tune of "Amazing Grace."

No one spoke as they gathered under the flag. There was the soft thudding of tennis shoes on the parking lot asphalt. A bird chirping overhead. Sniffles.

"So was that the infamous Principal Gaines?" Preston asked.

"Yes. He asked me to pray," she whispered.

"What did I tell you? One day they'd need your prayers."

Preston pulled Zora against his chest and rested his chin

on her head. She looked around and for the first time saw her in-laws, Monét and Jeremiah, and Belinda's family.

"I knew they'd need my prayers," she told Preston. "But I wish it didn't have to happen like this."

monét

Monét never knew Houston was such a huge city. Everything was so spread out, and it seemed to take forty-five minutes to get everywhere, more if there were the typical stalls on the highways.

Jeremiah had started his tour of the city early this morning after picking her up from the hotel for breakfast. Monét acted like she wanted to see all of Houston's tourist sites that she'd researched before she came—like The Bayou Place, the Galleria, or The Gite Gallery—but really, she was stalling.

As lunchtime approached, Jeremiah ended his tour and took her to his parents' house with a promise to take her everywhere she'd wanted to go before the day was over.

"Why do you have that look on your face?" Jeremiah wrapped his arm around Monét's shoulder and tried to pull her to his side.

Monét lifted his arm and put it back at his side. "What look?"

He grabbed her arm and stopped walking. "That look of dread." He stepped in front of her, blocking her view of the arched entryway of his parents' brick ranch home. "Like you don't want to be touched." He lifted both of her hands and intertwined his fingers with hers.

"Because my friends are being hit left and right with drama, and I'm on vacation. It's not right. I should be there with them."

"Zora has Preston to take care of her. She'll be all right."

"Even a husband is nothing like a best girlfriend."

"You're right. But I think she needs the security and comfort of her husband. You can spend some time with her when you get back."

"She's worrying herself sick," Monét said. "I know my best friend. And when I get home I'll be wrapped up trying to do last-minute stuff for the event. The timing is all wrong."

"Whose timing? Yours or God's?"

Monét hated when Jeremiah did that—trying to get super-spiritual when she just wanted to express her feelings. He was trying to counsel her at the wrong time. These were her friends, her sisters in heart. Maybe it was because women shared stronger attachments with their girlfriends than most men did. Sometimes Monét couldn't help but be emotionally drawn into their lives.

Monét guessed Jeremiah had a point. Her worry wouldn't help anything, and God was everywhere. She was in Houston.

"I'm okay," Monét said. "Let's go inside."

"There's nothing to worry about," Jeremiah said. He leaned forward and kissed the edge of her jaw line, just under the earlobe. "If I love you, they'll love you."

Monét didn't resist when his lips moved gingerly to her mouth. Their kisses were always sweet—like a first kiss every time. Jeremiah never forced anything, but you could tell he was holding back. The more time they spent together, the harder it was for them to contain their physical attraction.

Jeremiah's lips touched hers again. She pulled away from him and opened her eyes. His mother was watching them from the doorway.

"I love you, baby," Jeremiah said.

"I don't believe this," she whispered between clenched lips.

"Believe it, baby. I do love you. Why would you think I don't?"

"I'm not talking about you. Your mother is watching us."

"What?" Jeremiah hugged her tighter, but Monét let her arms drop like steel to her sides.

"Your mother is watching you trying to make out with me," she said, punctuating each word.

"I'm a grown man."

"It's not funny, Jeremiah. I'll go back to the car and stay there until you come out. I'm not lying."

"Yes, you are."

Monét heard the screen door unlatch and watched it swing open.

"Jeremiah, get in here and stop putting on a show for the neighbors," his mother said.

"See. Now she thinks I'm fast." Monét pulled herself from Jeremiah's embrace and playfully slapped his arm. She straightened her beige linen sundress.

"Hey, Ma." Jeremiah kissed his mother on the cheek and held the door open for Monét to enter. "You remember Monét?"

"Yes."

Is that all? How about, "How are you doing?" Or "It's good to have you in Houston"?

Monét was on Mrs. Cheryl Hartgrove's playing field. She'd promised herself and also prayed for God to help her to throw out all of her preconceived notions and anxieties about meeting Jeremiah's folks again. She was going to put her best foot— and best face—forward.

"Nice to see you again, Mrs. Hartgrove," Monét said.

A forced smile lined Mrs. Hartgrove's face before she said, "I decided we'd go to this new Italian restaurant I saw the other day. The last thing I wanted to do today was any kind of domestic work."

I guess it was too much to ask for a decent response, Monét thought.

"Is that okay with you, Monét?" Jeremiah asked, rubbing her back.

"I love Italian." Monét hoped she sounded genuine, because she actually wasn't in the mood for any kind of pasta. She was hoping they'd go somewhere with a nice salad bar spread. She smiled anyway, but could imagine that it looked just as artificial as Mrs. Hartgrove's porcelain-capped grin.

Either Jeremiah was oblivious to the tension, or he was ignoring it all. "Great," he said. "So where's Dad?"

"Upstairs washing up and changing his clothes. He just had to get the car spic-and-span clean so he could take it out today," she said, shaking her head.

Monét had seen the smudge-free midnight black convertible Saab in the driveway. Perhaps unbeknownst to Mrs. Hartgrove, the top was already down and looked ready for a midday over-the-speed-limit spin down the highway.

Mrs. Hartgrove smoothed the side of her head. It was pinned up into an elaborate upsweep with every strand in its place. Just like her. Every vase, picture frame, and home accessory had a specific and carefully thought out place in the tidy home. Monét could see that already, and she was still standing in the foyer.

"I'm not letting him mess up my hair," Mrs. Hartgrove said.

Monét decided to try again. After all, she had to survive the rest of the weekend. "It looks really nice."

There was a pause.

Mrs. Hartgrove fiddled with her small gold hoop earring before saying, "Thank you."

It was a bland response. One that she could've kept to herself as far as Monét was concerned. Mrs. Hartgrove walked to the kitchen, leaving Monét and Jeremiah standing in the foyer.

Monét looked at Jeremiah with a look that said, *This is what I was talking about.*

"Dad probably got on her nerves or something," Jeremiah whispered. "She'll get over it soon enough."

If Mr. and Mrs. Hartgrove had gotten into a disagreement before they arrived, Allen Hartgrove wasn't letting it show. He sang as he came down the steps.

"My dad and his quartet songs," Jeremiah said. "He plays them loud. Riding down the street in his midlife-crisis machine."

"Like father, like son," she said. "Sometimes you play your music loud enough for people in the next state to hear."

"I'm a musician. I have to feel my music."

Mr. Hartgrove finally appeared at the top of the stairs. "Monét, Monét, Monét, Monét," he said, singing her name like it was a rendition of the O'Jay's seventies hit. "Nice to see you again. Looking beautiful, but I'm not surprised. My son has my taste."

"Thank you, Mr. Hartgrove. And I'm glad your son has your taste. Makes me a blessed woman."

"Call me Allen. No need to be proper around here."

This weekend wasn't going to be so painful after all, Monét thought. Allen reminded her a lot of her own father in personality. They were the kind of men who never met a stranger. Grocery store lines were the perfect place to talk politics, and for Allen there was probably also no such thing as calling to talk for a few minutes. Physically, however, James Sullivan had taken too many midnight trips to the refrigerator to compare to Allen's athletic physique. She could see where Jeremiah inherited his love for sports and physical fitness.

During lunch at the restaurant, Allen gave Monét the acceptance that Mrs. Hartgrove withheld. Jeremiah's mother didn't contribute much to any conversation until her son asked her about the party. Most of the women attending were from her sorority. Jeremiah had already informed Monét that his mother was a devoted member, but that happened to be after Monét had packed her red dress. Instead of church, Mrs. Hartgrove's Sunday mornings were usually scheduled for brunch with her sorority sisters or doubles with her tennis partner of six years.

Maybe by the time Monét's plane departed on Sunday evening, Mrs. Hartgrove would warm up to her. So far, even the smothering Houston heat wasn't enough to melt her cold shoulder toward Monét. How could Jeremiah actually think it was because she was irritated with Allen? It was obvious that Monét was the cause of her discontent.

Monét was relieved when Jeremiah volunteered to pick up his paternal grandmother from the community's assisted living home. She'd rather do anything besides suffer through another forced conversation with Mrs. Hartgrove.

Grandma Geraldine—or GiGi as Jeremiah called her—spent every weekend with her son and daughter-in-law, he said. Jeremiah had mentioned on his last trip home during Christmas that her dementia was progressing.

"GiGi and Ma aren't exactly bosom buddies," Jeremiah said when they walked into the facility. He flipped open his wallet to show his identification to the security officer.

"Why am I not surprised?" *Did I just say that out loud?*

"It was a deserved comment. Mama hasn't been the easiest person to get along with today, but I know you'll grow to love her."

But will she ever grow to love me? Monét wanted to ask.

Mrs. Hartgrove had no justified reason to dislike Monét. She wasn't trying to live with her hands in Jeremiah's wallet; nor did she come with any children attached to her hip. The three-minute conversation they'd had at Zora and Preston's wedding wasn't long enough for her to build ill will against her. It was like there was some kind of invisible competition between them. Monét had heard about it before—a mother being attached to her only son and never thinking any other woman was good enough for him. What other reason could there be?

They stopped outside a door with a macramé cross hanging on a small nail. Wooden letters attached to it said *JESUS SAVES*.

Jeremiah tapped on the door that was cracked wide enough for Monét to see the edge of a black and white television.

"Come in."

"GiGi? It's Jeremiah," he said, poking his head through the crack.

"Sho nuff, that's you?" she asked, pushing herself up by the chair's armrests.

"Yes, ma'am. It's me." Jeremiah opened the door all the way. Monét could smell the scent of cinnamon potpourri and a wintergreen muscle soreness ointment.

"I thought your daddy said you'd moved 'way to Boston."

"Baltimore, GiGi. I came to see you before I left and then at Christmas. Remember?"

"That's right. Bossimore. Well, you're back now, I see. I know your daddy's glad you came on home. You staying back at your same place?"

"No, ma'am. I'm just in town visiting for the weekend," Jeremiah explained. "I'm coming to pick you up and take you to Dad's house. It's their anniversary party tomorrow."

"That's right. You know my mind's not as sharp as it used to be."

"You're all right, GiGi. I forget things sometimes too."

Like introducing me, Monét thought.

Jeremiah opened the closet door and took a yellow tote bag from a hook. Inside was a key that he used to unlock one of her dresser drawers. He winked at Monét as he dumped at least six prescription bottles into the tote.

Monét waited by the door until GiGi noticed her. When she did, the older woman's eyes brightened and cavernous dimples buried at the corners of her dentured smile.

"Come on in, sugar." GiGi beckoned Monét inside with her wrinkled fingers. "Don't you look nice? It's a blessing to see you again. You doin' all right?"

"Yes, ma'am." Monét didn't know whether she should address the fact that she'd never met this woman in her life. She'd never had experience with anyone suffering from dementia and didn't know if it was respectable to correct her.

GiGi steadied her rickety legs by holding on to the cherry-wood bedpost. She wrapped her free arm around Monét's waist. Like Monét's own grandmother, she smelled like she'd been marinating overnight in the complete bath gel set from the local drugstore, topped with two shakes of baby powder under her blouse.

"You're going to make such a beautiful bride. I can see the glory of the Lord all around you." GiGi circled a hand in front of Monét's face. She turned to Jeremiah. "You must be praying for her. I didn't see this same glow last time."

GiGi looked at her grandson.

"Y'all got a date yet? Just make sure it's not the same time as my television shows. I love watching those court television shows, you know. They got some real cute judges."

It finally hit Monét. *She thinks I'm the ex-fiancée.* Jeremiah came to her rescue.

"No, GiGi," he said, taking his grandmother's hand and helping her to a chair by the bedside so she could get her shoes. "This is my friend Monét from Baltimore. You've never met her before. This is her first time in Houston."

"Really, now? I'm sorry, sugar. These old eyes don't see like they used to. Not these natural eyes anyway. But my spiritual vision is perfect. It's on you. I see it on you," she said, repeating the waving motion she'd done earlier.

Jeremiah held his grandmother's hand while he locked her room door with a key attached to his personal set.

"What about her clothes?" Monét asked.

"She's got plenty of clothes and everything else at my parents' house."

GiGi sauntered down the hallway like a queen on parade, giving announcements and warnings to her hall mates as she passed each door.

"Behave yourself while I'm gone, Vivi."

"All right now, Willie."

"Did you all see Jeremiah? My grandson is home visiting from Brooklyn."

"Norma, be ready for Bible study when I get back."

GiGi stopped at the security desk. She took a peppermint out of her purse and handed it to the guard. "I'm his Sugar Mama," she said, laughing. She grabbed on to Monét's forearm. "Did I ever tell you I won the center's Miss Seasoned Saint beauty pageant at my church? They stopped having the competition after they crowned me. I guess they figured it wasn't any use because I'd probably win every time."

"That you would, GiGi." Monét laughed.

GiGi put one hand on her waist and tried to swivel her hips.

"Whew. Lord knows I need to stop before I throw my hip out again."

GiGi was full of enough animation and questions for Monét to host her own daytime talk show. She was as sweet as the peppermint on her breath; however, some of her lively chatter subsided when she got into the presence of her daughter-in-law.

Monét wondered what was going on between the two. She'd planned to ask Jeremiah later, if he didn't bring it up. Every family had their dysfunction, and this seemed to be the thorn in the flesh for the Hartgrove women.

monét

Although Monét felt more comfortable staying the week-end at the hotel, she didn't want to bother Jeremiah to take her back to her room so she could catch a nap. She wanted to rest before Jeremiah pulled her out of the house for the rest of his self-guided tour of Houston. He loved Houston to the point that Monét couldn't help but wonder if he had intentions to move back in the future. He'd said he didn't know where God would lead him down the road. He just had to be prepared to follow.

But what if they got married? Monét would have to submit to her husband's decision. She wasn't a Southern type of girl. She liked living close to the nation's capital and having access to the Big Apple for a shopping spree by a short four-hour drive. The one time Jeremiah had gone with her, he couldn't wait to leave New York City, saying it was too loud and polluted.

"Hey, girl." Monét had waited all day to check in with Zora. Although she was more concerned with her best friend's state of mind, she knew Zora couldn't wait to see how the day was going.

"Took you long enough to call," Zora said. "I thought maybe you'd call last night."

"I should've called you last night to get some prayer. Mrs. Hartgrove is a trip." Monét lowered her voice when she thought she heard someone in the hallway. She heard what she thought was the hall bathroom door close, then continued. "It's evident that she's not very happy that I'm here."

Zora sighed. "You're probably blowing things out of proportion. I can bet you're looking for something to be wrong."

"Trust me when I tell you it's not me."

"Give her some time. She'll come around."

"Maybe. But if she doesn't, at least I've got two people on my team. His dad and grandmother are as nice as they can be. Allen's been treating me like a queen since I walked in."

"Evidently you've impressed him if you two are on a first-name basis."

"Well, I'll keep you updated on the rest of the weekend." Monét picked up a baseball VIP trophy with Jeremiah's name and high school engraved on it. "I really called to check on you."

"I'm doing better," Zora said. "I never thought something would shake me up like this."

"It's different when you experience a news story instead of watching it."

"Tell me about it. But I know God's going to get the glory out of it."

There was a light tap on the bedroom door. "Hold on a minute," she told Zora. She covered her hand over her cell phone's receiver. "Come in."

Jeremiah walked in and closed the door behind him.

"Are you crazy?" Monét asked. "Open that door before your mama thinks there's something going on in here. She already doesn't like me."

"Stop saying that," Jeremiah said, opening the door.

"It's true," Monét said, putting the phone back to her ear.

"Let me go. Somebody just came in to pester me."

"I knew you came up here to check in with Zora. Acting like you're so tired," Jeremiah said, shoving her hard enough to make her tip over. He pressed his head to the side of Monét's so that her cell phone was sandwiched between their ears.

"Hey, First Lady," Jeremiah said.

"So she's got you saying that too?"

"No need to run from the calling." Jeremiah rubbed Monét's arm, then slid his fingers between hers. He kissed her knuckles. "I'm loving what God is doing in my life right now," he said. Jeremiah leaned over on Monét. "I wouldn't trade His blessings for the world."

Monét poked him in the side. "Get up," she whispered.

"My parents are downstairs. We're not doing anything."

"You better not be," Zora warned.

"Don't worry about that, Zora," Jeremiah said. "I did it wrong so many times that I wouldn't dare disappoint God by messing things up with Monét."

Jeremiah slid the phone out of Monét's hands before she could protest.

"Monét's gotta go now," he told Zora. "I'm taking good care of her. You need to start getting used to that."

Monét couldn't hear what Zora was saying from the other side, but when Jeremiah burst out laughing she knew she needed to end the conversation. They weren't going to talk about her without her getting the chance to defend herself.

"Bye, Zora," she said.

Jeremiah held Monét back at arm's length, blocking her from getting to the phone.

"Hang up the phone, Zora," she said. Monét made a quick dive so she could snatch the phone. Jeremiah fell backwards, and she landed on his chest, the phone still out of her reach.

"You better give it to me, boy," Monét said.

"Excuse me?" Mrs. Hartgrove stood at the door, and she didn't look the least bit pleased.

Oh no. This can't look good.

"Hey, Ma."

Monét pushed herself off of Jeremiah's chest, but he didn't bother to sit up. Monét tried to smooth out her clothes, but her linen sundress looked crumpled beyond anything her hands could repair. It was a good thing she had a change of clothes in the trunk of the rental car.

"Your father wants you. He's out in the garage. You should probably go. Now."

Monét's face was burning with embarrassment. She didn't know what to say, or whether she should laugh it off. Either way, she knew she had another strike against her.

"Okay. I'm on my way," Jeremiah said.

His mother walked away, but not before pushing the door wide open.

"Get whatever you're thinking out of your head," Jeremiah said.

"I wasn't going to say a word."

"Go ahead and catch a nap before we go out."

"Never sounded better," she said, pulling off her sandals and setting them beside a nightstand decorated with Jeremiah's high school graduation picture. *Maybe I'll wake up out of this mother-in-law nightmare.*

monét

Her dress was cute and classy wrapped up in one, Monét thought, looking at herself in the hotel mirror. Preston would be back upstairs any minute to get her so that they could go down to the hotel ballroom.

She knew the hotel had been a bit on the pricey side, but Preston had wanted her to stay in the same place where the anniversary soiree was being held. Tonight she was thankful. She'd be able to slip away and come relax in the Jacuzzi if she needed an escape for any reason.

Mrs. Hartgrove's attitude toward her had improved today, albeit slightly. Monét attributed it to the extra attention Allen had given his wife all morning. When they'd gone to Jeremiah's parents' house after enjoying brunch at a Houston hot spot called The Breakfast Klub, there was a crystal vase with one dozen red roses awaiting her in the foyer. Another peach bouquet on the dining room table welcomed her and yet another bunch of yellow buds on the fireplace mantle. With each vase, he'd written a card listing reasons why he loved her, so that she ended up with thirty reasons to signify the thirty-five years they'd been united.

"Now you see where I get my mack from," Jeremiah had said once his parents had slipped away upstairs, supposedly to change their clothes.

"Oh, is that what you call it?" Monét asked. She leaned her head against his shoulder. The oversized couch felt as comfortable as a king-sized bed, and before she knew it, she'd drifted into a sleep full of dreams.

Monét could hear the waves lapping at the shore and smell the salt of the sea when the breeze blew through. She was standing under an ivy-wrapped gazebo, and turned to see her parents and a handful of family and friends at the bottom of the gazebo steps. Josephine Sullivan dabbed under her eyes, holding on to her husband's arms for support. Monét had been able to contain her own tears until she saw her mother's face.

". . . to cherish and continually bestow upon her your heart's deepest devotion, forsaking all others, keep yourself only unto her as long as you both shall live?" The minister looked in the direction of the groom, and Monét turned toward her future husband.

Someone shook her shoulder. Monét opened her eyes.

"I do," Jeremiah said.

Monét rubbed her eyelids until the blur in front of her cleared.

"Wake up, baby," Jeremiah said.

"Did you say, 'I do'?" Monét asked, sitting up.

"Yes. Dad asked us if anybody wanted one of his homemade smoothies."

"Oh."

That dream was too real.

Now here she was standing in this white dress that she'd found at the mall yesterday afternoon.

Should I put on the red one?

Monét clasped a rhinestone barrette on the side of her coif just as she heard a knock on the door. There wasn't time to change, even if she wanted to.

"It's me," Jeremiah said through the closed door.

"Me, who?"

"I brought you all the way to Texas; you better know who it is."

Monét opened the door and knew immediately that Jeremiah wouldn't be walking her upstairs late tonight after the party. He looked too good to put herself in the position to make an immoral choice. Suited in a tuxedo, he literally looked too good for words.

"You might have to walk yourself upstairs after the party," Jeremiah said, coming in and closing the door behind him. "I don't know if a brother can handle it."

"Let's go." Monét gave him a flirtatious smile. They thought so much alike.

Downstairs was amazing. Monét had to admit it. Mrs. Hartgrove looked stunning. Age had taken a backseat to her youthful beauty. Looking at her tonight, a stranger wouldn't have guessed that she was fifty-eight years old. Monét's mother had always said that you could tell when a woman had a good man, because she wore the proof of it on her face. Allen looked proud to have his wife on his arm, but he was no small catch himself. Monét was looking at Jeremiah twenty-eight years from now.

The live band on stage ended their slow groove and kicked it up a notch. Jeremiah took her hand and wove her through the tables, stopping to welcome, thank, and hug his parents' guests. He never let her from his grasp, and she didn't want him to.

Most of the women were dressed in varying shades of pink or the occasional black dress or pantsuit.

"You didn't tell me I was supposed to wear pink."

"You weren't. My mother's sorors always have to represent."

"I see," Monét said. The women clustered together looked like a bed of newly bloomed roses.

Another arm wrapped around Jeremiah as they made their way to one of the reserved front tables.

"I know you weren't going to walk by and not speak to me." Full red lips plastered an imprint on Jeremiah's cheek.

That makes a nice accessory, Monét thought to herself.

"Jane, you know I wouldn't do that. I didn't see you." He kissed her cheek. "And I don't know how I could've missed somebody looking as good as you do."

She looked at Monét. "Because you're holding on to someone half my age and twice as beautiful."

"Jane, this is Monét Sullivan. Monét, this is Jane Wallington, my godmother and the woman who helped put this all together."

At first, Jane shook Monét's hand so tenderly, as if it would snap at the wrist. Monét resisted her tendency to put the corporate clamp on her. Unexpectedly, Jane leaned toward her, and Monét thought she'd have a lipstick stamp matching Preston's. Instead, she pressed her cheeks on either side of Monét's face and kissed the air.

"Nice to meet you, Jane."

"You too, sweetheart. You two have a nice time. I'll see you before the night is out." Jane looked around Jeremiah's shoulder, then back toward the ballroom entrance. "I need to go find my husband. He's so wild when I finally let him come out of the house." She laughed. "I'm just kidding."

Monét and Jeremiah finally got to the table, and Monét sat down beside GiGi, who was wearing a tightly curled wig and black pant suit with sequins around the collar of the jacket.

"Sure is loud in here," she said to Monét. "I can't hear as it is." She spoke too loud for ordinary conversation, but Monét enjoyed the talks with her nonetheless.

"They say you're not supposed to have favorites, but Jeremiah is my favorite. He used to always want to go with me. And I let him," she said, jabbing a crooked pointer finger in the air. "I taught him the ways of the Lord. Taught his daddy too, even though he'd rather sleep in than get up and go to church."

People on the dance floor and buzzing around the open areas

moved to the tables when the waiters started placing garden salads at the tables.

"I hope they give us more than this rabbit food," GiGi said as the waitress reached over her shoulder. "I wouldn't mind having a pork chop tonight."

Monét scooted her chair closer to the table. "I have a feeling that's not going to be on the menu, GiGi."

GiGi stabbed the lettuce. "Can you cook? 'Cause Jeremiah loves to eat."

"I can, but I don't do it as much as I should." Truth was, Jeremiah was a true carnivore. He didn't like a meal to pass without meat, but Monét was satisfied with a salad or veggie plate. In fact, she was still detoxing her body by eating only fresh fruits, vegetables, and baked fish. It felt great, and she'd seen a considerable increase in her energy.

Jeremiah slid onto the chair beside Monét. He hung his jacket on the back of the chair.

"GiGi. I wouldn't mind eating some of your smothered pork chops. I hadn't had any in a long time."

GiGi patted Monét's shoulder. "Told you that's my baby, Monica."

Monica?

Jeremiah corrected her, but GiGi was already gone to her next topic and had reeled in a man sitting beside her.

When a six-foot beauty sat down at the table, GiGi's memory seemed to snap into perfect order. "She ain't got no business sitting at this table. Some things are messy, and I don't like mess," GiGi whispered.

Jeremiah whispered to Monét from the other side. "Erica."

Jeremiah's ex-fiancée.

If she smiles any wider at Jeremiah her face is gonna crack, Monét thought.

"Hey, Jay." She beamed. Everything about her shone—her silky hair, glossy lips, and the body shimmer across her chest that was revealed by the off-the-shoulder top she wore. No surprise. It was pink.

"How are you doing?" Jeremiah said.

She stood like she expected him to come over and dip her over in a loving embrace.

Mrs. Hartgrove appeared on cue. "I thought you two could catch up." Jeremiah's mother hugged Erica like she was the daughter she never had. "I'm so glad you were able to come. I had to threaten her so she wouldn't go to work. She works so hard."

Too hard at work. Which is one of the many reasons why the relationship didn't work in the first place. Monét knew the story. She and Jeremiah had divulged the former problems that had made their past relationships fail.

"Don't forget the chapter is having a tea next week," Mrs. Hartgrove said to Erica.

"I'll definitely be there. Call me. Maybe we can go shopping afterwards."

Jeremiah mumbled something under his breath that Monét couldn't make out. "We can move if you want to," he suggested.

"No need. I'm fine. You had your time to deal with Bryce."

One time too many, but Jeremiah never let Bryce's presence shake him, even when he showed up at her house unannounced after one of the auction fund-raisers she'd put on for Dr. Manns's foundation.

"Definitely. I came to congratulate Monét, but it looks like she's already having a victory party."

Monét finally found her voice. "Thank you. And now that you've done that, I'll let you out."

Bryce wasn't shaken by her coldness. She didn't expect him to be. He was used to it.

"Am I missing the party in here?" Unaware of the room's tension, Jeremiah joined them in the kitchen. "Bryant, right?"

"Bryce. Mr. Bryce Coleman."

Mister?

"Jeremiah Hartgrove," he reminded him.

"You're the lucky man who's stealing Monét's heart from me?"

Monét sensed that Jeremiah had picked up on the tension.

308

It was probably by the way everyone froze like they were about to watch a ringside event.

Jeremiah laughed.

Monét caught the look he threw at Preston.

*"We just met today, so I haven't had the chance to try. Yet."
Jeremiah pulled out a seat at the kitchen table and sat down, propping one ankle across the other knee. "And I don't believe in luck."*

The teakettle whistled. It was a high-pitched shrill that matched Monét's scream inside. She turned to cut off the stove eye. It must have also been an alarm to Bryce.

"I'll give you a call tomorrow," Bryce said to Monét.

Bryce left, and one would think that Jeremiah would've walked out that night with no intention of getting involved in Monét's drama. Jeremiah had the charisma to woo her over the phone from miles away. Even though she'd been spending all of her time with Bryce, part of her heart had wanted Jeremiah. The day she ran into him during one of his weekend trips to Baltimore, she thought she'd lost him.

Bryce picked up her hand and pressed it to his lips. He moved from her cheek, and then to her lips. Monét's face grew flush. If his mother walked in on this scene their next stop would be the bridal boutique. She looked over at Mr. Coleman, who was preoccupied with tying his shoe. The only person who seemed to notice them was Jeremiah.

Jeremiah?

If it wasn't him, Monét had discovered the identical twin that everyone in the world is thought to have. Jeremiah moved in her direction, confirming her suspicions. He looked better than she remembered.

"I thought that was you," he said.

Bryce stepped up like the question had been directed to him. "Preston's friend, right? Justin?"

"Jeremiah."

"That's right. My bad," Bryce said, putting an arm around

Monét's shoulder. "So the lure of Maryland's history brought you all the way from Houston?"

Monét knew Bryce was trying to play Jeremiah. How was it that he couldn't remember his name, but he could remember where he lived?

"Work has me here."

Why is this awkward?

Your heart knows why.

Monét swallowed the lump in her throat and took an inconspicuous step to her right. Bryce's arm didn't budge. I'm not committed to either of them. I'm a free woman, *she thought.* There's no reason for me to feel this way.

She had to say something. It was rude for her to just stand there.

"Who did you come with?" *She looked around for Preston. As far as she knew, he was the only person Jeremiah really knew in this area besides a handful of business associates.*

"I'm here by myself. I didn't have anybody who wanted to roll with me."

Did he have to say that?

Jeremiah's eyes didn't leave hers. She didn't want them to. What she wanted was to walk out of the door with Jeremiah and leave Bryce there to deal with his mother and her shattered dreams.

"Have fun, bro," Bryce said, massaging Monét's shoulder. His hand traveled to the small of her back and rested on her waist.

"Maybe I'll talk to you later, Monét."

Why did he have to say maybe?

Jeremiah's intense gaze stayed with Monét from the moment he walked away.

Thankfully, he'd walked back into her life, and Monét wasn't going to let anyone drive her away now.

"This is my girlfriend, Monét," Jeremiah said to Erica. "She came down with me from Baltimore."

"Good to put a name with a face," Erica said. "Cheryl told me about you."

First-name basis? "Oh, okay." It was all Monét could say. She could only imagine the information Mrs. Hartgrove passed to "the ex," seeing that she didn't care to know much about Monét besides her name.

The table centerpiece made it hard for Erica to hold any meaningful conversations with Jeremiah. GiGi was a key defensive lineman, blocking Erica from reaching her goal line, aka Jeremiah.

Being at the posh event made Monét think about Savon's fund-raiser and the other projects she had in the works. Instead of listening to the toasts and dedications after dinner, Monét was stealing ideas that she wanted to duplicate, and reworking others that she would've done differently. Savon had a slew of projects lined up for her. He had the contacts and she had the skills to build a premier event planning and consulting business in the Baltimore and D.C. areas.

By the time dessert was on the table, a slight pain rolled across her midsection. A few minutes later, the cramp was too painful for her to ignore. The spicy chicken she'd eaten at dinner hadn't shown her any mercy. She should've known better than to eat the entire meal after being on fresh foods for so long.

Monét leaned over to Jeremiah. "I'll be back in a few minutes."

"How long? I've got a surprise for my parents."

"Give me ten minutes." Monét tucked her clutch purse under her arm, scrounged up enough change to buy a pack of antacid tablets from the gift shop, and squeezed onto the first available elevator and rode it to her eighth-floor room. She turned on the small bedside lamp, chewed two tablets, then lay down, praying they were fast-acting. It seemed her tiredness was more potent than the tablets. Ten minutes had passed the first time she forced her eyes open: 7:50. Sleep fought back with her.

Five more minutes, she told herself.

Monét woke up a few minutes later. Or at least that's what she thought.

311

It was 8:20.

Monét jumped up and checked herself in the mirror. She found her room key card and shoved it into her purse. *Jeremiah didn't even come get me.* When she walked back into the ballroom, she knew why.

The music was bumping, and so was the majority of Erica's body. With Jeremiah. He had his hands up in the air like the eighties flashback hits had taken over his body and his brain.

No, he's not getting his groove on with her. Monét was angry enough to go upstairs for the rest of the night, but that's what Erica and Mrs. Hartgrove would've wanted her to do.

GiGi and the waiters seemed to be the only people not on the dance floor. Monét pulled out the chair beside her. She tapped her foot under the table, a gesture she often did when she had built-up anger.

Until Monét felt GiGi's soft hand touch hers under the tablecloth, Monét didn't realize she'd been clutching her purse so tightly. "Don't you worry nothing about what you see. That ain't faith."

Hmmm . . . how ironic that was the same thing she'd told Paula.

Erica turned her backside to Jeremiah. She backed up closer, and closer, until Jeremiah put his hands on her shoulders and turned her around. *At least he has some shred of respect for me.*

"His mama nearly pulled him out of that seat to go and dance with that girl. You know Jeremiah is not a man to make a scene, so he went. He's just having fun, and it's got nothing to do with that girl. She's not the one." GiGi nodded. "You are."

Jeremiah looked to the table and saw Monét. He said something to Erica, then left her standing on the dance floor.

"You looked like you were having a good time," she said when Jeremiah sat down beside her. "Please. Don't let me stop you."

"I know you're not mad," Jeremiah said in low voice. "I was just dancing."

Monét didn't respond.

"You could've at least come and checked on me," she said, after giving him the silent treatment through two of the band's songs. "I wasn't feeling well."

"How was I supposed to know that?" Jeremiah said. "All you said was that you'd be back in a few minutes."

"After thirty minutes it seems you would've come to see what was going on."

"I didn't realize it had been that long. I was enjoying the salutes to my parents, and until now, I'd been enjoying the night."

"Oh, I saw that with my own eyes."

Jeremiah grabbed her hand. "Don't do this. You're looking for a reason to get mad about something. You know Erica is the last person on my mind." He slid his chair closer to her. "You need to let me love you like you deserve," he said. "And that's got nothing to do with getting you in bed."

paula

Paula walked out onto the back deck with Gabrielle wrapped close to her in a baby sling. When Micah was four months old, he was content to let the swing do the rocking instead of Paula's arms. Not Gabrielle. She wanted to be a girl on the go. It was Rosanna's fault for spoiling her granddaughter like she did.

Rosanna stuck her head out of the double French doors that opened to the deck. "Where's Micah's golf clubs? I can't find nothing in this house. It's too many rooms for three and a half people."

Paula hadn't heard her complain about having the entire finished basement to herself. "Look in his playroom, the first door on the left past my office. He probably took them in there."

Rosanna held her hands out for Gabrielle. "Give me my baby. She needs to know where the rooms are around her house so she won't get lost."

Paula handed Gabrielle to her mother. Gabrielle was a lot chubbier than Micah had been at her age. Her arms and legs were so plump that it looked like the bends had pieces of strings pulled tight to hold them together.

Paula sat down and flexed her legs, letting the stretch move from her toes up her thighs. It felt good to be home. For the past three days she'd felt her life shifting back to its normalcy. It would take some time to build the trust back, but it was possible. With God, all things were.

Delores had flown back to Chicago two days earlier with plans to return in a week. Until then, Rosanna—at her own suggestion—had come to Paula's house to take care of her grandchildren. The last time she'd come to stay over and help out, Micah had been three weeks old.

"I can handle it, Ma," Paula had told her over the phone on Sunday night. She could, but she didn't want to. "I don't want to inconvenience you. You've got your own life."

"If I didn't want to come, I wouldn't. You need to take care of your husband. Build a marriage that will last forever. It's something I could never do." Rosanna smacked her lips. "Besides, God had to give Darryl a near-death experience for him to come to his senses."

Paula had dropped off her mother-in-law and picked up her mother all within forty-five minutes, praying the entire way home. So far, so good. Darryl and her mother hadn't exchanged cross words once. Belinda had told Paula to create the atmosphere for a miracle—to pray around the house, fill the room with praise and worship music, and take all the Bibles she had and leave them open in rooms around the house.

This morning was the first time since Darryl had come home from the hospital that Paula had been able to escape for her morning power walk exercises. After a breakfast of peaches and cottage cheese, Paula went upstairs to the bedroom to change into her exercise gear.

"You got everything you need for now?" she asked Darryl. His empty breakfast plate sat on the tray beside him. "I'm all right. Good and full."

Paula stepped out of her turquoise nightgown. "Good. I'm going to go for a walk for a while, but Mama is downstairs. If you need something before I get back, buzz her on the intercom."

Darryl flipped one page of his medical journal. Paula still felt him watching her when she changed her undergarments.

"What's wrong?" She stuck her arms through the arm holes of a fitted microfiber tank.

"Nothing." He flipped another page, then looked back up. "Your body looks good."

"Thank you." It felt like he'd just walked in the door on their first date. Her heart fluttered while he examined her curves.

Paula purposely moved slowly while she put on the rest of her clothes. *He might as well get a look at the buffet he's been missing.* She fed his growing desire for her. It was in there somewhere. She knew it, because she felt her own desire to be with him flicker deep inside.

Darryl pushed the covers off of his legs. He was still in his pajama bottoms, although he wore no shirt. "Paula, don't leave," he said.

"I'll be back in thirty minutes."

"No, I mean, don't leave me. Never again. I couldn't stand it if you walked out on me again."

Paula sat down on the edge of the bed. The conversation was going to happen sooner or later. They'd never talked about the night she left. They hadn't tried together to save their marriage. She sat down on the edge of the bed and shoved her foot into her running shoe. She tied her laces so tight that her foot immediately began to throb.

"If you were that hurt you would've come after me. So why didn't you?" Her foot thudded as it hit the floor.

"Pride. Stupidity."

Paula stood. "You call it pride and stupidity. I call it another woman. Diane? Yeah, I know her name too. And she admitted it, so don't try to deny a thing." She began to pace back and forth in front of the bed. "While you were in the hospital dealing with your pain, I was dealing with the source of mine. The only difference is that nobody could pump painkillers into my system so I wouldn't feel it," she said. Her tears began to flow.

317

Silence.

Here they were—dealing with the shadow that had stolen the sunshine from their marriage—and Darryl had nothing to say. Her emotions were having a battle. Thankfulness that he finally seemed to see her worth. Hurt that he'd found comfort with another woman. Anger. Regret. Relief.

"I'm sorry," Darryl finally said. "I never meant for it to happen."

"It? What is *it*?" As she cried, she felt herself being cleansed.

"The relationship with her." He didn't even say her name. "I'm sorry."

Darryl had never looked so vulnerable, so helpless.

"Sorry is not enough. You had an affair, Darryl, and you act like you're apologizing for stepping on my foot."

He tried to sit up higher on the bed, but he didn't have enough strength to maneuver his entire body.

"Don't you have anything to say?" Paula flailed her hand in the air. Each moment was stirring up her anger, and she didn't want to feel like this.

Love covers a multitude of sins.

"I didn't sleep with her. I didn't have an affair."

It was the same thing she'd said.

"She didn't want to break her marriage vows."

"Oh. So that's the only reason you didn't sleep with her? If you're telling the truth about that." Paula knelt down beside the bed and buried her face in her hands. The anguish bearing down on her was too much for her to bear.

Cast your cares on Me. This won't be easy, but it will be worth it.

Paula tried to calm her breathing. She should've left the house when she had the chance. Maybe she should leave now. It might help to get out in the air and clear her head. Maybe not. If she went outside she might run—and never come back.

Paula breathed in through her nose and out through her mouth. "Affairs don't have to be physical," Paula said, between her sobbing. She pronounced each word slowly, as if English were Darryl's second language. "Affairs are emotional too."

"What can I do to show you I care? To show you I'm sorry? I want to make this work."

Paula gripped her scalp through a mass of thick curls. "This could be an act until you get better, and then you'll be back to the same mess," Paula said. "How do I know you're being real?"

"I guess you don't until I show you." There was one tear, hanging on to the corner of his eye. It trickled down his scruffy face. "When that truck slammed into me, you were the first and only person I thought about."

Paula wanted to believe him, but there was already so much distrust between them. She took another breath through her nose. She needed to know.

"I need to know the truth. Everything."

Darryl looked hesitant. She could tell he wanted to start over without looking back.

"It can't hurt any worse than it already does." *I hope.*

With every word Darryl spoke, Paula prayed for strength. How could her heart want two things at the same time? To love him . . . and to leave him.

"Diane worked at the hospital, so I ran into her all the time, usually in the cafeteria. One day I went down for lunch and she was sitting at one of the only empty tables. We started venting about problems at the hospital, and soon after that her husband had to go overseas."

Paula wondered what she had been doing on the days this was going on. There was no way to know if she'd been cooking a special dinner for him. Taking his son out for lunch. Planning one of his events. Had the door opened to this relationship on one of the mornings they'd had a fight and not resolved their anger?

"I felt like I was growing apart from you," Darryl said. "I didn't feel like you supported me. But Diane"—Darryl looked away—"she seemed excited about the ventures I wanted to try."

It looked hard for Darryl to continue. "We slept in the same bed, if you call that sleeping together, and there were a few intimate moments—which I know shouldn't have happened—but we never had sex. Never."

Paula knelt at the edge of the bed and buried her face in the comforter, not knowing what else to do or what else to say. After a few moments, she picked up her pedometer and clipped it to her waist, ignoring the ringing of her cell phone on the dresser. She didn't want to hear anyone's voice right now. Not even Darryl's.

"I'll be back," she said, taking the stairs by twos. She opened the front door. She suddenly felt free. Paula didn't walk—she ran until the heat and her fatigue dried out her mouth, but her eyes overflowed with tears.

Paula was sitting on the edge of the curb when she saw her own car coming toward her. If her mother was leaving to take Micah to camp, Paula had been out of the house for at least forty-five minutes. Her car slowed to a stop, and Rosanna leaned out of the window.

"What's wrong with you?"

"Nothing. Just thinking."

Rosanna looked at her with doubtful eyes. She made a U-turn, then pulled the car against the curb. "Micah, sit right here for Grandma," she said, opening the door. "Watch your sister."

Rosanna leaned against the back bumper. Paula didn't think Rosanna realized that she had a pink burp cloth hanging over her shoulder.

"I don't know what's going on, and it's really not my business." She slid her foot in and out of her bedroom shoe. "But it is my business as a mother to tell you you've got to make a decision. Your children don't need to see you like this—always crying, going back and forth. They can feel things."

Paula wiped her face with the bottom of her shirt.

"If you're gonna leave, leave. Go ahead and get it over with so you can start a fresh life.

A fresh life. It's not that easy.

"If you're gonna stay, stay," Rosanna went on.

She heard another voice over her mother's.

Stay.

monét

Monét collapsed into the section of folding chairs that the logistics crew hadn't started to break down. Exhilaration had carried her through the four-hour event, but now that it was over, her body and mind were giving in to sleep.

Normally she'd work the events she coordinated wearing comfortable shoes. Tonight was different. High and trendy fashion was on the minds of everyone there, and Monét literally wanted to put her best foot forward. Never again.

"Baltimore has never seen an event like that one," Savon said.

Monét had a feeling he was more thrilled about the number of women who jockeyed for the position on his arm for the night. Instead of committing to one, he'd rotated through them, and they seemed satisfied for the few minutes he afforded them.

"I think you're exaggerating," Monét said.

"Maybe a little." He pulled off his linen jacket that was a shade of brown lighter than his mocha-colored skin. "I've got to do what I have to do to charm you into what I want."

"Charm me?"

"Yes." Savon hung his jacket on the back of the chair and sat beside Monét. "I need you as my assistant, my right-hand woman."

"I don't know, Savon. I thought about it, but I don't want to be tied down and not have the opportunity to work on the events that I want to do."

"You saw how it went down tonight." Savon put his hand on Monét's knee.

She swept it off.

"You heard what the people were saying, baby girl." He rubbed Monét's shoulder. "We're a good team."

Monét lifted his hand off of her. "I can't do it."

Monét had put a lot of things into perspective. She had other things to consider. Or more like other people. Jeremiah had expressed his opinion on her working with Savon, and although he'd never pressured her into doing what he wanted her to do, Monét couldn't help but think about what would be the best for her and Jeremiah's relationship.

"It's your boyfriend, isn't it? He's intimidated by a man like me." Savon traced his fingers around his goatee.

"Don't fool yourself," Monét said. "But I am thinking about what I would want him to do if our situations were reversed." She held her two hands up like it was a balancing scale. "On one hand you've got a great business opportunity, and on the other you've got a potential partner who'll probably continue to try to cross the line of a business relationship."

Savon licked his lips. "I'm just trying to offer you a friendship with benefits," he said. "Know what I mean?"

He'd gone too far. Monét stood up. "The only benefit I need right now is my final check," she said, holding out her hand.

Savon reached into his back pocket and slapped an envelope into her hand.

"Thank you," she said. "I'm so blessed to have a man like Jeremiah. He would never be so disrespectful to a woman."

"You don't know what you're going to miss," Savon said.

Jeremiah walked back through the doors, his godly spirit and gentlemanly demeanor taking over the empty room.

"But I do know what I'm going to gain," she said.

"Everything's loaded up," Jeremiah said. "You ready?"

"I'm ready," she said, putting her hand in his. "More than ready."

After returning from Houston, they'd agreed to attend the next premarital counseling sessions at church before any type of official marriage proposal was done. In three weeks, they'd be in the class with other couples who were hoping to take their relationships to the next level. Word had traveled around the church that not all couples' relationships lasted after attending the intense, but beneficial, sessions. However, Monét had a feeling that she and Jeremiah were destined for forever.

paula

Paula didn't answer calls to her cell phone if she didn't recognize the number. It was the fourth time this week she'd received a call from the same number, and the first three times the caller didn't leave a message. To Paula, no message equaled no importance.

"Why don't you answer the phone?" Rosanna asked. She was wearing a new outfit that Paula had bought her. Paula was tired of seeing her rotate different shirts with her same tired set of jean skirts and khaki pants.

"Answer it," Rosanna fussed. "If they keep calling they must really need to talk to you."

Paula gave in.

"Hello, this is Paula," she said.

"Paula Gilmer Manns?" a woman's voice asked.

"Yes." Who would be asking for her using her maiden and married name?

"Oh, thank You, Jesus," the woman said. Her voice dropped to a whisper. "Can you hold on a minute?"

"Yes, I'll hold."

The woman pleaded again. "Please don't hang up."

"I won't." *What in the world?* If this was someone contacting her for Diane or another woman coming for a confession, there were about to be some real problems. She and Darryl had agreed to attend marriage counseling, and she didn't need any situations sending them two steps back from the one step they'd taken.

Paula heard fumbling in the background and what sounded like the opening and closing of a door. The woman came back to the phone.

"This is Mary Raymond," she said. "Floyd's wife. You saw me the day you came to the shop and gave me the letter to give to . . ." she paused. "Your father." Mary cleared her throat. "I thought it was a check. I'm sorry. And I got your number off the letter," she explained.

"I remember you," Paula said, hoping Mary would move quickly to the reason for her call. She hoped Mary wasn't calling to slash open the wound that was starting to heal. Paula had already laid aside the disappointment about her father and planned to move on. She should've listened to her mother.

"I wanted to speak to you directly. I called a few times this week, but I didn't want to leave a message."

"I noticed that, but I usually don't answer numbers I don't recognize," Paula said, trying to keep her patience. *Get on with it, Mary.*

"I'm glad you did this time. I have something I think you'd like to see."

"What is it?"

"A letter."

Mary's answer was too simple for the urgency in her voice. "What kind of letter?"

Mary answered Paula's question with another one. "Can you meet me today?"

Paula's day was already planned. Gabrielle had a wellness

checkup at three o'clock, she needed to take care of the household bills, and Micah needed some more summer clothes. His legs seemed to be sprouting overnight.

"What time?" Paula asked. "I've got a lot going on today."

"What about now? Can you come now? I can meet you in thirty minutes at Mamie's Kitchen; that's down the street from the repair shop."

Paula looked at the clock on the microwave. It was ten thirty. "I'll meet you in an hour."

"I'll see you then," Mary said. "I've got to go take the mid-morning snack to the shop."

"So who was it?" Rosanna asked, licking mayonnaise from her fingers. Rosanna had made herself a sandwich, and Gabrielle's eyes were following the turkey sub from the table to her grandmother's mouth, and back again.

"A placement agency I'd called about getting a temporary nurse for Darryl," Paula said, feeling guilty about lying. She couldn't tell her mother she was meeting the wife of the man who'd jilted her. Not yet.

"Oh," Rosanna said. She sat Gabrielle in the swing beside the kitchen table. It was the first time Paula had seen the baby leave Rosanna's arms since they'd been up this morning.

"I need to run out, Ma," Paula said. "I'll be back before it's time to take Gabby to the doctor, but I might try to find some clothes for Micah while I'm out."

"That's fine," Rosanna said. She bit a chunk so large out of her sandwich that she had to wait until she swallowed it and followed it with a sip of water to talk. "Tell Darryl you're leaving or he'll keep calling you on that speaker thing and be driving me crazy."

"I'll tell him," Paula said, walking upstairs to get ready. She had a feeling that nothing would prepare her for what Mary had to say.

✢   ✢   ✢

Mary was waiting for Paula when she arrived. She was wearing another outfit with flowers that dwarfed her petite size. She stood when she saw Paula.

"Thank you for coming," she said.

"Thank you for calling me," Paula said. *I think.*

Although breakfast was over, Mamie's Kitchen still smelled like fresh buttermilk biscuits and bacon. Two construction workers were the only other patrons in the restaurant, and the syrup on their plates was the only sign of the meal they had eaten. A waitress walked over, picked up their plates, and refilled their coffee mugs.

Paula followed Mary to a table in the back corner, near the kitchen.

"Floyd doesn't know I'm meeting you," Mary said, shaking her head. "If he did it wouldn't be a happy day in our house for a very long time."

Paula looked out of the discolored windowpane. "Mary," she said, "don't feel like you have to build a relationship with me just because Floyd doesn't want to. I know he's my father, but he's probably going to deny it to the grave."

"Oh, I know too." Mary looked a little embarrassed to admit it, but she said, "Back in the day, Floyd was a rolling stone, if you know what I mean."

"I've heard."

"But when we got together he'd really settled down. When we decided to get married, he told me that he had a few children, but he also said he'd never had a relationship with them, and didn't plan to. If I was going to marry him, I had to accept this."

Mary looked apologetic. "So I did." She reached over for Paula's hand. "But I never stopped praying about it. Do you know the power of prayer?"

"Yes. And the power of love."

"Yes, yes," Mary said, closing her eyes and shaking her head like she'd been caught up in her favorite gospel hymn.

Where was the letter? Paula thought.

"Things have happened over the past month that Floyd hasn't been ready to face." She took Paula's letter out of her purse, and another letter with it. "He'd even kept it from me, but I believe it was the Lord who allowed me to find these in his work pants when I was sorting clothes to wash." She unfolded the letters and laid them on the table. "He's so absentminded that he probably doesn't realize he doesn't have them."

Paula looked at the letter. Hers was handwritten, but the other was typed and on official letterhead from the Maryland Department of Human Resources.

"This one," Mary said, pointing at the typed letter, "was sent to him by one of his old flames who moved back to New Jersey with her grandmother right after she got pregnant. Mildred was a teenager, and back then, children listened more to what their parents had to say than they do now. Her mother told her she had to give the baby up for adoption, so she did." Mary handed Paula the letter. "Evidently, Mildred is not ready to face her past, either."

What? Paula read the letter twice to make sure she wasn't seeing things. She picked up both of the letters and stuffed them in her purse. "Thank you," she said, tears flooding her eyes. "Thank you, Mary, and thank You, God." Paula waved her hands in the air. She was about to have church right up in Mamie's Kitchen.

Paula was running out the door when she realized she'd left Mary sitting there. She ran back to the woman who was having a praise party of her own. Paula kissed her smack dab in the middle of her head. "I'll call you, okay? I've gotta go."

Nobody was going to believe this.

ZORA

Paula had called to make sure Zora was home.

"Are you there? Don't leave. I'm on my way over." Paula hung up without an explanation, and less than forty-five minutes later she skidded into Zora's driveway like she was being chased by the law.

"What in the world is going on?" Zora asked, throwing the door open. She could hardly get the words out when Paula threw her arms around her neck. Her friend's jumping up and down triggered Zora's excitement, and she leaped with her.

Jump.

"What happened?"

Jump.

"Girl, stop and tell me."

Jump.

Paula stopped, but she'd been jumping so hard that her words were breathy. "Floyd's wife called and—"

"Who's Floyd?" Zora interrupted.

"My father. Anyway, Floyd's wife has been trying to call me all week." Paula seemed too worked up to get her words together. "I met her today." She took two letters out of her purse. "She gave me these."

Zora took the two letters that Paula shoved in her face. Evidently Zora was moving too slow. Paula yanked the letters back out of her hands and unfolded one of them.

"Just look at this one."

The letter was identical to the one that Zora had in her purse, sent by her mediator. "How did she get a copy of my letter? This doesn't make sense."

"Oh, it makes sense," Paula said. She'd dropped her purse on the floor and grabbed Zora's shoulders. "Floyd Raymond is your father. We're—"

Zora fell to her knees on the floor. "Sisters." She couldn't get her body to respond to what her brain was telling it to do.

Stand up, it said. She couldn't. Her legs were weak—much like they'd felt when she first found the letter that she was adopted. Only this time, she couldn't describe the emotions that came with it.

Paula knelt beside her. Then she let her friend lead her to the couch in the living room. Still in disbelief, Zora looked out of an open window. She heard clinking from the kitchen. The faucet running. Footsteps across the tile floor.

Paula handed her a glass of cold water. It slid down her parched throat. She took another long swallow, drinking it all.

"Are you all right?" Paula asked, sitting down beside her. The excitement she'd had earlier had dissipated and been replaced with concern. "I shouldn't have dropped it on you like that. I apologize."

"No," Zora rushed to say. "Don't be sorry." She grabbed her chest. "Now I know what shock feels like."

"Imagine how Floyd feels," Paula said. "I can't say I blame him for not welcoming me with open arms. It's a lot to handle."

Zora's favorite soap opera was on television, but she was distracted by her thoughts. Any time she tried to picture her biological father's face, she couldn't envision anyone but the man she'd always known as "Dad."

"What's Floyd look like?" she asked.

"He's a man's man, and you can tell he's been working on cars for years."

"Why? Grungy hands with oil under his nails?" Zora asked.

"Exactly," Paula said. "Couldn't even wash it out with dish detergent if you tried." She sat back and relaxed. "His hands are rough with calluses."

Zora subconsciously rubbed her hands together. "But what does he look like?" She wanted to hear everything and was depending on Paula to paint a vivid picture that she could carry in her mind.

"He's about Preston's height, but he's bigger. Probably about fifty pounds more. You can tell his wife feeds him good."

Zora shifted her body so Paula could see her face. She pushed her hair away from her face. "Do I look like him?"

"No," Paula said, quickly. "You must look like your mother. His nose is wider and his eyes are rounder than yours. Yours are more almond shaped."

Zora cupped Paula's chin in her hand and turned her head from side to side.

"What are you doing?"

"Seeing if we look anything alike?" Zora said.

Life as the only child had its advantages, but Zora had always wanted an older sister whom she looked like and could steal clothes from. Until their young adult tastes headed in two different directions, Zora was always playing clothes swap with Monét. The day Monét came home with a retro outfit from the consignment store, that had stopped.

"I could see how I might look like Floyd a little bit," Paula said. "The female version, of course. More hair. More curves."

Zora had to ask the next question. She should have been satisfied for the chance to have a relationship with a sibling, but there was nothing like a parent.

"Do you think he'll ever want to know us, not just know *about* us?"

333

"A couple of weeks ago I would've said no, and I wouldn't have cared." Paula shook her head. "But I've seen too many miracles happen in my life lately to not believe it is possible."

"I wish I could see him," Zora said.

"You can. He doesn't know what you look like."

"That's true." Zora could walk out of the door right now to see her father—talk to him, study his face—and he wouldn't even know it. "Let's go," she said. "Let's go right now."

"If that man sees me he'll run the other way." Paula looked at her watch. "I need to leave now anyway to go take Gabby to her doctor's appointment. Maybe you should wait until Preston can go with you."

"Oh, goodness. I didn't even call Preston." Zora picked up the telephone, then hung it up. "Then again, maybe I should wait. Surprise him when he gets home."

"Definitely wait." Paula stood up with her purse on her shoulder. "Let me get out of here, sis."

"Okay, sis. Call me tonight, sis."

They laughed, then embraced, holding each other as if they'd disappear into thin air if they let go.

"We were sisters in spirit long before we knew we were sisters by blood," Zora said.

"I love you," Paula said, and for the first time in a long time, she shed tears of joy.

"I love you too."

They held each other for another long moment before letting go. Tears trailed down their faces.

"There is one thing we have in common," Zora said. "We're always crying about something."

"This time it's worth it, though."

Zora walked Paula to her car. The grass looked greener, the sky's blue more vibrant. As a single cloud wafted by, being pushed by a slight breeze, Zora looked for its silver lining. Life was good.

belinda

Belinda steamed the wrinkles out of T.J.'s graduation gown. She hung it on the back of her bedroom door along with his starched black slacks and white dress shirt that she'd picked up from the cleaners. T.J. had taken one last shot at breaking the rules, but this time it wasn't a big deal. Belinda heard him talking about a possible plan to wear gym shorts with a white T-shirt and tie under the gown instead of the requested attire.

"Don't even think about doing whatever you're planning to do," Belinda had told him when he came down for dinner the night before.

"Huh?"

T.J. tried to look confused, but he came off looking guilty instead.

"Don't 'huh' me. You know exactly what I'm talking about."

"Nothing gets past you, Ma 'Linda," he said, scooping Hannah up out of her high chair. "Hopefully they'll be too old to be private investigators by the time you get old enough to try and be sneaky," he said to his little sister.

Belinda swatted T.J.'s shoulder with the dry cloth.

"Ouch," he yelled, rubbing his shoulder like the lick was harder than it truly was.

"Ouch," Hannah yelled. "Ouch, ouch, ouch," she said, before throwing her head back in a fit of laughter.

"You've been looking for a reason to hit me," T.J. said. He sat Hannah back in her high chair and helped Belinda set the table.

"Trust me, I didn't have to look hard. You've given me plenty of reasons to take a smack at your hard head."

T.J. put three dishes on the table and set out Hannah's plastic plate and bowl. "Why didn't you put me out? You could've convinced Dad to send me back to Pittsburgh. I know the power of a woman."

Belinda turned the stove eye down to a simmer. "I thought about it plenty of times, but I knew that ultimately you'd be better off here for now. I love you, T.J. And love endures through things that we normally would've given up on."

T.J. walked over and swooped Belinda up into a bear hug. He'd gotten so tall that her feet dangled above the floor.

"You're squeezing the life out of me," Belinda said, squirming to get loose.

"No, I'm squeezing some of the love you gave me back into you," T.J. said, laughing that Belinda couldn't break free of his strong arms.

Thomas entered the house from the garage door. "Now this is the kind of scene I like to see," he said, unbuttoning his work shirt. "Love in the air, smiles on faces, and food on the stove."

T.J. squeezed Belinda's waist harder and walked her over to her husband, letting her down onto Thomas's feet.

"Here's your woman, Dad. She's a good catch. You might want to keep her around for a while."

"Mmmmm," Thomas said, kissing her forehead, then both of her cheeks. "Forever is more like it." Thomas kissed her on the lips. "This tastes better to me than any food."

"I'm going upstairs," T.J. said, covering his eyes and shaking his head. "Call me when you're ready to eat."

Belinda rested her head on Thomas's chest. The trials they'd endured had served to strengthen their marriage, even though it had seemed it was breaking them apart. The day she'd come home to her expanded family, her heart had grown to make more room. Looking back, God had probably worked on her more than he had on T.J. God had shown her the true meaning of love.

Zora

Zora still felt like she was in a dream. Preston was just as bewildered as she'd been when she'd announced the news. "Paula is my sister. My biological sister."

"What are you talking about? Your friend Paula?" Preston asked.

"I couldn't believe it either," she said, then went into the story about how God had strategically brought them together. "I've got to go see Floyd. And you've got to go with me," she said last night. After she shared the news with her husband, she'd called her closest friends and listened to the screams of Monét and Belinda, who celebrated with her like it was the missing piece they'd been looking for in their own lives.

Now that Zora had the chance to see the missing piece, she was feeling anxious. "I can't eat this," she said, pushing away her breakfast of toast and grits the next morning. "Everything is making me nauseous."

"You're just nervous," Preston said. He began shoving what

she hadn't eaten into his mouth. "You'll be all right. He won't know it's you, remember?"

"One day he will." God had done this much. Zora had no doubt that they'd meet when the timing was perfect. God's timing.

"We'll cross that bridge when we get to it," Preston said. He poured orange juice into his glass until it was half full.

"I don't want to go anymore."

"I took a day off work. You're going," Preston said.

He'd had to comfort her during the entire drive across town to the Oil Pit and Repair Shop. Zora spotted Floyd immediately. He was just as Paula had described. She felt like Paula must've felt when she'd called them the first day she'd met him. Thankfully, Preston was there with Zora to help her out of the car. He practically had to pull her out.

"How're you doing, sir?" Preston said, walking up to the man Zora had pointed out. "Do you all do tires here?"

"We don't sell 'em, but we can patch one up until you can get you one. That your car out there?" he said, pointing to Preston's black Nissan Maxima.

"Yes, sir," Preston answered.

Zora stared at him. Paula definitely resembled their father the most, but Zora thought the most prominent feature she shared with him were his thin lips. She always had to create an upper lip with lip liner whenever she wanted to reproduce the pouty effect that Monét had taught her.

Her stomach churned, and before Zora knew it, she'd unloaded the small taste of breakfast she'd had that morning—directly on Floyd's steel-toed shoes.

"I'm sorry," she said, keeping her head down in embarrassment.

"Maybe I'll come back," Preston said to Floyd. "Thanks for your help. And sorry about the shoes."

"No problem," he said and chuckled. "Ain't nothing that can't be wiped off. Get your little lady home. Evidently, she's not feeling too well," he said, stomping his foot on the ground.

Zora reclined her seat once they'd gotten into the car. "Just get me home, baby," she said. "I need to lie down."

"You've been getting sick a lot lately, especially in the morning," Preston said. "Are you sure you're not pregnant?"

Zora strapped her seat belt. "I don't know," she said, not wanting to talk with the sour taste still in her mouth. "I think it's been nerves. First, it was the shooting at the school. Now this."

"I'm stopping by the drugstore on the way home," Preston said, easing over the bumpy pavement and onto the street. "My mama said she had a dream about you being pregnant, and she's never wrong about anything."

I don't know about that, Zora thought. She closed her eyes and slept until Preston awakened her. They were sitting in the driveway at home.

"We're home," he said, opening her car door. "Do you want me to go out and get you some crackers or ginger ale? I didn't think about it when I was in the store. I was too busy trying to find a pregnancy test," he said, holding up a small paper bag. "I didn't know they had so many options."

"I'm fine," she murmured. If she could have, Zora would've crawled inside the house. She made it to the bedroom and onto the bed. Preston unstrapped her sandals and eased them off of her feet.

"You wanna take the test before you lie down?" he asked, a look of hope on his face.

"Not really, but I will if you want me to." *He did.*

"It won't take long. The box says two minutes," he said, taking the carton out of the paper bag.

Zora went into the bathroom, and Preston followed her. "Do you mind?" she asked, easing the door together.

"What if I'm pregnant?" Zora said. The realization didn't hit her until she was unfolding the directions.

"I'm gonna take off running down the street," Preston said through the crack in the bathroom door.

After she finished, Zora walked out and left the test on the back of toilet. "They have tests where you don't have to wait two minutes," she said. "It would've shown up immediately."

"Aw man, I didn't see that one." He lingered by the bathroom door like he was scared to go in.

"It's already been one minute, baby." Zora said. "Be patient."

"Be patient? We could have a son on the way."

Zora sat on the edge of the bed. She'd always pictured a chubby round face with pink bows in a baby girl's hair. Girls were made for dressing up in coordinated outfits, not boys. Somebody had to get some use out of the new fashion sense she'd picked up. "What makes you think it would be a boy?"

"I don't care if it's a boy or a girl, as long as—"

"Hold on, baby. We don't even know if I'm pregnant yet." Zora's excitement was growing, and she didn't want her hopes dashed. She walked over to the bathroom door. "Are you ready?"

"Get the test."

Zora picked up the test but didn't look at it. She walked back into the bedroom with the indicator window covered with her hand. She wanted her and Preston to look at it together. She lifted her hand.

The blue positive sign was as clear as the picture on the box.

"Get out your running shoes," Zora squealed, her heart leaping. "We're having a baby."

paula

Paula had seen Mary Raymond twice since they'd met that morning at Mamie's Kitchen, even though they'd talked at least twice a week over the last month. Mary believed in the power of God and had been praying with Zora that Floyd would seek out his daughters on his own. She'd gotten the letters back from Paula and said she'd stuck them in Floyd's top drawer of the dresser where he kept all of his important papers.

"You just keep believing," Mary had told her.

Paula had an intimate talk with Rosanna the day she came back from Zora's house. At first her mother looked like she'd wanted to spit fire when Paula returned from having lunch with Mary. But Paula had calmed Rosanna down and reassured her that no one could take the place of her mother. She'd sacrificed her life to see that her children were taken care of the best that she could.

At Paula's urging, Rosanna had stayed at their house even after Delores had returned. When the grandmothers realized they didn't need to fight for their grandchildren's love or attention, they'd actually been able to live cordially in the same house. They'd even taken the children out together on the evening Paula and Darryl attended their first marriage counseling session. Today was their second.

Darryl eased his way down the steps. The doctors had advised him to take it slow, and Darryl complied, taking an extra two months of leave from work for his health and his family.

Diane had tried several times to contact Darryl, but every time God had seen to it that Paula intervened in her attempts. Finally, they'd changed their home number, Darryl's cell, and had the hospital issue Darryl a new pager. Paula realized that she wouldn't be able to watch Darryl's every move once he returned to work at the hospital, but she'd have to trust God's eyes to be where she couldn't.

"I'm ready," Darryl said, looking as good as ever in a pair of starched jeans and a Carolina blue pullover golf shirt.

"Me too." Paula kissed Gabrielle, then handed her over to Delores. "We'll be back in about two hours."

"I was thinking we could go out for dinner before we came home," Darryl said.

"Oh, well, it'll be a little longer then," Paula said.

"Take your time," Rosanna yelled out. She was sitting on the living room floor helping Micah build a castle out of Legos. "I'll whip up something here. You've got plenty of stuff in the refrigerator."

It was a short ride to Paula's church, but it had been a very long time since she and Darryl had attended as a couple, not counting their first counseling session. The same as last time, the counselor, Felicia Grimes, started their session by playing a song of worship music. She left them in the room alone, saying, "When I'm not around, it'll only be you two and God to work things out."

After the song, she returned and sat down in the chair across from the couch Paula and Darryl shared.

"You all know my focus has been not to rehash everything that you all did wrong—but we will get to that," Felicia said.

"For the next few sessions we're going to talk about how to make a marriage work, and not just work, but prosper God's way."

Felicia opened a Bible. "This is one of the most powerful verses I know about love."

She began to read 1 Corinthians 13. "Love suffers long and is kind; love does not envy; love does not parade itself, is not puffed up; does not behave rudely, does not seek its own, is not provoked, thinks no evil; does not rejoice in iniquity, but rejoices in the truth; bears all things, believes all things, hopes all things, endures all things. Love never fails."

Paula looked over at Darryl. "Ain't that the truth."

Reading
Group Guide

D̲ear Readers:
   These questions are provided to help facilitate an entertaining and thoughtful exchange about the issues in *The Truth about Love*. If you'd like to arrange for Tia McCollors to visit with your book club discussion (in person or via phone), please contact the author at Tia@TiaMcCollors.com. She also welcomes readers to sign her guestbook on her Web site at
www.TiaMcCollors.com.

GENERAL QUESTIONS

What was the most memorable scene in the book?

Which character can you relate most closely to?

What lessons did you learn from the characters and their situations?

Read 1 Corinthians 13. Do you apply the biblical definitions of love to situations in your life? If not, how can you better exhibit love in circumstances and to people?

The media and society, in general, have sent mixed messages about love. How do you define *love*? Read Scriptures about the biblical standards of love and compare them to your personal definitions and actions.

A LOOK AT THE WOMEN OF
THE TRUTH ABOUT LOVE

PAULA

Although Paula felt hurt and betrayed in her marriage, it seems that inwardly she wanted to reconcile with Darryl. Why do you think she didn't immediately return home to Darryl? Read 1 Corinthians 7:10–15.

Why do you think Rosanna finally revealed the identity of Paula's father?

Did Paula's relationship with her mother grow?

Do you see any hope that Floyd Raymond would reconcile with his daughters and begin to build a relationship with them? If so, why? If not, why?

Darryl confessed some of the details about his relationship with Diana (Lady Di). Do you think he was being truthful? Is it possible to have an emotional affair?

Will Darryl and Paula's marriage be fully reconciled? Read Matthew 19:26.

BELINDA

At the beginning of the book, Belinda was aroused out of her sleep with anxious thoughts that eventually led her to pray. Have you ever experienced a similar situation, only to find out that your prayers may have spared a person's life or kept him or her out of a dangerous situation?

After praying for T.J. and then receiving the news that he'd been shot, Belinda later experienced an overwhelming sense of peace. Read and meditate on Psalm 91.

Was Thomas wrong for letting Juanita (T.J.'s biological mother) in their home while Belinda was away, or did Belinda overreact?

Even when raised in ideal and disciplined households, children may stray from the teachings and expectations of their parents. Have you experienced this with your own children or know someone who has? Talk about how the situations were handled. Read Proverbs 22:6 and Psalm 127:3–5.

How should situations be handled when parents disagree on a form of discipline or consequences for their children's disobedience?

ZORA

At first Zora seemed to have a problem accepting Preston's call to the ministry, and consequently her role as a minister's wife. Have you ever felt inadequate? Read Jeremiah 1:5; Psalm 139; and 3 John 1:2.

Has there ever been a time when you had to choose between following God's voice versus policy at work, rules at school, etc.? What happened?

Did Zora overstep boundaries by praying for her student, Toni, at school? What about praying at Toni's house?

At the end of the book, it's evident that Zora's life will be altered by three momentous changes—taking on the role of a minister's wife at the Fields family church, pregnancy, and finding two members of her biological family. How do you think Zora will handle the changes? How would you handle them?

MONÉT

Monét seemed to be reluctant about marriage and commitment because she felt she'd "lose" who she was as a person. Have you ever felt the same way?

How can holding on to old emotional baggage from past relationships affect a person's current and future relationships? Take a moment to analyze your life. Are you holding on to past hurts that are currently influencing any decisions? Read Philippians 3:13–14.

Zora talked to Monét about her fear of commitment. Do you have close friends whom hold you accountable or with whom you can openly discuss your issues without fear of judgment? Read Proverbs 11:14; 18:24; and 24:6.

Jeremiah and Monét made a joint decision to attend premarital counseling before getting engaged. Do you feel premarital counseling is beneficial to marital relationships?

Will Jeremiah and Monét's relationship finally lead to marriage?

Scriptures
about Love

Love suffers long and is kind; love does not envy;
love does not parade itself, is not puffed up;
does not behave rudely, does not seek its own,
is not provoked, thinks no evil; does not rejoice in iniquity,
but rejoices in the truth; bears all things, believes all things,
hopes all things, endures all things. Love never fails.
1 Corinthians 13:4–8

And now abide faith, hope, love, these three;
but the greatest of these is love.
1 Corinthians 13:13

Hatred stirs up strife, but love covers all sins.
Proverbs 10:12

"But I say to you, love your enemies,
bless those who curse you, do good to those who hate you,
and pray for those who spitefully
use you and persecute you."
Matthew 5:44

"By this all will know that you are My disciples,
if you have love for one another."
John 13:35

Owe no one anything except to love one another,
for he who loves another has fulfilled the law.
Romans 13:8

Beloved, let us love one another, for love is of God;
and everyone who loves is born of God and knows God.
He who does not love does not know God, for God is love.
1 John 4:7–8

Let brotherly love continue.
Hebrews 13:1

And walk in love, as Christ also has loved us
and given Himself for us, an offering
and a sacrifice to God for a sweet-smelling aroma.
Ephesians 5:2

But above all these things put on love,
which is the bond of perfection.
Colossians 3:14

"You shall love the Lord your God with all your heart,
with all your soul, and with all your strength."
Deuteronomy 6:5

Let all that you do be done with love.
1 Corinthians 16:14

"Greater love has no one than this,
than to lay down one's life for his friends."
John 15:13

ISBN-10: 0-8024-5913-7
ISBN-13: 978-0-8024-5913-8

Best friends Anisha Blake and Sherri Dawson have been inseparable for the last five years—until Anisha is swept away by Tyson Randall. When Anisha becomes the object of Tyson's affection, she believes her prayers for a knight in shining armor are answered. But as their romance grows, Anisha's intimate relationship with God becomes an afterthought instead of her first thought. With life crumbling around her, Anisha is faced with choices she was sure she'd never have to make. An inspiring and emotional journey through adversity and spiritual self-discovery.

Essence Bestselling Author Tia McCollors
Find it now at your favorite local or online bookstore.
www.LiftEveryVoiceBooks.com

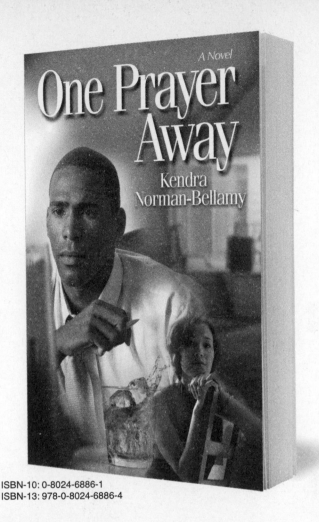

ISBN-10: 0-8024-6886-1
ISBN-13: 978-0-8024-6886-4

Mitchell Andrews made a bad mistake. His failure to cope made it worse. He turned to alcohol, and his angry outbursts drove his wife away—but it drove him to find Christ, sobriety, and newfound hope. He attempts to win back the love of his life, but the mistakes of his past threaten to undo his second chance. Will he come undone at his weakest moment, or will God give him the strength to endure?

ISBN-10: 0-8024-6839-X
ISBN-13: 978-0-8024-6839-0

"Many young people believe Michael Bolton was the first artist to sing 'When a Man Loves a Woman,' but actually it was written, produced, and recorded by two others before Michael was born. Percy Sledge arranged the familiar tune in 1966, but Jacob of the Old Testament penned the first version in Genesis, chapter 29. Everyone knows that Jacob of the Old Testament was a rascal, usurper, and deceiver. But Jacob knew how to do one thing very well . . . Jacob knew how to love a woman. If you want to know if a man really loves a woman, take a close look at what Jacob has to tell us from the passages of Scripture."

– Excerpt from *When a Man Loves a Woman*

by James Ford Jr.
Find it now at your favorite local or online bookstore.
www.LiftEveryVoiceBooks.com

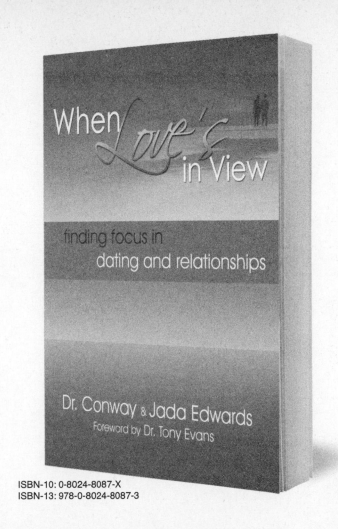

ISBN-10: 0-8024-8087-X
ISBN-13: 978-0-8024-8087-3

Dr. Conway Edwards, the singles pastor at Oak Cliff Bible Church in Texas, along with his wife, Jada, write from the heart to Christian singles about the best way to prepare for marriage. Discussing courtship and dating from a biblical perspective, they also share their personal story—including the mistakes they made along the way. The result is a thought-provoking, encouraging manual on making the most of your single years, and getting yourself ready for marriage.

by Jada Edwards and Conway Edwards
Find it now at your favorite local or online bookstore.
www.LiftEveryVoiceBooks.com

ISBN-10: 0-8024-9861-2
ISBN-13: 978-0-8024-9861-8

Four women, four lives, one God.
Zora Bridgeforth is twenty-nine and grappling with identity issues. While in search of her deceased mother's bridal veil, Zora happens upon a letter that reveals she was adopted. Zora is devastated and vows to find her biological family. To find an outlet for her feelings, she joins a multi-church women's discipleship group. Unexpectedly Zora finds that the joy of friendship with three women in her group (Monét Sullivan, Paula Manns, and Belinda Stokes) turns out to be God's hand at work. As the ladies drop their facades and learn to find healing through each other's testimonies, a series of events unfolds to an outcome Zora could never have imagined. Written from a young, fresh perspective, *Zora's Cry* is an inspirational read for the woman who appreciates the power of friendships and the power of God's love. Includes a discussion guide for readers groups.

Essence Bestselling Author Tia McCollors
Find it now at your favorite local or online bookstore.

www.LiftEveryVoiceBooks.com

The Negro National Anthem

Lift every voice and sing
Till earth and heaven ring,
Ring with the harmonies of Liberty;
Let our rejoicing rise
High as the listening skies,
Let it resound loud as the rolling sea.
Sing a song full of the faith that the dark past has taught us,
Sing a song full of the hope that the present has brought us,
Facing the rising sun of our new day begun
Let us march on till victory is won.

LIFT EVERY VOICE

So begins the Black National Anthem, by James Weldon Johnson in 1900. Lift Every Voice is the name of the joint imprint of The Institute for Black Family Development and Moody Publishers.

Our vision is to advance the cause of Christ through publishing African-American Christians who educate, edify, and disciple Christians in the church community through quality books written for African Americans.

Since 1988, The Institute for Black Family Development, a 501(c)(3) nonprofit Christian organization, has been providing training and technical assistance for churches and Christian organizations. The Institute for Black Family Development's goal is to become a premier trainer in leadership development, management, and strategic planning for pastors, ministers, volunteers, executives, and key staff members of churches and Christian organizations. To learn more about The Institute for Black Family Development write us at:

The Institute for Black Family Development
15151 Faust
Detroit, Michigan 48223

We hope you enjoy this book from Moody Publishers. Our goal is to provide high-quality, thought-provoking books and products that connect truth to your real needs and challenges. For more information on other books and products written and produced from a biblical perspective, go to www.moodypublishers.com or write to:

Moody Publishers/LEV
820 N. LaSalle Boulevard
Chicago, IL 60610
www.moodypublishers.com